IN THE SHADOW
OF THE **OMBÚ TREE**

By the same author

ANCESTRAL VOICES
'Ryan's pure, lilting, pensive prose is like a cool refreshing stream running through this affecting and healing meditation on Irish history...'
Publishers Weekly USA

ON BORROWED GROUND
'Once in a while there comes a book which is quite extraordinary in its ability to recreate times past, to bring us an evocation of a whole way of life now gone and to encourage us to remember with affection mingled with a little awe what was, as distinct from what might have been. This is such a book... Amid a welter of modern mediocrity, this is one of those rare gems.'
The Cork Examiner

REPRISAL
'...a human and humane account excellently told'
KEVIN MYERS, *The Irish Times*

'...a finely written historical novel that is at ease with time and place'
Sunday Press

THE KYBE
'...a well-researched, well-constructed and well-told tale'
The Irish Times

'...an attractive and well-told story with fresh dialogue and a strong Irish sense of place'
Irish Press

Hugh FitzGerald Ryan

In the Shadow
of the Ombú Tree

CHAOS

press

First published 2005 by
CHAOS PRESS
16 The Orchard
Bellefield
Enniscorthy
County Wexford
IRELAND

This novel is based on the story of my great-grandparents. I have gathered the scattered shards of fact and pieced them together with the malleable clay of fiction.

The author gratefully acknowledges a travel bursary from The Arts Council of Ireland.

British Library Cataloguing-in-Publication Data

A catalogue record for this book is available from the British Library

ISBN   0 9548529 1 5   paperback
ISBN   0 9548529 0 7   hardback

Cover typography: Alan Ryan
Cover illustration: Alan Ryan
Typesetting: Chaos Press
Printed in the Republic of Ireland by Betaprint, Dublin.

Acknowledgements

The story of my great-grandparents and Estancia Santa Catalina, as told to me by my mother, a Wexford woman, flitted in the background of my imagination for more than half a century. Yet I could never locate it in a real place until I encountered the web-site of William Revetria, chronicler of his native village. William anchored my researches to the Department of Soriano and provided me with a thesis by local historians, Ana Bentancor, Cecilia Clavijo and Malvina Ruiz. This thesis gathered together many disconnected pieces of information and charmed me with stories of the earliest inhabitants, both indigenous and settler. William, Luján, Gabriela and Cristina welcomed us to Uruguay and pointed us in the right direction.

I wish also to thank the Pupils and English teachers of Liceo Justo P. Rodriguez in Cardona for their interest and advice. Similarly the Governors, Teachers, Parents and Pupils of Escuela Pablo Purriel in Santa Catalina were unstinting of their time and generosity in helping us. A particular thanks must go to the Alfonsin family of Estancia Santa Catalina who enabled us to see at last, the dwelling places of John and Catherine and the land that shaped their lives. I acknowledge gratefully the encouragement of: Intendente Correa of Soriano; his cultural representative, Enrique de Leon; the Mayor and Social Club; the Librarian; the Church communities of Santa Catalina; Professor Manuel Pirez, Archivist of Mercedes; Sr. Aguiar of Cardona, horseman, farmer, sportsman, historian and finally, our guide and interpreter, Ignacio Gussoni. In Colonia del Sacramento the staff of the Museum of the Indigenous People brought vividly to life the history of the long vanished Charrúa people. Hilary Murphy and the members of the Wexford Family History Association and also many Cardiffs and Doyles from South Wexford provided me with invaluable nuggets of information.

My brothers and sisters kept the story alive in my imagination for many years, each contributing some fragment from their recollection of what they had been told. Our family, Tom, Alan, Alison, Sarah, Fergus, Jenny, Erika, Justin, Michael, Ellis, Eimear, Felicia and Paul, consistently encouraged and facilitated the work, although convinced that we would get irrevocably lost in the vastness of the Pampas. Maybe, on reflection, that was part of their plan.

My greatest debt in bringing this novel to completion is to my wife, Margaret, relentless scrutineer of proofs, tolerant supporter and indefatigable companion, who took Santa Catalina and the story of John and Catherine to her heart.

This book is dedicated to the memory of John and Catherine Cardiff of Wexford and Santa Catalina and to their great, great, great grandchildren, Sally Anne, Victor, Josephine, Kim, Leo, Sophie, Alice and those who are expected but have not yet arrived.

Nunca prosperará la casa sobre cuyo
techo cayó la sombra del ombú.

The house on which falls the shadow
of the ombú will never prosper.

Proverb

BOOK ONE

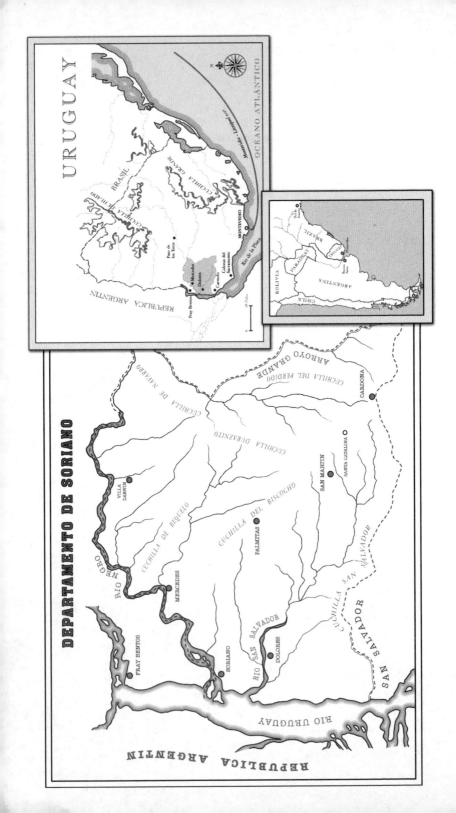

THE BEGINNING

Uruguay 1603

As soon as his feet felt the soft mud of the riverbank, the slave knew that this was the place. He heard the voice of his mother, the old witch, who had come from Africa all those years ago, saying to him: "This is the place. This is the time. Go now and be free."

She always knew. Everything that had happened, she knew and everything that was to be.

He tugged on the rope and the boat swung into the shallows, keeling slightly as the officer stepped ashore. The officer looked about, fingering the finely chased silver of his sword hilt. He strode to the top of the bank and fastidiously wiped his boots in the long grass. He removed his peaked helmet.

Downriver the first cattle and horses were coming ashore, struggling in the yielding mud. Their hooves churned the stretch of riverbank into a quagmire. The herdsmen shouted and urged them on. Behind them, almost to the middle of the stream, stretched a line of animals, swimming desperately, their eyes rolling whitely, their long curved horns like serpents rising from the glittering surface.

The slave scooped a handful of water and rubbed his neck, where the iron of his collar was hot against his skin. He took another handful and drank. This is the place, he thought again. The officer, irritable in the heat, ordered him to make the boat fast to an overhanging branch and help to drive the animals away from the riverbank.

Everything irritated the officer, his high ruffed collar, the breastplate hot to the touch, the idleness of slaves and the indignity of having to serve as a common herdsman to the Governor of Paraguay and The River Plate. It might be a shrewd investment for generations yet unborn, to release animals into this empty eastern province, but neither His Catholic Majesty nor his Governor or his misfortunate lieutenant, would live long enough to enjoy the profit. He watched idly as the cattle shook their flanks dry and began to graze. The herdsmen shouted, jabbing at them with long lances topped by half-moon blades. The horses, half wild already, tossed their manes and whinnied, sniffing the air of this new country and finding it to their satisfaction.

His reverie was interrupted by a shout. He saw a soldier lifting his firelock and settling it in the forked staff. He saw the slave running between two horses, holding a twist of mane in each hand, urging them towards the line of trees and scrub a few hundred yards from the water. He saw the black smoke. He heard the loud report. The noise reverberated on the water. The slave flinched, but retained his grip. He kept running.

The officer laughed. It was astonishing to think that anyone could hit a moving target at such a distance. Pure luck. He laughed at the effrontery of the slave and at the prospect of the chase. He shouted to a herdsman to dismount and surrender his horse. He dug in his spurs and swung the horse towards the trees. He drew his sword.

The slave felt his shoulder shattering and the power going from his left arm. His fingers, suddenly cold, let go of the horse's mane. He staggered but retained his grip on the other animal. He heard the hoofbeats behind him and the mocking cheers of the soldiers on the riverbank. The strength went from his legs. He fell and the horse veered away. The rider loomed over him. The sunlight caught the blade.

He saw a humming bird attending to a flower on a branch high above. The bird stopped in the air, its wings the merest shadow, its body a dark spot against the light. The flowers were waxen, yellow and pink. The branch bore savage thorns. He knew that the bird would save him. He heard the whirr of its wings. He saw a stone strike the officer's temple and that nobleman of Spain pitch sideways from the herdsman's sheepskin saddle. He closed his eyes and smiled. This is the place, he said. The humming bird flicked to another flower in search of nectar.

The soldiers watching from the riverbank, saw the savages emerging from the trees, two small stocky men, naked, dark skinned, darker than the Indians of the other side of the river.

"Charrúas," muttered a herdsman, "fieras, wild animals." He shuddered. The soldiers looked at each other. Their numbers were small. Their work was done. They knew the ferocity of the Indians of the Pampas, the terror of raids in the middle of the night and they had heard mention of the Charrúas of the Eastern Shore, the most terrible of all the savage tribes.

They saw the savages dragging the two bodies into the trees, a slave and an arrogant fool, not worth the life of an honest soldier. They turned to their boats and the safety of the opposite shore, a misty line in the distance.

The slave heard voices, the grunting of men, the twittering of children, the nasal tones of women. He opened his eyes. He lay in the dappled shade of a ceibo tree. Drifts of crimson blossom hung over him. The chattering ceased. The people were watching him in silence, an old man, naked except for a cloak of jaguar skin, draped loosely over his shoulders, several younger men and women, a group of children jostling to get a better look at him. He was conscious of a dull pain in his shoulder and turned his head. The wound seemed to be packed with moss and what he took to be spiders' webs. He grunted. The people gave a collective sigh, as if in relief. Dark skinned people, but not as black as his own people. High cheekbones and straight black hair, in some cases held back by a band of twisted plant fibres or the skin of some animal. The sunlight fell in patches on their shining bodies.

He smiled as if in recognition. His teeth gleamed in the shadow and against the blackness of his skin.

"Buenas tardes"! he said and the chattering began again. He made to sit up but the pain shot through him. He lay back.

The old man stood up, gathering his cloak around him with an imperious movement. He walked away, past the fire and the flimsy twig shelters, through the long grass, until he came to the riverbank. With the blade of his stone axe he knocked the top from an anthill. He lifted the gleaming skull of the Spanish officer and dislodged the angry black ants. They fell from the eyes and nostrils and the shattered temple where the slingshot had struck. He dipped the skull in the water, rinsing away the last of the scurrying insects. He knew that the strange dark man would not be strong again until he drank from the skull of his enemy. Carefully, with his axe, he chopped at the skull until he had fashioned a bowl from the crown. He threw the fragments and the jawbone into the water, white shards in the dark waters of the great river. He returned to the camp.

They caressed the slave's skin, comparing it with their own. They touched his hair and laughed. They tested the rough woollen cloth of his breeches. He laughed with them. This was like the home his mother had told him about. He sat upright with some difficulty and ran his fingers under the iron collar. They touched the collar, muttering among themselves.

"Fierro," he said, picking up a pebble.

He clinked it against the collar. "Fierro."

"Fiera," they replied and he clinked the pebble again.

"Fiera, Fiera" chanted the children in delight.

"Ah, Fiera," said the adults, pleased to know his name, but they could not manage the sound. They were calling him a wild beast, he thought with amusement.

The old man crouched beside him with a bowl of green liquid, a kind of sludge made from leaves. He gestured to him to drink. He sniffed an acrid earthy smell. He drank and grimaced. They laughed and gestured to him to drink again. He realised that he was thirsty. He drank. The leaves filled his mouth and he chewed on them, trying to swallow, to the huge amusement of the onlookers. He closed his teeth and filtered the liquid carefully. He felt a warm glow inside himself and the pain in his shoulder began to abate.

He took the stone again and tapped the collar. He scraped a bright streak on the dark metal. The people gathered closer and he repeated the motion, signifying that he wanted to cut himself free of the encumbrance.

"Ah!" they said understanding his intention. A woman knelt beside him and placed her fingers inside the collar. He felt the warmth of her forearm on his shoulder as she braced herself. She took a flint blade and began to scrape at the rivet which held the collar in place. The stone screeched on the metal and the people watched in rapt attention as she began to cut.

"Fierro," she said softly as if claiming him as her own.

Chapter One

Wexford 1864

When the tinkers came to the door at Lingstown, Dorothy Wray would run them. She was still Dorothy Wray, the Protestant woman who married Tom Doyle the farmer. She had no time for idleness or vagrancy.

"Go away," she would say sharply. "You'll get nothing here."

No matter how many prayers they promised she would not bend. Papist promises of Papist prayers, which she knew they would never pay anyway. Papists, she felt, were profligate with their prayers, throwing them around like snuff at a wake, as they say, devaluing them like a base coinage, telling their beads in a meaningless mumble. One good well washed and combed prayer on a Sunday morning was worth a thousand of the others.

"Be off with you!"

They would shuffle away, still promising a prayer or two in forlorn hope.

She knew however, that they seldom went away empty handed. She knew that her husband would have a few eggs for them or a wisp of hay for the ass or his favourite, a cut from a piece of ling that he had drying on hooks on the gable end of the house.

"Ah the poor children," he would say. "You couldn't refuse the poor children."

He always fidgeted with his knife, wiping the blade and snapping it shut, only to open it again, trying to make it look like a routine inspection.

"You'll have us in the poor house some day," was her usual accusation. Yet she was glad somewhere deep inside herself that he had given something. He knew that too, even though she set her mouth in a straight line of disapproval. Tom was no fool, even if he had a soft heart and always thought the best of people.

He tended to believe what people told him and was disappointed in a general way if he found it to be untrue, but still could not be harsh with the liar. He knew he would get no prayers for the pieces of fish, but it amused him that they thought they were diddling him and he knew that the fish would fill some empty bellies.

Tom Doyle had no political opinions. He had no grand plan to solve the troubles of the land or to alleviate the poverty that he saw around him. He believed that it was his duty to work and look after his family and lend a hand, when he could, to anyone that asked. With a farm of land at Lingstown, overlooking the lake and two boats fishing out of Kilmore Quay he felt he was not doing too badly. With two fine sons to take over after his time and good freehold land to leave to them, he was, he concluded, a happy man. Then there was Catherine, seventeen years of age, nearly a grown woman already, a daughter who would bring joy to the heart of any father.

Catherine was the centre of Tom's universe. He prided himself that he did not spoil her, despite his wife's warnings. She did her share of work like everyone else and did it cheerfully, often singing as she went about the house, some little French song, maybe, that the nuns taught her up in Wexford in the boarding school, or maybe a song in the Gaelic.

It was hard to have to send her away, but necessary nonetheless. Her mother had a great regard for education, even if it had to be with the nuns.

"That girl will go places," Tom used to say. "She'll do well for herself."

He had a great belief in the power of education even though he had little of it himself. As for the boys, they had always smiled tolerantly at the idea and gone back to the boats or to the horses. It was enough for them that Catherine would carry the standard of book learning in the family.

On that particular Easter day Tom sat, smoking his pipe by the gable end of the house. He looked down at the lake where the young people were having a picnic. It was grand to see them enjoying themselves, Catherine and her school friend with her brother and that other lad, Cardiff, the doctor's son from Wexford. His own two boys had been there for a while, Laurence and Michael, called for his brothers who had gone out foreign. He noticed that they had left the picnic party, probably remembering things they had to do.

"What happened to the fish?" His wife's voice broke into his thoughts. "Where's the fish? It could be drying in this sun."

"I took it down. I, eh, put it back in the salt."

"And why did you do that? Wasn't it salty enough?"

"Ah well, you know."

"Oh, I know, all right."

He saw her mouth close into that familiar line of disapproval, with small spider-web wrinkles at the corner and with a shock of realisation, he saw that she was getting old.

"I know right well. Young madam there, told you to take it down, so as not to embarrass her in front of the quality."

"There's nothing wrong with a decent bit of ling."

"So why take it down, then?"

He knew that she was right, but he did not want to admit it.

"She's only a child and this is the first time she has brought her friends home. I just thought I'd tidy up around the place."

He knocked his pipe on the side of the bench and trod on the dottle, grinding it into the gravel.

"Well, I'll be as happy if they don't come again in a hurry."

"Why is that?" He had to admit that she had the name of being a shrewd judge of character.

"That young fellow Boxwell is a decent enough young man, but I think his sister is sly."

She said it without elaboration or corroboration. He wondered how she had come to this conclusion.

"Why do you say that?"

"There's something about her, the way she looks at you. I don't know. All sweetness to your face. Too sweet in my opinion."

It might have been a prejudice, she admitted, about this branch of a fine old Protestant family who had turned Papist for no good reason that she could think of. She wiped her hands on her apron, still looking down at the group by the lakeside.

"I'd be afraid Catherine would be said by her too much."

Tom moved aside, motioning her to sit down, but she declined. "I've things to do."

"They can wait." He loosened his high collar and removed his bowler, brushing it with his cuff, although it was spotless. She sat down reluctantly, as if ready to spring up again and go about some urgent task.

"What about the other fella, then?"

He was teasing her, deferring to her astute judgement, yet knowing that she knew he would take no notice. It was a game he played which sometimes amused her, but this time she did not smile.

"There are two kinds of Cardiffs, the mad ones and the grand ones. I don't know which is worse."

He laughed, "The mad ones and the grand ones. Which have we got here today?"

"That's what I can't make out."

"He seems a very fine young man to me."

"Keep him away from our daughter, that's all I'm saying."

'Our daughter,' he reflected, realising her genuine concern. It was 'your daughter' when he was indulging her, when she was dissociating herself from the situation, but now she was closing ranks. He said nothing, feeling her concern. My daughter, he thought. Our daughter. He felt a sudden pity for his wife.

Her family had it hard as far back as Ninety Eight and the rising, when the roof was burned over their heads. Her father, the Reverend Wray, took the fever during the potato famine and left them near penniless. She was always on guard, he thought, expecting the bad times to come back, unable to relax in a bit of prosperity. Now there was another thing to worry about.

"But sure they're only children. Time enough to worry about all that sort of thing later when she's grown up."

Still this was a cloud on the horizon. She twisted the apron in her hands.

"Mad Cardiffs and grand Cardiffs." He laughed at the conjunction. "We could do without that."

She stood up suddenly.

"Anyway, enough of this nonsense. You can get the pony trap ready for them. I dare say they'll be starting back soon enough. Then you can put the fish back."

"Time enough for that." He crossed his legs and began to refill his pipe. "Maybe you'd bring me a light when you have a minute."

"Hmm!" she grunted and went indoors.

Catherine knew that Elizabeth had brought John Cardiff just to make her jealous. Although they were best friends, she knew that Elizabeth liked to put her down, always in the nicest way of course. Elizabeth had the ability to say things that were hurtful in intent and yet when you unpicked the words, there was nothing that you could put your finger on. She always thought of the right retort for Elizabeth, but always a day too late. Sometimes she thought she hated her. But this time with a surge of joy, she knew that Elizabeth's plan had backfired. That was what her uncle Laurence said when he came back from South America with only one eye. She was very small at the time, three or four when he made his last visit. He had a black patch over his right eye.

"Blasted thing backfired," he said, "savin' your presence, Ma'm." This to her mother, who never allowed profanity. He held the imaginary musket to his shoulder and swung it around to take aim. "A painted savage, he was." He laughed at the humour of it all.

"Blasted thing backfired." One in the eye for Elizabeth. John Cardiff preferred her to Elizabeth. She knew it in her soul. Robert was a nice enough fellow but John Cardiff had fire in his blood. When he looked at her, she knew that he was the only one for her, forever and ever. She smiled broadly. He watched her with interest.

"What's so funny?"

He lay propped on one elbow, elegant and casual. His straw hat lay beside him on the grass. She thought of one of those French writers or maybe a poet, but his athletic looking body suggested a man of action, maybe a soldier.

"What's so funny?" he asked again, smiling.

She felt that Elizabeth was watching her intently and for a moment, she caught the hostility in her eyes. She looked away, enjoying the moment.

"I was thinking about my uncle who lost his eye."

"And that's funny?" he persisted.

"No, no. It was the way he explained it."

"I don't see how that could be funny," Elizabeth said, sniffing in disapproval.

"He was fighting savages, with my other uncle, Michael. His musket backfired."

"I still don't see what's so funny," he said wrinkling his brow in puzzlement.

"Blasted thing backfoired," she said, mimicking her uncle's deep south Wexford accent.

"Backfoired." They never lost the accent, her two uncles, even after years in South America. She wondered how they managed with the Spanish.

"Backfoired," he said, smiling, "So that was how he lost his eye."

"I still don't see what's so funny," said Elizabeth rather coldly.

"What happened then?" asked Robert, practical as always.

"Oh, my uncle Michael shot the Indian. A painted savage, he was," she said, completing the formula.

"Where did all this happen?" asked Robert. He was a person who dealt in facts.

"In South America, in Uruguay, years ago when they were getting rid of all the Indians."

"Why did they do that?"

"I don't know. I suppose they had to make room for all the cattle. I don't know really." She was not interested in pursuing the matter. "They say there are millions of cattle there running wild. There for the taking, my uncles said. Pucks o' them, they said."

"Pucks," said Elizabeth, raising an eyebrow. "I never heard that expression before. Is that what they say down here?"

That eyebrow, thought Catherine. Elizabeth used it like a weapon, an evil eye, to turn people to stone. But she did not care this time. This time it had no effect.

"Yes, that's what people say down here." She emphasised the last two words almost defiantly. She felt a kind of elation. "Down here we country bumpkins have lots of strange expressions, you know. We even have our own language."

There was a silence. She thought she saw a flicker of a smile on John Cardiff's lips and she knew that she had won.

"So anyone can claim the cattle if they want to. That's interesting." Robert was unaware of the duel that was taking place. "Are your uncles still out there?"

"Presumably. We haven't heard from them for years. It's easy to get lost out there. It's a great big empty land."

"With no Indians," John interjected. "Now that your uncles have shot them all. We should all go out there and start an empire."

He rolled on his back, squinting his eyes against the light. He hummed a tune. Elizabeth plucked at a blade of grass.

"I think it's time we were going," she said abruptly, standing up, brushing at her skirts. "We don't want to be caught out in the wilds after dark."

"Beware of the painted savages" said John, "but sure Catherine can shoot them all for us."

"I still don't see what was so funny about losing an eye. I don't think it's funny at all."

She began to gather things into the picnic basket, throwing them in any old way. John looked at Catherine. He winked conspiratorially and her world seemed suddenly perfect.

Far in the distance a cockerel crowed, a small pin-prick of sound in the immense silence of the night. First with the news, like an eager child. There were still stars in the square of window and only the dimmest suggestion of dawn. Catherine lay there reliving the day. Nearer home another cockerel joined in, claiming his portion of credit. She listened to their insistent duet, waiting for their own fellow to take up the cry.

She thought of the boat on the lake and how she trailed her fingers in the water, languidly, like a lady in a picture, as John pulled on the oars. She should have worn a crown of daisies. It made no difference that Elizabeth sat beside her in the stern, a dowdy lady-in-waiting to a queen. Let her wait, she thought. Her Lancelot handled the little boat expertly, backing water, making the craft curvet like a restive horse. The lady of the lake.

"This is where they found the chalice," she said.

"You are indeed a fount of information."

She wondered if he were teasing.

"Just down there, shining out of the sand. Somebody hid it in the water when Cromwell was coming and they forgot where it was. Maybe Cromwell killed the person who hid it. It wasn't found for a hundred years."

"Who found it?"

"Some old ancestor of mine. He was fishing just about here and lo! A hand, clothed in white samite, mystic, wonderful, rose from the water, holding the golden cup."

"Liar," said Elizabeth but even she was interested.

"Excellent," he said. "Did you make that up yourself?"

"Not exactly. I read it somewhere."

"Let's see if there's anything else down there."

He leaned over the side. The boat swayed with him.

"Careful, man," said Robert, "or you'll have us all in the water."

"Nothing there," said John. "Maybe over this side." He tipped the boat abruptly the other way.

The two girls shrieked, gripping the gunwale. John continued to rock the boat, heaving on the oars, enjoying their alarm, until he tired of the game.

She could go to him now, she thought, standing in the little boat, her white robes drifting in the light dawn air, through the cut in the sand built ridge that separated the lake from the sea, borne on the tide to Wexford, in among the great ships, their spars black against the morning light and he would be there on the quay. He would know. Somehow he would know that she was coming and they would sail away forever to the end of the world.

The cockerel squawked outside her window. His voice was broken. He could never reach that final note. A dishevelled, down-at-heel fellow, he always came late to work, hurrying to catch up on the others. He squawked again, defiantly, putting his shoulder to the wheel, heaving the sun over the horizon, entitled to a measure of the praise.

Her mother did not approve.

"Plenty of time yet to be thinking about young men," she said. "You'll have your pick of them all in good time."

"Yes, some ignorant farmer with a few acres, that you'll pick out for me."

She was not prepared to take the topic seriously. There was no need to.

"I didn't do too badly with your father and he with no grand airs about him."

Catherine felt disloyal and disloyal too to her own brothers, shy country boys, ill at ease with the visitors.

"That's different," she said.

"As for that young Cardiff boy," her mother went on, "sure the Cardiffs wouldn't walk on the same side of the street as ordinary folk."

Catherine said nothing.

"A medical student, is it? I suppose he'll take over after his father in the fever hospital."

There was a silence. An old atavistic fear came back to haunt her.

"That's no life for anyone." She shivered.

"Times have changed," said Catherine guardedly. "Anyway, it's none of my business what he does with his life. It's no concern of mine. He is just a friend of a friend, that's all. I couldn't care less."

She thought her mother had looked at her strangely. She dropped the subject.

The last star faded in the window. Sounds of the awakening farm came with the sunlight, the whinny of a horse, the clank of a milk pail and the chirping of sparrows. From out beyond the lake came the ululation of wading birds, foraging the tidal mudflats. She closed her eyes. It was the whooping of Indian warriors galloping across some far distant pampas.

Chapter Two

The castle of Ferrycarrig stands like a chess piece, commanding the river crossing. Upriver the stream is broad and slow. Oarsmen in their flimsy skiffs, darted like insects on the placid surface.

"This is a Norman castle," said Mother Alacoque and the girls listened respectfully. Mother Alacoque believed in exercise. Exercise and hygiene, although neither to excess. The girls bathed regularly, but always in long cotton shifts. In each bathing cubicle there was a notice: 'God sees you', pinned to the door. Catherine thought that it was rude of God to be peering at schoolgirls in the bath, but accepted in a vague way, that He had a job to do.

Every Saturday, Mother Alacoque took them for a brisk walk in the country, walking two by two in a long demure crocodile. Idle chatter was not encouraged. Anything of an educational nature was noted. It was such a small castle, perched there on its rock. She wondered if their feet stuck out through the little windows when they lay down to sleep, armoured feet and silver spurs bristling out of the walls. She had heard all this stuff about the Normans so many times.

"Not the original castle of course," continued Mother Alacoque. "That was up there on the hill. Fitz Stephen's castle. It's all gone now, but we still have the names with us, haven't we girls?" They nodded. Some of them bore those very names, "Prendergast, Roche, the people of the rock. They spoke French, you see." They knew that already.

"Cardiff, FitzMaurice – oh hundreds of them."

Catherine started. This was the usual dry history lesson, but now she was listening.

"They took our land from us and gave it to the king of England."

Mother Alacoque combined in her lesson a deep pride in the history of Wexford and an inveterate hatred of England. Yet she liked the Normans as such. They spoke French, which was a point in their favour and they became more Irish than the Irish. They were a paradox which she never tried to resolve.

Catherine watched the oarsmen, lithe young men in white, cutting through the water in that start-stop way which she found almost mesmeric. Then she saw him again, sculling along in a tiny shell of a craft, tanned skin against the white of his singlet. Deliberately he cut in towards the bank, until only a few yards of reeds separated him from the watching schoolgirls. He looked up, smiling and she knew that he had seen her. He pulled away smartly, followed by twenty pairs of eyes.

Catherine felt a nudge. It was Elizabeth.

"I suppose you think he's after you," she whispered.

Catherine did not reply.

"You do, don't you?" persisted Elizabeth. "Come on, you can tell me. I'm supposed to be your best friend."

She had to tell someone. She wanted to share this happiness. She wanted everyone to know that she loved John Cardiff more than anyone else in the whole wide world, more than her family or even life itself and that she would die if he did not love her too.

"He's all right, I suppose," she conceded.

"I knew it," said Elizabeth in triumph. "I could see it straight away. Oh, I'm so happy for you."

She wanted to move on to the next stage. She wanted to know everything before there was even anything to know. She was prepared to consign her own romantic longings to dust in the interests of intrigue and excitement. In a moment of bleak recognition, she realised that she needed Catherine because she was beautiful and good and people gravitated to her, while she herself appeared cold and forbidding, making people wary. It was untrue and unfair. She had feelings too, even if her heart was not pinned to her sleeve.

"You could write to him. I could give it to Robert to deliver. I can go home on Sunday. In fact, you could come with me, if you get permission."

Catherine shook her head. It was too daring, too forward. He would think it forward of her, even common, to go chasing after him like that.

"No, I couldn't do that."

Yet, why not? Life is short. Already she was seventeen. Soon she would be old and he might marry someone else. Her life would be spent in loneliness and grief. It would be too unbearable. She felt tears stinging her eyes at the dismal prospect. She would be brave. She would be reckless and seize her opportunity.

"No, I couldn't do that," she said miserably. "I could never write to him, just like that. It wouldn't be proper."

"I was only trying to help, silly goose. Have it your own way then, but don't come running to me when he goes off back to college and meets somebody else," Elizabeth sniffed her disapproving sniff. She turned away. A dark cloud of despair settled over Catherine. She completed her walk in glum silence.

Despite official indifference and an almost total absence of printed material, Mother Alacoque taught her girls the Irish language. She sat them in a semicircle, conversing with them in the musical Irish of Munster. She wrote on the blackboard, old poems she knew by heart, in a strange and elegant script, in lines as straight as a ruler. She corresponded with Gaelic scholars in Dublin, sharing her findings with joy and enthusiasm.

"Without our own language we might as well be English," she explained, a fate too terrible to contemplate.

The girls responded to her, listening to her stories of blind poets and visionaries and rack-renting landlords, driven demented by the sharp barbs of the satirists. Most of all she loved the story of Art O'Leary, a brave soldier of Ireland, murdered by the oppressor and keened in heart-breaking verse by his faithful wife.

> 'Mo ghrá go daingean tú,
> My love was fast to you
> Lá da bhaca thú
> The day I saw you,
> Ag ceann tighe an mhargaidh

At the top of the market house.
Thug mo shúil aire dhuit.
My eye gave notice to you,
Thug mo chroidhe taithneamh duit.
My heart gave love to you.
D'éalaíos óm' charaid leat.
I fled from my kinsfolk with you,
I bhfad ó bhaile leat.
Far from my home with you.'

Catherine felt the tears coming. She tried to stop them, but in vain. She began to sob as the tears trickled down her cheeks. She plucked the handkerchief from her sleeve and blew her nose, attracting the unwanted attention of her classmates. Mother Alacoque looked up in surprise, pausing in her reading.

"Is there something wrong, girl?"

Catherine shook her head, unable to speak.

"It's, it's just…" she began and halted.

"I know," said the nun with unexpected gentleness. "It does you credit to feel so deeply, but perhaps you would like to go outside for a little while to recover your composure."

She knew how easily young girls could let their emotions get out of hand and she had no desire to let such strong feelings take hold of the entire class.

"No thank you, Mother," said Catherine, dabbing at her eyes. "I'm all right now." She looked around sheepishly and lowered her head, scrutinising her exercise book. She had no desire to draw any further attention to herself. She began to write, conscientiously taking the lines from the blackboard, forming her letters with elaborate care.

At the break of class, amid the clatter of chairs, Elizabeth slipped the book to her, a soft cover of embossed calf leather with gold writing, Tennyson's poems, with the initials J.C. on the fly-leaf. She felt her heart lurch with joy.

"Poetry," said Elizabeth, who had examined the book minutely the night before. "To be taken in small doses, if that's the effect it has on you."

Catherine smiled at the joke and touched her friend on the wrist, Elizabeth, the best friend that anyone could ever have.

She slid the book into her satchel, contraband, certain to be snatched away by the authorities, if ever discovered. Dangerous romantic stuff that could turn a sensible girl's head.

The Reverend Mother scrutinised the letter carefully through her reading glass. She looked up at Catherine, standing by the desk. She forgot for a moment to put down the glass. Catherine was startled to see a vast cyclopean eye staring at her, seeing into her innermost thoughts.

"And this is your father's signature?"

"Oh yes, Reverend Mother. You see my mother wrote the letter. She has a very good hand you see."

"Yes, I can see that." She felt that there was a kind of Protestant tidiness about the note, a certain stiffness and formality in the mode of expression.

"But my father signed it, because he is the head of the household, you see."

"There is no need to explain that, child. He is of course, the head of the household. I hope you appreciate what a very good father he is to you too."

"Oh, I do, Reverend Mother. I do."

"Your mother too, of course," almost an afterthought.

"Oh, yes of course, Reverend Mother."

Catherine shifted from one foot to the other.

"Kindly do not fidget, child."

"I'm sorry, Reverend Mother."

"Hmmm!" She folded the letter, tapping it several times on the desk. "I suppose it would be in order. The Boxwells are a very fine family. You will, of course, conduct yourself properly, as befits a pupil of this establishment and you will return here by six o'clock, as your parents direct."

"Oh, yes Reverend Mother. I will of course."

It was so easy really. Her father could never refuse her anything, although she suspected that her mother had been less than overjoyed. Words like 'importunate' and 'stringent conditions', words her father would never have used, suggested a certain reluctance, a sub-text of disapproval.

"You may go. Go now. Go on. Away with you."

The door clicked behind her. She was free. She wanted to

leap in the air and yell, but she must comport herself like a lady, at least until Sunday.

"I'm afraid we have been very dull company," said Mrs Boxwell with an elaborate sigh, "what with the rain and Elizabeth taking to her bed like that. I thought we might have had some tennis or a nice walk by the river." She was concerned for Elizabeth, but it had happened before, particularly on a Sunday afternoon when the prospect of school on Monday quite overwhelmed the poor child. The patient, tucked up in bed with a hot lemon drink and a fire in the grate, looked as if she might just about survive.

"Oh, but I have enjoyed myself, Mrs Boxwell. I really have."

She had enjoyed the dull afternoon enormously, even more so, because of Elizabeth's sudden chill, the result of walking from Mass in the rain. Everyone else had got wet too, but they were made of coarser material. Not that she wished her any harm, but after sitting with her for an hour or so it was a relief to escape downstairs where the others were gathered by the pianoforte.

"I insist that Robert walks you back to school. He must take an umbrella. Robert," she said, "you must walk Catherine back to school and take care that she doesn't catch a chill, like your poor sister. Take an umbrella."

"Please allow me," said John, getting to his feet with alacrity. "It's on my way. It would be my pleasure."

Robert looked at the rain bucketing down and made no argument. Catherine smiled demurely.

"I'm so sorry I have to go, but you know Reverend Mother and her rules."

"Quite right too," nodded Mrs Boxwell. "We must all live by the rules. Isn't that correct, John?"

"Indeed, yes, Mrs Boxwell. Indeed we must. So I shall make it my bounden duty to see that this young lady is back safely by six o'clock."

Catherine looked down. She fidgeted with her bonnet, turning it in her hands.

"Oh, my dear," said Mrs. Boxwell, "I hope you're not getting a fever. You look quite flushed to me. John, you're a medical man, do you think she looks flushed?"

"Permit me," said John, assuming a grave, professional air. He touched her forehead and cheeks with the backs of his fingers, lingering a moment, looking thoughtful. It was more caress than diagnostic technique. She felt a turmoil inside her. She looked into his eyes.

"Hmmm," he said smiling, "I don't think there is any cause for alarm."

Despite his reassurance, she felt suddenly a roaring sound inside her head, like the sound of the waves on a stormy night as they broke over the sand bar into the lake at home. Dark patches floated in front of her eyes. She turned away, fumbling with her bonnet, closing her eyes for a moment. The waves died down and her vision cleared.

"I'll just go and say goodbye to Elizabeth," she said, anxious to be by herself for a moment. She hurried out of the room.

At the turn of the stairs she paused with one hand on the banister and took several deep breaths. She became aware that she was trembling. She heard voices below as they came out into the hallway. She heard the rattling in the hall-stand as Mrs. Boxwell selected a suitable umbrella. She ran upstairs for fear that they might see her.

"This is a good stout car umbrella," Mrs. Boxwell was saying. "See the double spokes. We always use it when we drive out."

"A very reliable instrument, Mrs. Boxwell," John agreed, examining the umbrella, giving it an experimental flap.

"Oh please, don't open it in the house. Don't you know how unlucky that is?"

John slid the umbrella closed. "No, I never heard that," he said. "We wouldn't want to bring bad luck on such an agreeable afternoon."

He looked up as Catherine descended the stairs.

"I was just saying how much I enjoyed the afternoon, Miss Doyle and how agreeable it was to meet you again."

He made a swordsman-like flourish with the umbrella, declaiming:

"And drunk delight of battle with our peers,
Far on the ringing plains of windy Troy."

Mrs Boxwell looked puzzled. "It should certainly stand up to this weather anyway."

Catherine caught his eye and smiled. Mrs. Boxwell opened the door. The rain fell like a curtain. A small river swirled in the gutter.

"You had better take my arm," he said, as they stepped outside. Catherine complied, holding her skirts out of the wet with her free hand. The stones were slippery underfoot. The rain drummed on the umbrella. She felt safe and warm.

The streets were empty except for a few dejected animals standing outside a public house, two ponies drooping in the shafts of dishevelled traps and a donkey with crooked and cruelly neglected hooves.

"What was that line you were quoting when I came down?" she asked, after a long, awkward silence.

"Ah, so you haven't read my present," he accused lightly.

He was correct in his assumption. She had not read the book, but she had caressed it, revelling in the sensuous softness of the calfskin and the flickering gold on the edges of the pages as she fluttered them with her thumb. She had held it to her breast in the darkness of the night, longing for the time to luxuriate in its verses, perhaps by the river on a sunny day, or reclining in her little boat while he…

"I didn't thank you properly. It was very nice of you. Was that line from the book?"

"Ulysses," he replied. "My favourite." He quoted again:

"For our purpose holds to sail beyond the sunset,
And the baths of all the western stars, until we die."

They walked in silence for a while. Rainwater spurted at them from downpipes but they paid no attention. She did not notice that her buttoned overshoes were already soaking or that her hem dragged in the wet. She gripped his arm.

"Ulysses," he said. "He's the man for me."

"But aren't you going to be a doctor?"

He snorted in derision.

"I thought I was, but no. Do you know what I'll be studying if I go back? I'm supposed to go back on Wednesday."

"What will you be studying?" She thought of cadavers and grisly anatomy rooms.

"Pill rolling," he said, laughing. "We have to learn to make pills. They want to make an apothecary out of me. We have to weigh the stuff and roll it into pills on a little tray. Can you imagine the boredom?"

"But surely you have to know everything there is to know. It is a very noble calling, don't you think?"

"I look at my father dealing out dribs and drabs of medicine all his life and still the people die. Even the doctors die. What's the point of it all, tell me?"

"It is a noble calling to help others," she said primly.

"The noblest calling," he said with sudden vehemence, "is to be yourself, not what others want you to be."

She pondered for a while.

"You said 'if'," she pressed.

"If what?"

"If you go back on Wednesday."

"Did I?"

"Yes."

They walked on some distance in silence. He took out his watch and flicked it open.

"Come down by the quay," he said "to look at the ships."

"Why?"

"I like to look at them."

"Why?"

"There's something about a ship. Any boat really. As soon as you cast off, everything changes. All bets are off. Think about that day on the lake. I know what you were thinking then."

He became animated. "It's an act of faith. There are only a few inches of timber between you and a watery grave. Yet we trust the boat to keep us alive."

"I never thought about it like that. Anyway what was I thinking?"

He chuckled and said nothing. They emerged onto the rain-washed quay. Schooners lay against the wall. Far out on the harbour a white sail made towards open water.

They made their way through the clutter of cordage and barrels, stepping over mooring lines.

"What was I thinking?" she challenged him. A seaman in streaming oilskins watched them with idle interest, a Mulatto, a Lascar, some foreign race. He leaned on the rail of a little steamer, sheltering his pipe under the broad brim of his hat, impervious to the rain, his face impassive.

"You were thinking," said John, lowering his voice, speaking with sudden intensity, "you were thinking that if I asked you to come away with me, to leave home and family and come away to the ends of the world, you would come with me."

"I would?" She felt a chill of fear.

"You would. You know you would."

"But that could never happen."

"It can. It will," he said urgently, gripping her by the elbows. The umbrella fell unheeded to the ground. It bowled towards the quayside, vaulted once over its shaft and dropped into the water. The breeze caught it, taking it out into the stream.

"I would," she said softly, moving close to him. "I would. I would." She turned her face up to him, oblivious of the rain and he kissed her. The Lascar, impassive, drew on his pipe. The umbrella made good speed down river towards the open sea.

They walked, linking arms together. They plotted and planned their future. They laughed at anything and everything and nothing at all. He quoted again:

"It may be that the gulfs will wash us down.
It may be we will reach the Happy Isles
And see the great Achilles, whom we knew."

She knew that no gulf would wash them down. He stood on a bollard to declaim the poem. He raised his hands aloft, as he spoke in a fine ringing baritone. He leaped down and embraced her. They shook hands on the deal at White's Hotel, reaching across the narrow thoroughfare, as people delighted in doing. They splashed through the puddles, until, suddenly, it was half past eight and she arrived at the convent gates, soaked through to her undergarments and in serious trouble.

Chapter Three

The note in her missal told of Saint John, plunged into boiling oil on the orders of the Emperor, but saved by a striking miracle.

'Thou hast protected me, O God, from the assembly of the malignant, from the workers of iniquity, alleluia.'

The priest droned on, thinking of his breakfast. An unfair thought, she reflected. There was a chill in the church at such an early hour and a hollow echo which picked up the voice of the celebrant and carried it, reverberating, into the rafters.

'You see that on every side, we are afflicted by evils; grant we pray you, that the glorious intercession of blessed John, Your apostle and evangelist, may be our protection.'

Boiling oil would be the least of her troubles if Reverend Mother had her way. A stern letter to home, asking for an immediate interview had most probably arrived. Her parents might well be on the road already.

'The just shall flourish like the palm-tree,' she read, 'florebit in aeternum.' She savoured the words. She knew that there were palm-trees in that country.

The girls shuffled to Communion with heads bowed, but some of them looked curiously in her direction, a public sinner, kneeling in her place, barred from the sacrament until such time as her sin should be expiated. It was a deliciously interesting situation and some wondered if her parents would cast her forth from their door into a life of penury and shame. They hoped that nothing terrible would happen of course, but it was interesting all the same. She had spent a whole day, unchaperoned, with a man. Who knows where? It was known that he was a doctor from Dublin and that he smoked Spanish cigars. Elizabeth Boxwell knew the whole story but of course, she was saying nothing.

'And the heavens shall confess thy wonders.'

The Mass concluded. The priest closed the book with a resounding thwack.

"No talking please," said the old nun, as they fell into their accustomed line. She resented this extra responsibility, wishing fervently that the workmen would hurry up with the new convent chapel. The girls were hungry however and would make good time.

The streets were becoming busy. Shopkeepers were opening shutters or pulling down their sunshades. The nun yawned. She looked at the fish in the fishmonger's window. They stared back at her with their mouths open; haddock, hake, lugubrious gurnet. Disgraceful prices, she thought. Impossible to feed people at those prices. She resented her responsibility as bursar. Nobody appreciated how difficult it could be to balance the books.

A herd of cattle passed by, heading for the Liverpool boat. The girls scattered in alarm, cringing in doorways until the way was clear again. Meat, too, thought the nun. Scandalous!

A young man raised his cap to her and she acknowledged his greeting. A fine looking fair-haired young fellow, carrying a valise and helping an old woman in a black hooded shawl. He held her elbow as they crossed the street, stepping carefully to avoid the dung. It was unusual to find such courtesy in young people nowadays, even if he was smoking a slim panatella. She remembered the smell. She remembered her father's shop, how he would indulge in a smoke at the end of a long day and how proud he was when she told him that she was going to enter the convent. He took down a box and extracted a cigar, sniffed the length of it appreciatively and snipped off the end with a little metal device, which he kept in his waistcoat pocket.

"This is a cause for celebration," he said expansively, lighting a paper spill from the sputtering oil lamp.

The smell of the young man's panatella lingered in the air. Suddenly she longed for home, for her parents and the children she never had and she felt grief for the old woman in the black cloak, hobbling beside her boy, taking him to the boat, saying goodbye to him for the last time, probably never to see him again in this world. She said a little prayer for mothers everywhere and was glad that she would never feel their pain.

"Scandalous prices," she said aloud, clucking her tongue. She ushered the girls onwards, hurrying to keep up with them, reflecting that she was letting her mind wander from her responsibilities. She resolved to make some little act of self-denial as a penance.

Tom Doyle was intimidated by the convent parlour. He shuffled his feet awkwardly, fearful that he would scrape the polished floor. Dorothy sat quietly, with her hands joined in her lap. She approved of the neatness of the place and the absence of dust on the highly polished furniture, but the holy pictures she found oppressive.

The Reverend Mother entered like a whirlwind. The large beads which she wore at her waist, clattered against the door.

"She's gone," she said without preamble. "That wicked, wicked girl."

Tom started to his feet. He would not hear his daughter spoken of in such terms.

"No," he began and then the meaning of her words dawned on him. "No," he said again sitting down, shaking his head. He made a vague gesture with the hand that held his hat, "No, no," he said again. "No."

"What do you mean, gone? Where is our daughter?" He heard as if from afar, his wife's voice, stern and unwavering.

"She has gone," replied the nun, "She has run away. We have searched everywhere. We have notified the police. I have personally questioned every girl in the school and find no trace of her."

Tom got to his feet again.

"She must be somewhere around," he said anxious to go, to search the streets, to stop everyone he might meet. "She must be around somewhere." He felt a cold fear clutching at him and his mouth was dry. "She must be around somewhere."

"Your letter mentioned a young man." Dorothy rose to her feet. Her face was grim.

"I have already communicated with his parents. They dismiss the notion that he might be involved, quite out of hand. They are a very good family, you understand."

"How dare you? Are you suggesting...?" Dorothy's face was white with fury. "You had the care of our daughter and you have failed in your duty."

Tom looked at his wife in amazement. She had the rights of it, but he would never have dared to put it so bluntly.

"She is a very headstrong girl, that's all I was suggesting," mumbled the Reverend Mother, taken somewhat aback.

"This young man's name, please, and where may we find him?" said Dorothy coldly.

"He is Dr. Cardiff's son, John. I am informed that he returned to his studies in Dublin this very morning. They are one of the best families in the town," she added uncomprehending. "Very respectable people."

"Come away, husband," said Dorothy. "We have no further business here."

Tom followed her from the parlour in a kind of daze. He saw the bright May sunlight dazzling on the black and red tiles of the corridor. He heard the chatter of schoolgirls and their bright, echoing laughter. He trembled with dread.

"Good heavens, no," said Dr Cardiff. "My son is a scapegrace young fellow at times, but I assure you, he would never do anything dishonourable."

He put his hands behind his back, swishing the tails of his frock coat. A watch chain gleamed on his waistcoat. He paced a few steps along the corridor then turned to them again, simple country folk in some distress.

"I'm sure there is some explanation. In all likelihood she will be waiting for you when you get home. Young girls, you know, they take everything so seriously. You say she was in some spot of bother in school."

"Aye, that's right, Doctor," said Tom, hoping that the doctor could make sense of it all. An educated man. "She arrived back late on Sunday."

"With your son, they tell us," said Dorothy, coming directly to the point.

"Ah," said Dr Cardiff, pacing again. "But I can assure you…" He paused and rubbed his bearded chin. He dismissed the thought. "My son has gone back to college in Dublin. He went back this morning."

"This morning? Do you not think that a bit of a coincidence?" She knew that this must be the explanation and was relieved at the certainty that Catherine was alive. I'll kill her when I get my hands on her, she thought, furious with the girl and furious with the two slow-witted men who stood before her, frowning.

"We must follow them," she said.

"I can give you the address of my son's lodgings, but I am sure there is no need."

"Yes, yes," said Tom. They could get to Dublin in a few hours and have her home the following day, before any harm came to the poor child.

Dr Cardiff wrote on a piece of paper with the stub of a pencil.

"These are his lodgings," he said. "Perhaps he can shed some light on the matter, but I fear you are putting yourselves to a lot of unnecessary trouble. However, there is a train this afternoon, to the best of my knowledge."

"Aye, thank you, Doctor," said Tom. His wife looked at him sharply, as if he had put a knuckle to his forelock.

"We will leave you now, sir," she said. "If you hear of anything, perhaps you will be good enough to let us know."

"Of course. Of course," he said with professional gentleness. "In the unlikely event of what you are saying, being true, however, let me assure you that my son is an honourable man who would treat your daughter with respect." He dismissed the absurd notion from his mind. "I'm sure you will have better news presently. You'll see. These things work out in the end."

He shook their hands and showed them to the door. Tom raised his hat. Dorothy pulled on her gloves, thinking of fever. The doctor frowned for a moment. He shook his head, dismissing the thought and returned to his rounds.

The priest looked at the young couple sitting in the pew. Not the usual Irish emigrants who poured through Liverpool on their way to the New World. These were well dressed and well shod, with an air of confidence about them, particularly the young man.

"I think you would do better to go home and ask your parents' permission. It's better in the long run. There is no harm done, so you tell me." He coughed awkwardly. "There is still time to put things right with your people."

Catherine shook her head. She would not allow her happiness to be snatched away from her at the last minute by some old priest who knew nothing of the world or of love. Strange, she thought, that her day had begun in a church, with the Mass of St John, the boiling oil and everything and now the day was ending in a church, in a strange city, with the light fading and the hustle and bustle of a great sea-port all around them.

"You would not want us to burn in Hell for all eternity, would you?" There was almost a tinge of insolence in the way John put it, with a half smile twitching at his lips. "Would that not be the greater evil?"

"There is the matter of the banns. I would have to read the banns."

"Banns or no banns," retorted John, "We will be on a ship tomorrow morning, bound for South America, even if we have to ask the captain to marry us."

"That would be no marriage in the sight of God," said the priest severely. "I forbid it."

"Very well," said John, getting to his feet. "We must take our chances with the fires of Hell."

The priest looked down at the young girl, little more than a child. Tears glistened in her eyes, catching the light from the candles before a shrine.

"I want to be married in church, Father," she said, "but whether or no, I will be John's wife."

The priest sighed. They would need whatever blessing they could take with them to their new life in some wild and savage country. He wished that his words had the power to make them return to their people, but it was hopeless. In the deepest recesses of his soul, he envied them.

"Very well, then," he conceded, defeated on his own terms. He went to speak to the sexton, who all this time had been engaged at the back of the church, knocking a broom against the furniture, making the most intriguing echoes, in between testing the creaking hinges of the doors and the confessional. The sexton departed and reappeared presently with the housekeeper, a gaunt, spare woman, a poor substitute for family and friends.

The priest drove a hard bargain, insisting on confession and absolution before any wedding could take place. He spoke to them of the pain they had caused by their wilfulness and how they must write immediately to their parents, assuring them of their safety. This was a condition of absolution, he insisted. Furthermore they must continue to write. He had seen too many Irish disappear into that great void. Then he joined their hands together. They became man and wife and John gave her his grandmother's ring, the grandmother who had doted on him and had put the money by for his education.

Then it was done. She thought of how happy her parents would be when they heard. She thought that some day they would go home to Wexford, possibly with children and they would all celebrate together. She thought that her happiness would last forever and no matter what happened, no matter how they might lose patience with each other sometimes, or grow old and cranky, it would be enough for one of them to mention Liverpool and their wedding and all would be well again between them.

In a cheap hotel she tasted wine for the first time, strong wine from Portugal, a deep ruby red. It made her laugh. People looked at them, smiling. They had giggled about this at school, what men and women do. There had been jokes about wedding nights and talk about farm animals. She knew a certain amount about all that. She recalled her father taking the cows to the bull and how her mother would enquire as to whether everything had gone according to plan, as she put it. Even the old crack-voiced cockerel did his duty manfully, crowing about it afterwards.

Now it was no subject for joking or sly innuendo. Now she was a woman. In that small sloping bedroom at the top of the house, she made love with John and felt pain, joy and physical delight in his warm hard body. This was not something she could explain even to her closest friends. He knew what he was about and she responded to him, despite the pain and the sharp points of horsehair in the mattress. She wished that this could last forever, but suddenly he groaned and shuddered, rolling away from her with a long sigh. He laughed.

"If they could see us now," he said.

She pondered the idea in silence.

"What would your mother think of us?" he teased.

Catherine touched the ring, turning it on her finger. There was no going back.

"I am a Cardiff now," she said, "for better or for worse."

They lay together, secure in the warmth. The clock ticked insistently. A ship's bell clanged. A foghorn groaned far away, like a sick cow.

She turned to him again, eager for his touch, but he was asleep. She looked at him in the dim light and felt a great tenderness. He was exhausted. He had great responsibilities ahead of him. She touched his cheek as he had touched hers on that rainy day so long ago in that other world. She lay close to him, listening to his breathing. The clock ticked. Voices sounded in the street below, loud laughter. Footsteps retreated. The foghorn groaned again and amid thoughts of home, she drifted into sleep.

Tom Doyle read the letter again. It was creased and frayed from folding and opening. She signed herself 'Your loving daughter, Catherine.'

"Put it away," said his wife. "There's nothing to be done about the situation for now. When we get an address we can write to them and persuade them to come home."

"Aye," he nodded, replacing the letter in his inside pocket. "We can do that."

"She has a lot of growing up to do," said Dorothy "but they will be back. That young man has no staying power. You'll see."

"You could be right. We'll see her come in that gate in a month or two, when she comes to her senses."

"We can help them get started. Things are not so bad."

"Aye the money is there. We could maybe buy a bit of a farm for them. That's what we can do."

She knew that he was trying his best. She knew that his heart was broken. She felt a hard cold anger for what her daughter had done to them and particularly what she had done to Tom. He was incapable of anger, even towards the young man, but Dorothy was different. If she could eliminate him, she would. If he fell from the ship and was devoured by sharks or mangled in the paddle wheel, she would feel no grief for him.

"He sounds like a good lad, all the same," said Tom. "She says that they are all right for cash. Sure if Catherine loves him he must be a good lad. I dare say he'll be good to her."

"I dare say he will," she agreed. Her anger was ebbing away. "We must make the best of it. He is a part of our family now."

Tom looked at her in surprise. He had never seen her cry before, in all the years they had been together. He patted her shoulder with awkward gentleness.

"We'll make the best of it," he agreed. "He must be a good lad all the same, if she feels that way about him."

She patted his hand. "Well, we have things to do," she said briskly. "We can't stand around moping all day."

She took her apron from the hook on the back of the kitchen door, her hands fumbling as she made a bow at the back. She paused for a moment, then straightened the starched white cloth, smoothing it downwards with both palms.

"We have things to do," she said again, picking up her broom. Tom looked out of the window at the lake, the stiff reeds at the margin and the sea stretching endlessly beyond the sandbar.

"Aye, that we have," he said, but he made no move.

Chapter Four

The steamship, *Mersey*, butted into an unseasonable westerly gale, with the flag of the Royal Mail streaming bravely on the mizzen and all sails furled. Each time a wave caught the housing around the paddle wheels, the ship jolted or lurched to one side or the other. Sometimes the wheels flailed in vain, catching only air and the ship seemed to stop for an instant before ploughing ahead with renewed determination.

Below decks, the thump, thump of the engine reverberated through all parts of the ship. In their cramped cabin, no bigger than a wardrobe, John wished that he could die. The air was fetid with the smell of sickness. The curtain which shielded them from other passengers, did nothing to keep out the constant groaning of the sick and the crying of infants.

"Leave me alone," he said miserably, pushing her hand away, "I don't want it."

The smell of the soup made him retch and Catherine stepped back in alarm. He sank back onto the bunk.

"I'm sorry," he gasped. "I just can't manage it."

She wished that he would eat something. She had struggled through the crowd for that pannikin of soup, pushing her way to where the steward stood, bracing his knees against the huge pot and ladling the soup out to anyone who could stomach it. In fine weather the surge of people was even worse, but even now it was a struggle to be served. Food would be good for him, she was sure. She could not understand his attitude or why he had become so bad tempered. She thought the sea journey a fine adventure and delighted in walking on deck, even in rough weather. She left him to his misery and went up on deck. The wind was sharp and clean. The hood of her black silk school visite fell back. Her hair streamed in the gale. She warmed her hands on the tin mug. It would be a sin to waste it. She sat up on a folded life raft, swinging her legs like a child, sipping the well-salted soup and looking around. The deck was almost deserted. Black smoke rolled from the funnels overhead. The furled sails looked grey and soiled. She had expected canvas, white as the breast of a swan, carrying her over the water to her new home, but here she was in a snorting iron tub that wallowed in every trough. It amused her to think that things never work out the way you expect them and she felt a small triumph that she at least, was enjoying the experience.

The only other people on deck were a low-sized stocky man with a small moustache and a lady whom Catherine presumed to be his wife. They gripped the rail, enjoying the sea air and conversing in a language which she guessed was Spanish. The man wore rather baggy trousers, she noticed, tucked into his high boots. The lady gathered a shawl about her shoulders. Her hair was black and gathered at the back by a tortoise-shell comb. They looked in her direction. She lowered her eyes, concentrating on the soup. She heard their footsteps on the boards and they sat down beside her.

"You are enjoying your dinner?"

She looked up shyly. The man was smiling. His eyes were dark brown, with creases at the corners, as if he squinted into the sun a lot or maybe smiled a lot. She could not decide.

"Oh yes thank you, sir." She raised her voice against the wind and the thrumming of the rigging.

"It is pleasant to dine out of doors."

She nodded.

"You are travelling with your parents? Where do you go to?" enquired the lady.

"No, Ma'm. I am travelling with my husband, but he isn't here. I mean he isn't well. He's in bed."

"Your husband!" said the lady, raising her eyebrows. "But you are too young to have a husband."

"No I'm not," said Catherine defiantly. "We have been married since..." She hesitated. "Since Wednesday." She blushed.

"Ah," said the man. "So long! An old married woman." He laughed and Catherine took no offence. He stood up, took her hand in his and made an elaborate bow.

"I am José Luis Aguirre, at your service. This is my wife, María Jesús. May I ask who you are, Madam?"

"I am Catherine Cardiff. My husband's name is John and we are going to Uruguay to become farmers." She said it with an air of importance.

"Uruguay! Why do you go to Uruguay?"

"I have two uncles in Uruguay. They will help us find a place to live."

"Hmm," said the man. "There are some English in Uruguay. Many in Argentina."

"We are not English, sir. We are Irish."

She thought of Mother Alacoque.

"It is not the same?" He seemed surprised. "But you speak English so well."

"We speak English, but we are Irish, sir." It was too complicated to explain.

"We are also from Uruguay," said the lady, taking her hand, "We must be great friends, Catherine Cardiff."

"We will call you Catalina," said the man decisively and you may call us by our first names."

"Oh, thank you, sir," said Catherine. She realised that she was missing her parents for the first time. The idea had not occurred to her till then. She looked at the sea and the white spume torn from the crests of the waves as they surged eastwards in the direction of home.

"Please, not 'Sir'. José Luis and María Jesús. We must meet your husband when he is feeling better and we must talk about where you will live. Perhaps we can offer some advice."

"I'm sorry, sir, but I cannot be so familiar. You see, you remind me of my parents. May I call you Mr and Mrs Aguirre?"

"I understand. Well then, I am Don José. This is Doña María and you must begin to speak in Spanish."

"I will try. I will try very hard."

"And you will succeed," he said expansively. "You will be conquistadores in our country."

They got to their feet.

"We shall leave you now. When your husband is feeling better, I shall speak to him, as the head of your new household."

He bowed again and smiled at her. The Señora took his arm.

"Be very careful in this wind," she said. "Do not stay too long."

Catherine nodded. They departed and she sat looking at the sea. 'A gale o' wind,' her father would say. 'Blowin' a gale o' wind.' She thought of his fishing boats and hoped they were not at sea. She imagined them safe in Kilmore with the sea breaking over the harbour wall, trying to snatch at them. They seemed so small to her memory, compared to this great mail ship. She said a silent prayer that her brothers would be safe. She missed them.

The wind eased. John felt a little better. She sponged his face with a damp cloth and touched the fair stubble on his chin.

"You need a shave," she said smiling. "You would feel better too."

"I haven't the energy. I'll do it tomorrow."

"No, let me do it now."

He looked surprised.

"Very well. If you insist."

She busied herself about the preparations, working up a lather in his little shaving mug and soaping his chin with playful strokes of the brush until he could not help but laugh. She told him about the people she had met on deck and how they had promised to help them settle down in Uruguay. He was interested.

"Maybe they will know where to find your uncles. Did you ask them?"

"No, not yet, but I will."

She stroked carefully with the razor. He sat rigid, watching her apprehensively. She wiped the blade between finger and thumb.

"Careful," he said. "That thing is razor-sharp."

She looked at him witheringly.

"It would be, wouldn't it?"

"You know what I mean."

The ship lurched.

"This would be your chance to be rid of me," he said. "You could say your hand slipped just at the wrong moment. You could be a rich widow."

"Rich!" she scoffed. "On a few hundred pounds."

She scraped again and a speck of blood stained the white lather.

"Oh," she said, alarmed. "Sorry." She steadied herself against the roll of the ship. In the porthole the horizon tilted at an angle. She waited a moment then scraped again until she had completed the job.

"Not so bad," she said, pleased with her work.

He touched his chin where the razor had nicked. He looked at the pinpoint of blood on his finger.

"At least when the constabulary come, I can say I got a good look at my assailant."

She laughed. It was obvious that he was regaining his good spirits.

"Hand me up that valise, if you would."

She reached under the bunk and pulled out the valise. She noted that he was well supplied with clean linen and reflected that she would have a deal of washing to keep her own few items clean. There had been little time to buy anything in Liverpool. He took out his matching hairbrushes and brushed his long fair hair straight back from his forehead in a few rapid strokes.

"I feel better already," he said, swinging his legs to the floor. "I think I might try something to eat. Would you see if you could forage something for me? I'm not too steady on the pins. Haven't got the old sea legs under me yet."

She was glad to see him recovering. She went searching and by dint of bribery, managed to obtain some more soup and a few pieces of bread. The soup was almost cold but John managed it with a grimace. He sat waiting to see if there would be any ill effects. He took some of the bread. The colour had returned to his cheeks.

"A breath of air," he decided and they went up on deck. He inhaled deeply. "That's the stuff to give the troops," he said.

The ship was moving with a smoother motion. The water threshed in the drums of the paddle wheels.

"This is the life," he said, thumping his chest.

The sky was clearing. Stars flitted between the swaying yardarms high above.

"This is the life," he said again putting his arm around her shoulders.

With the return of his good spirits, John found some congenial companions and spent a lot of time in the cramped, second class saloon. He declared with glee that the voyage would pay for itself. His companions were avid card players, but John had the measure of them. She suspected that it was too easy, but he assured her that the stakes were low and anyway there was nothing else to do on board.

She passed the mornings on deck and in the afternoons she lay down for a few hours. It was said to be the custom in South America, an hour or two of sleep at the hottest time of the day. She wished that she had brought a book.

They were fortunate to have an outside berth with a porthole. Some people had to sleep in stygian darkness in the centre of the ship with only a fanlight as a poor substitute. She looked out at the sea and at a speck of sail on the horizon. They could go on like this forever, with nothing but the rhythmic thump of the engines to mark the passage of time. She felt her pulse. It kept time with the great heart of the ship. She wondered if she would die if the ship came to a halt. The speck of sail had grown in the porthole. It looked as if their paths might cross.

She heard footsteps in the companionway and John threw back the curtain.

"Come up on deck," he said in excitement. "It's a warship. An American."

He grabbed her hand. "Come quickly. They say she is going to stop and search the ship."

The absurd notion struck her that perhaps there was a warrant out for their arrest. Fugitives from the law. But they had broken no law. She hurried on deck, pleased that he wanted to share the adventure with her.

The passengers crowded to the rails, enjoying the drama, but some were apprehensive. Supposing the Americans were to open fire. There was no love lost between the Federal government and Her Majesty. It was not unknown for American ships to stop British merchantmen on suspicion of breaking the blockade of the South. Here on the vastness of the ocean there were no witnesses.

The warship came on, lean as a greyhound, with all sails set and smoke streaming from her funnel. The Union flag stood out, stiff as a board. There was a buzz of excitement among the passengers.

"She has no paddle-wheels, but look at the speed of her," said John intrigued. "How can she go so rapidly?"

"My friend tells me it is one of the new screw ships."

Catherine turned at the familiar voice. Don José was standing nearby, straining to see over the heads of the people at the rails.

"Ah, Don José. How nice to see you again."

"I am afraid I am imprisoned in the first class for much of the time, talking the serious business."

"This is my husband, John, that I was telling you about. John, this is Don José from Uruguay."

"I am delighted to make your acquaintance, sir," said John formally, shaking hands.

"And this is my friend, el Gales, Enrique Jones."

He tapped the shoulder of a young man who was watching the approaching warship with a keen interest.

"Enrique," he said, "you must meet these two young Irishes who are coming to live in our country."

The young man, raised his hat and nodded. He looked a serious young man, dark haired and brown eyed, she noticed. Short and stocky like Don José. She wondered if there might be some relationship.

"How do you do, Señor Jones?" She said.

"Henry, please," he said smiling. "Henry Jones, mining engineer at your service."

They shook hands.

"I am Welsh, you see. Don José has engaged me to explore the mineral wealth of his country." He spoke in the soft sing-song accent, which she had heard before when the Welshmen came over to the herring grounds in the winter.

"Look," said John. "They're signalling."

The Americans were running up a series of flags and the *Mersey* responded.

"There is no problem," said Henry. "They are satisfied. They'll not be running out their guns, see."

"You can read what they are saying?" queried John, intrigued.

"It's just something I know," said the Welshman modestly.

"Enrique is a man of many skills. That is why we have engaged his services. You must dine with us tonight. Doña María Jesús wishes to meet you. When my wife wishes something, I must obey." He made a self-deprecating gesture.

The American kept pace with them at a cable's length, the water churning at the stern. The gun ports remained closed. She turned away, heeling with the wind and her yards came about with an audible crack that echoed across the intervening water.

Don José watched the ship as it raced away from them.

"They are the new power in the world," he murmured, almost to himself.

"I beg to differ, Don José," objected Henry. "They are racked by civil war. It will take them a century to recover. They would be no match for the Empire."

"We shall see," said the older man. "But I hear that they have new guns. I shall have to find out more. The republic must be strong. We also have recovered from civil war. It did not take a hundred years." He leaned on the rail. Catherine noticed that he wore an enormous knife thrust into his belt at the back. The tooled leather scabbard was decorated with silver.

"Anyway," he said, turning to them again, "we can talk about such matters this evening over dinner, provided we do not bore the ladies."

He left abruptly with a smile and Catherine noticed that he walked with a limp, accentuated by the rolling of the deck.

"Who is he?" asked John. "He seems to be a person of some standing."

"Don José is a senator of the government," replied the Welshman. "He has been some time in England, purchasing machinery and small arms. As you have gathered no doubt, I have been engaged to help in the surveying and exploration."

"I see," said John, impressed. "But why all the talk about guns? There is no war, is there?"

"No. Not at the moment. But they have had their civil wars and the great powers are always interested in the River Plate."

"I see," said John again. "Civil wars."

"And rumours of wars," said the Welshman portentously.

Catherine felt a prickle of fear. She wondered what kind of a country they were landing themselves in, but at that moment her greatest anxiety was what she was going to wear to dinner in the First Class dining room.

Doña María Jesús motioned to her to sit. Catherine was looking about the cabin. The ceiling was so low that she was wary of bumping her head, but otherwise it was spacious, compared to their own cramped quarters.

"I shall talk to you as a mother," began the older woman. "Firstly, I know that you have run away."

Catherine lowered her eyes. It was almost like being in school.

"Secondly, you were not prepared."

"Oh, but we planned. John has money."

Doña María Jesús raised her hand, palm outwards.

"John has money," she said dismissively, "but you have not even a change of clothes. He has married you, yes and that is honourable. Otherwise your father would have to find him and kill him."

Catherine made to protest.

"Do not interrupt. It would be necessary. You have brothers at home?"

"Yes, two."

"They also, but it will not be necessary now. But now to more practical matters. You must tell me about your marriage and what you hope to do in our country."

Catherine told her of home and school. She recounted their flight, skipping through the herd of cattle, running and laughing, all the way to the boat.

"Now you have time to think, what have you decided? If you decide to return home, I shall find a berth for you, when we arrive at Rio. And for your husband too. Perhaps you should start again with the blessing of both your families."

"Oh, no," replied Catherine. "We want to make a new life together in Uruguay."

"You have an address for your uncles, I presume."

"Not exactly. We imagined that we could ask about them. Somebody will know them. Uncle Laurence has only one eye."

"Mother of God!" said the older woman, shaking her head. "This is your plan? I see. You speak Spanish, of course."

Catherine hung her head. It was not much of a plan.

"You will travel through Uruguay asking about a one-eyed man. Maybe they are in Paraguay. Maybe you must go to Argentina and ask the wild Indians of the Pampas if they know your uncles."

Catherine looked up defiantly.

"We will find work first. Then we will buy some land. I know about farming. John is a clever man. He will do well. He sees no difficulty."

"Ah yes," sighed Doña María Jesús. "The men see no problems. I am the wife of a soldier. He knows of no problem that cannot be resolved by his knife or perhaps a fusilade of lead. I have followed him on campaign. I know how the men think. But I am being severe with you. I want you to understand that there will be difficulties."

"I understand."

"So, because your mother is not here, I must advise you. She would do the same for my daughters."

Catherine was not so sure. She thought of the tinker children, a constant irritant to her mother, but then she remembered how her mother had always anticipated her needs, without fuss or preamble.

The woman stood up, stooping slightly. She opened the lid of a leather travelling trunk.

"First we must be practical. We must attend to your trousseau, if you will permit me. You are the same size as my eldest daughter. I have some things here for her but she can wait."

She emptied the contents of a suitcase onto a bunk. Catherine protested. She wondered what her mother would say about accepting charity.

"This is not charity. This is between friends. We must look well for our husbands, must we not?" She laughed, dismissing the awkwardness. She laid some items on the bunk and began to fold them carefully.

"Some undergarments and these towels of course, you will need, as you are a woman." She pronounced the word as 'goman'. Catherine felt a release of tension inside her, like a fiddle-string slackening. She had worried about all that. Her mother was more discreet, providing what she needed, leaving her to work things out for herself.

"I will send for hot water if you would like to bathe behind the screen."

She wanted a bath more than anything at that moment, even a quick up and downer as her father would say.

"Yes, please," she replied. What a relief it would be to rid herself of the rancid smell of a week's travel and the foul air below decks, even if God were to peer at her through the porthole.

"I shall teach you some Spanish as we travel along. You will be able to help your husband in his business affairs. Then he will need you more than ever."

She held up a long, black dress, shaking out the folds. The bodice was cut low in front and at the shoulders and decorated with a bow of red ribbon.

"There is nothing so silly as fashion," she declared. "What is new and exciting today will be cheap and vulgar tomorrow. But this will never be out of fashion. You must wear this tonight with a lace mantilla. Tonight you will be a great lady of Uruguay and all the men will admire you."

Mother Alacoque had done her work well. 'If in any doubt,' she used to say, 'start at the outside and work your way inwards.' It was not enough to learn the language of the French but one must understand their civilisation and to do that, one must understand how to lay a table and which cutlery went with which course. Nevertheless, Catherine kept an eye on the others. John seemed perfectly at ease with his silverware. Henry Jones ate everything with gusto. Doña María Jesús ate delicately, while her husband declined soup, fish, even lobster, declaring that he would wait for the main course.

She knew that John was looking at her with open admiration. She knew that he thought her the most beautiful woman in the dining room. She felt wonderful. If they could see us now, she thought smiling inwardly.

Don José twirled the stem of his glass, contemplating the contents.

"Ah yes," he mused. "I envy you young people. You have all your lives ahead of you. So many adventures."

They waited for him to continue.

"My husband feels sorry for himself," said Doña María Jesús, "because there are no more wars. Now he says he makes war on paper, fighting with his pen against mountains of official documents."

"It is true, what you say, woman," he replied. "I push paper around on my desk as I once moved armies in the field."

"You do important work," she said, patting the back of his hand.

"You were a soldier then, sir," said John with interest.

"I was. I was a general in the Great War. I fought at the siege of Montevideo for nine years. Before that I was an officer of cavalry. But now I am a politician. I do not call myself a general because it frightens people." He laughed at the idea.

"But first," said his wife softly, "you were a baqueano. Tell them about that."

"Ah, yes." His eyes took on a faraway look. He was silent for a while. "Ah yes," he said again. "Before I was a soldier. Before I educated myself and learned the manners of a gentleman. Before the wars began, I was a baqueano." He swirled the wine again and drank.

"Baqueano?" said Henry frowning. "What is that?"

"They are gauchos with a special gift," said his wife proudly. "The baqueano is different. He is a quiet man. He knows his way by the stars and by every hill and hollow. He will guide you to a place, even a place he has never been to, even if it is five hundred leagues across the Pampas. He will take you as straight as an arrow, hardly stopping to sleep."

"Ah, you exaggerate, woman. The baqueano must learn, like everyone else. My family were wandering gauchos. I learned the signs, that is all."

"Tell us about the gauchos," said Catherine.

"You will love the gauchos, my little Catalina. We are the horsemen of the Pampas. We go where we please and we take what we please."

He paused as the steward began to serve. She noticed that he accepted only the meat, an enormous mound of various cuts, which he began to attack without recourse to condiments of any sort.

"But you are a soldier, sir," put in John. "How did that happen?"

Don José chewed and swallowed. He gestured with his knife.

"The baqueano is the eyes of the army. I joined Rivera and fought in the War of the Two Colours. I joined for adventure, I suppose. I fought Indians for Rivera. I am not proud of that, but it had to be done. They were wild people, you see, savages."

Catherine was about to ask him if he had ever encountered her uncles. They had fought the savages too. She stopped herself in time, glancing at Doña María Jesús. This was not like a fair day in Wexford where people stood around chatting and asking 'Do you know such-and-such,' or 'I have an uncle up that way. Maybe you've come across him.' She held her tongue.

"Thirty years of war," he sighed. "Now I have little need of a horse. Without my horse, I am less than a man."

"That is not so," protested his wife, "You are still a great guide for your people."

"Ah," he grunted, concentrating on his food, but he was pleased nonetheless. "And of course, Venancio Flores threatens to bring the Brazilians down upon us again."

"He is a patriot," asserted his wife. "He will not harm his own country."

"We have a government of consent now. Flores relies too much on the foreigners. Berro is a man of peace. Let us enjoy our prosperity."

They argued some more in Spanish, but apologised, realising that their guests were at a loss.

"You said 'five hundred leagues,' Madam," said John. "How extensive is this Pampas?"

"We must not say 'leagues' any more," she said playfully. "My husband's government insists that we say kilometres. We are very modern nowadays. Enrique, shall you measure in metres and kilos when you dig in the mines?"

"Indeed yes," said the Welshman. "We must move with the times, see. We must be scientific."

"But to your question of the Pampas," said Don José. "Imagine a world completely flat, a grassland stretching away in all directions, without a hill or a valley. A thousand, two thousand kilometres. I find these measurements difficult myself. You travel for days and see no change. Perhaps an ombú tree, a flock of ñandú, our native ostrich, a herd of wild cattle. Only the stars to guide you at night. The white bones of animals…"

"Please, you will alarm our young friends. Our country is more gentle. We have hills and plenty of water and good timber. We have some good roads and my husband promises us railways. We are very modern indeed."

Don José was silent. He thought of his horses, his gaucho saddle and a world where nothing changed. He remembered what it was to live off the country, to ride down his quarry with bolas or lazo and dispatch the creature with a stroke of his knife.

The steward brought cigars and the ladies decided to take a turn on deck, as the evening was warm. John drew on his cigar, a fine Cuban. This is the life, he reflected. We will travel First Class in future. Don José spoke of cattle and how the trade in dried meat was falling away. He spoke of the English and their new factory at Fray Bentos.

"We take our culture from Spain but our economy from the English," he explained. "They own many businesses in Uruguay. We need their money and perhaps we may need their navy. They have helped us in the past."

He spoke of the Great War of 1839, which lasted for eleven years, the nine years' siege of Montevideo, of Garibaldi and his Italian Legion.

"San Felipe y Santiago de Montevideo, to give it its proper title. The modern Troy, but that is behind us now. We are men of peace, are we not?"

"But who won the war?" asked John.

Don José turned his cigar between finger and thumb. He blew gently on the lighted end, watching it glow.

"There were no winners and no losers," he said with a degree of pride. "No conquerors. No vanquished."

"Except for those who died," suggested the Welshman softly.

"Men die in war," replied Don José. "The Uruguayan knows how to die."

"But who gained?" persisted Henry.

"It is a question of honour," explained Don José patiently. "We gained a sense of our national identity. We learned, both Blancos and Colorados, that we do not want foreigners deciding the fate of our country. You both, the Gales and the Irish, come from conquered countries. You do not control your own affairs. You are subjects of the Queen."

The younger men were silent, stung by the observation and he relented.

"I am sorry, I do not wish to offend. We were a colony for many centuries also, but now we defend our independence. It is a question of honour."

"But you have many English, you say," retorted John.

"We are realists," said Don José, accepting the point. "We need their money and their machinery. I have bought their guns, but we will turn those guns on the English or anyone else if necessary." A thought struck him. "You will need a good rifle. I shall see to it that you are provided with a suitable weapon. Do you shoot?"

"I do indeed, sir. I have a sporting gun at home. Unfortunately I was unable to bring it with me."

"You will have plenty of sport in Uruguay. There is plenty of game."

"But no savages," said John lightly.

Don José was silent for a moment.

"Who knows?" he said slowly. "Who knows? I was there at the matanza, the killing place of the Charrúas. Their blood is on my hands. It was necessary, as it is necessary to kill animals for food, but it was an ugly sight."

He smoked in silence. They waited.

"There was an Italian soldier with me. He was once a fisherman. He told me of the matanza, the netting of the fish and the killing, the boats drawing together, the pulling up of one great net and the blood in the water." His hand shook and the smoke curled upwards, in folds, like a translucent ribbon.

"Did any survive?" asked John. "Did you kill them all?"

"A few survived. The cacique, Sepé with perhaps, twenty of his followers. I saw him for a moment. He was naked except for a cloak, a quillapi, of the skin of the jaguar. He looked back at me, then disappeared into some trees. We never could find them, although we hunted for days."

"Was it an honourable thing?" asked the Welshman.

"No," said Don José, "it was not an honourable thing in itself but it is honourable for a soldier to follow the orders of his superiors. But Sepé retreated with honour. He killed nine of our men and two government officials. That was honourable. They had nothing but sling-stones and arrows against our modern weapons."

"Do you think he might still be alive? Could he be out there somewhere, in the forest waiting his chance for revenge?"

Don José gave a short dry laugh.

"No," he replied. "Sepé lives only in my dreams. Sometimes in my dreams I see him still, with his sling in his hand and his skin of the jaguar."

"And are you afraid?" John listened wide-eyed, like a child listening to a bedtime story.

"No," said Don José. "We are both men of honour. Sepé knows that I would fight him again in the place of the matanza or in the next world, if our paths ever cross."

They smoked in silence until the ladies returned. They said 'good-night' and retired to their cabins.

"We have met him," said John, squeezing in beside Catherine in the lower bunk.

"Met who?"

"The great Achilles. Don't you see? We are sailing to the new Troy. Have you noticed his limp? He is a warrior although he claims to be a man of peace."

"You're daft," she said, laughing and digging her elbow into his ribs.

"No, I'm not. I've been listening to him all evening and he is right. You have to fight for anything that is worthwhile. Then you must hold onto it, by force if necessary."

"I don't like that kind of talk," she said slipping her arms around him. "Come here to me, my husband. You will be a farmer, not a warrior."

She began to kiss him gently at first, then more urgently and they forgot about the wars, about Achilles and even the passengers in the neighbouring compartments.

It was the relative silence that woke her. She lay there listening intently. John was still asleep. She felt the vibration of the engines, but there was something missing, the threshing of the paddle-wheels. It had been there in the background for weeks, sometimes insistent and at other times just a dull rhythm of metal and water. She felt the ship jolt as the anchors took hold and in some dismay, she realised that the voyage was over. The confined routine of ship-board life would be no more. She wondered what lay ahead in a foreign city and a vast unknown country.

"We have arrived," she said shaking him by the shoulder. He mumbled and turned on his side.

"We're here," she said again and he sat up with a start. "We must have arrived. Listen."

"What is it?"

"The paddles have stopped."

The porthole showed the dim light of dawn. There was rain on the glass. They peered out, wiping their breath from the pane.

A sharp wind cut the river into deep, brown furrows, cold and uninviting. There was no land visible.

"We must be still at sea," she said, puzzled. "Maybe we have to wait for the tide, to get into the river."

As she spoke the ship swung on its chain, coming around into the current and the distant city swam into the circle of the porthole. They saw a low coastline of rocky promontories and the hill that gave the city its name. The bleary morning light glinted on white breakers and stretches of sand. Above the walls and the jumble of houses of this modern Troy, stood the two towers of the cathedral, one tower for Felipe and one for Santiago.

In the bay, lay the ships of many countries, men o' war and merchant vessels, riding at anchor, their cables taut in the pull of the river. Nearby, *H.M.S. Bombay* lay, trim and smart, fresh from her refit at Chatham, with yards squared away and the admiral's flag at the mizzen. She was an impressive sight, with her eighty-four guns, testimony to the power of the British Empire, which could reach into any part of the world and decide the destiny of nations.

Already a lighter was coming alongside to take off the mails. They hurried to dress and pack their belongings, as there was a deal of shouting on the deck above and a general excitement at the prospect of going ashore.

Chapter Five

It was a relief to be on their own again after living in close proximity to so many. It was strange that after weeks at sea she began to feel unwell only when she stepped off the tender, which brought them ashore. The unyielding nature of the ground under her feet made her feel heavy and slow. She felt sweat on her upper lip, cool in the breeze and she sat down for a moment on the suitcase, which Doña María José had so kindly provided. The feeling passed and John took her firmly by the arm. He carried both her case and his valise in one hand supporting her with the other. She felt safe at his touch. He dealt with all the business of customs.

He hailed a cab and showed the cabdriver a piece of paper with the address, which Doña María Jesús had given them.

"Ah, Inglés, Inglés," said the cab driver. "You are welcome."

He slapped the reins. The little horse took off at speed, rattling over the cobbles. She felt her insides turning over. She closed her eyes and gripped the rail, expecting at any moment to be upset and thrown into the street. She heard John laughing and she moved closer to him. He put his arm around her shoulders. He looked about at the fine houses and at the men, lounging with hands in their pockets, watching the traffic clattering through the arched city gate. The rain made him think of home.

Catherine lay on the bed in the small hotel room. The breeze from the window was cool. John had been gone since early morning. He had laughed when she offered to go with him.

"You must rest," he said, "and get your strength back. Anyway this is mens' work."

She wanted to say that she could help him; that she could interpret for him in matters of business, but that was only a dream. As yet she could manage only a few basic greetings. There had been that mix-up at the desk when she confused casado and cansado, married and weary. The concierge seemed to think it all very funny as she made the correction with a scratchy metal pen.

"Oh cansado, sí, sí," she laughed, nodding wisely.

Catherine was glad that they had declined the invitation from Doña María Jesús. It was better to be independent. Doña María Jesús seemed to understand. Young marrieds need their privacy.

She turned the pages of *The Graphic*, which John had picked up on board. It was six weeks out of date, an echo from another world. On the cover, the Constable of the Tower was inspecting the Beefeaters. They would do well in South America, she thought, as they seemed to eat nothing but beef. They looked a comical lot with their ruffs and knee breeches, but their long pikes looked dangerous enough. The Constable's daughter, standing beside his lady, looked stunted and frumpish, like a squat adult with that ridiculous bustle. Shadowy figures stood at the windows in the background, just a few lines of the engraver's art, ghosts of long dead prisoners, their heads miraculously restored to their shoulders.

'Holloway's Pills improve the appetite, promote digestion, are direct purifiers of the blood and perfect regulators of every function, and have withstood the test of time and the most relentless opposition.' She wondered about the relentless opposition. She resolved to ask John. He would know about pills. She wished that he would come back.

'*Home They Brought Her Warrior Dead.*' The words seemed to leap from the page. She started. He could go missing in this strange city. Perhaps Don José and the people he had recommended were ruthless predators. They carried knives. He could be lying in some alley with his throat cut and his blood staining the stones of the pavement, his beautiful fair hair all matted with blood. She fought her panic down. He was gone such a long time. Moreover the city was full of soldiers. There was talk of war in the North and massacres in the countryside.

'Song. Words by Alfred Tennyson Esq. D.C.L. Poet Laureate.

Music by Miss Lindsay (Miss. J.W. Bliss) No. 1 in E flat. No. 2 in G. Four Shillings each. Most touching and pathetic.'

All the new music was there, all written it seemed for them: 'The Pioneer', a new baritone song, sung by Mr Maybrick with the greatest success. 'A Warrior Bold,' also sung by Mr Maybrick throughout the provinces and always encored. 'Faces in the Fire,' 'Though Seas Between Us Roar.' All songs of loss, of warfare, of exile.

She thought of her family and resolved to write them. It gave her comfort to think that a letter would retrace their journey and find its way to her home by the lake. She would wait until John returned with news of his meetings. When they were rich she would write home frequently. She would order fine writing paper from J. Macmichael, stationer to the Queen, five quires and one hundred envelopes with Macmichael's celebrated raised and rustic monograms, noted for their elegance and good taste. A bargain at five shillings, post free.

She put down the newspaper and went to the window. She saw him striding purposefully up the street. He looked up and saw her. He raised his hat, waving it cheerily. His face seemed flushed with excitement.

My Dearest Parents,' she wrote.

I know that the manner of my going caused you distress and I am truly sorry for that. I want you to know that I am happy here and that John is a loving and kind husband. I know that this knowledge will make you happy too.

At the moment of writing we are still in Montevideo. We made the acquaintance of a very important man in the government and his wife when we were coming over on the ship. They have been very kind to us and have introduced John to people in the government offices where they make grants of land. I do not fully understand how this is done. It appears that the land is empty of people and we can buy it at a very low rate. They have arranged a loan for John with an English bank and he will discharge the debt when he sells his cattle. The cattle are wild and there for the taking, not like at home. Our farm will be called an estancia and it will be very big indeed, thousands of hectares. Hectares are bigger than acres so your daughter will be married to a country gentleman.

There are some people in that part of the country whom he will engage as herdsmen. They are a mixture of Spanish and Indian blood and are deemed to be skilled in the management of livestock. We will be far away from the armies and their wars, thank God.

We have not yet heard any news of Uncle Laurence or Uncle Michael but I am sure we will hear from them soon. There are not many people living in this country yet, so I am sure that word travels quickly when new people arrive. They will probably hear of us before we find them.

Don José, the senator whom we met on the ship, gave John a present of a gun. He is very proud of it. It is a rifle like the ones the soldiers carry. He intends using it for hunting. Do not worry about Indians. We are in no danger from painted savages, as Uncle Laurence used to say. They were all killed years ago in a war.

Although I miss you both and my dear brothers, I know that I shall be happy here. However, I would like some little reminder of home. When it is autumn, please send me some acorns from the oak tree in the upper meadow. I would like to have an oak tree on our new estancia. I would like my children to climb in it the way we climbed our tree at home. It is winter here but soon it will be Spring and we will have a proper address.

We will be setting out for our new home presently, travelling in an ox-drawn wagon, fording rivers and having all sorts of adventures. It will be so exciting.

She signed herself , *Your loving daughter*

Catherine (Cardiff).

She read the letter over again. It was a fine letter, reassuring and affectionate. She wondered about the parenthesis and the 'Cardiff'. Would they feel that she was making too much of a point of her new identity. What other Catherine did they know in Uruguay anyway? She folded the letter and sealed it in the envelope. She addressed the envelope, lingering for a moment, looking at it pensively. The she turned it over and put her name on the back, American style, but this time she wrote it as Catalina, just for fun. She wondered what they would make of that back home in Wexford. She resolved to write to Elizabeth with all her news. Definitely she would sign herself as 'Catalina' and see what she would make of it.

The roads were rutted and progress was slow. A cold wind from the South West chilled her through her black alpaca dress. It was fine for summer wear in school, but no match for the wind off the pampas. She was glad of her Wexford cloak. They travelled in a convoy of eight two wheeled wagons, each drawn by six oxen with an out-rider in front. The wheels were fully eight feet in diameter and the wagons swayed with the motion of a small boat. John was highly amused by the system for urging the animals on. From the roof of the wagon, a leather-covered tunnel, there protruded a long pole and hanging from that on a leather strap, was an even longer pole, delicately balanced and sharpened at the front, with which the driver jabbed the two leading oxen, encouraging them to greater exertions. He handled the pole like a billiard player, selecting his target with deliberation. The animals plodded on stolidly, their hooves squelching in the mud.

The day was bright but the wind battered at them, as cold as any winter's day at home.

"It is the Pampero, Señora," remarked the driver, as Catherine's hood was blown back. "Sometimes he come to visit us, but soon he go and it will be warm again."

Idly she watched the birds in the marsh by the roadside, white egrets, a sort of yellow heron, a stilted grey plover, some ducks and an old familiar friend, a water hen, moving with assertive nods trailing a long vee behind him on the surface.

John wondered if he might try a shot. The ducks seemed bigger than those at home. He put the notion aside. If he missed, the men would be amused. If he hit the mark he had no way of retrieving the bird. Anyway he was unsure of the protocol. He was nonetheless, itching to try out his new rifle. He never left it out of his sight. He loved the feel of it, the dull gleam of the gunmetal and the smell of oil. It made him feel secure.

For the first two nights she slept in the wagon and John brought her some meat from the fire and a little bread with olive oil. It was a strange combination but she was glad of it. She made herself as comfortable as possible between the sacks and boxes of trade goods. The wagon tilted on its two gigantic wheels, with its shafts on the ground, but she was relieved that the swaying motion of the day was over.

The leather covering overhead fluttered in the wind. The Pampero whistled all about. By the fire a man began to sing but soon gave up. After a while she slept.

They forded a fast flowing river between well-wooded banks. She was astonished to see the out-rider strip naked and throw his bundle of clothes into the lead wagon. She noticed the darkness of his skin and looked away in embarrassment. The man waded into the water, driving the oxen forward, whacking them unmercifully with a broad leather whip. He repeated the operation for each wagon, at times holding onto the traces but all the time beating the animals. The brown river surged as high as his chest. She imagined that he must be frozen.

The oxen struggled, at times almost swimming and the wagons swung in the current, but eventually they were all across. The man retrieved his clothes and stood drying himself with his woollen cape. The muscles on his hard, tanned body stood out like cords. She tried not to look as they passed and John laughed.

"The baqueano," said the driver by way of explanation. "It is his responsibility to get us across."

It was as if this explained the man's behaviour and his singular lack of shame. She could feel her face burning. She could not imagine Don José behaving in such a manner.

On the third day the wind died away. The countryside looked fresher and greener, even though it was winter. A flash of red, followed by another, caught her eye.

"The cardinal," said the driver. He had begun to feel that he should offer some information to the two young Ingléses. He departed from his usual habit of taciturnity. "He is a bird of our country, called for the great men of the church. He wears the hat of the cardinal."

She watched the two birds darting in the bushes and in the long grass. They lifted her spirits. The sun was warm. John leaped down to walk beside the wagon. He stretched his arms wide and breathed deeply.

"This is the life," he said again, smiling up at her. "This is the place to be."

"Señor, señor," said the driver. "Boom! Boom!" He was pointing towards the crest of a low grassy ridge. He seized the rifle and handed it down to John, holding it by the barrel. "Ñandú"

On the crest of the ridge glided a troop of rhea, their long necks swaying gently with a motion like tall water plants in a gentle current.

"Meat," said the driver urgently and John realised what he was suggesting. He brought the rifle quickly to his shoulder, sighted and squeezed the trigger. There was a click. He had forgotten that it was not loaded. The driver laughed. John flushed with annoyance.

"Ah, señor, the meat," said the driver good-naturedly.

The birds broke into a sudden loping run, flapping their short wings, not quite flying and yet, not thrall to gravity. Soon only their necks protruded over the long grass, too small a target for any marksman. Then they vanished. John clenched his fists on the rifle. He would not be caught out again.

That night she sat by the fire. The drivers left them in peace, preferring their own society and their own fire. She felt happy again and filled with optimism. She looked up at the canopy of stars, strange constellations, bockety looking, she thought. The sky looked wrong. The sliver of new moon lay on its back like a segment of an orange.

"Do you know any of the stars?" she asked.

He lay back, resting his head in her lap. The stars were so bright that he imagined he could have touched them with the long pole from the wagon, goad them into moving, maybe put them back into their proper order.

"That one I know," he said pointing. "Orion, the giant. I recognise him. He comes into our sky in winter. So this is where he goes." He chuckled. The wood crackled in the fire.

"Henry Jones knows all about them. He told me the names when we were on the ship."

"Oh," he said mockingly, "Henry Jones, is it? You have an admirer then?"

"Silly," she said, rapping him on the head. "He is a very knowledgeable man. He was worth listening to. Especially as you were downstairs playing cards with your cronies."

"So what did he tell you, then?" he said, mimicking the Welshman's sing song accent.

"Well, he showed me Regulus, the brightest star. Called after a man of honour, he said. And Taurus the bull and that constellation there, the Centaur."

John was impressed. "Hmm," he said.

"Although Don José did not agree. He said that the Centaur is a gaucho. The gaucho is a centaur you see. It is the same thing."

"Don José has his own names for them, has he?"

"Some of them. The bull is attacking the giant, but the giant is not Orion. He is Sepé the Charrúa and he will kill the bull with his rompecabeza. See how he raises it."

"His what?"

"His rompecabeza. His head-crusher. It is a knobbly stone club."

"Sepé the Charrúa. His ancient enemy."

She stroked his head and ran her fingers through his hair. She was glad that he never used that horrible macassar oil. He fished a half-smoked cheroot from his pocket, grimaced and tossed it into the fire. A shower of sparks drifted upwards to join their fellows in the night sky.

"This is the place," he said contentedly and closed his eyes.

She woke to the sound of a shot. John was gone. It was not yet fully daylight. The fire was low. She scrambled to her feet and looked around, then she saw him with his rifle in his hand and over his shoulder the carcass of a small deer. He held his gun aloft in a gesture of triumph and she shared his pride.

They saw cattle everywhere, grazing by small lakes, sometimes standing belly deep in the water or sheltering under clumps of trees. Occasionally they might see a rider moving through the herds. Sometimes the rider might raise a hand in greeting and move on, harrying the animals with a whip or a rope. She loved the fluid motion of man and horse and the counterflow of cattle as they sought to defy his will. But the man always prevailed.

"Señor," said the driver. "You must have a horse. It is not good that you go hunting on foot. There are dangers."

"Dangers? What dangers?"

The driver laid it on for effect.

"Snakes," he began, "víboras. By the river you may meet the snakes. Scorpions also and spiders. The spiders, they are also big as your hand."

He was enjoying the effect the conversation was having on Catherine.

"Also the toros. You must carry a lance to protect against the toros."

"I see," nodded John. "There are horses on the land we are going to. We will be well provided."

"That is also good. There is a house on this land? It is important for the Señora to have a house."

"Of course there is a house," said John rather sharply. "We are not fools. Locos. No locos." He tapped himself on the chest, speaking loudly for emphasis.

The driver nodded. "Sí. Good. It is important for the Señora to have her own house."

She looked forward to being mistress of her own house. She could picture it already, bright with new paint; a shady porch for the summertime; a fire in the hearth. They could sit in the cool of the evening, watching the sun go down and talk and plan.

"Also you may meet the jaguar in the Cuchilla del Perdido to the east," resumed the driver, returning to his theme of danger.

"What is a cuchilla?"

"A line of hills. Like the blade of a knife. Some leagues to the east of here," said the driver, gesturing vaguely, "lie the Hills of the Forlorn and the River of the Perdido, the Lost. There you may meet the jaguar."

"If I do," said John, "I will shoot him."

"Who was lost?" queried Catherine. "Why are they called the Hills of the Forlorn?"

"Who knows?" shrugged the driver. "Someone was perdido. If he came back to tell us then he would not be lost."

He laughed at the undeniable logic of his point.

John leaped down and strode beside the wagon. He slung the rifle over his shoulder and whistled as he marched. At the tailboard the carcass of the deer swung from side to side as the wagon-wheels lurched over the ruts. A rope of dried blood dangled from the nose and from a gash in the throat. Flies settled on the eyes. Dust began to rise from the hooves of the oxen. The sun was pleasantly warm.

That night she could eat none of the meat from the deer. The smell of wood smoke reminded her of the tinkers. She could smell it off her clothes and on her skin. The meat tasted strong, like rabbit and she put it aside.

The driver offered her his gourd. "A maté," he said. "It will give you hunger."

She had watched them with their matés, sitting by the fire, passing the gourds from one to another. She flinched at the thought of sharing the siphon with anyone, but the offer was kindly meant.

She sipped the warm liquid. It tasted of earth and grass, of tobacco and stagnant water from a green standing pond. She shuddered.

"Ah!" she gasped, passing it back.

He laughed. "Good for you," he insisted and passed it to John. John tried it in turn and put it away with an expression of shocked distaste.

The taste lay on her tongue. She tried to classify it. It had something of cold tea about it. Disgusting and yet, she wanted to try it again. It was like John's kiss after he had been smoking. She took another sip. Acrid, warm, difficult to swallow. She handed it back with a polite 'gracias'. She felt a little better and nibbled at some hard, dry bread.

Towards evening of the final day, they reached the pulpería, a stagecoach inn in the middle of nowhere. There was light from the windows and from the open door. Silhouettes of riders moved across the rectangles of light. There was a sound of laughter. She looked forward to a wash and a comfortable bed.

"You may hire horses here, señor," said the driver. "The baqueano will take you the rest of the way."

"Shall we be there tomorrow?" she asked.

"Tonight," replied John. "We can be there in a couple of hours. It's only about four leagues from here."

"But can't we rest here for the night?"

The driver shook his head. "The pulpería is not a place for a lady. You would prefer your own home."

She had to agree. They began to unload their belongings. The sun slipped away. Suddenly it was dark. The baqueano returned with horses, one of them bearing an elaborate side saddle of red velvet with a single silver slipper for a stirrup.

There was a low rail at the back, which put her in mind of a chaise longue in the convent parlour. She had never ridden side saddle before, her only experience being the amiable plough-horse at home on the farm. She imagined that she would look quite the elegant lady and would make a great impression on whoever was taking care of her house. The other horses had the by now familiar sheepskin saddles, which she admitted, looked a lot more comfortable. The fourth horse was for their belongings and supplies, which looked pitifully few when strapped to its back. John lifted her into the saddle and slipped her foot into the stirrup.

"Ah, my princess," he said bowing gallantly, sweeping the ground with his hat. "You shall be the ruler of all you survey."

The baqueano, wordless as ever, attached a broad leather apron to protect the horse's breast and shoulders and the rider's legs. She wondered what kind of country they were going to encounter.

Dark trees stood out on the crests of low hills in the light of the growing moon. The horses were linked together, putting her in mind of the school 'crocodile' from which she had so cleverly escaped. It was such an adventure, but the awkward, twisted posture was beginning to hurt her back. It would be a relief to get down and walk, but the horses were belly-deep in thorny brush. The branches swished on the leather apron and she gripped the side rail for fear of falling.

They came out into open, undulating grassland. Cattle coughed in the darkness. Birds whirred away at their approach. Waterfowl slapped and splashed as the horses forded a small river and climbed a long grassy slope. They saw a light under the straggling silhouette of an ombú grove. Their guide hailed the rancho, as he called it. She saw that it was no more than a low hut with a flimsy awning in front of the door. Smoke, white in the moonlight, swirled through a hole in the roof. A figure appeared in the doorway and conversed with their guide in heavily accented Spanish. They seemed to reach some understanding.

John dismounted and flexed his legs. He walked stiffly. He groaned at the returning circulation. He lifted her down and unloaded the pack horse. He hitched his rifle on his shoulder, touching it repeatedly, as if for reassurance.

"So this is it," he murmured. "Stay close to me."

The advice was unnecessary. She felt a cold dread settling on her at the prospect of staying even one night in this dark and sinister place at the extreme end of the world. She held his arm and felt safer. The guide swung his horse abruptly and trotted away into the night, taking with him their only means of transport. The figure at the door grunted something. The long knife in his hand glinted in the dim light. John shifted the gun on his shoulder. The man gestured to them to come inside.

At first she saw only their eyes as they turned to stare at the two young strangers. The voices, just now raised in argument, abruptly died away. Firelight flickered on dark faces, throwing the shadows upward in a sinister inversion. Ten or twelve men, their elbows propped on saddles or the skulls of beasts, lounged around the central fire drinking the maté. A haunch of beef hung over the flames and fat sizzled into the ashes. They stared in silence, a band of assassins with their long, gleaming knives.

The first man said something to the group and was answered with a few grunts and a nod from one or two.

"Good evening," said John, formally. "I am John Cardiff, the new owner and this is my wife, Catherine."

He put down his valise, waiting for a reply.

"This is going to be difficult," he said to Catherine. "Can you manage anything at all?" Her mind went blank. She could feel her heart pounding. Her mouth was dry.

"Anything at all?" he asked again. "Tell them we are happy to be here."

Greetings, she thought desperately. Doña María Jesús had laid great stress on good manners. The smoke stung her eyes and she blinked.

"Encantada," she said. Her voice shook. She wished they could abandon the enterprise there and then. All bets off, as John would say, before their throats were cut and their possessions plundered.

"Ah, encantado," chorused the men. "Encantado." They laughed and began to speak volubly. An old man, grizzled and almost black, brought forward a pair of stools and placed them near the fire. The stools were ingeniously made from the dried bones of animals. He motioned them to sit. Another cut a slice of meat and handed it to Catherine. She realised that she was starving. The man passed his knife to John, inviting him to help himself. The knife was fully eighteen inches long. They ate hungrily and took some more. It was not as Mother Alacoque had instructed, mused Catherine, as she licked the juice from her fingers. She felt her fear receding. She noticed that John had put his gun away, leaning it against the valise. She studied the men closely. They wore the oddest assortment of garments, long white breeches or voluminous baggy trousers and high boots with the toecaps cut away, it seemed. Their toes peeped out in a most comical way, but there was nothing comical about the enormous spurs which jingled every time they moved. Such spurs, she concluded, could only be an impediment to walking.

The man who had brought the stools, the old black man, came forward again. He spoke haltingly.

"I am Fierro, capataz," he began diffidently. "Foreman. I worked for Inglés, Drabbles and River Plate Company. A little Inglés I speak. You are Inglés?"

"No, Irish," said John realising that it was pointless. "We come from Ireland."

"Ah, sí," nodded the foreman. "Inglés."

He passed the maté. Catherine braced herself and drank. The pungent taste went a long way towards offsetting the smell of smoke, of unwashed bodies and of burning meat.

"Señor Fierro," said John again formally. "We will have great need of your help." He unbuckled his valise, producing a bottle of gin. "I would like you to have a drink with me." He uncorked the bottle and raised it.

"Sláinte," he said, smiling broadly. He took a swig and passed it to the foreman who also raised it in a toast before drinking. The foreman passed it on and amid laughter, they all drank and toasted the newcomers. Catherine nodded and smiled as they saluted her particularly. The smoke, the firelight and her throne of bones made her feel like the princess of a barbarian tribe in some mythological fantasy.

"What is the name of this place?" asked John, speaking slowly and deliberately. He unfolded a map which bore an official stamp at the corner. Señor Fierro looked at it closely. John inclined it towards the fire. He traced the line of the river with his finger. It led into a larger river. Some hills were indicated with dark hached lines.

"This is Laján," said the foreman, "but now it is called the Place of the Ombú."

"Laján?" queried John. "What does that mean?"

"It is the Charrúa word for the ombú."

"Ah, the Charrúas again."

The foreman was silent. He looked into the fire. "They are gone," he said after a while. "You will wish a new name for your estancia. The name of a saint is a good thing."

Catherine was touched. It was a generous thing to give up an old name. She thought of the legions of Irish saints, one for every mile of the road and every tree as well. Every quaking bog, every islet and windswept mountain claimed its hermit, austere and implacable, storming Heaven daily with his prayers.

"We will call it Catalina," said John suddenly. "Estancia Catalina. I like the sound of that. No, you are correct. A saint is good. It will be Santa Catalina."

He stood up and took the almost empty bottle. He raised it aloft, declaiming extravagantly. "I name this land Estancia Santa Catalina."

He bowed to her and drank. She blushed, wishing that he would sit down. She remembered his dramatic recitation on the quayside in the rain and wondered suddenly what had happened to the umbrella. The men applauded the performance, nodding approvingly, when Fierro explained what had taken place.

"Santa Catalina," they said, smiling in her direction, "Santa Catalina." They raised their matés in salute.

"Gracias," she replied. "Gracias." She wondered when they would leave and where she might find a bed. Her back hurt and her head was light with weariness. She wanted to relieve herself but was afraid to go out into the darkness.

Fierro cleared a space near the fire and spread a poncho on the ground.

"For you, señora," he said, motioning her to lie down. "When your niño comes, we will make a better place for you."

She half understand what he was saying, but she was too tired to argue. She lay down under the curious gaze of the men, some of whom were still carving and eating the beef. She tried to keep her eyes open, afraid of what might happen if she slept, but her eyelids were heavy.

"What did he say?" asked John sharply. "He said something about a better place."

"When the baby comes," she mumbled. "He will make a better place, when the baby comes."

John sat in stunned silence. This was an unlooked for complication. He shook her shoulder, but she was asleep. He turned to the foreman. Fierro put a finger to his lips.

"She needs sleep," he said quietly. "I will send my wife to her in the morning."

"But what is this about a baby?"

"She did not tell you? But then you have many negocios to concern you as head of the family."

"But how did you know?" He tried to conceal his ignorance with a touch of indignation. "My wife would not discuss such matters with a stranger."

"I know things," answered Fierro, without offence. "It is a gift of my ancestors."

"Hmm!" John was sceptical. The man was rambling and damned impertinent too.

"Tomorrow," said Fierro, "we will make a screen to give you your private place, but tonight this is all we have. In time you will make a fine house for your family, but you must keep it with strength." He clenched his fist in a gesture of determination. "In this country a man must be strong."

John liked the sound of what he said. A strong man, armed, keepeth his house. He adjusted Catherine's cloak around her and slipped his folded jacket under her head. She stirred and mumbled but did not wake. He brushed a strand of hair from her forehead and watched her in the firelight.

The men, one after another, lay down, pulling their ponchos about them. Their spurs jingled as they got comfortable. Soon the hut was silent, except for a few snores and the occasional sizzle as a drop of fat fell from the bare bone, into the ash. John watched his wife's gentle breathing and swore that he would never fail her.

Chapter Six

She dreamed of home, of her family and the patient plough-horse. She heard the bees around the straw-built hives and the crack-voiced cockerel crowed. She lay in a contented daze listening for the sound of the sea. The noise came again, a harsh, metallic ratcheting sound like a spring releasing suddenly on some mechanism. She opened her eyes and looked around.

The men were gone. The fire had died away. The door was open and the pale light of the dawn showed her a room of about twenty five feet in length, perhaps fifteen feet wide, with an earthen floor and a round hearth of stones in the centre. There was a hole in the roof directly above the hearth. The furniture consisted of some blankets, the two stools of bone and a number of skulls, with horns still in place, which also served as stools. She was appalled at the poverty of the place. She could not imagine how they would survive or how she would make a home in such a place. She heard the strange metallic sound again and timidly she went outside. The low sun was red. Fog lay in the hollows. All about was long grass and on the crests of the ridges, stands of timber. She heard geese in a lake where the river widened and birds rose from the grass with a sudden whirring of wings. From far away came the lowing of cattle and the shouts of men. She looked about carefully, making sure she was unobserved, then squatted to relieve herself and the world seemed better.

The rasping sound came again from the grove of ombú surrounding the hut. Some bird, she thought, angry at her intrusion. The hut was surprisingly solid, built mainly of large stones crudely mortared together. The roof was of overlapping cowhides. At one end was the rickety porch which she had observed the night before, a flimsy structure of cane and willow. She could not decide if the ombús were individual trunks or parts of one great tree, almost surrounding the hut. She peered into the foliage, looking for the indignant bird, half afraid that it might attack and peck out her eyes.

"Chicharra, señora," said a voice beside her. "Nobody see him."

A woman had come up to her without her being aware. Her bare feet left a dark trail in the dewy grass. She wore a long red petticoat with a white blouse and her head was bare.

"Oh," said Catherine, startled.

The woman might have been fifty or sixty years of age but she carried herself like a young girl. Her high cheekbones and dark skin suggested Indian blood.

"It is chicharra," she said again. "Insecto. Nobody ever see him."

"I see," nodded Catherine, alarmed to think that an insect could make such a noise. A formidable creature, she reckoned, moving back from the tree.

"I am Guidai, the wife of Fierro," said the woman, "and you are Catalina."

"Yes," replied Catherine. "I suppose I am."

"Fierro sends me to help you. I teach you how to live in this country and I help you when your niño comes."

"But how can you tell? I…"

The woman raised her hand. "Fierro knows. His ancestors were witches." She laughed, making light of the idea. "You are young and your husband is strong. I see in your face you have a baby. It is natural."

Catherine pondered this thought for a while. She felt panic rising inside her. Tears came to her eyes.

"It is natural," said the woman taking her hand. "I am here. There is nothing to fear. I will teach you everything and Fierro will teach your husband to be estanciero."

The chicharra rasped again and Catherine felt her fear leaving her. This could be a good place. She would learn. She would have children and they would be tall and strong like their father.

The horses milled about in a circular enclosure, small wiry horses with angry eyes. Buckskin was the predominant colour. Bigger than the Connemara pony, thought John as he watched the foreman selecting a mount for him. A couple of gauchos looked on with interest to see how the newcomer would fare. Fierro moved among the horses, trailing his lasso. He swung the noose and dropped it over the neck of an animal with deceptive ease. The gauchos surrounded the creature immediately, manhandling it to a stake at the side of the enclosure, winding the rope until the horse was held hard against the stake. They forced a bit into its mouth and strapped on a saddle.

"I give you the saddle of the Inglés," said Fierro.

"Very well," said John, clenching his teeth.

They held the horse by the bit and by the tail as he mounted. The animal's eyes rolled with fear and fury. The gauchos let go. The horse exploded under him. It leaped and sun-fished and John flew through the air. He hit the ground with an unmerciful thump and lay unable to breathe. He heard the laughter of the gauchos. He stood up slowly, filled with a cold fury.

"Again," he said to Fierro, pointing to the horse, which was still cavorting and bucking, enraged by the unfamiliar feel of the saddle. It was obvious that they had done this to try him. He remembered an incident at a circus when he was a boy, 'The bucking mule,' shouted the ringmaster. 'A pound to anyone who can ride him.' A local farmer, a mighty man, succeeded. He dominated the animal with his weight and sheer determination. The ringmaster tried to fob him off with a pound of butter but the man was having none of it, much to the delight of the audience. 'He kicked up stink,' was how they described it afterwards. The man got his pound.

John grinned at the memory. He flexed his arms and legs. There were no broken bones.

"Again," he said. Fierro went after the horse and the gauchos brought it to the stake. This time it fell in its struggle and they tried to haul it to its feet. Two men pulled at the head. Another hauled on the tail. John held out his hand.

"The whip," he demanded and pointed. A gaucho handed him a broad leather whip, an outsize riding-crop with an ornate handle. The gaucho raised his eyebrows. John stood over the horse and lashed it smartly across the haunches. The animal struggled to its feet, snorting and trembling. Again he mounted and took a twist of mane in his fist. The gauchos let go. Again the horse twisted and bucked. Again he hit the ground and lay there gasping.

He rose stiffly to his feet dusting himself down. He spat.

"Again," he said with a snarl and Fierro swung his lasso. Now it was personal.

"Rebenque, señor?" asked the gaucho holding out the whip, with grudging respect.

"Rebenque," agreed John and administered a thrashing to the quivering horse. He struck it on the neck and flanks with a controlled ferocity. He looked it in the eye.

"Now, you bastard, you can kick up stink."

The gauchos looked at each other. He mounted again, hauled on the reins and twisted them around his fist. He took a handful of mane and kicked the horse's flanks. The gauchos let go.

The horse bucked. It curvetted. It essayed a gallop. Other horses swirled about it and dust rose in a cloud. The horse's head dropped. It seemed to go limp. It slowed to a canter, then to a walk. John pulled it around and rode back to the stake. The gauchos applauded.

"Madre de Dios," muttered Fierro, under his breath. The horse was flecked with sweat and dust, but it stood obediently as John dismounted. He grinned broadly and patted its neck.

"Now we understand each other," he said and Fierro wondered if the remark referred only to the animal.

Catherine could see that he was in great good humour. He dismounted and tied the reins to a branch.

"This is mine," he said. "I broke him myself."

He looked incongruous in the clothes of a Wexford farmer, sturdy tweed trousers tucked into leather gaiters. He wore his waistcoat with shirt sleeves rolled up. Already his arms were reddening with sunburn.

"You will have to buy the proper clothes for this climate," she warned. "Be careful of the sun."

"What's all this about a baby? You said something about it last night. I've been too busy to talk to you since."

Catherine made a small grimace. It was true. He could not wait to get out to look at his new possessions. It seemed so casual in a way, to have acquired so much, lock stock and barrel, and so easily too, just by signing papers.

"It is true. I am going to have a baby."

"Are you sure?"

"Señora Fierro says so. She asked me about everything. You know."

"I see," he said slowly, sitting down on the bone stool, which she had brought out into the shade of the porch. "But this is wonderful news. We will be a proper family."

He grinned broadly at the idea.

"You will have children and we can found a dynasty here."

"Hold on a minute. Hold your horses," she said, pleased with his reaction. "One at a time."

He laughed. "You should have seen me breaking the horse." He laughed again. "We kicked up stink."

"Oh, I wish you had told me. I would have come to watch."

"I would break one for you, but you cannot ride now. I will get you a gig of some sort to ride around in. But you must promise to be careful."

"I would like that very much. Of course I will be careful. I will do everything right. I will be a great wife to you."

"Of course you will," he said and swung her onto his knees. The stool creaked under their weight.

"This land goes on forever," he told her. "There are cattle everywhere. All we have to do is brand them and they are ours. Fierro says I should consider keeping sheep. He says the wool is valuable now. Better than hides or tallow, because it comes every year."

He was almost bursting with enthusiasm and an eagerness to do things.

"I must go with the men to look at the land. It goes on forever," he said again. "There is game for the taking too. I must get a shotgun."

She laughed and brushed his hair back from his forehead.

"Take it slowly," she admonished. "One thing at a time and you must not forget your little wife with all these negocios."

"What is this woman like?" he asked, suddenly concerned. "She will look after you, I take it."

"Señora Fierro. She is an excellent woman. Her name is Guidai, which means The Moon. She has a daughter, Estrellita, which means Little Star and some grandchildren."

"A constellation," he joked. "Excellent. When we build a proper house, you will need servants."

The word jarred. She knew nothing of servants. There was a woman at home, old Aggie, who had always been part of the family, but she had never thought of her as a servant.

"I thought we would be friends," she said diffidently.

"Hah!" he laughed. "You must remember who you are. You are Señora Cardiff and never forget it. You are the mistress of a great estancia and you shall have servants." She made no protest. He stood up suddenly and put his hands on her shoulders.

"You are so precious to me. You shall have only the best."

He dusted his trousers with his hat and turned to go, but hesitated, turning back.

"You may write to your parents and tell them all this good news. The mail-coach stops at the pulpería every week. I shall take the letter there myself. There are so many things I need. Now that we have an address, we need not be isolated."

He went inside the hut and emerged with the rifle slung across his back.

"You never know," he said, unhitching the horse. He swung easily into the saddle and turned away. He waved and kicked the horse into a trot.

She watched him go with a sense of pride and a certain awe that this was her man, a man of strength and decisiveness who would protect her against all dangers. She would write to her parents, although she had only pencil and paper to tell them of all the good things that were happening to their daughter and of how they would soon be grandparents.

On a hot autumn day she sat under the awning out of the heat of the day. She was tired and heavy. The child stirred inside her. She looked at the letter, recognising her mother's neat handwriting. Queen Victoria, with her hair in a neat bun, was smudged and partly obscured by the post-mark, 'Wexford, Nov. X 64.' Christmas was long gone, but it was not really Christmas in this heat. She thought of Christmas and presents, the goose roasting, the Kilmore carols in the chapel and people shaking hands. She was no longer part of that world. She was reluctant to open the letter, afraid of the blame and recrimination it would surely contain.

She had enjoyed Christmas too. There was a goose, shot by John with his new shotgun. There was beef of course and some wine and a cake. Sultanas were always available from the pulpería. People ate them by the handful. It was not a great cake, baked in the iron cauldron over the fire. Guidai was amused by her efforts, but she enjoyed the end result.

She fanned herself with the letter. It was considerate of John to leave her alone to open it. It was considerate of him to buy her this comfortable chair. He would no longer allow her to do any heavy work. She had learned to scrape and stake hides in the sun and salt and dry the beef into strips of tasajo, the slave food for Brazil. She could cut out the tallow from a carcass and render it over a fire, but now he said she must rest and think of their child. He had also arranged for materials to build new ranchos for the men, so that the hut was now entirely theirs. Altogether she had little to complain about.

The pulpería was interesting too. She was amused, on the one occasion she had gone there, to see the gauchos drinking on horseback. The proprietor served them through a window. They rarely dismounted. They were indeed centaurs. There were travellers there too, sitting by the enormous fireplace, while the post horses were being changed. It seemed a leisurely operation. She spoke to a woman who understood English. She was travelling to Fray Bentos, with her husband. No, she had never met anyone by the name of Doyle. She had met one-eyed men and a man who limped, but no Irish.

She laughed. "The men, they fall from their horses. They fight. They break each other's heads."

Loud voices from outside interrupted her. "Some little altercation," John had said. "Some fellows in dispute over a bet." The gauchos played a strange game with bones, something on the lines of horseshoe throwing or skittles.

The woman spoke of the revolution of Venancio Flores and how President Berro had relinquished power to him. "Berro is a man of peace," she said, repeating the commonly held view.

Catherine had heard nothing of the latest upheavals. It was like news from a foreign land. Now there was to be war with

Paraguay. Flores was giving the Brazilians free passage. Montevideo was swarming with Brazilian soldiers. "Very good for business," said the woman with a coy smile. She would follow the armies upriver as far as Paysandu, near enough to be of service to the brave soldiers, but not too close to the fields of battle.

Catherine was impressed by her dedication. She had read about women taking more active roles in war, nursing the wounded, comforting the dying. Her husband seemed a sharp, ferrety little man, who spoke no English. John seemed to be amused by the couple. He insisted on buying a drink for them and was most attentive to the lady.

Catherine looked at the letter. She slid her finger under the flap and tore it open. There was only one page. She read:

My Dearest Catherine,

Your father and I are relieved to hear that you are safe and that you have a roof over your head. We cannot deny that the manner of your going was a great shock to us and caused us great apprehension. Whether it was your father's softness of heart or my severity, the fact remains that you left us for a strange country with a man who is a stranger.

Nevertheless, he is your husband and we respect him and must love him too as our son. We are relieved to hear that your venture is going well. Your letter reassured us greatly on that point, although the system of farming in that country seems very strange.

We earnestly hope and pray that your confinement will be an easy one and that your child will enjoy good health. We trust that you will have the best medical attention.

Please ensure that the child is baptised in the Roman Catholic Church as you and your brothers were. I know nothing of religious matters in that part of the world but I imagine there are priests enough, as there are here.

Your brothers send their kindest regards. They continue to work hard. The fishing is good. Please remember that if things change and you decide to return, we have the means to help and that there will always be a place here for you both and for your child.

We wish you both a happy Christmas and New Year.'

There were some lines scored out, which she could not decipher. Her mother signed the letter

Your loving Parents.

No names. No surname in parenthesis as a little dig. 'Loving parents.' Her mother had never used that word to her but now she realised that behind the stiff formality of the words her mother missed her greatly. 'Apprehension' was the word she used. 'Great apprehension' and they blamed themselves.

She folded the letter and closed her eyes. Chicharra whirred his metallic message in the branches. Guidai came to her.

"You have news of home. This maté is to console you."

Catherine opened her eyes. She was grateful to the woman. Guidai sat on the ground beside her. She tucked her feet under her skirt, sipped from the gourd and passed it to Catherine.

"Where is home?" she asked. Catherine told her of Ireland and rain, their house by the tidal lake and how she had run away, leaving her parents to grieve. She sipped the maté and passed it back. It was like a storybook. She spoke of her brothers and their fishing boats. Storms at sea, ships wrecked on the rocky coast, sailors on the quays from all parts of the world and the rain and green grass. Always the rain.

"It is a hard thing to leave home," Guidai agreed. "But now you have a new home."

The maté was warm and comforting, or maybe it was the gentleness of the woman and her understanding.

"When your baby is here, Estrellita will nurse it for you. She will have a baby too."

She laughed. "Estrellita will have milk enough for two."

"I have been wondering," began Catherine, "which of the gauchos is the husband of Estrellita."

"Ah," said Guidai. "She has no husband. Estrellita is candombera. She dance. The men like to watch her dancing, so she has babies. When she has many babies she will not dance."

She laughed again. "I have one child, so I can still dance. I am not beautiful like Estrellita, but I still dance."

Catherine had heard the drums sometimes at night, but she had never seen the dancers. John dismissed it as some African mumbo-jumbo brought over by slaves in the old days. There was no denying that Estrellita was beautiful and that the men liked to watch her. She wondered if John would allow such a person to nurse his child. She would wait a while before mentioning it. The maté was good.

"Tell me about the people who lived here before us."

Guidai said nothing. She rose and walked about the ombú grove, scuffling her bare feet in the grass. She stopped and picked something up. She returned and sat beside the chair. In her hand was a stone about the size of a crab-apple. There was a deep groove cut into it, dividing it into two hemispheres. She handed it to Catherine.

"Before you came here there were others. Blancos and Colorados. In the Great War this land changed hands." She counted on her fingers, "Yu, sam, deti, betum, betum-u, maybe five times. Yes, five times. Then there was nobody. We lived here in peace. We used what we needed. Now it is your land because the government says it is." She shrugged. "That is the way it is."

Catherine turned the stone in her hand. She felt the groove.

"What is this? Why do you show it to me?"

"That is a bolas stone. It is of the Charrúas. Everywhere in this country you may find the stones of the Charrúas. They are here since the world began. You look for them, you find them."

Catherine was not sure whether she meant the people or the stones.

"What was that counting?" she asked. "It was not Spanish."

"Ah no," said Guidai. "I speak in Spanish and now you make me speak the Inglés, but I think in the old language. I teach you."

She counted again insisting that Catherine should repeat the words. She counted on her fingers. "Yu, sam, deti, betum, betum-u, betum-sam, betum-deti," Catherine could see the pattern emerging. She counted again, pleased with herself.

"Betum-artasam, baquiu, guarroj."

Catherine counted again, concentrating like a child, finishing triumphantly on 'guarroj'.

"How do you know these words?" she asked, but Guidai would not be drawn.

She looked into the maté.

"It is finished," she said. "That is a story for another day and another maté."

She rose and straightened her skirts. Catherine watched her walking through the long grass and reflected that she moved with the lithe grace of a dancer or perhaps a cat, the way she placed her feet so lightly and delicately.

She hefted the stone in her hand. John would be interested. He was learning to use the bolas and was proud of his skill. He would be hungry too she realised, getting up to prepare some food. Meat as usual. As soon as the baby was born she resolved to start a garden. She would write to her father for seeds. There would be green vegetables for the baby and a bit of variety. She thought of a nice piece of salted ling and her mouth watered. Definitely vegetables. They would do well even in the mild winter and God knows there would be no shortage of manure. For the moment though it was beef, with beef for dessert and cold beef for supper. Sultanas too of course and some lemon drink from the pulpería, which she liked very much, although there was gas in it. She began to mix dough for the hard flat bread that Guidai had shown her how to make. She put aside her thoughts of home. Now she was the wife of an estanciero, almost a gaucho and she was his china. She smiled at the idea. But she would have her garden all the same and she might even learn to dance before she had too many children.

The Brazilians camped by the arroyo, their bivouacs in neat military lines, with a park of gleaming cannon. Birds circled over the place where the cattle had been killed and smoke rose from cooking fires.

"It is no use, señor," said Fierro. "The armies take what they need and often more. There is nothing to be done."

"We'll see about that," answered John, his mouth set in a stubborn line.

"Señor, I do not advise," Fierro said, but John was already urging his horse down the slope. Fierro followed reluctantly. Two soldiers, resplendent in green and yellow with freshly pipeclayed webbing, stepped forward to challenge them. Fierro spoke to them and they gestured with their bayonets, indicating that the two men should follow. John struggled to understand the exchange, which was in both Spanish and Portuguese. He dismounted, but Fierro stayed in his saddle.

The colonel was shaving, with a mirror attached to the tent-pole. A black servant held his towel. He looked at the newcomers. John began without hesitation.

"Your men have stolen my cattle, sir. I demand compensation."

The colonel took the towel and pensively wiped his face. He snapped his braces over his shoulders and felt his chin appreciatively.

"Demand!" he said, clucking his tongue. "That's a mighty hard word, demand."

John was taken aback. The man spoke in a slow, American drawl. John swallowed.

"Yes. I demand payment for my animals."

The colonel chuckled. He began to button his tunic.

"Son," he said good-naturedly. "It seems to me that you don't know the way of the world."

"I know that those are my cattle with my brand on them."

"And those there are my men with my guns. This here is a war and my soldiers must eat."

"I'm not at war with anyone," retorted John, "and I have a right to my property."

The colonel sighed.

"Sit down, son and let me explain."

He turned to the servant, speaking in Portuguese. The man placed a tray with glasses and a bottle on the camp table.

"No offence, son," he began amiably. "Let's have a drink together. Men of the world."

He poured two tots and downed one at a gulp. John tasted his drink, winced and drank.

"Kentucky Sour Mash," said the colonel. "Hard to lay hands on down here." He poured again. He looked to where Fierro waited, lounging on his horse. "That man o' yourn. You sure he ain't contraband?"

"That's my foreman. He is a citizen of this country," replied John indignantly.

"I'd be obligated to take him back to Brazil if he was contraband."

Fierro knew that he was the subject of their discussion. He clenched his bare toes in the stirrups and shifted uneasily.

"Perhaps we can discuss the matter of my cattle."

"I like your spirit, son," said the colonel. He raised his glass and drank. "I surely like your spirit."

John decided on another approach. It galled him to say it, but it was worth a try.

"I would point out to you that I am a subject of Queen Victoria."

The colonel laughed outright.

"There I was startin' to like you, boy. Well, your queen ain't goin' to help you none out here." He laughed again. "You won't have heard that her flagship blew up, the *Bombay*. Burned to the waterline."

"It what?" He remembered the great ship riding at anchor.

"Yeah, just outside Montevideo. I witnessed it myself. Boy, when that magazine went up! Those poor boys boiled alive." He shook his head. "No sir, your queen ain't goin' to do much for you out here."

John was silent. He drank again, hiding his distaste. The whiskey warmed him.

"I tell you what I'll do, son," the colonel went on. He undid the top buttons of his tunic again. "I'll give you a note for these here cattle. You can claim it against your government, though I don't reckon they'll pay. Or you can claim it against mine."

"What? America?" John was confused. The colonel laughed.

"No. Those Yankees are too busy carpetbaggin' an' stealin' The South. I mean Brazil. I serve the great emperor of Brazil, Pedro the Second."

He took up a pen and began to write. The paper bore the imperial crest. He signed the document and handed it to John.

"It could take a while," he volunteered, "but the money is there. No shortage of money there. Look at this," he said indicating the camp. "Think what the Confederacy could've done with this kind o' money." He sat in a brooding silence for a while, revolving his glass in his fingers.

"I see," said John with interest. "You fought with the South."

"I surely did, son. Right to the end. Till I hadn't a boot on my foot or a bullet in my pouch. Now I'm on my way to fight Paraguay." He shrugged.

"Why Paraguay?"

"Why not Paraguay? Sure as hell, can't fight the Yankees. And I don't want to fight you either, son. The least I can do is offer you some food."

He spoke to the servant, who returned in a moment with cutlery, a bottle of wine and two plates of meat.

"It's your own beef," said the colonel. "No disrespect, but what you need is a few white-faced Hereford bulls."

John found himself liking the man. He was enjoying the incongruity of eating his own beef and the easy hospitality. The servant brought a skewer of meat to Fierro. Fierro sat in the saddle and carved carefully with his long knife.

"You sure he ain't contraband?" asked the colonel again.

"No sir," said John. "Fierro's family has been here for centuries."

It was a pleasure to talk to this man and a relief not to have to fumble in broken Spanish.

"He is an excellent fellow."

He found himself opening up, seeking a kind of approval, talking of how he had come to Uruguay and how he would improve his holding. He spoke of Catherine and how he planned to build a fine house for her and for her child. The colonel listened approvingly. Yet John felt a certain envy of the colonel who had seen so much action and would see so much more. He wondered what it would be like to lead men into battle.

"It seems to me that you are a fortunate man," said the colonel. "I had a home once, just like you. Take my advice and get off home to your little lady and put your arms around her and never let her go."

He stood up and extended his hand.

"You put that letter through to the proper channels, now y'hear." He patted John on the shoulder in avuncular fashion, making him feel like a schoolboy and walked him to his horse. He regarded the small criollo horse quizzically.

"No disrespect, son," he said. "He may be good for work, but a gentleman needs some good horseflesh under him. You get yourself somethin' with a bloodline."

John nodded. He would take that advice. He mounted his horse, touched the brim of his hat and took his leave.

"You have the money for the cattle, señor?" asked Fierro as they walked their horses along the riverbank.

"No," said John defensively, "but I have a paper and the word of a gentleman."

"Ah!" murmured Fierro. He said nothing more.

The sun slipped away and the moon rose. A bugle sounded far behind them. The note echoed and dwindled in the far hills. Catherine would be worried he thought with a flicker of resentment. She worried too much. Probably her condition. What would she think if he were to go with the army to fight in Paraguay? What if the Paraguayans were to come here? He would fight them for sure and she would have to accept it. No bones about it. He slouched in the saddle and closed his eyes. He realised that he was slightly drunk. He laughed. What would she make of that? Moreover, he had a letter of credit from the Emperor of Brazil. Wait till she sees that. He saw a pinpoint of light far off and the dark shape of the ombú grove. He kicked the flanks of his little horse.

Catherine was not impressed, not even by the imperial crest. Neither was she impressed by the way he stumbled and knocked over the stool or the way he repeated himself with such an air of satisfaction.

"Mind you, he was a thorough-going gentleman."

"I know," she said. "You told me."

"An absolute gentleman."

"I know," she yawned. "Do you realise how worried I was?"

"You're not married to some tuppenny-ha'penny clerk," he snapped. "You can't expect me to keep office hours."

"I was worried, that's all."

"Well don't," he said sharply. "I can look after myself."

She was silent. He had never spoken to her like that before. He was upset about the cattle and probably felt foolish at being palmed off with a piece of paper. She held her tongue.

"Anyway, I got a receipt. That's as good as money in the bank."

She said nothing.

"What are you sulking about?"

"I'm not sulking. I just think he was patronising you."

"Nonsense, woman."

He pulled off his boots and lay back on the bunk. He yawned. "Nobody gets the better of me."

She added a piece of wood to the fire. It crackled and filled the room with the wet tomcat smell of eucalyptus.

"Nobody, do you hear? I'll collect that money someday."

"I'm sure you will," she agreed, lying down beside him. She could smell the whiskey on his breath. She wanted to sleep.

"Did I ever tell you about Malacca?"

"No," she yawned. "No, you didn't. Where's that?"

"It's not a place. Well maybe it is. No, he was a scholastic when I was in school. An apprentice priest. He had a cane. He used to say: 'This gentlemen, is a clouded Malacca.' He was very proud of his cane. He liked to wallop us with it."

"Hmmm," she mumbled, half asleep. "I'm sure you deserved it."

He laughed. "The scholastics had the power to beat the younger students, but I got him."

"You got him?"

"I did. He used to take us for sport. I got him with a hurley. Right in the mouth. I made out it was an accident. He never touched me again." He chuckled at the memory. "You should have seen him with his teeth all broken and he spitting blood. 'It was an accident,' says I, but we understood each other after that."

"What happened then?"

"What does it matter what happened then? That's the story. But if you must know, they threw him out. I think it was because he couldn't manage the Latin without his teeth."

'Corpup domini noptri,' he mimicked and she laughed despite herself.

"The poor man," she said.

"Poor man, be damned. He asked for it and he got it."

He turned away and was immediately asleep. She looked up to where the smoke swirled through the hole in the roof. She thought of the poor Doyles, distant cousins, who lived beyond the bend of the lakeshore, near the forge. She smelt like they did with their smoky cabins and fires of salty driftwood. She wondered if the dawn had already reached the lake. They might be out in the shallow water with sprongs, spearing flounders for breakfast. Her father's cattle would be standing among the rushes and buttercups of the water meadow.

She watched a star in the circle of smoky darkness. She would have to have a proper house with a fireplace and a chimney. Guidai had said something about the ombú. 'No house will prosper where the shadow of the ombú falls upon its roof.' She offered no explanation. It was some old wives' tale, some pishogue, as her father would say. Yet she felt a vague fear. There is always a reason for a pishogue, however far-fetched.

The poor cousins would derive some satisfaction if they could see her lying on animal hides in an earth-floored hut, after all her fine linen and her convent education. She would talk to John about a proper house, maybe in the morning when he might be feeling a trifle guilty.

John was away when Richard was born, slipping easily into the world by the light of the fire and an array of tallow candles, which Catherine had made herself. She was proud of her candle-making skill, dipping hanks of them at a go into the seething fat.

There was no doctor or midwife in attendance but Guidai and her daughter were there with a wizened old china who directed operations and gave her something to drink.

"It is a boy, señora," said Guidai holding him up, all wet and slippery. The baby seemed to glare about him angrily and how he yelled.

"This is a strong one. He is almost ready to walk."

The old woman grinned a toothless grin. She nodded in agreement. She wrapped the baby in a towel and handed him to Catherine. Catherine looked at the tiny fingers and marvelled. Now they were a real family at last. She rocked him gently. He made little noises.

"Oh," she said, "when your Daddy sees you!"

John was overjoyed. Everything was going well. His first delivery of cattle to the Liebig plant at Villa Independencia was profitable, well worth the fatigue of the round-up and the many dusty miles to the English factory. He was impressed by the size of the place and the steamers lying at the wharf. English coal was piled high to the second storey windows and smoke billowed from the tall chimneys. The Uruguay stretched like an ocean as a backdrop to this piece of industrial England transplanted to a warmer climate. The English were easier to deal with than renegade Confederate colonels or Brazilian emperors. They paid on the nail. Now he had a son to succeed him. He lifted the baby high in the air, exclaiming, "Who's a great fellow, then?"

He kissed Catherine on the forehead, handling her carefully like a piece of delicate china.

"You are wonderful," he said. "Amazing!"

It was as if she had pulled off some astonishing conjuring trick. "Amazing!" he said again. He grimaced at the smell of maté. "That stuff again."

"It's good for me. It brings on the milk. So Guidai says."

He relented. "Good, good. I don't want that daughter of hers nursing my son. No, indeed."

He laughed, lifting the baby again.

"She was very kind to me," protested Catherine. "She is a very good person."

"Wait 'till I tell you," he said, changing the subject. "Wait till I tell you what I have been up to." He told her about the drive and how they had hunted rhea on the way.

"Off they went," he said, "at a rate of knots and I went after them. There was one fellow. He ran like this." He ducked his head and flapped his elbows. She laughed at his antics. "He was looking back at me. He reminded me of a youngster dodging a blow from the teacher. I swung the bolas and down he went in a tangle." He demonstrated with a wave of his arm and a swishing noise. "Tremendous fun!"

He told her of the factory, the herds milling in the pens and ships from all parts of the world. "I brought some back for you, the meat extract. It's supposed to be ideal for nursing mothers, invalids, growing children. We'll have you jumping over five-barred gates before you know where you are."

He talked of the money and of how she must keep the books. She was pleased. Most of all he talked of the men who were coming to make the bricks for the new house.

"There is no end to what we can do," he went on. "I have negotiated the purchase of new stock, new bulls and I will definitely try some sheep. Wool is on the up and up. We're all on the up and up. This war is good for business you see, though poor old Paraguay is taking a hammering."

"Why?"

"Nobody seems to know. I suppose that's what emperors do for a living."

"God help them," she murmured. "I hope we never have to deal with that sort of thing."

"The so-and-so owes me money," laughed John, "but I'll get it from him some day. The gauchos won't handle sheep of course, no matter what I pay them."

He looked down at the baby. "Anyway, you need a holiday. What do you say to a week by the river in Mercedes or Carmelo? We could go boating. We could have this fellow christened while we're at it."

"Oh, that would be wonderful."

"And maybe start another one," he said slyly.

"You can hold your horses, there. I'm in no rush, I can tell you."

She loved to watch the procession in the afternoon. Up and down the boulevard they went, arrogant young men on their spirited horses, with their sweethearts clinging on behind them. All dressed in their finest clothes for the week that was in it. Older people too walked their horses or strolled by the river. Everyone watched everyone else with studied indifference. Fish plopped in the water, making rings. The rings grew and connected into ripple chains on the surface. Anglers angled in desultory fashion and boatmen sculled lazily in the heat. It was like another world. She studied the fashion, feeling well in her new clothes. She smiled at her baby and watched the humming birds at the flowers. John twirled his cane and nodded amiably at passers-by. The cathedral bells rang. Some painter, she hoped, would capture the scene forever so that she could re-visit it again and again.

They christened their son on Easter Day and the bells rang out as if exclusively for them. She loved the sounds and echoes of the cathedral. She went back again, although John preferred to walk by the river. She carried the baby in a shawl like the tinker women. She looked at the statue of the Virgin. They had something in common now, although the statue wore chains on the left wrist. She had the face of an Indian.

"She is the patron of slaves," said a soft voice beside her and she knew it at once. It was the Welshman, Henry Jones.

"Mr Jones," she exclaimed then dropped her voice again, awed by her surroundings.

"Mr Jones," she whispered. "I am so pleased to see you again."

"Henry, please," he replied. He held his hat in both hands. He bowed slightly. "You are well, I take it, Mrs Cardiff?"

"Oh yes. We are all very well. Please call me Catherine. Some people call me Catalina. Oh, this is wonderful. John will be so pleased to see you. This is our son, Richard. We christened him here. It has been so long since I have been in a church." She stopped. "I am chattering on. But what have you been doing?"

The Welshman smiled his gentle smile.

"Oh this and that. They have me building bridges now, see. I can turn a hand to most things that require a bit of mathematics."

"And the stars? Do you still study the stars?"

"Indeed yes. I have plenty of opportunity. The heavens seem very close when you are sleeping in the open."

"I know what you mean," she agreed.

Richard stirred and protested.

"Perhaps you will walk back with me to our lodgings. The pavements are very irregular and John will be so pleased to see you again. Perhaps you will dine with us."

"I would be happy to," said Henry and she reflected that he was perhaps a lonely man.

John was delighted to see him, insisting that they dine together. He was a most affable host. They talked of the war and how Brazilian money was flowing into the country. They talked of shooting and scientific farming, of how tillage was replacing cattle in the south and how good the Uruguayan wines had become.

After dinner John excused himself, asking Henry if he would be so good as to entertain Catherine for a little while. He explained that he had to see a man about a little bet. He returned presently, rubbing his hands in satisfaction.

"What was all that about?" she asked.

"You'll find out tomorrow," he said mysteriously. He ordered another bottle. Henry rose to go.

"You must join us again tomorrow," said John. "There are races on the river."

"I look forward to it," said the Welshman taking his leave.

"I hope you're not gambling our money on some silly race," she said when they were alone.

"Good God, no," he said laughing. "There's no money involved. Just a battle with my peers. A test of skill."

He would say no more and finished the bottle.

They engaged a girl to take care of Richard and John escorted Catherine to the river. Flags and bunting stirred in the light breeze. Cats' paws played on the water. He insisted that she wear her most fashionable dress and carry a parasol like the most elegant of ladies. He seemed so proud, showing her off to the members of the boating club. She enjoyed the attention and enjoyed also meeting the young people, some of the English who had settled in the region. She thought that some of the ladies looked down their noses at her to an extent, but it did not bother her.

John explained to her that he was engaged to race against a young Englishman and that the prize was a horse, a fine stallion of impeccable lineage. He was excited. So this was his big secret. It seemed an extravagant business, but she knew that to some of these people, money was a trifling matter.

John introduced his opponent, Fortescue, a laughing, casual fellow in white flannels with his sleeves rolled up.

"Madam," he said, bowing over her gloved hand, "your husband has challenged me and I must prevail or die in the attempt."

She withdrew her hand. There was something about him that made her uneasy. He seemed to be mocking her with his florid language.

They sat into their boats, heavier craft than the racing shells of home, with a flamboyant rake to their bows. They gripped their oars. John shifted his grip and flexed his arms. She saw the sinewy strength of him from long months of physical work. She was proud.

The starter fired his revolver and away they raced, upriver to the first mark. Fortescue pulled skilfully, feathering expertly but it was obvious that he was out of condition. Luxury and easy living destroyed his chances. John pulled away, opening the gap to a length, to two lengths before the upriver mark and turning with that sudden backwater that she remembered from their first day together on the lake.

The current worked with him. Before his opponent had rounded the mark he was streaking towards home. Catherine jumped and clapped her hands. The crowd cheered and derided the struggling Fortescue. John leaped from his boat to embrace her in triumph.

"I knew I could do it," he declared, clenching a fist. "I just knew it."

Fortescue took his beating in good spirits.

"I am vanquished, Madam," he said "and I must pay the price."

He beckoned nonchalantly and a man came forward leading a horse, a glistening chestnut stallion. Fortescue handed the reins to John and shook his hand. The onlookers applauded his sporting gesture.

John put his foot in the stirrup and mounted. He put down his hand to Catherine, inviting her to join him and Fortescue lifted her easily onto the croup. She put her arm around John's waist, laughing with excitement, embarrassed at being the centre of so much attention. John waved his hat and nudged the horse into a walk. She felt a little like a circus performer. What if the animal bucked? She clung on tightly. The crowd parted before them. She saw their upturned faces and heard the applause and in their midst, the solemn face of Henry Jones. He raised his hat respectfully as they passed.

The island was joined to the riverbank by a small wooden bridge, a popular place with strollers and fishermen. Trees drooped their branches towards their mirror image in the water.

They sat on the grass, watching the anglers. It seemed as if nobody worked in Mercedes. They either fished or strolled or rode up and down the boulevard. John smoked a cigar. He watched the smoke. Catherine kept her eye on the girl who was wheeling the baby and flirting with some young men. She noted the elaborate contempt with which she greeted their remarks and the toss of her head as she dismissed them. It was all very good-natured and harmless. She wished that she could understand their rapid exchanges and their jokes. It occurred to her that she was no more than a year or two older than the girl, yet she was bound by the conventions of marriage.

Henry studied a line of black ants. He fed them crumbs, which they carried away, trundling through the grass, holding their trophies aloft. Their bodies gleamed like elderberries.

"Danegeld," said Henry.

"What's danegeld?" she asked, intrigued by the insects.

"It was money paid to the Vikings to buy peace."

"How do you know so much?" said John with a snort of laughter. He enjoyed drawing Henry out. Henry was not offended.

"I read books," he said simply. "If I pay the Vikings they won't attack us."

John stirred uneasily. "I hadn't thought of ants. What about scorpions or spiders?"

"Not around here. Further east in the hills perhaps. There are spiders here of course, but they aren't dangerous."

John shrugged at the thought. Catherine drew her skirts back from the line of ants.

"It is going to rain," said Henry. "They take food below ground when rain is due."

"Tortas fritas," said Catherine. "The gaucho women make little pancakes when it rains. They eat them for comfort, they say. They put a hole in the middle to let the rain out."

"It doesn't look like rain to me," said John squinting into the sunlight. He sat up and scratched his bare forearms. The talk of insects made him uneasy.

"I don't care for ants," he remarked.

"They do a useful job all the same," Henry insisted. "Think of all the bones you see. The ants leave them clean and dry. Imagine what it would be like if they didn't. My apologies, Catherine. It isn't a very pleasant subject."

"It's a fact of life," said John. "You know, the first time I brought cattle to the saladero it was almost enough to make me give up and go back to Ireland."

Catherine raised her eyebrows in surprise.

"You never told me that."

"It's true. The way they dealt with the animals. It nearly put me off meat."

"But not entirely," she remarked.

"No, you get used to it. You have to. It was just such a brutal business and inefficient too. You had these fellows on horseback roping the bullocks and dragging them over to the butchers to be dispatched with knives. You had women scraping hides and staking them out in the sun and children, good God, not more than five or six years of age, cutting out the tallow. Piles of meat ten or twelve feet high, under mountains of salt."

He stopped and shuddered.

"And the noise, cattle bellowing, birds all over the place and pigs, big fat pigs snuffling at skulls and offal."

He exhaled sharply.

"Please, please," protested Catherine. "It sounds disgusting."

"It is. It is," he nodded, "and damned inefficient too, if you'll pardon my language."

She had seen her father killing a pig or a goose. He put a noose over a rafter in the barn when he wanted to kill a goose. She had seen the gauchos killing an animal. She had scraped and staked out hides and had melted tallow. But that was piecemeal and of necessity. Killing was part of life and the ants cleaned up the residue, but she wondered how people could live with it day in and day out, particularly children.

"Very unhealthy," said Henry solemnly.

"It sounds like a vision of Hell," Catherine mused.

"You can get used to anything," said John, drawing on his cigar. "But anyway, that's all on the way out. This Liebig plant is the way of the future. They use everything, meat, hides, bones, hooves, the lot. Nothing left for the caracaras. You've been to Villa Independencia, I take it, Henry?"

"I have. It's Fray Bentos, really. I would like some day to put a bridge across to Argentina."

"There wouldn't be enough money in the country to do that. Or enough steel in Europe."

"No, no indeed. But I would like to try."

"Not in your lifetime I'm afraid."

"No, no indeed. But I would sell my soul to the Devil for the chance."

"Don't talk like that," Catherine chided. "That's flying in the face of God."

"I apologise. It was just a figure of speech." Henry was contrite. "It's an enthusiasm, you see."

"Why do you say Fray Bentos?" queried John. "I understood it was Villa Independencia."

"It is. That's the official name, but the people always called it after the little hermit."

"I sense a story coming on," said John tolerantly.

"Who was the little hermit?" asked Catherine.

"A little monk, a frayle called Bento. He was sent to teach the Indians of the Banda and to baptise them. He lived in a cave on the riverbank, praying and fasting."

"Did he succeed?"

"He did with the Chanas and the Yaros, yes, but never with the Charrúas. They refused to change their old ways."

"Ah, the Charrúas," she said.

"His name, they say, floats on the river. No matter what they try to call the place it will always be the home of the little friar."

"And after all his prayer and fasting," said John with a shrug, "we will always see him as the jolly fat friar filling his face."

She laughed at his alliteration.

"Well you know what I mean," he grinned. "But that's how he will be seen all over the world."

"It is an extraordinary business, certainly," said Henry. "He will feed the world, given time."

"And these English will spend the money. They certainly know how to spend."

Henry was silent.

"That's a thing," said Catherine. "He didn't care about the horse, that man. He must have lots of money."

"They live like kings," agreed John. "They certainly know how to enjoy life."

"But what did you bet him?"

Henry coughed and stood up.

"I think I shall take a little turn along the island," he said "if you will excuse me."

"By all means," said John, starting to rise.

"But what did you bet him? It must have been a lot of money."

"It was nothing much," answered John.

Henry hurried away. He stopped to admire the baby. He raised his hat to the girl.

"What was it?" she persisted. "We can't afford to spend like these people. Remember that I look after the books."

"He was an arrogant fool. I just knew I could beat him."

"But what was the bet?" She felt her annoyance rising. "I'm not a child. Tell me."

"All right. All right. It was just a bit of fun. He wanted a kiss from you. That's all. He was prepared to stake his horse for a kiss."

"No," she said, shaking her head. "No."

"It was a bit of fun."

"And you said nothing to me," she stood up. He could see that she was trembling.

"You paraded me around like some prize heifer and let people snigger."

"Nobody else knew. It was a gentleman's agreement. He said you were the most beautiful…"

"Gentleman! That was not the action of a gentleman."

"For God's sake! I knew that I could beat him."

"You don't understand, do you?"

He frowned. "But I knew that I could beat him. I knew I could beat him."

She felt a sharp sting on her foot, like a hot needle. An ant had bitten her, even through the stocking.

"Oh!" she gasped, tears coming to her eyes. She brushed at the ant, slapping it away in panic. "Oh," she said again.

A drop of rain fell from the almost clear sky. The ant bite stung like a burn.

"I want to go home," she said, biting her lip. "I want to go home now."

She set off abruptly towards the bridge. John followed at a distance, with Henry and the girl bringing up the rear. The rain began to fall in a steady drizzle.

The rain delayed their departure for another day. There was a strain between them. She concentrated her attention on the baby. John was solicitous and wary, fetching things before she needed them, which began to amuse her, but she said nothing.

At times he would go out to the stable to look at his new horse, but he never mentioned it to her. She wondered if he would return it to the Englishman, but there it was, hitched behind the carriage when the time came for them to go home.

The roads were wet and rutted but they covered the distance in two days. The further they got from the town the more the tension eased. It was as if their disagreement had happened in a different world. She was glad to be away from the fashionable people and their idle chatter. She was relieved to see the rolling grasslands, the trees, the cattle and towards evening, solemn little owls perched by their burrows, turning their heads this way and that to watch for danger. It was as if they could rotate their heads through a complete circle.

"I did think," she began at one point, "that you might have given back the horse. I thought it would get rid of this awkwardness between us."

He thought for a moment.

"I couldn't do that," he said. "A bet is a bet. He would think that I placed no value on my part of the bet."

She was confused by his answer, wondering if he meant it as a compliment.

"It was a mistake, I admit and I apologise, but once I was in I couldn't back out."

It had taken him two days to say the word. Apologise. What did it mean? Could a word take away the hurt? Was it just a formula, a lubricant to make things easier, like grease on a squeaking axle? Or was it the first span of a bridge stretching out over a dark void, whereby they might reach each other and continue their journey together? She thought of Henry with his talk of German steel and bridges held together by complex geometry. He explained how the weight thrust downwards and sideways and of how he could offset these forces by mathematics. Eventually the components of the bridge worked together to hold the entire structure in place. It was a comforting image. Words in the right place would hold them together.

"It was a mistake," she said "I accept your apology, but nothing like that is to happen again."

"It won't," he mumbled. His voice caught in his throat. He slapped the reins impatiently and she lurched against him. She was glad of the contact. She looked back at the baby, content in his basket. Through the small isinglass window in the hood she saw the horse's eyes as he trotted behind. He tossed his head and snorted. She looked away.

The gaucho studied the horses under the shade of the trees. They shook their heads and snorted. They flicked their tails to dislodge the flies. Their skin flickered and twitched at the irritating insects. The gaucho liked the white colt best. He nudged his horse closer. The animals under the trees began to move. He swung his rope gently, waiting for a clear throw. The horses moved out from the shade. He moved to cross their path. They broke into a trot, almost in unison. He dug in his spurs, just as the lead animals accelerated and dropped the noose around the neck of the white colt. He vaulted from the saddle, quickly taking a turn with the rope around the bole of a tree. The colt struggled and bucked, but it was in vain. The gaucho drew it closer to him until it was within arm's length. The terrified animal stared at him, its eyes rolling. The gaucho drew his long knife and at a stroke, he severed the jugular. The colt faltered. It staggered. A fountain of blood spurted from its neck. Its knees buckled and it fell in its own blood in the grass.

The gaucho worked swiftly. He cut a circle at the top of the hind legs and again, just above the fetlocks. With the aid of his knife he loosened the skin at the top tugging sharply, until he had flayed the entire leg, turning the skin inside out like a stocking. He chopped through tendon and bone to remove the hooves and pulled the skin free. He moved some little distance away from the colt to avoid the gathering flies. He squatted and worked on the skin with his knife, whistling tunelessly through his teeth. He scraped away all traces of flesh or fat until the hide gleamed white and dry. He pulled off his old boots and threw them away. He drew on his new botas de potro, fitting his heel snugly into the bend of the knee, so that the skin of the pastern covered his feet, except where his toes protruded to afford a better grip on the stirrup. He laced the top with the old thongs turning down a couple of stylish inches of white skin. He slipped on his silver spurs and regarded his handiwork with immense satisfaction. He retrieved his horse and swung into the saddle.

Birds dropped on the carcass of the white colt as he rode away. A wild dog slouched out of the bushes. It sniffed the air. The birds squabbled and flapped as they tore at the exposed flesh.

John stopped at the place where the builders had opened a clay-pit, a bright red gash in the side of a hill. Bricks were spread like a pavement under a long open-sided shed. Smoke rose from piles of smouldering timber. The builder, an Italian, came forward. He rubbed clay from his powerful hands.

"We have begun your foundations, señor," he began without preamble. "The rain has delayed us, but soon we will begin with the walls."

"Good," said John, prepared to be agreeable. He had heard of the migratory ways of builders and had no desire to upset the man.

"There is clay enough to build an entire village," said the builder. "We make the good bricks."

"Excellent," said John. "Perhaps in time."

"Yes, perhaps," said the man. He touched his hat to Catherine. "You see the foundations, señora. You walk in the rooms. You tell me what you think. What you want."

There were no plans. She could design it as they were building. She was pleased with the idea of the house growing from its native clay, taking shape under her direction.

"You do as the señora wishes," said John and the man nodded. He smiled for the first time.

"It will be a pleasure, señora," he said. "We are artists and we will create for you a palazzo."

"A house will do," she said responding to his good humour. She felt excitement rising at the prospect of having a real home.

"I will show you tiles, señora. You must choose. I can bring tiles from Italy and France. I can build you a house finer than any in Montevideo."

"I am grateful," she said, smiling and the man touched the brim of his hat again. His fingers left a red stain on the straw. He turned to his workmen, gesticulating and shouting in Italian. There was no time to be lost. John urged the horses forward.

"When the house is finished we can go to Montevideo to buy furniture," suggested John, "What do you think?"

"That would be good," she agreed. "Perhaps Doña María Jesús would advise me."

"I'm sure she would," he said, glad of her agreement. "Of course we should avoid the city during the hot weather. It would not be good for Richard."

They came to the top of the rise. In the distance was the ombú grove and their hut and beyond, some piles of earth where the builders had been digging. There was an avenue of newly planted eucalyptus. Near the river, smoke rose from the ranchos where the women were preparing food.

"It's good to be home," said John. She touched his arm.

"It is," she agreed. "My Santa Catalina. We will never leave here."

Chapter Eight

The birds scattered at their approach, rising with harsh cries and circling overhead. John moved upwind of the stench, holding the reins of his chestnut stallion. He pushed his way through the long grass and looked down at the carcass of a young colt. The eye sockets were empty. The blood was black where the animal's throat had been cut. The birds had torn open the abdominal cavity. Flies swarmed on the gash.

"What happened here?" he asked. "A jaguar?"

Fierro shrugged. He dropped the butt of his lance to the ground.

"Jiménez, he need new boots."

"He what?"

"See where he take the skin from the legs. Now he has new boots."

John looked at the carcass. He saw where the skin had been flayed from the hind legs and how the hooves had been chopped off.

"You mean he killed a colt just for the skin off two legs."

"It is our way, señor," answered Fierro. He pointed to his foot. His bare toes gripped the stirrup. "It is how we make our boots. We roll the skin from the leg and it is a boot."

"But this colt was mine," said John angrily. "He had no permission." He pointed to the brand.

Fierro frowned. He scratched the grey stubble on his chin.

"It is indeed your brand, señor. But the horses were here before there were brands. They are here since they crossed the great river in the time of the ancestors. We use them as we need."

"Not any more," said John. "I will see that he pays for this one."

"But señor," protested Fierro, "he will not understand."

"He will understand when I take the price of a colt from his pay."

"Señor is this wise? This has always been the way of the gaucho. We do not ask for much but we must be free to take the necessities of life from the land."

"Times have changed, Fierro. Jiménez must understand also. The land is mine and the animals on it are mine. If they carry my brand, then they are mine. I pay you to protect my property."

Fierro felt something shift inside his head.

"So if I need boots, señor, I must pay you for the colt."

"No, Fierro. You do not pay me for the colt. You go to the pulpería and you buy new boots. It is better that way. It is less wasteful. There is no dead animal for the birds. That is the way the world works."

"Then maybe we move to another place," said Fierro, "where there are horses enough for everyone."

"My way is better, Fierro, believe me."

John remounted and turned away from the dead animal. The birds circled lower and landed, hopping awkwardly in the beaten grass.

"Jiménez will not be happy," said Fierro. "It will insult his honour."

John shrugged. "If he doesn't like it, he is free to go."

"He will not be happy," said Fierro, shaking his head.

"You like my horse?" asked John. "His name is Slaney. That is a river of my country."

He always found himself speaking in a stilted manner, striving for clarity.

"He is a fine horse indeed, señor."

"Worth more than a pair of boots, then?"

Fierro nodded. "You have paid a great price for him?"

"I have indeed." John smiled a secret smile and patted the horse's neck. "He is mine and nobody takes him. Not even the Emperor of Brazil."

Fierro looked at him quizzically. This was a strange one, the young Inglés.

"No señor," he nodded, resting his lance over his shoulder. They rode on in silence.

Jiménez woke before dawn. He yawned and stretched. The rancho was dark. He listened to the silence. Estrellita stirred beside him, moaning softly in her sleep, a low animal sound. Outside in the dim light his horse snuffled. He smelled wood smoke. It was warm enough to leave the fire outside but the smell was always there, like a miasma, but a healthy smell that kept sickness away.

He swung his legs over the side of the low bunk and sat up, rubbing his short beard. Estrellita reached out and ran her hand over his back.

"There is time," she said softly.

She scratched, playfully, like a kitten. Jiménez smiled.

"There is time, Jiménez," she coaxed. He laughed.

"Later woman. There is work to be done."

He shuddered at her touch. There were many things to be done before they would make love.

"I may not be here," she said, teasing. "I may find another man who will content me and feed my children."

"And I will cut his throat," said Jiménez.

He looked down at her nakedness, sepia in the dim light of dawn. He stroked her warm neck.

"Just here," he said, rocking her head gently from side to side. "With my knife."

She rubbed her chin on the back of his hand, like a cat demanding a caress.

"Later, woman," he said, swallowing hard.

He stood up and began to dress himself, pulling on his white cotton trousers that she had made for him, gathering his chiripa around him, securing it with a broad belt. She watched him pulling on his shirt and felt her body wanting him there and then. Jiménez was a hunger to her. He was better than any of the others. She put her hands behind her head and twisted sideways, offering herself to him. He struggled with his new boots. They were still a bit stiff, but they had shrunk to a perfect fit. He flexed his legs in satisfaction and bent to fit on his spurs, his silver nazarenas, of which he was so proud. The metal jingled as he rolled suddenly on top of her, straddling her and bending to kiss her breasts.

She laughed as he tickled her under the arms.

"Later woman," he said and rolled away. A child stirred in the corner. The baby in the cradle suspended from the ridge pole, began to cry. Jiménez touched the cradle and it swung like a pendulum. The leather rope creaked. The baby went back to sleep.

Jiménez took his long knife and thrust it into the back of his belt. He draped a kerchief over his head and the back of his neck and put on his small high-crowned hat. Lastly he folded his poncho, throwing it over one shoulder. She watched him with pride, her man, her gaucho. Jiménez looked down at her and smiled. His strong teeth gleamed in the darkness of his beard. Jiménez was proud of his good teeth. He pushed aside the leather flap at the doorway and stepped out into the light.

He heard the cockerel crowing and geese by the lakeshore. The first insects had begun their tentative stridulation. He saddled his horse with the same assiduous attention as he had given to his own appearance, carefully smoothing the lambskin caronilla to eliminate all danger of wrinkles. Over this he placed the soft jergas of leather, which had often been his only cover against the elements, when he slept under the stars. Then came the coverings of tooled leather, which he regarded with pleasure. He cinched home the wood-framed saddle and covered it again with a light rug and the skin of the aguará, the gangling, solitary wolf of the Chaco. These he secured with the sobrecincha, buckling it securely in place. He slipped his fingers under it, testing it for grip. He was satisfied. The bridle was decorated with silver pesos. He looped the lasso over the horse's haunches, put his toes into the ornate stirrup and swung gratefully into the saddle. He felt like a bird taking flight, transformed from a hobbling earth-bound creature into a soaring eagle. It was a feeling that informed his songs and the music of his guitar, when he played for Estrellita to dance. Jiménez had everything a man could want.

He drove the horses to pasture. He rode several miles to the east and moved cattle to an area where they had not yet grazed. He saw sheep and watched them with contempt. Sheep were for newcomers, for men who went on foot and saw nothing wrong with working in filthy sheds, shearing the ugly, naked, blood-flecked creatures. He paused and watched eagles soaring. He determined that if there were more sheep, he would take Estrellita and her children and go. He would go west across the river, into the great pampas, where a man could live with some pride. He realised that he was hungry. He turned the horse's head towards home.

Estrellita made a stew, a puchera with herbs and vegetables, which she grew on a patch of ground by the river. He ate it to please her, although he preferred proper food. It was the African in her that believed in vegetables. The children squabbled about him. He sent them away. He smoked a cheroot and sat in the sun. Estrellita brought the maté. They sat together, passing it back and forth. He watched the Italians in the distance, working on the house, digging and carrying, climbing ladders and hammering nails. He wondered how men could live like that. He could see the hammer rising and falling in silence. Then, in a moment, came the sound, echoing like a gunshot. He wondered why this was so. The house had become a feature of the landscape, visible for miles beside the avenue of trees. It made him uncomfortable. The land was becoming crowded.

Estrellita pulled at the drawstring of her blouse. He looked at her and smiled.

"Come inside," she said, taking his hand and he followed her. She set the baby's cradle in motion. The infant gurgled contentedly. The rope creaked as they made love, slowly and languorously and Jiménez drifted into sleep, to the chirping of insects and the distant noises of the builders.

He woke to the sound of Fierro talking to his daughter. He went outside, yawning. Fierro would always find something for him to do.

"Jiménez," said the older man, "take these letters to the pulpería for the señora."

Jiménez shrugged. The señora was a great one for letters. She sent many letters and received interesting packages too. Sometimes there were rolls of newspapers with stamps bearing the head of the queen of the Inglés. Jiménez could not read, but there were pictures in those papers, he knew. He knew there were pictures of people in many parts of the world. He would ask the señora some day if he might look at the pictures. She was a good person. She would not refuse.

"You can bring some things for me," said Estrellita, but do not drink too much or you will forget."

"What of my money, Fierro? Today is the day the señora pays the money."

"You take the letters to the pulpería and I will follow with your money. Take what time you need. We will have a drink together."

Jiménez laughed. "Maybe I will take your money also at the taba."

Fierro smiled a bleak smile. "Perhaps," he said. "Perhaps."

He seemed preoccupied. Jiménez took the package and mounted his horse. Estrellita called after him her list of requirements and Jiménez waved dismissively. He was glad of the journey as a relief from too much domesticity and he looked forward to the conviviality of the inn.

Catherine sat at the table arranging the little piles of coins. She opened her ledger and placed her pencil in readiness. She looked at the names and the marks made by the men in acknowledgement of payment. She enjoyed this little ceremony. She remembered how her father had told her of the tithe-proctors with their grim and suspicious faces and their ledgers, as they exacted the tax for the Established Church and how the people parted so grudgingly with their shillings. She had seen tenants on gale-days queuing to pay their rents to the landlord's agent. Something inside her rebelled at the notion. But this was different. She was paying willingly for work done and appreciated.

The men waited. John called each one by name and he came forward and made his mark.

"Guillermo."

The man came forward, his spurs ringing and received his pay. "Gracias, señora." He licked the pencil and made an X in the ledger. He nodded to John. "Señor," he said touching the brim of his hat.

"Aníbal," called John. The second man came forward in like manner and made his mark.

"Jiménez," called John, looking around.

Somebody laughed. "He is in bed with his woman." There was general amusement at the idea and some envious comment. Fierro stepped forward.

"Where is that idle fellow?" asked John. Fierro's eyes flicked to the rifle which John carried loosely in his right hand.

"I have sent him to do some work," said the foreman, reaching for the pencil. "I will make his mark and bring the money to him."

John intercepted his hand. He picked up two coins and held them up to the men. Catherine looked at him in surprise.

"Dos pesos," said John, holding the money aloft. "This is not the value of my colt but I wish to make this point."

There was a murmur of puzzlement.

"Fierro, explain to them. Nobody is to kill an animal without my permission."

Fierro looked at him and shook his head.

"Explain," said John, setting his mouth in a grim line. Catherine noted how he bit his lower lip. She had not seen him do that before.

"Explain it to them," said John again, swinging the rifle, tapping it against his boot.

Fierro spoke rapidly and lowered his head. The men muttered and fell silent.

"Gutiérrez," called John firmly.

Gutiérrez looked at his companions then shuffled forward to receive his pay.

"Gracias, Gutiérrez," said Catherine gently, aware of his embarrassment.

"Gracias, señora," he muttered, touching his hat. He looked at John. "Señor," he said and turned his back.

"Well, that's that," said John. "Now we know where we stand."

Catherine looked at the columns of names. There was no X beside Jiménez, unfinished business. She gathered his coins and handed them to Fierro, who took them without comment. John closed the book with a bang. He felt good about things. He reckoned he had earned a drink.

Jiménez sang to the guitar in a high nasal voice verging on falsetto. He sang of the skinny Gringo women and the fierce women of the Basques. His companions joined him, clapping and laughing. He wished that Estrellita had come with him to dance the gato for them. He sang of how Creole women bound a man's heart like a lasso of two rings. Some day he reckoned, he would buy her a ring and possibly look for a priest to say the words over them. All in good time.

He drank the rough native wine. He argued. He had done well at the taba and his pocket jingled with pesos. He tried to remember what Estrellita had asked him to bring. Fierro would remember.

"It was a mistake," his companion was saying. "It was a mistake to keep the Blancos out of the government."

"Flores won the revolution," retorted Jiménez. "There would be no point in a revolution if he let the Blancos back into the government."

"Ah, but there you are wrong, my friend," said the other. "This Berro is a man of peace. He let the Colorados share in the government. It was good for the country."

"And where is he now? No, Flores is a strong man. He uses Brazil and Argentina to make The Banda strong. He will destroy Paraguay with their money." He laughed. "He is as cunning as the gato."

"But why?" asked the other.

Jiménez pondered the question. He knew nothing of Paraguay, except that it was up-river somewhere.

"Because they are the enemy," he said at last. The simplicity of it all pleased him. "They are the enemy, so they must be destroyed."

He looked about for corroboration. He spotted Fierro entering the low-ceilinged room.

"Fierro," he called, beckoning him over.

"You are a man of knowledge. You tell us why we must make war on Paraguay."

Fierro scowled. "There is too much talk of fighting," he said. "I want to speak with you." He drew Jiménez aside.

"I would give you the two pesos myself, but I know that you will hear anyway. It is a matter of little importance, but I know you too well."

He explained about the colt and the decision of the señor.

Jiménez laughed. "No, this is some joke you are playing on me."

Fierro took out the coins.

"You have plenty of money to buy whatever you need. The señor will protect his property. I want no trouble between you."

"No, no," said Jiménez, struggling with the idea. "The animals were there before the señor. This is not right. He is no more than a boy. He insults me before my companions." His hand went instinctively to the hilt of his knife.

"Jiménez," said Fierro, taking him by the arms, "my friend, you must be calm. This world of ours is changing. This is the new way. Think of Estrellita. The señor has papers from the government. He has the authority."

"Papers! I care nothing for his papers. He insults my honour."

Fierro sighed. "Drink with me, my friend and in the morning we will talk. You will see that this is a matter of no importance."

Fierro's voice, rather than his words, calmed Jiménez. He shrugged. His fingers relaxed about the hilt of his knife. There was a burst of laughter from a group of newcomers and Jiménez looked around.

"I think he has come for his boots, Jiménez," said one of the newcomers, nodding towards the doorway. John Cardiff stooped under the lintel and entered the room. Jiménez drew his knife.

Tom Doyle struggled with his emotions. He adjusted his reading glasses. The letter lifted his spirits. He was proud of Catherine and of how she was coping in a strange and violent country. He had begun to talk to his neighbours about how well she was doing and about how big their farm was. The neighbours were sceptical. Not even the gentry owned that much land. Sure, a man might plough a furrow in one direction every day for a week and he wouldn't reach the far side of his field at that rate. They nodded at his story, but they were still sceptical.

On the other hand, it broke his heart to know that she had put down roots so far away and that he would never see her again. Nor would he ever see his grandson. He unfolded the letter and read it again. It was three months old.

My Dearest Parents
I write to tell you that everyone here at Santa Catalina is well, as I hope and pray that you are and my dear brothers also. I hope that

the fishing is good for them and that you are prospering. I think of you very often.

Your grandson, Richard, is strong and is beginning to take his first steps. It is a joy to me to inform you that he will soon have a little brother or sister. Soon he will learn to ride as all the children here do. John takes him on his horse and he is a great favourite with all the people of the estancia.

We both speak Spanish quite well now, which is necessary for dealing with the men. John is a good employer and they like and respect him greatly. He has learned to do all the things the men do and has become quite expert with the rope and the bolas. This is a thing with three weights on cords, which they use to trip the animals.

We are keeping sheep now and wool is fetching good prices. The gauchos do not like sheep so we employ immigrant workers to mind them. John has talked of bringing over someone from home, who understands the management of sheep.

I have become quite an expert at spinning and I am also learning to weave. John does not approve. He says this is work for the servants. My friend, Guidai, is teaching me the patterns of her people. She is an extraordinary woman. She tells me stories of her people when we are working together. Her parents were Indians, who were driven out of their lands long ago. You remember how Uncle Laurence told us of fighting the Indians. It was around that time. It is a very sad story when she tells it. Only a few of them escaped.

She tells a beautiful story of the princess of her tribe, Aymará. Aymará fell in love with a man, an estancia owner, who asked her father to let him marry her. She was no more than sixteen. The man was very much older and he respected the chief very much. The chief agreed and Aymará was sent to a convent in Buenos Aires to be educated. Can you imagine how lonely she must have felt so far from home? I feel so sorry for her. When she came home, the Indians were all gone. She married the man and had his children. They live somewhere to the east of here.

We have heard nothing of my uncles yet, although I am hopeful that they will hear of us. There is a war going on, but we see nothing of it. It is away upriver. I hope my uncles are not involved. I know how they enjoyed fighting the Indians, but they would be too old anyway.

Our house is coming on very well. It is exciting. I wish you could be here to see it. John is taking me to Montevideo in February to buy things, furniture and all, for the house. When it is finished we will ask the priest to say Mass in it. The priest comes every few months and says Mass under the ombú trees. It is like the way they used to say it in the old days at home when it was forbidden. It reminds me of Fraughan Sunday, when we used to go to the top of the hill to hear Mass. Do you remember how the priest would be struggling with the book and the pages flittering in the wind? I used to be so afraid that the book would blow away. They were very happy days.

But I am very happy here of course. When we go to the city, I will have a photograph taken and send it to you and then you will know how well we are and you will see that your grandson is a Doyle. You will be very proud of him, I know.

I have planted the acorns and I live in the hope that some of them may grow. Thank you for ordering The Graphic for me. It is good to read the news of the outside world and, of course, to keep up with the latest fashions. I will be quite the lady in Montevideo when I call on our important friends, the Senator and his wife. You would be very proud of

Your loving daughter

Catherine Cardiff.

Tom put down the letter and removed his glasses. He rubbed his eyes. He thought of the little Indian girl, so far from her family and he hoped that the nuns were kind to her. The education would stand to her. It was sad how she came home and all her family was gone, but she was safe now with a good man. The thought gave him comfort. He looked into the fire. Aye, he thought, and I carried her on my shoulders to the top of that windy hill. His hands shook as he folded the letter again, placing it carefully in his waistcoat pocket.

Chapter Nine

John fired as the man lunged towards him. He had no time to lever another cartridge into the breech. He swung the butt of his rifle and felt it connect. He felt a jolt of pain in his arm and saw the long knife falling, stained with blood. In the lamplight he saw Jiménez, writhing on the floor, clutching at his belly. His mouth was a bloody gash where the rifle butt had caught him. He saw the faces of the ring of onlookers in the awful silence and painfully he worked the lever, backing towards the door.

Fierro went on his knees beside Jiménez. Jiménez groaned. Blood seeped through his fingers.

"It is not good," said Fierro. He gestured to the onlookers. "Take him to a bed. We will do what we can for him."

The men lifted Jiménez, who gasped with the pain. His head lolled back as they took him away.

"Señor," said Fierro, "you are wounded. Let me see."

John watched him warily.

"It is all right, señor. You were attacked. The right is on your side."

The onlookers nodded agreement. They admired how the señor had handled himself, although Jiménez was well liked.

Fierro took a bottle of brandy from the bar. He opened John's sleeve and examined the gash. He spread the lips of the cut and poured brandy into it. John's knees sagged. He felt his calf muscles trembling with shock. He bit his lip and made no sound as the pain seared through him. Fierro bound the wound with his kerchief.

"You must tell the señora to stitch this when you go home," he said in a matter-of-fact way. "The wound is clean."

He poured some of the brandy into a tankard.

"Drink this," he ordered and John did as he was told.

"Now I must see to Jiménez," said the foreman. Young bulls, he thought. They must always be fighting. If it is not women, it is politics or gambling or a nice decision on the fall of the taba. Matters of honour.

He took the remains of the bottle and went out.

"There is no blame, señor," said the proprietor. He wiped his hands on his soiled apron.

"No blame at all," said another man and John felt nothing but goodwill towards these fair-minded men.

"We will have a drink," he said to the assembled company and the proprietor hurried to oblige.

"Sláinte," he said, raising his tankard. They raised their drinks in salute. His arm no longer pained him.

Catherine heard the horse and taking a lantern in her hand, she went outside. The air was so still she could hear John talking and laughing now and again. Then she saw him in the dim light, swaying in the saddle. She saw the whiteness of the bandage on his arm. She ran to meet him in case he might fall.

"...and drunk delight of battle with my peers..." He slurred the words "battle with my peers," a second time, relishing the phrase. He laughed. "He went down, you know. He went down."

Catherine felt a chill fear descending on her.

"Jiménez?" she asked, her voice shaking.

"And he'll get the same again if he ever steps on my land."

He leaned sideways and slid from the horse. He drew himself unsteadily to his full height.

"He went down, you know."

She took him by his good arm.

"Lost a drop of blood," he explained.

"You'd better come inside. You're hurt. I'll see to the horse."

"Damn fine horse, too. Knows his way home. Good boy, Slaney." He patted the horse's neck. The horse snorted.

"Not drunk," said John urgently. "Lost a drop of blood."

"I know, I know," said Catherine, anxious to get him inside. She led him to the bed and lowered him onto it.

John laughed. "He went down, you now. Came at me with a knife. Not a word of warning." He chuckled. "I was too quick for him though. Everyone says I was in the right. Battle with my peers, eh?"

"Is he dead? Jiménez? Did you kill him?"

"If I had, he deserved it. No, but they say he'll never ride a horse again. The bullet smashed this bone here, the what-do-ye-call-it?"

"The pelvis."

"That's it. If he doesn't take infection and die he'll be a cripple for the rest of his life and serve him damn well right."

"The poor man," she exclaimed.

"Poor man? Poor man? Blast him, he tried to murder me." He closed his eyes.

Catherine looked down at him. The light of the fire played on his features. This was not the boy she had run away with. This was some stranger, who had stumbled out of the darkness.

"In the saddle-bag," he mumbled. "It's in the saddle-bag."

She did not ask him what it might be, for fear of waking him. She went out and took the saddle off the horse. She brought the saddle indoors and opened the pouch. There was a package. She recognised Elizabeth's handwriting. She sat on the bone stool and looked at her name, Catherine Cardiff. Who was this person? she wondered. Was it the child who had arrived into this firelit hut so long ago, shaking in fear of the wild looking men sitting around the fogón? She looked at John. He had protected her that night and she had been glad of his strength, but now she feared it.

She opened the package. She recognised the book, the calf-bound Tennyson, with its stories of voyages and adventure.

Elizabeth wrote of her life in Wexford, of having finished school and of how they often talked of her and envied her, her great adventure. She was well and was walking out with a young man. Robert sent his best regards to them both and Mother wondered, if they had finished with her umbrella, would they please send it back. She read it again and began to laugh. The tears ran down her face. She wiped them away but they came again. She put her face in her hands and sobbed.

In the morning he was up and washed when she awoke. He looked smart in a clean new shirt. He ate an egg for his breakfast.

"An egg is the acid test," he declared. "If you can manage an egg after drinking, you're not too bad."

She said nothing.

"I feel bad about Jiménez" he began. "I will tell Fierro to send his daughter to him. We'll see that he is provided with whatever he needs."

"Good," she said. She had misjudged him.

"But he is not coming back here." He paused. "You might have imagined that I had too much to drink last night, but I hadn't."

"Huh," she replied.

"No, not at all. I lost a fair deal of blood, you see."

"I see."

"No, really. It was quite a gash. Fierro says you should stitch it, but I don't think that will be necessary."

"I will if you want me to." She grimaced.

"We Cardiff's are quick to heal." He made light of it, smiling at her. "What is it?"

She was shaking. He went to her and put his good arm around her.

"What's wrong?"

"Oh I was so afraid. You could have been killed and I thought you were glad about Jiménez."

"Delirium," he said lightly. "Disregard anything I may have said last night." She moved closer to him.

"If anything happened to you," she said, "we would be lost."

She looked at Richard, still sleeping peacefully in his hammock.

"You can't kill a bad thing," he said patting her shoulder. "Now we have a lot to do before setting off for Montevideo. If you could speak to Fierro's daughter it would help. Tell her that we will provide for Jiménez."

She nodded, "I will," she said gratefully. But when she went to speak to Estrellita, the rancho was empty and the fire was dead.

Doña María Jesús was aghast.
"You mean you have travelled all this distance, just the two of you and your baby, without protection?"

"We had no problem," said John, puzzled. "In fact we found the bridges a great convenience."

"Indeed yes," she agreed. "We have put some of our new wealth to good use."

Catherine told her of how they had camped one night by the river and how blessedly cool it had been compared to the intense heat of the road. She spoke of the raucous parakeets perched high in the trees in their untidy nests and of how they came and went incessantly, scrutinising the intruders.

"When we travelled that way four years ago we had to ford the river," she continued. "The baqueano swam with the oxen, as I recall."

"But it is not safe," said Doña María Jesús. "The country is very disturbed. You could have been robbed. Some of the local commanders, the caudillos, exact taxes from travellers at gunpoint."

John smiled. "We have no politics. Why would anyone attack us?"

Doña María Jesús looked around at the small hotel room.

"This is not good," she said. "You cannot stay here in this heat. It would be dangerous for the baby. There is talk of disease in the city."

Catherine drew breath sharply.

"Disease? What disease?"

"Cholera. Perhaps it is untrue. I heard it only today. This city is full of rumours." She sighed. "Blancos, Colorados. It goes on all of the time."

"Then we must leave, John. We cannot stay in the city."

"We have come here to do some business," said John. "We will not leave just yet."

"Please, you will come to my house on Florida. We have the new water supply. It will be cooler for you."

"You are kind, Señora," said John, inclining his head, "but we would not wish to impose."

"It would be no imposition," said the lady graciously. "I would be glad of the company as Don José is away at the war."

"The war?" said Catherine in surprise. "But I thought he had retired from the army."

"Ah yes. So I thought myself. But he was not in favour with Venancio Flores, because he had worked with the Blancos. He believed in the politics of fusion, you see, although he is himself Colorado."

"With Berro?" asked John. "Everyone talks of Berro."

"Yes, with Berro. We thought it would be for the best. Then came Flores with his Brazilians and Argentinians."

"So Don José has left politics?"

"He returned to his old rank in the army. I am glad of this too, because there is so much politics, so much division in the city. So you see, I would be glad of the company and your baby would be safer in my house. It is your house now."

Catherine looked at John. The air from the open window was heavy, fetid with the whiff of cesspools, the smell of summer in the city.

"There is a cool breeze from the river in the evening time" said Doña María Jesús with a smile. "We can sit on the balcony and watch the people passing."

"You are kind, señora," said John. "Yes, we will accept your offer gratefully."

"Good," she said rising. "It is settled. I shall send a man to guide you in the afternoon. We will be able to continue our conversations of the voyage and you will tell me of your estancia."

She took her leave directly. Catherine looked at John.

"I am nervous of staying at such a fine house. What will we talk about?"

"It is better this way. At least I won't be worrying about you sitting here by yourself when I am out on business."

"True," she agreed. At first she had talked of going with him but he had pointed out that he could hardly call on bankers or lawyers with a lively infant and a heavily pregnant wife in tow.

It was settled. They moved to the high, cool house on Florida. Doña María Jesús embraced them like new members of the family.

"I shall send for my daughters to come and meet you," she said to Catherine. "You are of a similar age. You shall be great friends. They reside at our country house for the summer, but I shall bring them to the city again." She laughed. "Perhaps I shall find them husbands from all the army officers. Then I shall have grandchildren too. Your parents are pleased that you have a family?"

"Oh yes," said Catherine. "They are very happy indeed."

"Good. It is important that you communicate with your old family."

The little boy Richard, was playing with a small toy cart. He filled it with wooden bricks and tipped them out again. He liked the way they clattered on the tiled floor. He scattered them in all directions, enjoying the way they skittered on the polished surface.

Catherine made to pick them up.

"No, no," said Doña María Jesús. "Do not disturb yourself. You are tired and the infant must have his freedom. You must rest all the time you are here and let others take care of things."

"John is very good with Richard. He takes him away a lot of the time."

"Ah yes, but he also has his business affairs. Let us help you while we can."

Catherine was glad of her assistance. It was obvious that the older woman enjoyed having a child in the house.

She went to her room and wondered how John was getting on. She dozed fitfully. She thought she heard a distant crackle of gunfire. It was like the sound of breaking twigs, scribs, as her mother called them. "Go down to the meadow and get me some scribs for the fire." Brown, withered stalks of cow parsley that exploded in the fire. She always felt like a giant snapping the fragile stalks, a giant striding through the forest, pulling up trees and snapping them in two with a twist of the wrist.

But it was not the sound of scribs. It was gunfire and John was out there somewhere on the streets. She leaped up in fright, reaching for her garments. She had to find him.

John was downstairs talking to Doña María. "Berro led the attack himself," he was saying. He seemed flushed with excitement and his voice slurred. Catherine felt an enormous relief that he was safe and a stab of anger that he had been drinking. She was ashamed.

"Yes, with a revolver in one hand and a lance in the other."

"Berro?" said Doña María Jesús in astonishment. "Not Berro," she shook her head.

"I assure you," said John. "Assure you I spoke to people who were there. Berro and some twenty-five others. The Fuerte is in their hands. The government has been put to flight. They say he has sent for troops to come into the city. 'Down with Brazil,' he was shouting. Quite frankly, I do not understand the politics of this country." He gave a short laugh at the absurdity of it all. "Down with Brazil."

"This is very bad," said their hostess. "We must lock the doors. It will be dangerous on the streets." She hurried away to instruct the servants to make everything secure and in particular, to lock the stable yard.

Catherine spoke coldly to her husband.

"Come upstairs please. I want to talk to you."

He raised his eyebrows.

"Now," she said urgently and he followed her to the bedroom.

"You have been drinking. Do you want to disgrace us in this house?"

He looked at her, shaking his head.

"I have not," he said, "although I could do with one now. It matters nothing to you, I suppose, that I could have been shot out there."

"Keep your voice down," she said. He went to the window and looked down into the street.

"Seems to have quietened down now," he remarked. "Storm in a teacup, I suppose."

He watched a wagon loaded with hay, lumbering up the street. The driver slouched on top of the hay. The broad disc of his sombrero obscured his face. He must be sweltering in that heavy poncho, mused John. Too stupid even to consult his own comfort. He shivered. The day had got cold. The wagon rattled over the stones. The sound of the wheels reverberated in the street and in his head. The wagon turned the corner onto Mercedes, vanishing from his gaze.

"I think I will lie down for a while," he said, turning back to the room.

Catherine was saying something, but it made no sense. He could see her mouth moving. He could hear the sounds, but he was too tired to make anything of it. He wished she would stop. He sat down on the bed and tugged at a boot, but it would not come off. Damn it to Hell, he thought. He would strike her if she did not stop, this stranger prattling at him, when all he wanted to do was sleep. He lay back drawing the covers around him and shivered. Could do with a drink. He felt her tugging at his boots. He heard the door close as she went out.

As his coach rounded the corner, General Venancio Flores said to his companions, "I will offer this fool, Berro, terms of surrender. A revolution, he says." He stroked his moustache. "I will offer him terms and then I shall shoot him. And his followers."

"He has sent for the troops of Coronel Bastarrica," Márquez interrupted. "You must use the Brazilians against him, General."

Flores looked at him. He raised his eyebrows. "There is no need. I will talk to him."

"Artillery," said Flangini. "Level the Fuerte and everyone in it, before Bastarrica can get here."

"He will not come," said Errecart, with a shrug.

"Why not?" asked Márquez.

"Because of the cholera. I am told that Berro's messenger drank from a contaminated well. He died on the road."

"It is like a tragedy of the Greeks," remarked Flores, "except that this idiot in the Fuerte is no hero. We are in more danger from the cholera than we are from the Blancos."

There was a sudden thunder of gunfire. The coach slewed sideways, as the driver pitched forward from his seat and fell under the hooves of the horses. The occupants saw holes appearing and daylight spearing towards them, as bullets tore through the fabric of the vehicle. Faces appeared at the windows. Hands holding pistols were thrust into the semi-darkness of the coach. Fire blazed from the muzzles.

Flores pushed at the door on the side away from the attackers. He drew his revolver and pulled the trigger desperately. The hammer clicked on an empty chamber. He swore. He had forgotten to check it. The door, hard against a wagon-load of hay, would not open. He saw his companions tumbling through the other door and going down on the cobblestones under a fusilade of fire. He was aware of numbness in his arms and legs. He concluded that he had been hit. Then they were upon him with their knives, men in long ponchos, faceless in the shadow of their sombreros.

Within seconds they were gone. A horse stamped and tossed his harness, alarmed by the smell of blood. The body of Venancio

Flores lay twisted and bleeding among those of his companions, the head virtually severed from the neck.

Doors opened. People came timidly onto the street. A priest knelt by the bodies. Blood stained his cassock as he murmured the prayers and made the Sign of the Cross on the foreheads of the dead and dying. Flangini stirred.

The priest rose and went to pound on the door of the store of Quentín Correa.

"For the love of God, open this door," he shouted and the shopkeeper emerged into the sunlight, rubbing the siesta from his eyes.

"They have murdered Venancio Flores," cried the priest. His words echoed in the tremendous silence. Others took up the cry. "They have murdered Venancio Flores!" The word took flight from street to street, throughout the fever-stricken city. "They have murdered Venancio Flores!"

Correa brought out a camp bed and they lifted Flores in pity and fear and carried him indoors, where the priest attempted to arrange the mangled corpse with some semblance of decency. The shop took on the appearance of a field dressing-station. Then the supporters of Flores arrived, grim, angry men with murder in their eyes.

Catherine ran up the stairs and threw open the door. "John, John," she cried, "Wake up! Something terrible has happened."

The stench struck her immediately. She pulled back the shutters, letting light into the room. He had soiled himself in the bed and with a shock she knew that he was seriously ill. His face was pale, with a tinge of blue. His teeth chattered with the cold. She screamed. Doña María Jesús came running.

"Madre de Dios!" she said putting her hands to her face, "the cholera. Madre de Dios and at such a time."

Catherine stared at him, still in shock. And she thought he had been drinking. She cringed with guilt at the hateful things she had said. She heard the sound of marching feet and shouting in the street below. She sat down on the side of the bed.

John twitched and groaned. She should do something. She felt his wrists. The pulse was weak and fluttering.

"The doctor," said Doña María Jesús. "I shall send for the doctor. Then we must clean him and give him water. He must have fluid. All these things must be burned."

She hurried from the room, calling to a servant in the hallway below. Catherine raised John's head and tried to help him drink some water. His eyes were sunken. He looked at her helplessly, but could not speak.

Doña María Jesús returned. She wore a white, starched apron. Her sleeves were rolled up. She handed a similar garment to Catherine.

"We should not be here, señora," said Catherine. "I am sorry for all this trouble." She was shaking. Her hands fumbled with the strings of the apron. She could not tie a bow at the back. The woman tied the knot, tugging it firmly. Catherine felt like a child. It was the way her mother had tied her apron for her.

"Now," said Doña María Jesús, "let us begin. I have dealt with this before on the campaigns. You will be no use to your husband if you stand here wringing your hands."

Catherine was glad that he was asleep. She imagined how furious he would have been at the indignity of being undressed and cleaned by others. She was glad to follow orders and glad to hear the doctor's heavy tread as he ascended the stairs.

Don Bernardo Prudencio Berro strode into the hall of the Cabildo, flanked by his supporters. The body of Flores lay draped in the national flag. Beside it stood the members of the council, among them the puppet president, Varela.

"This is outrageous," began Varela without preamble. "You have brought shame and violence to your country."

"Silence!" roared Berro. A pulse ticked in his temple. "The dictator is dead. I offered peace and co-operation and how did he answer me?" He glared around at the hostile faces. "How did he answer me, this general?" He spat the word contemptuously. "This general, who made war on his own people. This general who brought the foreigners into our country to make war on his fellow Uruguayans. I say to Hell with him and to Hell with those who stood with him. I am the government again, Varela."

He turned to leave. His men levelled their rifles. "Come to me at the Fuerte before dark and I will grant you your lives and the terms under which you will serve my government." He ground his teeth in fury. "In the meantime remove this garbage." He turned back to the body of Flores and twitched the flag from it. He threw the flag at Varela. "And show more respect for the flag of your country." He strode from the hall, followed by his men.

Varela, stunned, held the flag in both hands. There was blood on the smiling face of the sun. He touched it with his thumb. It was dry. He heard a single shot outside. He hurried to the door, knowing already what he would see. The body of Berro lay on the ground. Over him stood the son of Flores, little more than a boy, with a revolver in his hand. Behind him stood a detachment of troops, their rifles trained on the supporters of the dead man. One by one the Blancos relinquished their weapons, letting them clatter to the ground. They raised their hands in surrender and Varela knew, with a sinking heart, that he was powerless to prevent the anarchy.

"You are fortunate, señora, if I may use such a word in the circumstances," said the doctor. "This is the English cholera. It is not as severe as the other. Now, you must see that all water is boiled and that the, ahem!" he coughed, "that the contents of the commode are destroyed by fire." He replaced his instruments in his case. "I have got him to drink and will return in some hours. You must also get him to drink, in case I am delayed. There are many cases in the fever hospital. Your husband is safer here. He must have this fluid and salt at regular intervals." He patted her hand in a fatherly manner. "You must be brave for him and do what is necessary."

She nodded silently.

"If you could get some chloride of lime it would be useful to soak some sheets in it and hang them over the windows. Some say that this disease is a miasma rising from the drains."

"Chloride of lime," she repeated. "Yes, I will do that."

She had no idea what it might be or where it might be obtained, but she would look for it if it could help John.

"Keep him warm," warned the doctor, "but you must not share his bed for fear of contagion."

She nodded, wordlessly. She knew that she would not sleep until John was safe. She would sit with him and suffer with him in expiation for misjudging him. She would not sleep for fear that that which she dreaded, might happen and she would not be there to hold his hand.

"But you too must rest, señora," he added, turning at the door. "You will be no use to him if you do not rest."

She nodded again. She heard him descending the stairs and low voices in the hall. She heard the outer door closing and she returned to her patient. There was shouting and laughter in the street outside.

John turned his head sideways and retched. She held the bowl to his cheek. She wiped his face when he had finished. She stroked his forehead, brushing his fair hair back from his brow. There were several grey hairs at the temple. She stared at them. This was something new. She wondered about them. Perhaps they were merely bleached by the sun.

The noise in the street broke in on her thoughts. She went to the window and looked down. A cart, piled high with refuse was being trundled along the street by a mob of men. They were cheering and waving torches. In the cart was a naked and headless corpse. In front of the group strutted a man carrying a head impaled on a gaucho lance. He looked up as he passed, pointing to his grisly trophy.

"Look, señora," he shouted up to her. "Here comes the outcast, Bernardo Berro, the murderer of General Flores."

He laughed and the procession moved on. She stared after it, transfixed. The corpse rolled on the pile of garbage, pale in the light of the torches. The crowd turned the corner. The cheering died away.

I am in Hell, she thought. This is a punishment. I want to go home. She heard a groan from the bed. Fear closed about her. She found that she was trembling. She clenched her fists and breathed slowly, taking in the cool night air. Gradually, the trembling abated. She went back to the bed and lifted him. His bones felt sharp and angular under the clean nightshirt. She steadied him on the commode turning her face away. In sickness and in health, the priest had said, that evening in Liverpool when she had given her word. She had given her word because she had loved his beautiful face, his smile, his fair hair and taut, athletic body. Now he had two grey hairs and his body was racked with spasms. It was wrong to think like that. She had wronged him and misjudged him. In humility, she cleaned him again and laid him in the bed.

She took the vile contents of the commode and went down to the fire in the corner of the stable yard. The fire sizzled and smoke swirled upwards. She looked up and saw the stars. She prayed. The city was strangely silent.

John Oldham, manager of the Proudfoot Telegraph Company for the River Plate area, scrutinised the message. President Varela was acting with commendable speed in summoning his commanders and political chiefs to the city. Oldham believed, as did most people, that the presence of troops in overwhelming numbers, was the only way to prevent the spread of violence. Already rumours were circulating that the Blancos were deliberately contaminating the water with infection from the cesspools.

Oldham had already dispatched a telegram to Buenos Aires, in which the President had asked for immediate help from the old allies of Flores. He had set guards on all foreign embassies and effectively had declared a state of siege in the city. People were surprised by his decisiveness. If only, thought Oldham, his handwriting matched his unexpected ability. He cursed his own imperfect Spanish and began to tap out the message. He lingered over the word. Was it "vénganse" or "vénguense"? It was probably much the same thing. He sent the fatal message, repeating it to all concerned and inadvertently brought about a bloodbath as the veterans of many campaigns poured into the city to avenge their fallen leader.

The city sweltered in the heat and the cadaver of Flores, embalmed in haste and inexpertly, mouldered in the Cabildo, presiding over a city in love with death. Firing parties worked incessantly as prisoners were dragged out into the light and placed against the bullet-pocked prison walls. Still, still, the cholera worked, feeding the terror, a miasma in the late summer air.

They came to the house of Don José. Catherine heard the pounding on the door and loud voices in the hallway.

"My husband is a loyal patriot," Doña María Jesús was saying. "He is with his troops in Paraguay. You have no business with us."

The leader of the group, a civilian, looked up, seeing Catherine at the top of the stairs.

"Who is this, señora?" he asked, pointing.

"This is my friend. She is a guest in my house. She has no politics. She merely nurses her husband who has the cholera."

"The cholera!" The man took a step back. "You have cholera in this house?" He sniffed the air. There were sheets on the windows. They seemed to be impregnated with some foul-smelling chemical. He looked at his companions.

"Well, anyway," he said menacingly. His voice trailed off. They left hurriedly and Doña María Jesús bolted the door after them. She sat down on an ornate wooden chest.

"I am ashamed of these politics," she said. "The people are driven mad. We are lucky they did not burn the house."

"But Don José, is he not Colorado?"

"Yes, but he worked the politics of co-operation when we thought that Berro was good for the country. That makes him a traitor in some eyes. Enough of this. How is your husband this morning?"

"He is a little better, señora. He is drinking by himself. I have given him a little food. He does not know what is going on and I try not to distress him by telling him about all these terrible things."

"You are wise. He is a fortunate man to have such a wife as you. You have saved his life."

"No, señora. We owe everything to you." She sat down on the chest and clasped her hands. "Without you we might both have died in that wretched hotel. And Richard too."

"Now you must sleep," said Doña María Jesús. "I will watch over him while you get some rest."

Catherine yawned a long, shuddering yawn. She put a hand to her mouth, excusing herself.

"Go now, child," said the lady. "Get some sleep."

Catherine went and lay on the bed that had been left ready for her. She had lost track of time and of the date. It seemed as if she had been in that house for ever, watching over John, taking care of him, watching the blueness gradually recede from his face and listening to loud voices and hoof-beats in the street outside. The smell of the sick room was in her nostrils, in her taste and in her brain. She longed for her home and the clear air of the pampas. She longed for the cool water of her own river, the shady places under the trees and the rasping welcome of chicharra.

John made a good recovery. He began to take proper nourishment. In a few days he began to walk about the house and sit in the courtyard. He asked about what had happened to him. His hostess explained how Catherine had stayed with him night and day.

"You owe your life to her great love for you. You must never forget this time."

He was silent.

"Her time is near. It is not safe to travel. I beg that you will stay in my house until her baby is born."

"It is too much, señora," he said humbly. "We are too much in your debt."

She smiled. "I do this only for my country. I am a patriot. We need young, strong people like you and your Catalina. I will be as a mother to her, so that she may have many little Uruguayans."

He liked how she made little of her generosity.

"But I must return to the estancia. There are things to be done."

"When you are strong. When all this trouble is over. Stay with us."

"But..." he began and faltered.

"You came to buy things for your house. It is not possible yet. Soon you may go out on the streets and then, maybe..."

"Perhaps," he agreed. He was too tired to argue.

The weeks passed and at last, the rotting corpse of Venancio Flores was laid to rest, with sonorous brass and gunfire. The dementia of the people died down. The abandoned Cabildo stank of his presence and slowly the gaunt and haggard prisoners in the dungeons below, realised that they were forgotten. Their cries came back to them, mockingly through the echoing stone vaults and empty corridors and gradually they sank into despair. The season turned to the cooler days of autumn. Fallen leaves lined the streets. The cholera relaxed its hold. Life began to return to a tentative normality.

Chapter Ten

At night Estrellita dreamed of the jaguar. He came in the darkness to her hut by the River of the Forlorn and in the morning there was food in a pouch, hanging by the doorway. Food for her children and for Jiménez, but Jiménez would not eat. He was no longer a man. He could not walk, nor would he ever sit on his silver-decked saddle or hear his nazarenas jingle as he rode. Estrellita did not question things. She knew why the jaguar came to her and she knew that when the candle flame died, Jiménez would be gone.

She placed the shells around the candle and some silver coins. She examined each shell, precious objects from far away, where the world was of water. They glowed in the light of the candle, with the soft shine of horn or wet pebbles from the river. In the darkness of the hut she heard the drums of the ancestors and the spirits of the Orishas, as they came for the soul of Jiménez. She saw a man running, a man with a collar of iron and she heard the thunder of hooves. She was dreaming, but yet she was awake. The candle flame twisted and struggled in a well of molten tallow and gave up the ghost. The last glow faded into darkness and Jiménez was gone. In the gap of the doorway she saw the jaguar, just for an instant and then there were only the stars. She heard the river rushing, swollen with the first rains of winter and she knew that she must return to her home place, Laján, that which they now called Santa Catalina.

Catherine loved her new house. It had been so long since they had left and so much had happened. Now she had a daughter, Sarah and a son to inherit after them. The rooms were so big and the fireplace crackled with a cheerful log fire. It was indeed a palace, compared to the low hut by the ombú and worth all the waiting. As if to remind her of the hut, a puff of smoke backed down the chimney and curled about the mantle piece, warning her not to get above herself. Outside, the rain fell on the verandah roof with an incessant drumming. She had noticed that only when the wind came from the east, did the smoke blow back in the chimney.

The kitchen had a cast-iron oven and blue tiles on the floor and on the walls. Blue tiles all the way from France, "just for gosther" as she had said. It was a palace fit for a queen and for her little princess. She did not mind the rain. She made the tortas fritas and punctured them in the approved manner. Like the ants, she and her family would be warm and comfortable until the sun should return again.

Guidai was overawed by the house. She had never seen anything so magnificent. The tiles were cold under her bare feet and she imagined that this would be the most wonderful cool place during the long days of summer. She hoped that the señora would find work for her in the house, although she felt that things had changed. She did not expect that they could any longer share a companionable maté in the shade or sit by the fogón, as the meat sizzled on the spit. Catalina would be a great lady and important people would come to visit. She would have little time to sit and listen to the stories of an old china.

Catherine was feeding her new daughter. She was sitting in a chair that rocked backwards and forwards. There was a rug on the floor. Guidai avoided it. It was too precious to be trodden underfoot.

"I have come, señora, to ask if you will need my help in this great house."

Catherine looked at her in surprise. "Oh, but I assumed... Of course, if you feel that you can." She was confused. "I am not a señora, Guidai. I am your friend, Catalina. When I am old, maybe, but not yet." She put out her hand. "You helped me when I came here. You made me welcome. I will always need your help and most of all, your friendship."

Guidai was moved. She took Catherine's hand. It was a contract. Catherine handed the baby to her. She buttoned her blouse.

"Now you must sit and I will make us a maté. My new fogón is difficult to manage. You must try my rocking chair."

Guidai sat down gingerly, laughing in surprise when the chair moved under her. She clutched the baby in alarm but gradually settled to a comfortable rocking rhythm. The baby slept peacefully in the crook of her arm. Guidai ran her hand over the arm of the chair. It was a wonder of smoothness. Catherine went out.

"You have milk enough, señora?"

"I have. There will be no need for Estrellita." She stopped herself. "I'm sorry. With so many things happening, I forgot. Have you had news of her?"

"I hear that Jiménez is dead. She is coming home. She will find a new man."

Catherine came out of the kitchen.

"I am sorry to hear that he is dead. My husband wanted to provide for him, if he could."

"No one could provide for him, señora," said Guidai. "He had lost his honour and he could not ride his horse. He had no wish to live."

"But my husband felt responsible. He wished no harm to Jiménez."

"There was no blame. Your ways and those of the gaucho are not the same. Life changes. This, Jiménez could not understand. Things do not always remain the same."

Catherine sat on a stool. She offered the maté to Guidai. Guidai struggled to her feet and put the baby in a Moses basket. She stood by the fire.

"Sit down, please," said Catherine, indicating the chair. Guidai regarded it warily and sat again. She sipped the maté and smiled in contentment.

"How did Estrellita survive? Where did she take Jiménez?"

"She took him to the East, to the Arroyo del Perdido, that which the Inglés call the River of the Forlorn. It is where my people went in the old days."

"But how did she live?"

"She says the jaguar came to her with food. The jaguar is the spirit of my people."

Catherine waited.

"The blood of the African is in Fierro and in our daughter. It gives them knowledge." She shrugged. "For myself, I know only of Indian matters. I am Christian like you, but I remember."

"Tell me," said Catherine softly.

Guidai stared into the fire.

"I have been with Fierro since the matanza, since the soldiers came to kill our people."

"The Charrúas?"

"Yes, the Charrúas. We were children together, in the time of Sepé and Aymará, the children of the old cacique."

"Sepé, the great chief?"

"Yes, Sepé, the last chief of the Charrúas."

"And then the soldiers came?"

"Sepé took us into the Hills of the Perdido, but the soldiers followed. Almost all of my people died, but some of the soldiers also died. We hid in the trees. Fierro had a great knife. His ancestor, the African, took it from a Spanish soldier. He said that he would protect me with his great knife, but I knew that he would kill me if the soldiers tried to take me. In this way he would protect me from them."

"And you knew this?"

"Yes and that is why I have loved Fierro all the days of my life. It was our way."

"I don't understand. I thought Fierro was a gaucho."

"This is what I say. Life changes and we must also change. Now we are gauchos. Now we are Uruguayans."

"And what of Sepé? What became of him?"

"Sepé entrusted his sister to the estanciero, as I have told you and she became a great lady. I have not seen her since. Sepé took his weapons and went further into the hills, to the place of the thorn trees and jaguars. He is with the spirit of his people."

"I see," said Catherine thoughtfully. "He was never defeated."

"No, he was never defeated."

She sipped the maté. Catherine watched the play of light on her face as Guidai rocked backwards and forwards. It was almost like home, with a fire in the hearth and the sound of the rain.

"And the señor?" asked Guidai. "He is well?"

"He is, thank you. He was very ill in Montevideo, but he is recovered. I hope though, that he is under shelter from this rain."

"There were terrible things in the city, they say."

"There were." Catherine closed her eyes. She could still see the headless corpse of Berro lolling on the refuse cart. She shuddered. "Terrible things."

"It is good, señora, that the wars do not come here."

"It is," she agreed. "God forbid that trouble should come to us."

In the pulpería, John swirled the last of the rum in his glass. He had lost heavily on the cock fight. He downed his drink and stepped out into the rain. He swore and turned his collar up. He climbed into the saddle. He was half sorry that he had not decided to stay the night.

"He looks like your side of the family," Tom Doyle insisted. He adjusted his spectacles. He removed them and held the picture close to his face. He was amazed by the magical process that had brought this image of their daughter to them over thousands of miles of ocean.

"Aye, he has the cut of your family right enough."

Dorothy took the picture and scrutinized it. Her eyes were sharp, undimmed by years of sewing and darning, making and repairing. Catherine stared from the print with all the determination required by Daguerre's relentless technique. She held what looked like a bundle of washing, containing a small white face with the eyes tightly closed. John stood behind her chair, grim and proprietorial, resting his hand on the head of a small boy, a Doyle to the life, with a fringe of fair hair. Behind them stood an elegant balcony, giving onto a lawn and some stately trees, but a fold at the bottom betrayed it as a painted backdrop.

"He's a Doyle," she declared. "Thank God."

Tom demurred. He was prepared to be generous.

"Why 'Thank God'? Your family were fine looking people." He spoke in the past. She had no other living kin.

"I meant that I hope he has the Doyle temperament and not the Cardiffs'." She regarded the boy closely. His right arm was blurred like a bird's wing in flight. No wonder his father had a hand on his head. It was necessary, she knew, to stand still for a photograph. With a chill premonition, she wondered if a propensity for flight might be hereditary. It was a silly notion. She put it aside.

"He's a fine little fella' all the same," said Tom. "We must get a decent frame for this, before it gets damaged. Read that letter again for me, like a good woman."

He rubbed his eyes and sat back, stretching his legs towards the ashes. He closed his eyes and his mind flew to a strange city in a land far away.

So now that the city has quietened down we have been able to go about our business. It is almost Winter now and...

"Isn't that the strangest thing? And we here thinkin' about the early spuds." He chuckled at the strangeness of the world.

"It is," agreed his wife, irritated by his interruptions, yet pleased to see him so happy. Catherine's letters were like beams of light into the darkness of his melancholy, his desperation to have her back safe again. Had she gone in the fullness of time it would have been different, but it was as if he had mislaid his daughter somewhere and was still searching for her.

Don José has returned from the war. He tells us about Paraguay and what a beautiful country it is. They have so many oranges there, they feed them to the pigs. Even the children smoke cigars. He says they make the best cigars in the world. I have sent you some tobacco so that you can taste Paraguay and some yerba to make tea. It comes from Paraguay also. I hope you enjoy it.

"Sounds like a marvellous place. I dare say the bacon there would have a comical taste."

"So why do they destroy it?" asked Dorothy.

Tom shrugged. "It's a woeful business, right enough. This Don Josie fella' sounds like a hardy man. I'm just as glad he has the power to protect them. Y'know, it sounds to me like the stories they used to tell about the Ninety Eight."

They were silent, remembering tales of murder and battle and the madness that had swept over the land in their parents' time.

"It does," she agreed. "I pray to God…"

"But it would never be as bad as that. At least, I mean, they're all the one religion, aren't they? That should make a difference."

"That should be a great help," she replied and set her mouth in a grim line.

Don José has promised us a military escort when we are going home. He has to send soldiers around the country to keep the peace. We set out for home in a day or two, whenever he gives the word. By the time you get this letter we will be set up in our new house with all our new things.

John has recovered from his illness and sends his kindest regards. You would be so proud of him if you could see how well he is doing. We will travel by day because the weather is much cooler now. When we came down, we travelled by night sometimes, because the days were so hot. It was beautiful to look up at all the stars. They are so different from home. It was interesting to see all the changes that are coming about. There is a lot more tillage and in some places the farmers are fencing in their land. I suppose it is necessary now to keep the animals out of the crops, but I doubt if it will happen in our part of the country. The gauchos would never learn to plough and sow. It would be an insult to their honour. Ha Ha!

"Begod," interrupted Tom again. "Isn't that a good one? They wouldn't do too well in this country, I can tell you. Heh Heh! If a man wasn't prepared to get a bit o' muck on his boots, he wouldn't get very far in this country." He regarded the picture again. "Our man here." He tapped his finger on the image of John. "Doesn't he wear the strangest get up? Look at the hat of him." John was wearing a low-crowned hat with a broad, flat brim. "That would be for the sun, I suppose."

"I suppose it would." Dorothy too, had been struck by his style and the touch of arrogant flamboyance in his garb. Nothing too overstated, but definitely foreign.

"That's about it," she said, putting the letter aside. "She sends her love, of course and love from John and from Richard and Sarah." She took up her knitting. "At least I can see them now as real people." The needles clicked. "She looks a good deal older."

"Ah, that's only the photograph. It makes everyone look older. Should we get one made and send it back?"

"I don't think so. If she wants to see us, she knows where we are." Her needles clicked rapidly and she lowered her head to her work.

The rain stopped abruptly. The sky cleared. John smelled wood smoke. He saw the glimmer of a fire in the distance and approached warily. The horse, Slaney, snorted and whinnied. The sound rang in the echoing darkness. John patted his neck.

"Easy, boy," he said and, for reassurance, touched the stock of his rifle in the saddle holster. He could see in the moonlight, a cart, its shafts resting on the ground and a figure sitting by a fire. He called out and the figure turned in his direction.

"Who is that?" he called. "What are you doing on my land?" He slipped the rifle out and laid it across his saddle. He heard an answering whinny and Slaney pranced underneath him. The figure stood up and threw a shawl back from her head. He recognised Estrellita, the daughter of Fierro.

"What are you doing on my land? he asked sharply.

"Ssh!" she admonished, putting her finger to her lips. "My children are asleep. Do not make noise, Cardiff. They are tired from their journey."

"Who the Devil...?" he began but she put her fingers to her lips again and he lowered his voice. "What are you doing on my land?"

"Jiménez is dead," she said. "You must care for us now, Cardiff."

"How dare you speak to me in this manner? I take no responsibility for Jiménez or for you or your children. He was a fool."

"Maybe, but he was mine and you took away his pride and so he died. Now, Cardiff, you must care for us."

"I will have none of your insolence. I owe you nothing." He was angry with himself for arguing, but he felt, deep down, that he owed something to her father, if not to her.

"But you will feel better if you care for us. This I know."

She stirred a pile of shells with her toe. They glinted in the firelight. Among them stood a glass of water. She stooped and lifted the glass and offered it to him. He hesitated, suspecting a trick. She put the glass to her lips and drank. Her gaze never left his face. He could see yellow in the whites of her eyes. He felt that she could see into the depths of his soul.

"You are thirsty," she said and he realized that his mouth was dry. She offered the glass again and he drank. He felt a kind of defeat as if she were dictating the terms.

"If you live on my land, you will earn your keep."

"Of course, Cardiff." She lowered her eyes submissively.

"And you will address me with respect."

"Of course, Cardiff."

"And that horse. Is that the horse of Jiménez?" He indicated the animal hobbled among the bushes. "If so it belongs to my estancia."

She laughed derisively. "The horse of Jiménez would never draw a cart. No, that is an old yegua, which I bought to bring us home. She is in season, as your horse knows very well. He smells her before you smell the smoke of my fire." She put her head to one side and looked at him. "The yegua is foolish for the men."

"What work can you do?" He felt an urge to strike her across her insolent face with his rebenque.

"Well, let me see." She began to tick off her qualifications on her fingers. "I can cook and I can dig. I can make the seeds to grow. I can take good care of children and scrape the hides of the cattle and boil the quebracho for the tanning. There are many things."

"And you will do this work or by God, you will get off my land."

"Betum-sam," she continued, ignoring the threat. "Betum-deti." She looked up at him and smiled. "Also I can dance and make a man happy and I can tell you where the world has come from and, guarroj, what the future holds for you. These are ten things I can do for you, Cardiff."

"You are an insolent woman. So help me God, if you do not behave, I will sell you to Brazil."

"I would fetch a good price, Cardiff, with all these many things I can do. But you will not do such a thing."

He wiped his mouth. He imagined that he could taste her from the glass. He handed it back to her and her fingers touched his. He wiped his hand on his coat.

"And why not?"

"Because you will want to know. You will want to know what the future holds for you."

"Nonsense," he scoffed, gathering the reins. His horse stirred restively.

"You do not believe me now, but some day you will come to me."

He dug in his heels. Slaney resisted at first, reluctant to leave, but John pulled him around and rode into the darkness. He looked back, but a rise in the ground hid the fire from his sight. He heard the plaintive whinny of the yegua, and angrily, he spurred his mount to a canter.

Catherine watched him fumbling in the semi darkness. He was not yet familiar with the room. He stood, looking down into the cradle.

"Ssh!" she whispered. "I've only just got her to sleep."

"You're still awake?"

"Yes. She wouldn't settle and I was worried about you, out in all that rain."

"No need." He sat on the edge of the bed and pulled off his boots, letting them drop on the floor.

"Please, please, don't make noise," she whispered again.

He muttered something under his breath.

"What is it?" She queried. "What's wrong?"

"What's wrong? Everything is wrong. This blasted country. That's what's wrong."

She waited. She knew he had been drinking. There was a time when a few drinks made him cheerful and full of optimism. Now it made him morose.

"Liebig has refused most of my stock. They will take only the Herefords."

"Well then, take the others to the saladero," she said brightly.

"And sell them for their hides?" He growled. "Nobody wants the dried meat any more."

She searched for some way to lift him from his black mood.

"You have sheep. Wool is doing well. Don't worry. We will survive."

She reached out and touched his back. She rubbed her hand gently over the flannel of his shirt, feeling the line of his spine. He shrugged irritably and stood up.

"They've been taking sheep and killing them for saddles."

"Who? Nobody kills sheep."

"Bandits. Revolutionaries. Whatever they want to call themselves. Thieves. That's what I call them. They will bankrupt the country and everyone in it. They even kill the Angora goats to make saddle bags."

She was quiet again.

"I will arm the men, God damn it! It's the only way to survive. Every tin-pot politician has his own army, so why shouldn't I?" He gave a dry, sarcastic laugh.

"Ssh!" she warned again as the baby stirred and moaned. "Come to bed. Things will look better in the morning."

"A rabble. What we need is a strong government to crush the whole damn lot of them."

The baby stirred again. He rocked the cradle gently and the infant settled into sleep. Catherine was touched. In the midst of his anger and worry he could be so gentle.

"Come to bed," she said softly. She wanted him so much. It had been so long since they had made love. Long before the cholera and the terrible events in the city.

"Come to bed."

The moonlight caught one side of his face leaving the other side in darkness. He moved towards her and knocked against a chair. It clattered to the ground and the baby awoke, screaming. John swore and lifted her from the cradle. He put her over his shoulder and patted her back. He walked back and forth, but to no avail. He muttered under his breath.

"Here, you deal with her," he said angrily and handed her to Catherine. "I've had enough for one night." Abruptly he left the room, kicking the chair aside as he went.

She found him later, dozing by the half dead fire with an empty glass beside him on the hearth. He sprawled in her rocking chair and snored. She left him there and returned to her bed but she did not sleep.

In the morning he was thoughtful and withdrawn. He toyed with a mug of coffee. She tried to distract him. She dressed the baby, Sarah, in her prettiest clothes.

"Isn't she beautiful?" she said, holding her on her knee.

He looked at her, frowning.

"What?"

"Isn't she beautiful, your daughter?"

He looked at the baby thoughtfully for a moment and smiled.

"Yes, she is," he said, reaching for her. "Give her here." He put the infant on his knee and bounced her up and down. He spoke to her in baby talk and wiped her mouth when she dribbled. "Who's my girl?" he asked, laughing. "I've just had a great idea," he announced.

"What's that," asked Catherine responding to his good spirits.

"Why don't I write to Robert and ask him to come out? What I need is a man with a good head for figures."

"But I thought…" She was going to protest that she could look after the figures, if only he would let her. He was excited.

"Robert is the man. I could offer him a partnership. He has a few bob, you know. We could build the place up and ride out any recession. Get the bank off our backs."

She felt a sense of something being taken away, a dream flying in the cold light of dawn.

"How bad is it? You haven't told me anything. I thought I was to look after the books."

"No, no don't worry. Don't worry. Everything is fine. I can handle these pen-pushers. But what do you think of my idea?"

"You have no guarantee that he would come. You haven't even asked him yet."

It would be good to see a familiar face from home, even the solemn Robert Boxwell. It would be worth a try and maybe a partnership was the way forward.

"If he is agreeable," she said slowly. "I suppose it might be an idea."

"It's brilliant," he said. "I will write to him directly."

"Have one of the men take the letter to the mail. I have some post to send too."

"No, no," he replied, dandling his daughter on his knee. "I'll go myself. I want to order some rifles for the men."

"You're serious about that?" She was alarmed at the idea.

"Deadly serious. This country is in turmoil. A strong man armed and all that sort of thing."

She changed the subject.

"By the way I went out early this morning."

"Who's my girl?" he said to the baby, without looking up.

"I said I was out early this morning. I went for a walk down by the river."

"Oh yes?"

"I met Estrellita, Fierro's daughter. She has come back."

"Has she now? And what does she want?" The baby grasped his finger and tugged at it. "Hey, hey," he said, pleased with her strength.

"She just wants to come home, she says. I said she could use the hut under the ombú tree. I didn't think you would mind."

"Another mouth to feed. I suppose we can manage."

"And her children of course," added Catherine.

"Why not? Why not? Come one, come all. We might as well feed the entire parish."

"Jiménez is dead, she told me. She has no one to care for her now."

"Not for long, I'm sure. I heard about Jiménez."

"Where?"

"Oh, I don't know. Somebody in the pulpería, I suppose. You know how news travels."

"I felt sorry for her."

"Waifs and strays. Let's take them all in, brats and all and her mangy yegua. Why not? Why not?" He laughed. "We have plenty of room here, if the hut is not to her liking."

He stood up and handed her the baby. "Take this young lady and I will go and write to Robert. As long as he doesn't bring that hairpin of a sister."

She was pleased by his good spirits. The plan had merit, she had to admit. As long as Elizabeth did not take it into her head to come along. On the other hand, it might be nice to lord it over her a little as the lady of the estancia. She smiled at the idea. It had a certain attraction. John was kind too, to that unfortunate woman and her children and even her mangy yegua. They probably laughed about her at the pulpería, which was cruel. She wondered how Estrellita had bought the mare. She had her ways. It was strange though, her story of the jaguar and how he had brought food to her by the River of the Forlorn. Catherine's skin crept at the thought and goose bumps rose on her arms.

Estrellita really seemed to believe her own story. A strange one indeed.

She wondered about the bank and what pressure it might be putting on John and she began to feel guilty about the expense of the new house. Perhaps they had been unwise. The banks were free with their paper money, but they demanded payment in gold, which was difficult to come by.

Doña María Jesús had explained to them about the split between those who favoured paper and those who insisted on gold. She had tried to explain also, the politics of the day and the differences between the two parties. Even within the parties, there were sects and schisms: the doctores, intellectuals lost in the airy realms of theory; the principistas, devoid of practical common sense and the netos, purists who cared only for ancient tradition. These netos were despised by the doctores and dismissed as candomberos, as backward and populist.

The word brought her mind back to Estrellita, the candombera. She had never seen Estrellita dance. It was an idea. Perhaps they should have a fiesta to show their appreciation for all the work. It would give Estrellita a chance to shine, to be important. Now that he was in better spirits, she decided to put the idea to John, but he was already gone. He had forgotten to take her letters.

The day was bright and dry with a sharp westerly wind. She hitched her own little horse to a pony trap and took Richard with her to show him what would one day be his. Guidai was glad of the chance to have the baby all to herself, to feed her and bathe her and sing her strange songs to her.

She drove out along the red clay tracks beaten by millions of hooves over the centuries and by the men who herded the animals. Fierro fell in beside her. He touched his hat.

"It is a fine day, señora."

"It is indeed, Fierro."

"I am going to attend to some branding. We are late this year."

"Perhaps we will come and watch. I want Richard to see the work that must be done."

"He is small yet señora. Small to do the work of a man."

She touched the boy's head and he smiled up at her. He gripped the brass rail and watched Fierro at close range. He reached out and tried to touch Fierro's horse.

"He wishes for a horse of his own, señora. He wishes to be free. We will make a gaucho of him."

He smiled. It was his highest compliment. The horse snorted. His breath showed like steam in the coolness of the morning.

They came to a height and looked down on a circular corral, made from upright tree trunks. Cattle milled about inside the circle and a wood fire blazed, its flames blown horizontal by the wind. Catherine removed her bonnet, letting her hair blow about her. She could smell the smoke and the animals and meat cooking slowly over the flames.

She watched, fascinated, as the men singled out an animal, lassoed it and brought it to the ground, sometimes working their horses in opposite directions to immobilise the fiercest beast. There was a languid quality about the way the gauchos moved through the flood of cattle, cruising in the river of tossing horns, then, a sudden burst of speed and the noose was secure. She had seen an osprey take a fish in similar style, gliding, unconcerned and then the strike.

She saw the puff of blue smoke as the iron was put to the hide and felt pride at the sight of the letters SC, intertwined and burnt indelibly onto the haunches of their animals. John was right. It was right to arm the men and to protect what was theirs.

Fierro brought her meat from the asado and she got down to eat with the men. Richard gnawed on a slice of beef and wiped his chin with his sleeve. A fly, golden in the sunlight, hovered in front of his face and white clouds fled overhead. She was moved almost to tears by the beauty of the scene and by the gentle goodwill of these men, who could dominate the wildest animals with their brutal efficiency. She found that she loved the panoply of their simple lives, a paradox in itself and the many paradoxes of this wild and beautiful land.

She drove further and saw white sheep on distant hills and rarity of rarities, a troop of ñandú. She remembered her first sighting of the birds and how John had forgotten to check that his gun was loaded. She told the story to Richard. He pointed his finger at the graceful creatures and said "Bang!" She paused, watching them dwindle in the distance, feeling unaccountably sad that they were gone. She turned towards home.

She saw Estrellita down by the river, washing her clothes. Smoke rose from their former home under the ombú grove. A boy was riding the mare around and around, to the delight of his little brother and sister. He rode bareback of course and the animal responded to his skill. It was not a bad mare at all. Catherine wondered why John had called it a mangy yegua in such a disparaging tone. The children waved to her and Richard jumped up and down, keen to join them in their game. She waved back and her heart lifted at the sight of her house. This was a place worth fighting for.

Chapter Eleven

Robert wrote that he would come. He had some assets that he could realise, which would take some time, but he would come to them "with the utmost dispatch." There was little excitement at home except for the draining of some sloblands and the usual political wrangling.

"We don't want him for excitement," said John. "We want him for his pedantic book-keeping. God forbid that Robert would start looking for excitement."

"And his money too," she added. "Isn't that the main reason?"

He was stung by the remark. "Yes, we need his capital. So what? I will give him a share. It will all be done legally."

"But will Santa Catalina still be ours? I don't like the idea of having to share it with anyone."

"Look," he said, "Think about it. We already share it with people. Everyone who works here has a stake in it. At least Robert will be putting something into it, instead of taking it out."

"The gauchos contribute their work."

"When it suits them," he scoffed.

"No," she protested. "Nobody else could do the work they do. That skill is bred in the bone. We could never manage without them."

He was thoughtful for a while.

"You could be right," he conceded. "You know we almost have a village growing up around us, what with the new workers and the shepherds as well."

"And they depend on us."

"Don't I know it?" He spoke with a truculent growl like a man sorely put upon by others. He put Robert's letter on the mantelpiece and stood with his back to the fire. She noticed that he was putting on weight, despite the long hours he spent in the saddle. He stood with his legs apart, his hands behind his back, a posture that accentuated the increase in his girth.

"God forbid that he would be looking for excitement," he snorted.

"I was thinking," she began.

"What?"

"I was thinking that maybe a bit of excitement would do no harm."

"What do you mean? Come to the point." He frowned.

"A fiesta. I thought we might have a little celebration."

"What for? What have we got to celebrate?"

"Oh come on. Look at all we have. I know you would enjoy it. You owe it to your people."

He drew himself up. She knew he would like the idea of his people. She smiled to herself, remembering her mother's comments on the "Grand Cardiffs."

"And who would pay for it, of course?" he challenged, but the idea had taken hold.

"A fiesta. A bit of music maybe and a drink. Not a bad idea. Not a bad idea at all." He clapped his hands and rubbed them together. "Not a bad idea at all."

The priest came on his mule from Dolores. He said Mass in the shade of the porch and the people knelt before him, mostly the women and children and a couple of Italians, who looked after the sheep. Two or three gauchos sat on their horses in the background. They removed their hats out of respect for Nuestro Señor, but did not dismount, even for the Consecration.

Catherine held her daughter on her knee. She and John had chairs, as befitted their station. John kept a stern eye on Richard, conscious of the importance of his position as head of the family. He wore a dark suit and a high white collar and made an imposing figure. His hair, greying at the temples, was neatly brushed back from his forehead.

The priest dined with them, but declined their invitation to stay.

"There is so much trouble in the land," he explained. "I must keep going, to bring the consolation of the word of God to the people."

He was a gentle soul, worn thin by travel. Catherine feared for his health. He would not stay, even for the fiesta and set off in the heat of the afternoon for a distant estancia. He had no fear, he told them, of bandits or the soldiers of the latest revolution. There was nothing they could take from him except his blessing. There was security only in owning nothing and thereby having nothing to lose.

John raised his eyebrows and caught her eye. He helped the priest onto his mule, shook his hand and thanked him. The priest kicked his heels and the mule set off at an ungainly walk, refusing to go any faster, despite the priest's persistent efforts. There was no danger, thought John, of bandits stealing that creature. He tugged at his collar and opened the pin. Now they could take their ease and let the people enjoy the music and a little refreshment.

By the light of a bonfire and lanterns strung along the porch, the people danced and sang. There was wine and beer and a fizzy lemon drink for the children and meat sizzling over the fire. A travelling cantor, glad of the hospitality, sang of the great events happening in the land and a sad song of Flores, the lost hero. He played on his accordion and the gauchos vied with him on their guitars. An Italian shepherd played on his mandolin, a haunting tune of his homeland. The gauchos raised their tankards and their matés in generous salute, if not of his profession, at least of his musical ability. He sang of his boat on the sand and of his love looking from her latticed window. Nobody understood the words, but they were carried away by the melody.

John, filled with good humour, obliged with a song of Wexford, again to general approval. In his strong baritone he sang a rebel song of Ninety Eight, a song for which the author had come close to the gallows. He drew himself up with that pride that fills all Wexford men and his voice carried in the stillness of the night. The people applauded. He bowed in acknowledgement of their praise and raised his glass.

"La señora," called the people and Catherine stepped forward. The only songs that would come to her were the old Gaelic ones that Mother Alacoque had taught them. She saw the faces in the firelight, waiting expectantly and she began. She sang in the old style, with quivering grace notes, the widow's lament for her brave soldier, Art O'Leary. She was the only person who understood the words and her voice caught in her throat. They could see that she was moved and murmured encouragingly. She made a small dismissive gesture, excusing her hesitancy and finished to enthusiastic applause.

"Excellent," said John, clapping his hands. "I didn't understand a word, but excellent all the same."

"It was for you." She said. She quoted in Gaelic and translated. "I fled from my kinsfolk with you, far from my home with you."

"Ah," he said thoughtfully. "So we are the subject of a ballad, are we? And what happened then?"

"Oh it's just an old song. It doesn't mean anything."

"But what happened?" He had to raise his voice as the music had struck up again. His eye strayed to where Estrellita and three other women were dancing a kind of quadrille with the men. The gauchos were dressed in their finest clothes. They wore long white trousers, fringed with lace. Their ponchos swirled as they turned and they flourished with handkerchiefs as they bowed. The women, barefooted, danced a little tapping jig in front of their partners and then they were off again swinging with the music, their long skirts swirling about them. The music swelled.

The bastonero, directing operations, tapped his staff and the cantor sang of life and love and the stars in the heavens. John drank.

"I said he was killed," said Catherine for the second time.

"Who?"

"I told you, Art O'Leary, her husband."

"Oh, yes. Yes of course." He watched the dancers, tapping his foot to the rhythm.

Catherine followed his gaze. Estrellita was the only woman who could match and even outdo the arrogant flamboyance of the men. She danced her little jig in front of her partner and her arms swayed above her head.

"She's very good," remarked Catherine.

"Who?"

"Estrellita."

"Indeed." He emptied his glass and looked down at it pensively. "Here, let me get you something to drink."

"Thank you," she said, her attention on the dancers. A small line appeared between her brows as she frowned.

John stood in the tiled kitchen. The music pulsed in his head. It reverberated in the room. He put his head against the coolness of the tiled wall and closed his eyes. All he could see was Estrellita, swaying to the rhythm, lifting her bare arms over her head, turning this way and that, as she encouraged and then spurned the advances of her partner. He could see the column of her neck and the white blouse that barely covered her shoulders. His hands shook.

He heard a child crying and he straightened himself.

I am the señor, he thought. I am John Cardiff, descendant of conquerors. I am the head of this family, as I am often reminded.

He filled his glass and another for Catherine. The baby, Sarah, cried again and he went to her.

She was standing in her cot, with tears running down her cheeks. Her cheeks were red with teething. He lifted her and comforted her. Sarah put her head on his shoulder.

"There now. There now," he said, patting her back. The music came, more like a dull thumping, from the other side of the house. He felt safe with his daughter. He talked to her gently and she responded with little gurgling noises.

He wrapped her in her blanket and went through to the kitchen. He collected the glasses. He went out onto the porch and found Catherine, still where he had left her. He gave her the glass.

"This young lady wants to join the dancing," he said jovially. He raised his glass to her.

"To us," he said, toasting her. "To the Cardiffs of Santa Catalina."

Guidai took the baby from him and he put his arm around Catherine's shoulder. She shivered in the chill of the night air and he drew her closer.

"To us," she said and raised her glass.

The gauchos began a malambo, a wild and whirling duel of lightness and agility. The musicians drummed their hands on the guitars, strumming wildly. Women and children joined in and the spectators clapped and applauded each individual virtuoso performance. The dancers danced as if possessed by some wild energy. The señor and his lady clapped their hands and smiled on everyone who looked their way.

They made love that night when everyone had gone. It was like the old times. They lay listening to the silence of the house. The timbers of the roof contracted in the chill night air. They creaked as if some creature had crept across, unseen in the darkness. The clock chimed in the living room. It seemed to clear its throat with a whirr of springs, before deciding on a number. Four o'clock.

"Betum," she said.

"What?"

"Four. It's the way the Indians say it."

"Betum," he savoured the word. "Betum."

It echoed the chime appropriately. "How do you know that?"

"Guidai taught me."

"I was just thinking about all the languages here tonight. If we had your friend, Henry Jones, he could have given us a Welsh song."

"Henry. I wonder what he is doing now."

"Who knows? It would be easy enough to get lost in this country."

"The Hills of the Forlorn. It is a lonely name."

He turned on his side.

"Go to sleep," he said, yawning. The music was still pounding in his head.

Something was niggling in the depths of Catherine's mind. Art O'Leary had been killed in a dispute over a horse. She wondered if his widow had gone back to her father's house. Jiménez had died because of such a dispute.

"How did you know about the mare?"

"The what?" He thumped the pillow and sighed.

"The mare. Estrellita's mangy yegua, you said."

"It is a mangy yegua. What of it?"

She remembered the morning clearly. It was the morning she had gone driving with Richard and they had watched the gauchos branding the cattle. She remembered the blueness of the sky and the startling white of the clouds. She remembered the smell of the coffee, his brilliant scheme of writing to Robert and the cold feeling that had come over her when he spoke of getting the bank off their backs.

"I told you that she had come back and you said, with her brats and her mangy yegua. Why did you not tell me that you knew?"

"How the devil should I know? They talked about her at the pulpería, I suppose. Go to sleep for God's sake."

He punched the pillow again and pulled the blanket around his shoulder.

"So you didn't know?"

"No, I didn't." He was quiet for a moment. "She's a bit of a yegua herself, so they say." He laughed dismissively.

"That's a cruel thing to say."

"It's the truth."

Catherine lay quietly. The timbers creaked again. The sound was reassuring. She was safe in her own house.

"It's cruel all the same," she said again.

"They look on these things differently. She's half savage, for God's sake. Now go to sleep."

She lay, listening to his breathing, but she knew that he was not asleep. A dim light began to creep in at the window and she lapsed into a fitful doze.

In the morning the soldiers came for horses.

"The Lanzas, señor," shouted the gaucho. "They are looking for horses. They are coming, two men on each horse. That is why I was able to get ahead of them."

His mount had a fine film of sweat on its neck.

"How many are they?" asked John, looking about.

"Twenty, maybe thirty, señor. I did not stay to count."

"Very good. Well done."

He could see dust rising in the distance. The Lanzas. Another blasted revolution. There was no possibility of resistance.

"Get Slaney," he said. "Take him into the kitchen. Keep him quiet. I will go to meet them."

He took the gaucho's mount and set off in the direction of the rising dust cloud.

They were a battered looking crew, covered in fine red dust, which gave their assorted outfits an appearance of uniformity.

Some were bandaged and hollow-eyed from pain and exhaustion. They carried a variety of weapons, even ancient flint-locks, slung across their backs and the column bristled with long lances, the straight military type with fluttering pennants and the gaucho lances with the crescent moon blade for slicing hamstrings. Some of the horses carried a double load, a desperate expedient.

Catherine watched them coming on with John riding beside their officer. John pointed towards the river and the bulk of the detachment turned aside, but the officer continued straight on, flanked by four of his men and drew up in front of the house. John dismounted.

"These men have no time to lose. They want whatever flour we have," he said. And they are taking some horses." His face was impassive. The officer listened carefully, trying to follow what he was saying.

"Speak in Spanish, Inglés," he directed.

"I was explaining to my wife that you require fresh horses."

"I want your best horses. We have no time to lose." He acknowledged Catherine with a nod.

"Our horses are all down by the river, as you can see. I will send my people down to you with whatever food we have."

"That is good, Inglés," the officer replied. He was a mild looking, middle aged man, who affected a bristling moustache to make himself more fierce looking. He looked tired and anxious. "You have weapons in this house?"

John shrugged. "I have an old shotgun. It would be of little use to you."

The officer made to dismount.

"But I will give it to you also," said John quickly.

The officer looked around. There were a few loungers watching the exchange, but no visible danger. A small boy stood beside the woman, sucking his thumb. A woman carried a baby. She was a harmless old china. The tension went out of him.

"No, there is no need. I will take the horses and some food. I will give you a receipt of course."

"Of course," said John.

The officer's horse shook its head. Flies were encrusted on the gum that trickled from its tired eyes. The bridle jingled and the horse snorted, to be answered by a whinny from inside the house.

"What is this?" said the officer in surprise.

"What is what?" asked John looking around in puzzlement.

"You keep a horse in the house?" He gestured to his men to go and investigate. "Is this the way of the Inglés?"

"We are not Inglés as a matter of fact." John bit his lower lip. "We are Irish, Irlandes."

"Aha," said the officer. "Maybe we find some pigs too. I have heard of your people."

John clenched his fists. Catherine gripped him by the arm.

"Say nothing," she hissed.

The soldiers threw open the double doors and led Slaney into the light. They were laughing. John smiled.

"So that's where he got to," he said, turning to the officer. "He is a hungry fellow."

The officer looked appreciatively at the stallion.

"You take me for a fool," he growled.

"Coronel," said one of his men. "Look at this."

He was carrying a bundle of rifles, which he had taken from the gun case, old single shot weapons, which the gauchos had declined to use.

"These are of no use, Coronel," began John but the officer's rebenque caught him across the face. He staggered backwards, tripped and fell in the dust. He put his hand to his mouth and looked at the blood on his fingers.

"I could have you shot, young Inglés. It is treason to oppose the revolution."

John got to his feet. He wiped his mouth with the back of his hand.

"I have no politics," he said defiantly.

"There is no middle way," said the officer. "Consider yourself lucky that I do not burn this house and have you all shot. The next time, do not take me for a fool. My men will take what they need." He stood in his stirrups, white-faced with anger.

John spat into the dust and wiped his mouth. He stared at the officer and made no reply. The soldiers turned away and led Slaney down to the camp by the river. By mid-day they were gone, leaving their bedraggled horses to crop the lush river meadow and shake their ears at the flies.

John took his rifle from the bedroom. He sat at the table and loaded it. His face was grim.

"What are you going to do?" asked Catherine. She sat opposite him and put her hand on his. "You can't go after them."

"I want my horses back," he said, not meeting her eyes.

"No, it is pointless. There are too many of them. That man will kill you. I could see it in his eyes."

"He is more afraid than I am," replied John.

"That is why he is so dangerous. You must stay here. Think of us. We can get more horses at any time."

"But Slaney. I want him back."

She looked into his eyes.

"Slaney was the cause of trouble between us once before. I have never said anything since that time, but let him go. I don't want any trouble between us ever again."

He lowered his eyes from hers.

"It isn't the horses. He humiliated me in front of my men. It is a question of honour."

"This is foolish talk. There was nothing you could do."

"He struck me, for God's sake. Don't you understand? How can I have respect from these men if I do nothing?"

"But what of me and what of your children?"

He stood up and picked up the rifle.

"I don't know. I can't read the future. But I have to do something."

Guidai came to the door.

"Señor, they come again."

Catherine clutched at his sleeve, but he shook her off and hurried outside. In the distance he could see dust rising over a column of mounted men. He clenched his fingers on the rifle and stood waiting.

It became clear that these were not the saddle-weary fugitives of the early morning. These were well equipped, government troops and at their head rode their old friend and benefactor, Don José, a general of the Army of the Republic and a hero of the war against Paraguay. Catherine felt a flood of relief when she recognised him and ran forward to greet him. John put aside his rifle and stepped out of the shadow of the porch into the afternoon sunlight.

The general raised his hand and the dusty column came to a halt in the scant shade of the young eucalyptus trees lining the avenue. He rode forward and dismounted. He bowed and kissed Catherine's hand. She wanted to embrace him, but was inhibited by the interested gaze of the soldiers.

"Don José," she said, "I am so glad to see you."

John shook his hand, "Don José," he mumbled.

"You have had trouble," said Don José, looking at John's bruised and purple lips. "The Lanzas have been here."

"How did you know?"

"You forget that I am a baqueano." He smiled.

"Ah yes," said John. "Of course. They took my horses."

"Naturally. This will give them some advantage. I must not delay."

"But señor," protested Catherine, "will you not eat with us? They left us enough to offer you some dinner."

"You are kind, my Catalina, but we must not delay. I must arrest these men or bring them to battle as quickly as possible. They have caused much damage in the countryside. No, my men will water their horses and then we must press on."

"Perhaps, a glass of wine," she persisted. She was reluctant to let him go without some gesture of hospitality. He relented and stepped into the shade. The column flowed by, heading towards the river. People stood to watch them. Estrellita paused in the act of pounding some corn in a mortar and some of the men whistled. She placed one hand on her hip and regarded them with amusement.

Don José looked around.

"This is a fine house," he said appreciatively, "you have done well."

"Thank you, sir," said Catherine. "We have been fortunate."

"You have been celebrating, perhaps?" He tapped one of the hanging lanterns. It swung, pendulum like, from the roof.

"We had a fiesta last night," said John. "I had almost forgotten."

Don José chewed on a sandwich of cold meat. He watched his men.

"You have a cannon, I see," remarked John. He indicated a wheeled gun, covered by a tarpaulin and hitched behind a wagon.

"Aha!" exclaimed Don José. "This is my beauty." He directed the driver to remove the tarpaulin, gesturing to John to step forward and inspect the weapon.

"My beauty," he repeated with pride, standing back, enjoying John's reaction.

The gun seemed almost to strut with arrogant confidence. Its metal gleamed from loving attention. It appeared to have six barrels, designed to rotate about a central shaft. There was a handle at the rear, obviously to make the barrels rotate.

John ran his hand along the machined gun metal. The front end looked like a face, two black eyes peering over a sweeping brass moustache, with a large hexagonal nut in the middle for a nose. He had never seen anything so perfectly made.

"What is it?" he asked in awe.

"A revolving battery gun," said the general with the pride of a small boy showing off his new toy. "It is made by the American, Gatling. With this there will be no more revolutions." He laughed. "Well, there will be revolutions, but only of my gun." He gestured to the driver to replace and lash the tarpaulin.

"Don José," said John, "I would like to go with you. I need to recover my horses."

The general pondered. He understood.

"This is a dangerous business. It will not be pleasant. You have responsibilities." He glanced towards the porch. Catherine, holding her daughter in her arms, was watching them.

"It is important to me," said John urgently. He touched his bruised mouth.

"I understand," said the general, "but you would be entirely under my orders."

"Of course, señor," nodded John. He returned to Catherine. "I am going with Don José to get my horses."

"No," she protested. "Forget the horses. Let them go. I don't care about the horses."

He retrieved his rifle.

"I am going," he said grimly. "Let's not have any hysterics in front of these men."

The remark was unfair and she felt it.

"You have never seen any hysterics from me," she replied. "Have you?"

He shrugged. "I'm going," he repeated and a cold numbness passed over her.

"I may never see you again," she said in a small voice. She picked at a button on his shirt. "What will I do if you never…if you…?" Her voice trailed off in dismay at what might become of him.

He kissed her gently on the forehead. "I'm sorry. I did not mean to be harsh."

She turned away, hiding the tears that had sprung up in spite of herself.

"I will get some things for you," she said, passing the baby to him.

Fierro arrived at a gallop. He was leading a horse, already saddled.

"Señor," he called. "I will come with you."

"Where are you going?" asked John.

"To the wars, señor. If you go, then I must go too."

"How did you know?"

Fierro shrugged. "I just know."

John was touched. "What is that you have there?"

"My sword, señor." Fierro drew the blade from his belt.

"This is Fierro, my capataz," said John by way of explanation. Don José asked to see the sword. He examined it and swished it back and forth. The blade was pitted with rust but had kept its edge.

"This is a very fine blade," he remarked. "A fine blade of Toledo. Where did you get this?" He handed it back to Fierro.

"An ancestor, mi general. He took it from a Spaniard."

"I see," said Don José. "But my friend, you are too old for military service."

"With respect, mi general, I am not much older than yourself."

Don José laughed. "That is true," he replied ruefully.

"Fierro," put in John, "you are more use to me here. What if I do not return? How will the señora manage?"

Fierro hung his head. "Señor, I am old. I have never been to the wars, like so many of my people have done. This is my last chance."

Don José interrupted him.

"My friend," he said, "the wars come and go, but you and your kind are the backbone of this country. Put up your sword. You have better things to do. The señor is right."

Fierro looked into his eyes. He slid the sword into his belt.

"I apologise to you for the things that I must do, but some day there will be no wars and there will be no need of soldiers. But always, there will be need of you and men like you."

He put out his hand and Fierro grasped it.

"Mi general," he said. "As you direct." He handed the reins to John.

Catherine returned with his saddlebags and he slung them across the horse. He kissed her once more on the forehead, handed her the baby and mounted. Don José called for his horse, anxious to be on his way. The wagon lurched forward with the machine gun, sinister under its cowl, swaying behind it.

Catherine watched them go. She heard a bugle echoing along the riverbank and the shouts of men.

"He will come back, señora," said Fierro. "You need not fear."

"What did the general say?" she asked him and he told her of the exchange. There was pride in his voice.

"I am glad you did not go, Fierro. We have great need of you here, all of us."

"He will come back, señora," he said again. "He is in good hands." Fierro took his leave.

She tried to be reassured by his words. She walked under the eucalyptus. The leaves, like green blades, caught the sunlight, as they tossed in the breeze. She looked at her house and wondered what might befall it. She saw something in the grass that she had not noticed before, a little oak seedling, with two scalloped leaves fluttering in the wind. She had forgotten about the acorns. She sat in the grass, pulling her skirt around her and cleared some space for the brave little tree, a little oak of Wexford, an omen.

She thought of home and of the shouts of her brothers as they helped her into the branches. It was as if she heard their voices from another world. She had always followed them on their expeditions. "Wait for me. Wait for me." Indeed they had always waited. She touched the leaves. She would make a fence around this welcome visitor, to protect it from the sharp hooves of the animals, an alambrada, like the farmers of the south made for their fields of wheat and maize and the tall, dishevelled sunflowers. The sun dipped towards the horizon and spiders' webs adorned the grass with threads of gold.

Chapter Twelve

"They say they would rather die than surrender, mi general," said the rider.

The Lanzas stood at bay with their backs to the Rio Negro, a tatterdemalion, but defiant, little army. John could see the officer riding back and forth, exhorting his men. He recognised his chestnut stallion, Slaney. It would be good to see that officer brought to account.

Don José sighed. He took out his watch. "Tell them one more time. In fifteen minutes I will open fire."

The messenger went back again. Don José watched him through his spy-glass. He clucked his tongue and handed the glass to John. John saw the messenger turning away, the staff of his white flag braced in his stirrup. He saw the officer in dumb show, addressing his men and the reality of the situation hit him for the first time. These men were about to die and they would try to take him and the others with them. There was a cold feeling in the pit of his stomach. He looked around for a place of refuge, but it was open country. He must stand his ground. He drew out his rifle. Don José gestured to him to put it away. He had no wish to allow a civilian to disrupt his precise choreography. He looked to his right to where the gunners had positioned the Gatling gun and raised his arm. The Lanzas formed a skirmish line. They charged.

John raised the glass again. They were coming directly at him, the space between them foreshortened by the lens. He saw the wild eyes of the horses and the sun gleaming on Slaney's shining coat and the men lowering their lances as they charged through the long grass.

The Gatling gun opened up, hammering six hundred rounds per minute, the fire-power of a regiment, into the disintegrating line of horsemen. John's horse started at the racket and he pulled on the reins. He saw the gunner traversing the gun and turning the handle, with all the determination of a washerwoman putting clothes through a mangle. The barrels revolved and all sound was subsumed into the hammering of the gun. Birds rose in alarm from the long grass. The broad river threw back the echo.

The general sent his cavalry forward at a walk, their carbines at the ready, but the Lanzas were no more. What had just now been a line of brave and desperate men, was a scattering of corpses, dismembered by the heavy .58 slugs of the Gatling gun. Here and there a soldier put a horse out of its agony, punctuating the silence with a single shot.

John looked down at the body of his horse. He could feel nothing. The officer lay with one leg caught under the fallen animal. None of this made sense. This man had offered him a receipt, a piece of paper, redeemable when the revolution achieved its glorious objective, a balancing of the books, a final reckoning. He shook his head, uncomprehending. Only the crows stood to gain from this transaction.

"There are some horses under the palm trees," said Don José. "You are entitled to them."

John looked at him.

"I'm sorry. What did you say?"

"There are some horses. You may take them if you wish." The general came closer to him. "This is your first time to see what war is like. It is always difficult."

"But I thought..." He was not sure what he thought, some nonsense about gods and heroes. There was a butcher at home who had a cast-iron mincing machine. The meat came out like worms when he turned the handle. Once when he was a child, John had run out of the shop and the maid had to run after him, all the way home. She was afraid of the mistress and he of the grinding machine.

"It is the only way," said Don José. "With these machines we can make war impossible."

John nodded. He wanted to go away. Was it cowardice? he wondered. Were these men braver, who were already digging graves for their fellow countrymen? He wanted to get away.

"I must go home," he said. "I will take the horses, thank you."

"Travel carefully," said Don José. "You should have no trouble from the bandits now, but nevertheless, be careful. You have responsibilities."

The journey made him feel better. He rode at the head of a string of horses. The sound of the hooves soothed him. He made a fire and chewed on a piece of dried meat, the slave rations that had once made fortunes for the landowners. He lay back and looked at the stars. In the darkness the horses shuffled in their hobbles. It was good to be alone. He probed the bruise on his mouth. It was no more than a yellow stain. That bastard was dead anyway. He felt a small satisfaction at the thought. He had asked for it. It would have been good to look him in the eye before he died.

He imagined his return home, a conqueror, with the string of horses behind him. It was a good feeling. There were the Centaur stars, galloping down the Milky Way. Catherine knew the names of all the stars. She was a great one for reading. He lit a cigar, a Parguayan one, booty of war. It had a certain attraction, this idea of pillage and taking what you want.

He wished Catherine had thought to pack some brandy. His ancestors had come to Ireland to conquer and hold the best of the rolling green countryside and cover it with their cattle and rightly so. He would get another Slaney too. He was alive and they were dead. That was what it came down to in the end.

He watched the Centaurs, the gauchos as the general had called them, riding across the limitless expanse of the heavens. They would be his guiding stars from now on.

There was an item in *The Graphic* about an enormous Home Rule meeting in Belfast, where the principal speaker dismissed the idea on the grounds that the wealth of Ireland would be dissipated in political contention. "The Irish temperament is so inflammable that he prefers a bonfire to the warmth of a modest hearth." There was a Fenian amnesty meeting in Stockton, which had been attacked by some Welshmen. Welshmen, for Heaven's sake! Catherine could make little sense of any of it. The politics of home were just as incomprehensible as were those of her new country.

There was a grisly story of a woman who had fallen victim to marital affection, a Madame E..... of Paris. Her husband went to seek his fortune in China, from whence she received a note telling her that he had been burned alive by Malay pirates and his bones calcined to ashes. The writer, Mr C.... C..... of Old China street, Canton, enclosed a small box of white powder. The unfortunate woman, deranged by grief, inhaled her late husband with some snuff, but such violent bleeding ensued, that she succumbed, despite the exertions of a doctor. Inevitably, a letter arrived the same evening, proving the husband to be alive and prospering.

She wondered how anyone could think of such a grotesque and cruel joke. She wondered where John might be. He had been gone for over a week and still there was no word. She imagined his bones whitening on some distant battlefield and the ants scurrying about their work. No, it was not possible. Don José would have let her know. Unless, of course... No, the Lanzas were no threat to Don José and his army. She sipped her maté. Her eye settled on an engraving, Lord Cardigan's charger, Ronald. What a silly name for a horse!

'Into the Valley of Death.' Tennyson was always wittering on about death. She had grown tired of Tennyson and rarely looked at his poems. Despair and death and idiots charging into the cannon's mouth. She wanted her husband back where he belonged and not stravaging the countryside, as her mother might have put it.

"She is coming, señora," cried Guidai, bursting into the room. Her eyes were bright with excitement. Catherine started from her reverie.

"Who is coming?"

"The princess, Aymará. I told you about her a long time ago."

Catherine remembered. This was the little Charrúa girl, who married the estanciero. She straightened her dress and removed her apron. She went quickly to the door, in time to see a coach drawing up outside.

An old woman, dressed in black, stepped down from the coach. She supported herself with a cane. She was as dark skinned as Guidai. There was undoubtedly something regal in her manner.

"You are welcome, señora," said Catherine, stepping forward, extending her hand.

"Have you travelled far?"

The woman looked at her and took her hand. Smiling, she looked about.

"Yes. I have come a long way. I have come to see these Irishes. Ah, the ombú tree. It is so much bigger."

She pointed with her cane to where smoke rose from Estrellita's hut. "It was so small when I was last here." She noticed Guidai standing diffidently in the background. She went towards her and embraced her. "My old friend," she said. "How we have changed!"

Guidai lowered her head. She said nothing, but her pleasure was evident.

"You must come in and rest, señora," said Catherine. "I have heard much about you."

She stood aside and ushered the woman into her house.

The woman sipped the maté and rocked back and forth by the fire.

"Ah," she said, "my bones are shaken by the journey."

"Señora," began Catherine. "How shall I address you?"

"I am Doña Silveria Oliveira, widow of Don Cayetano," she said with pride. "My husband was a great guerrillero in his younger days."

"Doña Silveria," said Catherine respectfully, intrigued by her exotic visitor.

"But here in this place, I am Aymará, daughter of a great cacique and sister of Sepé. Here in Laján, the place of the ombú, I am Aymará, the Indiecita."

"Aymará," repeated Catherine.

Guidai was in the kitchen preparing food, but she had left the door open.

"You must tell me your story," said Aymará. "I wish to know why you have come to this place of the Charrúas and if you are happy here."

Catherine bit her lip. "Yes, we are happy here. We are very happy indeed."

The children peered around the door. Richard held his little sister by the hand. Aymará beckoned them forward and they came shyly to her knee.

"They are so fair," she said, putting her hand on Richard's head. Her skin was dark against his curls. She stroked Sarah's head and patted her cheek.

"You must tell me your story," she said again and Catherine began. It was a kind of release to tell the story to this stranger, to go back along the trail of memory to her home by the lake. She told her of school and of the nuns and how she had run away with John.

"And where is this John now?" asked Aymará. She had something of the manner of a nun herself, that instinctive ability to question and to demand the truth.

"He is not here," said Catherine. She explained about the soldiers and how John had gone with the army to retrieve his property.

"That is understandable," said Aymará. "You fear for his safety. But you need not fear. The Lanzas are defeated. Your husband will return soon, I am sure."

It was as if a weight was lifted from her mind. The danger had passed.

"I too was educated by the nuns," said Aymará. "In Buenos Aires they taught me to be a lady. They taught me to be a Christian and to speak a new language."

Catherine hesitated. "And did you miss your home and your family?" She remembered how she had cried for weeks, the first time she had gone to the boarding school.

"Since the beginning of the world," Aymará began, "the Charrúas lived here and by The Great River. We wanted for nothing and we had nothing, certainly not garments like these." She plucked at the fine fabric of her dress. "We went naked except in the winter. We were the Wild People, you see. Too wild for the new people who came into this country. They were afraid of us and so they set out to kill us with their guns."

Catherine thought momentarily of her uncles and their entertaining adventures. They wanted to run sheep on the land of the savages. She was ashamed to mention them.

"Before he died, my father gave me to Don Cayetano. He knew that the days of the Charrúa were over and he wanted to save me. Yes, I cried in the convent in Buenos Aires. I cried for my people fishing by the river and the hunting of the ñandú and the stories of great battles fought by my ancestors and when I returned I was a Christian lady and my people were gone."

"All of them?"

"All but a few and nothing is heard of them now. They were lost to the eyes of men." She stared into the fire. "Except for those who learned to change, like myself and my friend Guidai here."

Guidai put down a plate of food. She was pleased by the attention of this princess.

"We are all Uruguayans now. No longer Charrúa or Irish or Inglés or Spanish."

She held the children close. They stared up at her dark face, not understanding. Richard was fascinated by the yellow in her eyes and the blackness of the irises.

"All these many races and languages. All one now. My sons have served in the army of this country, the army that destroyed their ancestors." She sighed. "It is strange, but that is how it is."

She passed the maté to Catherine.

"With your permission I will stay one night and then I will continue my journey."

"Of course. Of course."

"I am glad that you are happy in this place, although you too are far from home and your family."

Catherine made no reply. Aymará watched her.

"When the Moon is high, I wish to go to the ombú grove to offer a prayer for my people. Guidai can accompany me as she is named for the Moon."

"And Fierro," said Guidai suddenly. "You remember Fierro, the boy with the big knife. He is my husband."

"Ah, Fierro. Of course we must have Fierro."

Catherine felt excluded. It was her land and yet she was left out. Estrellita would be there, with her heathen mumbo-jumbo. She wondered if she would ever be fully part of this country. She could do with a prayer, as could her wandering husband.

The men raised the canvas walls of the little arena and the champion was tossed into the centre of the ring. He flapped his wings and strutted. The sun gleamed on the oily colours of his neck feathers and on the silver needles of his spurs. His implacable stare sought out his challenger. The young contender circled warily and attacked, beating his stunted wings and slashing with his spurs. He pecked furiously at the champion's throat and a gash of red appeared. But the champion, veteran of many battles, came back at him. The blood of heroes flowed in his veins. His reputation was known far and wide. He bore the challenger to the ground, inflicting a terrible wound on his head, but it was not decisive. The challenger rose again, his comb a tattered mess. He had lost an eye. Blood spurted from the socket. He backed away, searching for his adversary through a film of red.

The men watched impassively, aficionados all. There was a lot of money riding on this contest. The challenger squawked, calling on his harem for help and the men laughed. But no help came. The champion closed again in a flurry of dust and feathers. The challenger's legs gave way. He rolled on his side and the champion bestrode his fallen adversary, tearing at the open head wound and piercing him with his spurs. The challenger's wings flapped ineffectually. He twitched convulsively and expired in the dust and heat of the afternoon. The champion crowed his victory song, to the cheers of his backers. John Cardiff swore under his breath. He rubbed his stubbled chin and drained his drink. There was nothing for it but to go home.

Chapter Thirteen

Catherine was shocked to see how he had changed. He looked ten years older, gaunt from hunger and exhaustion. She ran to him as he stumbled out of the darkness and embraced him. There was the sour smell of old whiskey from his breath and it was obvious that he had not washed for a long time.

"Oh, John," was all she could say.

He sat down heavily in front of the fire. He was shivering.

"I was afraid you would never come home."

"Well I'm home now, am I not?" he growled.

"Was it dreadful?"

"What do you expect? It was butchery, nothing more." He pulled off his boots and flexed his toes.

"Oh you poor thing."

She went into the kitchen and put some soup to heat on the stove. She decided not to tell him yet that he was going to be a father once more. He took the mug in both hands and sipped. He grimaced at the heat of the liquid and put it down on the hearth. He spread his arms and leaned towards the fire, garnering warmth.

"Do you want to tell me what happened?"

He did not look at her. "All dead," he replied. "That infernal machine."

"And your horses?"

He made no answer.

"And Slaney?"

"For Christ's sake, don't go on about it. Of course he's dead."

She flinched at the violence of his words. She felt guilty for not understanding how upset he was and how he had suffered.

"But you are safe. That's all that matters," she said gently. "We still have the horses the Lanzas left behind. They will do just as well as our own."

He shrugged. "They offered me a few survivors by way of compensation, but I declined." He yawned.

"Why? We could have done with them?"

"It would be like scavenging the dead."

"But they were yours to begin with."

"No. These had some other brand on them. It would be dishonest to keep them."

The matter was closed. They could have done with the profit, but she admitted that John had done the honourable thing.

"Take your soup," she urged. "You should never drink on an empty stomach."

"Drink! What do you mean 'drink'? I had one drink on the way home. What's all this about?"

"I was just saying...."

"I know what you were saying." He stood up and his foot knocked against the mug. The soup spilled into the ashes. "I know what you're implying?"

"I'm not implying anything. I was just saying..."

"Well don't. Every time I go anywhere it's the same inquisition."

"Please," she said, alarmed at his reaction. "Keep your voice down. You'll wake the children.

"The children. This is my house, by God. I'll wake whoever I want to. You and your children. A blasted millstone around a man's neck. The next thing you'll tell me is that there's another one on the way."

She backed away from him, frightened by his anger. He was mad. He must have been through a terrible time. She stared at him, wide-eyed. He understood.

"So there is, then." His voice dropped to a sneer. "Another snivelling brat around the place."

"Why are you talking like this? she challenged. Her courage returned to her at the injustice of it all. "Yes, there is another baby. Your baby and you should be thankful. You should be thankful that you are alive and that you have a family to come home to."

"Christ!" He swore. "You're no better than that whore, Estrellita. That yegua." He laughed.

"How dare you?" she replied and made to strike him across the face.

He seized her wrist and pulled her towards him. He blinked. In his head he heard the rattle of the Gatling gun. He saw the cocks tearing each other to bloody shreds and the laughing faces of the gamblers wishing him better luck the next time. He squeezed her arm and brought her to her knees.

"Don't ever," he said through clenched teeth, "don't ever raise your hand to me. Do you understand?"

She winced with the pain. He twisted her arm back and she cried out.

"Do you understand?" He looked down at her. "I will not be questioned in my own house. Do you understand?" He shook her again, demanding submission. She nodded.

"Good," he declared, relaxing his grip. "Just so as we understand each other."

She stood up and backed away, looking at the white weals on her wrist.

"Excellent," he said with a sneering courtesy. "And now perhaps, I will have some of that soup."

She went into the kitchen. Her movements were like those of an automaton. She poured a ladle of soup into a mug and brought it to him. He was standing with his back to the fire. He held a glass of brandy. He swayed and when he spoke, his voice was slurred. She had put that down to fatigue at first.

"You should try this," he said, smirking. "Much better than that green slop you drink."

He raised the glass in mock salute and drank defiantly. She put the mug down on the hearth, avoiding his eyes. She went outside. The air was cool. His horse still stood by the porch. She removed the saddle, placed it against the wall and turned the horse loose. He was tired and glad to be home. He would not stray very far. She rested her cheek against an upright and listened to the insect sounds of the night. She longed for the sound of the sea and the waves plucking at the sandbar beyond the tidal lake.

Estrellita sat by the fire of her fogón. Her children were asleep. She arranged the shells and the polished river pebbles and watched the flames dancing. She examined a silver coin. There was a castle on it and a scales, a horse and a cow. It was the history of her country. She picked up a cowrie shell, a strange object, speckled like the feathers of the little wren, the ratonera, but hard and shining, like polished bone. The orifice was long and gleaming white with serrations like the teeth of a saw. She put it to her ear.

This was a wonder. She closed her eyes. The wind moaned in the hollow of the shell and she saw the great water. White spray lifted from the waves. It was wider even than The Great River. It was grey and menacing. Dimly she saw the two men, borne away by the water. She saw their hands reaching up and then they were gone. The waves thundered in her head and she swayed from side to side in the firelight.

Catherine could see the glimmer of light under the ombú. That had been her first home. She remembered the fear and how John had minded her on that first night. She thought of those dark faces and the firelight glinting in their eyes. It was a great adventure then and they had faced it together. Now she was afraid, but John was not there to mind her.

She went back inside. He was asleep in the rocking chair. The soup was untouched but the glass was empty in his hand. She thought to remove it, but was afraid to disturb him.

She went to her room and lay on the bed fully dressed. Something in her warned her that she must be ready if he woke again. She must be ready to defend herself and her children. She listened to the creaking of the roof and gradually, sleep overcame her.

In the morning he was wary. He washed himself and shaved, but he kept the beginnings of a moustache. He examined it in the mirror.

"What do you think?" he asked.

She was laying the breakfast table in the kitchen. She looked up as he entered.

"What do you think of my moustache?"

She shrugged indifferently.

"Do you like it?"

"Do what you like," she said, distributing cutlery.

"I think I'll keep it," he said brightly, holding up his side of a non-existent conversation.

"Yes, I think it suits me."

She put bread on the table with some cold meat and placed a pot of coffee in the centre.

"Ah! coffee," he remarked unnecessarily.

He ate hungrily, talking with his mouth full, like a man too busy to pause, but she made no reply. He pressed on brightly.

"I know where I can get a little pony for the children. I'll get one each as they get big enough. Three little gauchos. Hey?" He acknowledged the coming child.

Catherine tried to eat. The bread felt like paper in her mouth.

"Do you know how some people make butter out here? No? They put the cream in a skin and tie it on a donkey's back and drive the poor creature around the place all day." He laughed at the incongruity of the idea, "Comical, as they say at home."

She looked aside, focussing on a crack in one of the floor tiles. She resented that crack as she had resented the horse that caused it. He followed her gaze.

"Ah!" he said, "the horse. Never mind. I can have it repaired. It will be right as rain. Good as new." He was talking too much and he knew it. He finished his coffee and watched her as she tidied up.

She brushed the crumbs off the table and fetched a broom to sweep the floor. It irritated him to watch, but he was reluctant to leave without some sign of a truce.

"It would be easier just to clean the table and not brush everything onto the floor."

She continued sweeping, searching out each corner for the smallest particle. She decided to wash the tiles as soon as he was gone. She would get down on her knees and scrub them.

"I said, you're making work for yourself." She paused with her back to him. She could make no sense of what he was nattering about, just wishing he would go.

"Just a suggestion," he said rising and taking his hat from a chair. "I'll be off then," he said, pausing at the doorway.

She resumed her sweeping, knocking the broom against the furniture, concentrating on the task. She heard his boots on the boards in the other room and a door closing. She sat down, exhausted and looked at the cracked tile. What did it matter? She would wash the floor later, but now she wanted to rest. She heard the children calling and wondered what to do.

Guidai came in.

"The señor has returned, I see," she said.

Catherine nodded.

"He is well, señora?"

She nodded again.

"He seems different, señora."

She gave a half smile.

"He has a moustache."

She remembered two countrymen at a fair. They were sharing a joke at the expense of one of the gentry, a military man with a flowing moustache. 'Isn't he the great man to cultivate somethin' under his nose, that grows wild all over his arse?'

They had guffawed at their small revenge and she had savoured the remark. It was funny, but she knew enough, even as a child, not to repeat it to her mother. Her mother had pulled her along by the hand, for fear of hearing more, pulled her through the throng of hard-drinking men and milling beasts and streets splattered with dung.

She smiled at the memory. The moustache suited him, but she would not give him the satisfaction. She was with the two raucous countrymen.

"You are happy, señora, to have him home," said Guidai, interpreting the smile. Catherine nodded.

"Yes, yes, of course. Guidai, will you look after the children for me this morning? I want to walk for a while.

The Indian woman nodded. The señora was not herself.

"Perhaps it would be safer to drive, señora. The men are moving cattle to the western pastures. It would be dangerous to go on foot."

Catherine agreed. Besides, the thought of walking was beginning to make her feel even more tired, but she had to get out of the house.

She watched the river of cattle flowing westwards and the beauty and drama of the scene, as always, lifted her spirits.

She heard the high pitched yelps of the gauchos and admired their nonchalant dominion over the animals. The Hereford bull went past, regal and slow, secure in his potency and strength. The Gauchos treated him with respect. He shook his head and glared imperiously around.

John came towards her with another man, possibly the buyer from Fray Bentos. She composed herself. It would be important to make a good impression. That much she would concede in front of outsiders.

As they came closer she realised that the dark-suited figure was none other than Henry Jones, the grave Welshman.

"Look who I found," began John cheerily. "Our old friend Henry."

Henry raised his hat and greeted her. "Mrs Cardiff," he said. "I am working in the vicinity and am making it my business to pay my respects."

"Oh please. I hope it is not too much of a task."

He looked at her, suspecting irony, but she was smiling.

"I have asked Henry to dine with us," said John. Henry might be a useful catalyst. "He looks as if he could do with a decent meal."

"I have to admit that I am not very good at catering for myself," said Henry, as always stating the facts of the case. Her heart went out to him. He looked older and more alone than before.

"But I do not wish to impose."

"You are more than welcome, old fellow," said John heartily. "Isn't he Catherine?"

He looked at her and she put aside her reserve. The moustache did suit him all the same, despite what the two vulgar farmers might have said. She smiled again at the remark and he responded. Compared to Henry he was a striking figure of a man.

"You must come home with us at once," she said and it sounded like old times.

"It's funny really," said Henry, sitting back in his chair. He turned the glass in his fingers, swirling the wine. "It's funny all the same. The English want to build railways, so the government plans a road to compete with them. Everywhere they build a railway there will be a good road alongside it."

"Now let me be clear on this," John interrupted. "You are surveying for the road?"

"That is so."

"And when will the railway come? They will have to pay to go through my land."

"It will be a long time yet," replied Henry.

"The government wants to beat them to it."

"But why do you not work for the English company?"

Henry seemed slightly offended. "I am an Uruguayan now," he stated. "The English will take what they can out of this country and then they will go."

"But the railway is the better bet. It would go to Fray Bentos." John stroked his moustache. "It would make life a lot easier for us."

"It would, I agree. But the government has not got the capital. And anyway the Departments would not cooperate. They are saying that the Blancos want control of four Departments as a condition for stopping their revolution."

"They should spend their money on railways," put in Catherine, "and not be wasting it on wars."

The two men looked at her in surprise.

"And other useful things," she continued. "Roads, schools, hospitals, instead of wasting it."

"You are absolutely correct," agreed Henry. "It is pride, see. I find it difficult to tell the difference between Blancos and Colorados. The one thing they agree on is not giving the English the satisfaction."

"But the English have the money," said John returning to the salient fact. "If they want to build a railway here, they will pay in hard cash." He was pleased with the notion. "Hard cash, I tell you." He drummed his fingers thoughtfully on the table.

"I would like to start a school," said Catherine suddenly. "The children will need to learn and the gaucho children too."

John laughed heartily.

"My dear, you have no idea. Of course you will teach our children. But the gaucho children! They have learned everything they need to know by the age of five. The boys can ride and throw a bolas and use a knife. What would you do? Turn them into office clerks? No, no, no. It would be a waste of time. Can you imagine Estrellita's little savages in a schoolroom?"

He chuckled at the notion. Henry looked from one to another.

"What do you think, Henry?" asked John.

Henry cleared his throat. It was a big subject.

"Well things are changing, you see," he began cautiously. "Yes indeed. We may see a time when the gauchos will change also."

"And they will need education," interrupted Catherine.

"Possibly so," said Henry, reluctant to take sides.

"Nonsense," said John. "A gaucho is a gaucho. He can never be anything else."

"I still want to try," insisted Catherine. She looked down at her plate.

"By all means," said John expansively, "but I warn you, it is a waste of time. I will teach them to ride and you can teach them their ABC."

He topped up his brandy and reached to do the same for Henry. He went to fetch some cigars.

"I understand that John was involved in a campaign," said Henry, lowering his voice.

"He refuses to talk about it," she replied.

Henry nodded. "He mentioned something about losing some horses."

"Yes, he did. You remember the horse he won in the boat race?"

"That one too?"

"Yes." She paused. "He was very angry about that."

"An upsetting business. Still he seems well now. And how have you been, Catherine?"

"Oh, I am fine. You know. Up and down. Prices haven't been great as you know."

"But otherwise?" he probed.

"Oh, fine, fine. We're getting to be a big family now."

"So I see," he agreed. "The school is a good idea, but it will take time."

"Oh, it's only a dream, I suppose."

"Dreams are important too," he said, "Sometimes it is the dream that keeps us going."

She had never associated Henry with dreams. Facts and figures were his stock in trade. She looked at him in surprise and he lowered his eyes in some confusion.

"Here we are," announced John, returning with a wooden box. "Some of Don José's Paraguayan cigars." He sat down again and took out a box of lucifers. "I managed to get some of these," he said and struck one on the strip of sandpaper. The match flared as he held it up. "Ingenious," he remarked. "Called after the Devil himself." He touched the flame to the tip of his cigar and drew upon it. "I'm sorry, my dear," he said. "You don't mind if we smoke, do you?"

She shook her head. Lucifer, the morning star, the brightest angel that fell from Heaven. It was a silly notion. She put it aside and thought about her idea of a school. Headline copybooks and children forming their letters between the red and blue lines. She could almost hear the scratching of nibs. 'Procrastination is the thief of time.' 'Cleanliness is next to godliness.' Little maxims for the better conduct of one's life, particularly when executed in fine copperplate.

"No, to tell the truth, I was terrified." John was laughing. She brought her mind back to the conversation. "Don't mind admitting it, but what can you do?" He made light of the danger. "I give them credit for courage, but they never stood a chance." He shook his head in regret. "Poor fellows. The gun just swallowed them up." He took Catherine's hand. "I felt sorry for them to tell the truth, but most of all I was glad to be alive. Too much to lose, Henry, you understand. Too much to lose."

Henry nodded. He noticed how she flinched at his touch and how she withdrew her hand without looking at him.

The picture stayed with Henry as he rode back to his camp. The Moon was high and the air was still and warm. He was perturbed by the atmosphere in the house, despite the hearty welcome. He looked back at the dark outline and its frieze of black trees. There was no welcoming light in the window. He felt more alone than ever before. He shivered despite the warmth of the night and turned his collar up.

Tom Doyle rubbed his hands and held them towards the fire. A January gale battered at the house.

"That's a cold one," he remarked, blowing on his fingers. "Are the lads in yet?"

There was no fishing, so both of his sons made themselves

useful around the farm, even though there was not much they could do in such weather.

"No, they went to collect woar. Piles of it came in during the night." Dorothy turned the bellows handle, brightening the fire.

"Good," said Tom. "Good lads." He loosened his boots, feeling guilty that he was not there to help them gather the seaweed, but pleased at the thought that they were men now, men who could take the weight of the heavy work off his shoulders. That was the way God intended it and any man who resented the growing strength of his sons was a fool. There were men he knew, who kept their sons down, browbeating them, keeping them as boys around the farm. Nobody lives forever. He slipped off his boots and sighed.

"There's a ship came ashore on the Forlorn Point. She'll break up entirely if this wind keeps up."

"Oh, God help them!" exclaimed Dorothy. "Was anybody drowned?"

"No, thanks be to God. They managed to get ashore over the rocks. If they had to go aground it was as good a place as any."

"I suppose the whole barony was there for the pickings."

"Oh, indeed. There won't be much left for the receiver."

Tom never cared for that business. It was like scavenging the dead. And yet it made sense. The sea was a hard taskmaster and people were entitled to salvage, but there was sometimes an unholy glee about another's misfortune. Strange that men would put their own lives at risk, putting out in a storm to rescue shipwrecked mariners and yet show no sympathy for the unfortunate owner in some far distant port, waiting for a cargo that would never arrive. Tom had a great respect for property and the fruits of labour.

"I suppose the lads will sell some of the woar."

"I suppose so."

He accepted a cup of tea.

"No news from abroad, then?"

"No. I thought I might write to them. Not that much happens around here."

"It's quiet enough all right. You could tell them about Christmas and the foul weather. I wouldn't mind livin' in a country where there was a bit o' sun. The rheumatics are at me again."

Dorothy smiled bleakly. "We could tell her that we're two old pensioners creaking around on sticks. Make her feel guilty. Is that it?"

"Ah, no." He chuckled softly. "It's long past that stage. I've accepted that fact long ago. They've made a go of things out there and that's all there is to that. That's the holy all of it." He laced his fingers together over his waistcoat. "You could tell her about the politics and all the trouble about evictions, I suppose. It doesn't sound like much compared to the wars they have over there."

He took out his watch and looked at the time. Rain began to beat against the window.

"Begod, they'll be soaked if they don't get in soon. Maybe I should go and have a look around. Call them in, maybe."

"They're hardy lads. They have the sense to come in for their dinner."

"Maybe they went down to see the wreck. The whole barony went down."

"So you said."

Dorothy fetched a pen and paper and sat at the table. She turned up the oil lamp and the room filled with a warm glow. Her pen scraped in the ink bottle. She tapped it to remove the excess and began to write. Tom looked at his watch.

"At least we've no worries about evictions," he mused. "God help the poor people in weather like this."

Your father is fretting here, she wrote. *He is never at ease until his boys are safe under his roof at night. They are men now, but still he frets when they are away. He is happy that you are safe too, with a fine house around you and your children.*

She paused and tapped the handle of the pen against her teeth. There was not much to say really. Their paths had diverged. Their concerns were not hers any more. She put down the pen.

"I'll finish this later," she said pressing the letter on the sheet of blotting paper.

They heard the cartwheels on the cobblestoned yard and she got up to stir the stew.

There was a loud knocking on the door. Tom hurried to open it. A petty officer from the coastguard stood in the doorway. His face was grey. His oilskin coat battered around him in the gale. He clutched his cap, as the rain sliced at his face.

"I have bad news, I'm afraid," he said, shouting against the uproar of the gale and Tom Doyle's world stopped. The words reverberated in his head –'I'm afraid. I'm afraid. I'm afraid.'

He heard the ladle clattering to the floor. He saw Dorothy putting her hand on the table to steady herself. He could not move. His mouth was dry. 'I'm afraid. I'm afraid. I'm afraid.'

The petty officer stepped into the room and took off his cap.

Chapter Fourteen

Estrellita came for the washing. She brought some flowers. "They are birds of paradise, señora. I will give you some for your garden."

They were brightly coloured and fibrous and looked for all the world, like gaudy herons, stretching their long necks and peering about for little fish.

"You are very kind, Estrellita."

Catherine never knew what to make of her. Sometimes she was a little afraid of her. That was ridiculous. Estrellita was a common washerwoman, who depended on them for her livelihood.

"It is not a very good garden," she said lightly, "but I am trying. It will improve."

"It will be a great comfort to you," said Estrellita. "You must work at your garden."

"Why do you say comfort?"

"When bad things happen. When there is bad news, you should work in your garden."

"Why do you say this? What bad things?"

"Nothing remains the same. I will take the clothes down to the river."

"We could take water from the well. There is no need to walk so far."

"I prefer the river. I will drive there with my mare. I will bring my children to bathe. That is where my people lived before."

"Before? Before when?"

"Before everything. Before cattle and gauchos and estancieros. Before soldiers and guns."

She said it in a matter of fact way.

Catherine bit her lip. There was so much she did not understand.

"Do you resent us?" she asked and regretted the question immediately.

"You have been kind to me señora and some day I will do something for you. For the moment the land belongs to you. You have papers. But some day it will belong to someone else. That is how it has been."

"My husband will never give up this land. This land is for our children."

"He will give up the land, señora, but the land will not give him up."

She picked up the basket and put a block of soap on top of the clothes.

"No," insisted Catherine. "You are wrong. He will fight for this land. He will fight anyone to protect this land. He has been to war already to protect what is ours." She said it with sudden pride.

"Ah, señora, he does not need to go to war. The war is inside him, the good and the bad." She put her hand over her heart.

"You must not speak of my husband in this manner. Remember that he is the señor. I will not have you talking like this."

"No señora," said Estrellita, lifting the basket. "I will go to the river and wash these clothes."

"Very well," said Catherine, dismissing her.

She felt that she had played the part of the señora quite adequately. John would never tolerate insolence. He would have approved, although he would never have allowed such a conversation in the first place.

She looked at the flowers. They reminded her of the irises in the water meadow at home, but these were wilder, more savage flowers, with colours of flame. She had loved to pluck those irises, deep purple with veins of yellow. They held their perfection only for a day, but even as the old one withered, a younger flower was bursting out higher up the stem. Estrellita was right about that at least. Nothing stays the same. Perfection gives way to decay and rebirth. She reflected that she was getting morbid. She went around to the back of the house to where she had begun her garden. It was a constant struggle against the tall wiry grass. The oak tree, fenced off from intruders, was doing well. She cleared the grass away from it again and felt better about things.

The Devil! thought John. Another letter from Wexford. Just when things were improving between them, this had to come. Letters from home served only to upset her. That was the last thing he needed. He looked at the letter from his lawyer in Montevideo. He tapped it thoughtfully on the counter. He tore it open. The bank was prepared to extend his credit. That was a relief. Now if only Boxwell, bad cess to him, would come across with some money, everything would be fine.

The diligence arrived in the yard outside, in a great commotion of snorting horses and shouting. The other drinkers drifted out to watch the drama of changing horses and passengers alighting to stretch their legs. John looked out, half expecting to see Robert Boxwell stepping down with a Gladstone bag full of money, but there was no such luck.

He looked at the Wexford letter. The postmark was three months old. It had lain at the pulpería for a fortnight. It was old news. He thought to throw it in the fire, but hesitated. He might as well know what it contained. Probably more thinly veiled inducements to come home. He smiled. If only they could see the absurdity of such an idea. He opened the letter.

The date was crossed out and changed to another. The first paragraph was also crossed out but he could read it nonetheless. Something about a January storm and a ship going aground.

It has taken me many weeks to complete this letter and to send you the sad news that your two brothers were drowned. They tried to go across the estuary to the Burrow with a load of woar, but they were carried away by the tide. They are laid in Tomhaggard, fornenst their grandparents and I can say no more than that we are heartbroken.

We send our love to you and John and your children. We remain

Your loving parents
Thos. and Dorothy Doyle.

He remembered the two quiet boys; sturdy young men with very little to say for themselves. Decent fellows by all accounts. This was too bad and coming at the worst of times too. It would be better to break it to her gently. He went to put the letter into his pocket. Better to burn it. He crumpled it in his fist, but hesitated again. That would not be fair either. He folded it again and slipped it into an inside pocket.

What the Devil is woar, anyway? More of that old country talk. Why would they try to cross the estuary in a storm, in the middle of winter? 'Fornenst their grandparents.' He felt a vague irritation at the phrase. This was an unnecessary complication. Tomhaggard. He remembered her story about the chalice in the lake and the Cromwellian soldiers killing the priest, as he was saying Mass. The church was covered in ivy now. It teetered over the road amid a cluster of toppling tombstones. Dark and gloomy. He had no desire to see the place again or to listen to their stories of Cromwell or the rebellion, stories as sombre as the ivy that strangled every growing thing. They were better off away from all that.

The chalice was another matter though. Gold and silver glinting in the water. The Welshman had come to Uruguay with dreams of finding gold and jewels and he ends up plodding the cattle tracks of the back country, drawing lines on maps. He should have held on to his dream.

He contemplated another drink to celebrate the letter from the lawyer. Maybe not. She seemed to object to a man having a drink. Probably got that from her Protestant mother. There was a friend in medical school who used to talk about the 'auld one' test. A Dubliner. God! That was so long ago. 'If you ever think of marryin' a girl, go and have a look at her 'auld one'. That'll usually cure you.'

He laughed aloud at the memory and at his own negligence in not applying the 'auld one' test. To hell with it, he would need a drink to banish the idea of being married to a scrawny 'auld one' in a cross-over apron, feeding chickens in the muck of a Wexford farmyard. He gestured to the barman.

A strange one, thought the barman, this Inglés who drank by himself and laughed at nothing at all. A dangerous one too, who had shot the gaucho, Jiménez, in that very doorway. He hastened to pour another drink, and accepted the generous tip with elaborate gratitude.

In the old days, Estrellita knew, in the days of the jaguar, the people had often camped in that place by the river. There would be a fire with food cooking and the children would play in the water. The men would trim their arrows or twist fresh thongs for their slingshots. The women would scrape hides or spread meat in the sun to dry.

She had no memory of this except for what her mother had told her and what she saw in the smoke of the fogón, but in her heart this was where she belonged, with the Wild People by the river.

She stretched the washing on the grass. It would dry in an hour. The white people divided the day into hours. They were always trying to catch up on the hours as if some day they would have a great pile of hours to spend. She could never understand this fear of losing time and the anxiety it brought. Jiménez had never suffered from this sickness with regard to time. She wished that he were still with her. Her body ached for his touch. He was lazy and did only what pleased himself, like the big red bull, but he satisfied her and he was her man. There would be others, she thought, but never another as proud and beautiful as Jiménez.

She slipped out of her clothes and waded into the water to where her children were splashing about and laughing. She soaped their hair and ducked them under the water. They spluttered and struggled to escape, slippery as little fish.

"You must be clean, the señora says. You must be clean if you are to go to her house to the school."

"What is school?" asked the eldest, a sturdy little boy of about eight years.

"School is where you will learn to read. You have seen the pictures in the papers the señora reads. Well, you will be able to read all the words as well."

"Can you do this?" he challenged.

"No. I have no need to do this, Rafael, but for you it will be necessary."

"Why?"

"Because if you cannot read you cannot vote."

"What is this vote?"

She soaped his hair again, ducking him under to rinse it. The bubbles flowed downstream.

"To vote is to pick the great men who rule this country. You could be one of those great men."

The boy pondered the idea.

"I would have soldiers and my brother and sister would have to do what I would tell them. Ha! Ha!" he laughed and dived away from her.

She soaped her own hair. She would have liked long hair like that of the señora but that could not be. But she would not want the señora's life. Too many things to worry about.

"Where do these bubbles go, Mama?" asked the little girl, Angelita.

"They will go down this river, around and around." She sketched the wandering course of the river in the water and the bubbles flowed with her hand. "They will go into the River of Durazno. Then they will meet the River of the Perdido, where we lived before Jiménez was taken from us. They will swim into another river, the Black River and then into the greatest river of them all and at last they will find a great water that never ends."

The child gazed at her, enraptured by the journey of the bubbles. Estrellita lay back in the water, letting the river flow over her. Her dark skin gleamed in the sunlight. She put her head under and listened to the river. She wondered what it would be like just to drift away with the bubbles, down this river and into another and another until she came to that great water that she had heard in the shell.

No, it was a cold and dangerous place. She would stay here and watch her children growing in peace, learning to read and becoming great people in the land.

She sat up in a cascade of water and wiped her eyes. Down river she saw John Cardiff sitting on his horse in the middle of the ford. The horse was drinking. He was watching them. The light dazzled off the water. She stood up, making no effort to conceal her nakedness and called her children from the water. They scampered out onto the gravel, laughing and splashing. The horseman moved on. She watched him go. He did not look back. She bent and picked up her clothes.

The washing was already dry. She gathered and folded it. The children vied with each other to carry the basket to the cart, where the mare stood waiting patiently in the shade, twitching her ears at the flies. Estrellita felt clean and strong. Her skin tingled from the rough soap. I will not fear this man, she thought, because I know what will become of him. I will hate him because he destroyed Jiménez and I will pity him because he will destroy himself, this man of the fair hair and the brightness of an angel. And always the jaguar will protect us.

Rafael would not learn to read or write. He was ashamed to sit at the table in the kitchen with niños. Estrellita brought him several times, keeping a firm grip on his arm as he struggled and yelled. He punched his younger brother, knocking him from his chair. He stabbed his pen into the wooden table and spavined the nib. He tore the paper that Catherine gave him and ran for the door. Eventually they gave up.

"I am sorry, señora," said Estrellita. "I can do nothing with him. He wishes to be with the horses and the men. It is his nature."

Catherine sighed. She was secretly relieved. It was too late for Rafael, but maybe not for his little brother and sister, Miguel and Angelita. Estrellita liked angels, she reflected. Richard liked the children. He seemed to enjoy learning with them and little Sarah was keen to join in. Perhaps there was a future for her educational venture.

"He is a gaucho, not a scholar," she said smiling.

John came into the room. He threw his hat on a chair.

"He's a wild one all right," he said tolerantly. "A bit of a savage, eh, Estrellita?"

Estrellita took a step backwards.

"Señor," she said, looking him in the eye.

"And how are the scholars doing today?" he asked, addressing himself to the children. He bent over their work, admiring everything. Sarah showed him her drawing, a scribble of lines.

"This is you on your horse," she lisped. He held up the drawing.

"It is upside down," she pointed out and he laughed heartily, apologising for his mistake.

"Excellent," he declared. "Excellent."

He turned to Catherine. Estrellita was gone.

"Excellent," he said again and the tension went out of her. He seemed to be happy with her little school, despite the chatter of the children.

"I have something here," he said, making much of searching in his pockets. He took out a bundle of cards with little coloured pictures.

"Liebig cards," he explained. "They are giving them away with the meat extract. The more you buy, the more cards you can collect." He tapped the side of his nose conspiratorially. "But I have influence." He spread the cards on the table and the children reached for them eagerly.

"Careful," said Catherine. "Don't bend them."

She picked one up. The colours were exquisite and the drawings delicately executed.

Hannibal's Campaign. One of a set of ten. There was a recipe on the back of each one. John was proud of his find.

"Look at this," he said. "Water Management in the Ancient World. Historical Figures. Natural Phenomena. We can collect whole sets of them. Look at these water-spouts," he said, showing them to the children. "Don't they look like snakes?"

The children nodded and went back to the cards, each child thinking that the others had better ones. They skittered some onto the floor.

"Careful," warned Catherine again, bending to gather them. "We will get paste and make books of cards. Won't we, children? Great big books of pictures."

"Yes," they chorused, but they were not yet ready to relinquish these wonders to the formality of pasted books.

She looked at John. She was touched. It was a kind thing to have done.

"Thank you," she said gently.

He shrugged and spread his hands.

"Anything to further the cause of education," he said, smiling his old smile.

"Look at these, Daddy," called Richard. "What are these ones?"

John took the cards and glanced at the back. "Notable Belgian Town Halls," he announced, laughing aloud. "Very important to know your notable Belgian town halls."

Richard looked up at him, awed by the extent of his father's knowledge. He frowned and studied the elegant buildings. Catherine could see how the children worshipped their father. She resolved to do everything she could to make allowances and to put everything right between them.

Rafael shuddered at his narrow escape. He knew that he had come close to disaster and that had he not asserted his manhood, his life could well have been destroyed. Never again would he allow them to imprison him like that when the sun was shining and there were so many things to do. He unrolled the poncho and looked at the wonderful things that had identified Jiménez as a man. Jiménez would understand. He would want him to have these things. He knew that Jiménez was not his father. He was something better, a man who went his own way, allowing a boy to grow up without trying to break him or contaminate his mind with notions of learning. Jiménez had no ambitions to inflict on a growing boy. Rafael missed Jiménez and the indolent rhythm of his life.

He drew the long knife from its sheath. Unusually for Jiménez, it was a plain bone-handled working knife without decoration of any kind. He touched the blade. It had kept its edge. He replaced it in the sheath, thrusting it into the back of his ragged trousers, just as the men wore their knives. The handle pressed against his spine, but he liked the feeling of security. He put his hand behind his back, drew the knife and flourished it about. He replaced it again, feeling with both hands for the mouth of the sheath. This would require practice.

He tied on the enormous spurs. They were so big that they lifted his heels from the ground when he tried to walk. He hobbled to a stool and sat down. He spun the spiked wheels, imagining what it would be like to sit proudly on a horse with these silver nazarenas jingling as he rode. Some day he would also wear those fine boots of Jiménez, those boots of fine, white colt skin, for which Jiménez had given his life. It was a great price to pay. He could not understand why Jiménez had wanted them so much, but they were fine boots.

A figure darkened the doorway. Estrellita came into the dimly lit interior.

"So you will not be a scholar," she teased.

"No, I will not," replied Rafael

"What if I make you go back to the señora?"

"No one will make me go back. I will run away." He clenched the knife in front of him.

She laughed. "If you carry such a thing then you must learn to use it. I will send you to my father, Fierro and he will be your teacher from now on."

She looked at the spurs and smiled.

"Not yet," she said gently, making to pat him on the head. "When you are bigger, Rafael, my angel."

The boy twitched away from her, shaking his head, tossing aside the caress.

"I am not a baby," he said gruffly. "I am a man, like Jiménez."

"Go to my father. He will teach you to use your head as well as your knife. But for the moment, leave the nazarenas with me."

Rafael grinned. Reluctantly he undid the spurs and replaced them on the poncho.

"You will be a great gaucho," she said drawing him to her. She held him for a long time, until he struggled. She let him go.

BOOK TWO

Chapter One

Sarah preferred her father. She knew that she should love her mother equally, but her mother was always tired. She seemed to worry all the time. She used to sing to them when they were very little. There was a song she sang, where there was one very high note. It was an Irish song with strange words. It was a game she used to play, working up to the high note:

'*Is an bhfaca tú?*'

"Did I get it?" she would ask them, her eyes bright with fun. "Did I get it that time?"

"Yes, yes," they would say, clapping their hands.

Now she did not sing. She made them read and write, with great emphasis on accuracy and neatness. She praised them when they did well, but sometimes her mind seemed to be elsewhere. There were arguments too, usually at night when her father would come home. She could hear their voices in the darkness and she would wait and wait for them to stop. Then there would be silence and she would wait for them to start again. She would drift into sleep, only to wake again in fright at the sound of the voices raised in anger.

She wondered why her mother made him so angry. There was always such fun when he was around. He bought ponies for them and taught them to ride, holding the pony on a long lunge-rope as they rode around and around.

"Remember. You're holding a big egg between your legs." He had no time for girls riding side-saddle. "Don't drop that egg." He always made them laugh when he talked about the big egg and they would lose their grip and slide off into the long grass.

He let Estrellita's children ride the ponies too but Rafael, the eldest, laughed at them. Even William, her little brother could manage a pony and soon they would have to get one for the new baby. Maybe that was why her mother was so tired. She always seemed to have a baby to look after.

Now and again, her father would take them all on a great expedition, across the river and over the rolling hills to the pulpería. There was always such excitement there, with people drinking and laughing and travellers coming and going. There were men playing that strange game with the bones. They lounged on the grass and argued as each bone fell.

"What are they doing?" she asked him once.

"Arguing the toss," her father said. "This game was invented by an old friend of mine, Achilles. He played it long ago in a place called Troy and people have played it ever since."

She smiled because he was smiling at some private joke. He took a great interest in the bones. Sometimes he took money from the other men and sometimes he gave them money.

They sat on a crate and drank a lemon drink. It was fizzy and sometimes it went up their noses. This always made them laugh. They were half afraid to laugh, which only made them laugh even more, snorting the fizzy drink and spilling it on their clothes. Their father was never cross if they spilled their drinks, but their mother was always annoyed. She tried so hard to keep them clean.

She would never come with them to the pulpería. She always stayed to mind the baby or clean the house, dusting and sweeping. There was a lot of dust, especially in the summer time.

In the pulpería the men argued. They were always arguing about the government. The government was a gang of men who lived somewhere far away. They were always causing trouble. They were always looking for money. They sent soldiers all over the country, looking for people and taking their money. They were very bad people. The men in the pulpería talked of how they would throw the government out. She hoped they would do it soon, because sometimes the government made her father very angry and he would not talk to them for a while.

In the pulpería sometimes there were letters for him. He would read them. Some he would throw into the fire. Others he would bring home and then there would be arguments. They were probably letters from the government or from the bank. She hoped that the men in the pulpería would throw out the banks along with the government.

If the news was bad in the letters, he would whistle through his teeth on the way home, a shrill tuneless whistle. He would always have to take William up onto his own horse before they got home. William always went to sleep, nodding away to the motion of the horse, secure in his father's arms. Their mother would always complain that he had kept them out too late and that he had overtired them.

Catherine watched the little cavalcade arriving. William was asleep in his father's arms as always. She resented the way he seemed to recruit the children, binding them to him with games and fun and long horse-back rides. She knew that he did not try to turn them against her, but she felt excluded. He tolerated her concerns, but it was clear that they preferred to be with him. He garnered the fun to himself and left her with the more mundane aspects of family life. He left her to do the worrying too. She knew that there were problems with their debt to the bank, but talking about it only made him angry. It was all part of the conspiracy against him. Wool was down by a third. The paper money was almost worthless. The country was importing far more than it was exporting and the market for hides and dried beef was contracting all the time.

John had even resorted to paying the shepherds with lambs as they refused the paper money. It annoyed him to think that they were grazing the lambs on his land. He could see difficulties arising in the future and fully expected that he would be the loser. But for the moment it solved a problem.

He stumbled on the doorstep, almost dropping the little boy. She took the sleeping child from him and carried him to his bed. She pulled the blanket around him, looking down at him. He was a Doyle. She brushed the hair back from his forehead. He turned in his sleep and muttered.

She remembered the night they had made him, the night of the fiesta, almost four years ago. She remembered the lanterns and the music and the comical dance of the old man, Granillero and Mama Vieja, the African woman. There had been so much laughter that night, as the couple danced to each other and away again, like two butterflies, touching and separating with all the time, the staccato pounding of drums. The drums were still in her head when they made love that night, but after that night it was never the same again. There was no pleasure in their lovemaking. He took her with an urgency that bordered on violence, almost like a vengeance and she wondered what she had done wrong. Now there was another baby, another little boy, Michael. She knew that there would be more and the thought frightened her. There was nothing she could do about it. It was her duty, but she longed for the time when it had been her joy.

"No news from home?" she asked, returning to the kitchen.

"No," he said with his mouth full of bread. It irritated her that he could not be bothered to give her the courtesy of table manners.

"Come on, come on," he said to the children. "Eat up there and get off to bed."

Sarah was resting her head on her arms. She yawned.

"Off to bed," he said again. The children stretched and yawned and went off, dragging their feet. He lit a cheroot.

"That's all in the past, I'm afraid. You might as well put it behind you. They have forgotten about us."

She sat down opposite him and picked at a piece of bread. Pensively she swept the crumbs into a pile with the crook of her little finger.

"There must be a problem with the mail," she said. "I have written so many times."

"That's probably what it is," he agreed. "You might not think it here, but this country is on the brink of anarchy. Not much better at home by all accounts."

"How do you mean?"

"Agrarian violence. Coercion acts. You've read about it in *The Graphic*."

"Hmm," she mused, nibbling on the dry bread. "Strange how the newspaper gets through and yet no letters from home."

He paused in the act of tapping the ash from his cheroot. The ash fell onto the table top.

"Nothing from that blasted Boxwell either. I think we can regard that plan as a dead duck."

"It's bad then, I take it."

"What? The bank? No, no. Nothing we can't cope with."

"I wish you would tell me where we stand. There was a time you used to tell me everything. Remember how we used to make plans."

"You have to trust me," he said. "I can handle the situation. There's nothing to worry about."

"I still wish you would talk to me. I could write to my father, if necessary."

"No, God dammit," he said angrily and stood up. He went to the stove, opened it and dropped his cheroot into the flames. "I'm not reduced to that yet," he said, slamming down the lid.

"It was just a suggestion. I know he would help." She stood up and swept the pile of crumbs and ash onto the floor. Taking the broom from the corner, she began to sweep the tiles.

"I'm not reduced to that yet," he repeated. He stood with his back to the stove, his hands behind his back. He watched her. "Clodhoppers," he growled under his breath.

"What did you say?" she paused in her sweeping.

"Nothing."

"You said something. You said 'clodhoppers.'" Her knuckles whitened on the broom handle.

"I won't go cap in hand to some clodhopper of a farmer, that's all."

"How dare you? If you could run your affairs as well as my father runs his, we wouldn't be in the pickle we're in now."

"Indeed!"

"My family are decent hard working people with their feet on the ground."

He was about to make some retort, but checked himself.

"Not like the Grand Cardiffs." She loaded the words with sarcasm, resuming her sweeping.

"You did it again," he said evenly.

"What?"

"The crumbs. You swept them onto the floor. I thought I told you not to do that."

She said nothing.

"It may be all right in the Doyle household, but I will not have my house like a pigsty."

She swung the broom at him in fury and the blow glanced off his arm.

He seized her and the broom clattered to the floor. She smelled the tobacco on his breath and the sour smell of whiskey.

"I will be obeyed in my own house," he snarled, gritting his teeth, emphasising each word with short chopping blows, eight blows, alternating the back of his hand and the palm, catching her on either cheek.

Astonished, she counted the blows and found that she was counting in Charrúa, as Guidai had taught her. 'Betum artasam' eight. The word sounded like a slap.

He stopped, breathing hard.

"You never listen," he said releasing his grip. She backed away, staring at him in shock. Her legs trembled and she was afraid that she would fall. She gripped the table.

"Why are you like this? What have I done?"

"Just don't annoy me," he said taking his jacket from the back of the chair. "All I want is some peace in my own house."

He went out into the darkness and she heard the outer door slam behind him.

Richard felt his heart pounding in the darkness. There was sweat on his forehead. He heard a shuffling sound. He opened his eyes to see his sister holding William by the hand. By the light from the window he could see his little brother rubbing his eyes with the back of his wrist.

"Will you mind us, Richard?" said Sarah. "They are fighting again."

"I will," he said pulling back the blanket to let them climb in beside him.

"What will we do?" asked Sarah and Richard told them how he would take them away. He would get a big knife like Rafael's to protect them and they would take their ponies and go north. They would take some lucifers and at night they would make a big fire. They would cook meat and they would never fight or shout at each other. Then some day they would get on a ship and go over the sea to Ireland to visit their uncles and their grandparents.

Catherine found them asleep together in the one bed. The sight of them broke her heart. She wished that she could gather them up there and then and carry them away with her to a place where they would be safe, a place where people were gentle with each other; where the fields were always green; where the lake water came almost to their door.

In the quiet of the night Estrellita sat watching the stars. The moonlight fell in patches through the leaves of the ombú, so that she was invisible against the tree trunk. The stars danced for her in a wide and swirling dance, a dance that never paused or changed its tempo. They danced around the homes of the Orishas, who knew everything and the Orishas beat time like the bastonero. When she sat quietly she could almost hear the music. She could hear her heart beating in time with the stars, the stridulation of the insects of the night and the gentle rustle of the ombú leaves over her head. She closed her eyes.

She heard the sound of voices raised in anger. Thinned by distance, the voices rose and fell and suddenly stopped. She heard a door slam in the house of the señor. She saw a dark figure on the skyline. She watched him walk back and forth, back and forth, no bigger than an ant against the light of the moon. He seemed to stoop and work in the garden of the señora. It was a strange time to be working in the garden.

The figure disappeared from the skyline. The light went out in the house. It was strange how in a place of such beauty and plenty, they could not be happy.

She heard him approaching through the long grass and gradually she could make him out, outlined by a glimmer of moonlight. He stopped beside one of the curving trunks of the ombú putting his forehead against the rough bark. He was breathing heavily. She sat motionless and invisible, watching him. He was looking towards the dark bulk of her hut. He knocked his forehead once, twice, against the tree. She heard the smack. He struck his fist against the bark, swearing under his breath.

He leaned against the tree, fitting his back to its curve. His breathing eased. The tree swayed under his weight and the leaves whispered. 'Not yet, not yet.' She heard something scrape and his face was illuminated, yellow and haggard in the flare of the lucifer. He held the flame for a moment to light a cigar. There was a patch of blood on his forehead.

She smelled the smoke of the tobacco, heavy and sweet on the night air. He blew on the match, extinguishing it, but a yellow patch remained on her vision for a moment. As it faded she saw the tip of the cigar and his features, red in a pulse of light, when he inhaled.

He stood for a long while, smoking and resting against the tree, until the cigar was no more than a stub. He dropped it and ground it underfoot. She could smell his sweat on the night air and reflected that his clothes could do with a wash. She felt a sudden chill as dew formed in the air. He grunted, standing away from the tree. He took two steps and stopped, then walked away rapidly in the direction of the house.

Estrellita followed at a distance. She went around to the garden. The fence around the oak sapling had been kicked away and the little tree had been uprooted. She knelt and began to dig with her fingers, making a place for it again. The soil was moist from the dew. She set the roots in the hole, firming the clay around them.

Chapter Two

Tom Doyle wrote:

My Dear Catherine,

I hope you get this letter. I do not know why you do not rite. I know there do be wars in that country and mabye everything is disturbed. I pray that you and your faimly is safe. Since your brothers and your mother past on I have been managing for myself as I told you before.

I want you to know that the land will be yours. If you want to come home I will set you and your husband up in a farm of land and when I am gone you will have this one to.

I have sold the boats and I have money in the bank to do this. I hope you will consider this offer.

I remain your loveing father Thos. Doyle.

He put down the pen. He read over the letter again. It was a good letter, but he recognised that he had not as fine a hand as Dorothy. He printed the address in large block capitals, taking great care with each word. He put the letter into the envelope and stood it against the teapot. He wondered who this MRS JOHN CARDIFF might be, what she looked like and whether she was still in the land of the living.

Don José approved of the new government. After forty years and more in the army and in politics, he could at last see order coming to the land. He approved also of the influence of the military on civil affairs. There was need of discipline in all aspects of life.

He wrote the message, short and to the point. 'If your men are not capable of this task, telegraph me immediately and I will replace them and you also.'

Any commander who shirked his duty or compromised with rebels would be replaced and would face a firing squad, if his behaviour merited it. There would be a strong central government if he personally, had to machine gun every local caudillo and every band of predatory gunmen. These bandits, these wandering gavilleros, under the guise of revolution were bleeding the country dry. Here in the city, with its cosmopolitan population and its societies of intellectuals and orators, it was easy to forget the harsh realities of life on the pampas. There was danger there in everyday work and in the constant threat of raiding by bandits from the untamed border country to the north.

But the telegraph wire would eventually ensnare them. He would use the railways to crush them into the ground. They could not stand up against the machines of the modern world. With a faint twinge of regret for his far off youth, he realised too that their freedom of movement was being restricted by the relentless process of enclosure. Not for very long would they be able to lose themselves in the trackless wilderness. The alambrada would do for them, if the Gatling-gun did not find them first.

He signed his name and rank and handed the slip to the telegraph orderly. He stood up, flexing his bad leg. Inactivity made it worse. He went outside and called for his horse. Sighing, he climbed painfully into the saddle. He was getting old. He wheeled the animal and urged it into a trot. The parade-ground gravel crunched under its hooves. He felt good. There was still work to be done.

The one-eyed man slid his drink along the bar and edged closer. He knew that accent well. The sailors could only be Wexford men.

"If you ever get to Hokitika," said the bigger man, "there's a grand little bar right on the waterfront."

"I know it," said the other, "but I'll tell you where you can get a decent drink."

They spoke of bars on waterfronts from the Baltic to San Francisco and the one-eyed man listened intently. These were men who had travelled the world but, it seemed, had never penetrated further inland than the waterfront bars of all the ports they had visited.

"I was never that happy ashore. You get out of the way of it. I like to be able to see me ship. Keep an eye on her."

"Aye," agreed the other.

They looked at the one-eyed man, raising their eyebrows, enjoying a secret joke. He was a typical Argentinian, brown as a nut, with skin weathered by the winds of the pampas. He slouched at the bar wrapped in his poncho, looking into the depths of his glass.

"And where are ye bound for now?"

"Uruguay," said the big man. "Fray Bentos. Hides and meat. Time was we went round the Horn to California for the hides but this is better, by God. We'll have a nice run up to Boston."

"Boston," said his companion. "I can recommend a place." He extolled the virtues of a waterfront bar, frequented by the Irish. "But they're all from the West. Half o' them can't speak English. Talkin' away in the Gaelic. It's like a foreign country."

"Mother o' Jaysus," said the one-eyed man, "it is a foreign country." They looked at him in astonishment. "Here ye are in Buenos Aires and ye can't speak a word o' the language." He spoke to the barman in Spanish. Three more drinks appeared.

"Well I'll be damned," said the big sailor. "We took you for a foreigner."

"I'm as Wexford as ye are," said the one-eyed man, introducing himself.

"Laurence Doyle from Lingstown near Tomhaggard." He said it like Tomagger in the round, mellifluous tones of south Wexford.

They spoke of home. They had another drink and another. They argued about the relative merits of life on shore and on the ocean.

"I like to keep me feet on the ground," said Laurence. "I came out in thirty two. One trip home was enough for me. He told of herding sheep in Patagonia, where the trees grow sideways in the wind. He had herded cattle in the north. He spoke of mining in the western mountains and earthquakes, where whole towns slid into the Pacific. "I like to keep me feet on the ground," he declared again, "unless I have a good horse under me."

"So you must speak the language then?"

"Indeed. The only way to learn the language is to sleep with a dictionary, if ye take me meaning."

The larger of the two laughed, while the other man frowned.

"I was never much for the book learnin'," he admitted ruefully. "Just about write me own name."

His companion guffawed and slapped him on the back. "No you fool. He means a woman."

"Ah," said the small man, grinning sheepishly.

"So how many languages do you know?"

The one-eyed man made a rueful face,

"I'm too old for learnin' any more languages," he said, "but I have a bit of Guarani and the Spanish o' course. But me Portuguese is a bit rusty." He took a long drink, letting his mind drift back over the years and the women who had thrown their lot in with him. But he had always moved on. That was all long ago.

"I don't suppose you met many of your own kind."

"Oh, there's Irish here in Argentina all right, but I never had much to do with them."

"Wait a minute. Wait a minute," interrupted the smaller man. "There was some story I heard of a young one from your part o' the country, ran away with a young lad from Wexford. Son of that doctor that was in the fever hospital. Cardiff. That was his name. Terrible decent man. Ran away to Uruguay, I heard."

"Not many Irish in The Banda," said Laurence. "What was her name?"

"Broke her parents' hearts, the way I heard it."

"What was her name?" asked Laurence again.

"Farmin' people. Down by the lake. Her mother was a Protestant. Terrible decent people, they say."

"It wasn't Doyle by any chance?"

"It could be. The way I heard it and it's a good few years now, her name was Catherine and they named a place after her, Santa Catalina."

"Catherine," said Laurence. He fell into a brooding silence.

"Terrible decent people, they say," said the sailor looking into his drink. "Terrible thing to do to you parents."

"An' what age were you when you ran off to sea?" challenged his companion.

"Eh, ten. But that was different. They were glad to see the back o' me."

"Santa Catalina," mused Laurence.

"That's a saint," declared the big man triumphantly. "I know that much Spanish. Be god, I'll have to find one o' them dictionaries before we set sail."

He looked around speculatively.

"She was no saint now, if she would do that to her poor parents," said the other sailor, his voice thick with emotion and drink.

"Go on outa' that. When did you last bid your parents the time o' day?"

"Ah that's different." It was different. A crowd of children in a back street slum. All he could remember was babies crying and his father's voice raised in drunken anger. "That was different," he said again.

"Fray Bentos?" said Laurence. "Would your skipper take me upriver, d'ye think?"

"He'd take the Divil himself if he paid hard cash," laughed the sailor. "How an'ever," he said draining his glass and hitching up his belt, "I'm away now to improve me Spanish."

"A terrible thing to run away like that," said the other sailor, sniffing. Laurence signalled to the barman putting some coins on the counter. The sailor drank, thinking of the child he had once been and of his parents, their lives, shrivelled and warped by poverty. He thought that he might send them something from his travels, something to put up over the empty fireplace, a trophy to show to neighbours. He should have bought one o' them tattooed heads in Hokitika, fierce Maori warriors, forever frowning. A head up there on the mantelpiece. That would impress the neighbours. Laurence left him to his thoughts and went down to the ship.

Robert Boxwell wrote, requesting letters of introduction to the lawyer and bankers in Montevideo. He was prepared to come over, but only on condition that he would be told the full facts. He was optimistic that they could form a partnership and if, as John said, trade was about to improve dramatically with the increasing political stability etc. etc. He was delighted to hear that things were going so well. He took his time, thought John, swearing under his breath. All the same, Boxwell would not find out the truth until he came all the way over and then he might as well stay. He did not relish the idea of a partnership, but Boxwell had the money and he needed money desperately. Boxwell was a dull and plodding fellow, who could be bent to his will. He wrote back immediately, urging him to come over with all speed.

Laurence stood in the doorway of the pulpería. A fly zinged in the dead heat of the afternoon. Three gauchos sat in the shade, playing cards and passing around an earthenware jar of rum. A fourth man was tuning a battered guitar. He was having difficulty, adjusting and re-adjusting the strings until he was satisfied. He drew his thumbnail across a chord and began to sing a mournful Peruvian yaraví. His eyes were closed as he sang, a monotonous, repetitive tale of lost love and loneliness. He dragged out the high notes to telling effect.

The gauchos argued about the cards. They argued about politics. They argued good naturedly about horse racing and cock fights. They laughed at the recollection of some man who had bet his wife on a horse race.

"So his horse won, but I say that he is not hidalgo. He is not noble. He may think he is, but I say he is not."

"If I bet my china with another man I tell you she would geld me with my own knife." He said it with pride.

Laurence left them and went inside. The stone flagged room was cool. He sat at a table. The proprietor brought him some food. The proprietor wiped his hands on his apron and sat down.

"As you are going to Santa Catalina, señor, perhaps you would bring some letters."

He poured himself a glass of wine.

"This is our own wine," he said proudly. "It is from the vineyards of Carmelo."

"It is good," agreed Laurence. "How far is this place?"

"About six leagues by the new road. Shorter if you go across country."

"I will go by the road. Do you know the people there?"

"I know the señor." He shrugged. "He comes here sometimes with his children, sometimes without them. The Inglés, he likes to drink."

"Inglés?" Laurence was disappointed. "We say Inglés but he is not Inglés. He is something else. He does not like to be called Inglés. But letters come with the stamp of the queen of the Inglés."

He took the letters from the pocket of his apron. "See. It is the queen of the Inglés."

Laurence peered at the envelopes. There was one from Montevideo, addressed to John Cardiff, but the other bore the severe image of Victoria and was postmarked Bridgetown. He remembered Bridgetown with its little thatched post office.

MRS JOHN CARDIFF, SANTA CATALINA, SORIANO, URUGUAY. This must be the right place, the place the sailor had talked about. He stood up, dropping some coins on the table.

"I will take them," he said. "No doubt she will be glad of news from home."

Catherine straightened up, putting her hands to her back. She groaned. The garden was doing well, even the oak sapling. She had hibiscus of many colours and herbs that scented the evening air. She found peace in the garden with her children helping and hindering in equal measure. She saw the horseman turning into the avenue, coming towards her between the rows of eucalyptus. There was something about him. She shaded her eyes against the low sun.

He wore a black eye patch. He was a tall, thin man. A tall, thin man with a black eye patch. She began to walk towards the oncoming rider. She began to run. She waved her hands, calling to him. He dismounted and caught her by the waist, lifting her high in the air.

"High, high," he said laughing and she put her arms around him and hugged him. It was a game they had played when she was little, that time he had come home from the far end of the world.

"Oh, I am so glad to see you," she sobbed. The tears flowed down her cheeks. "Oh, you have no idea."

He wiped the tears with the back of his hand.

"Now, now, girl," he said and she thrilled again at the sound of his voice. "There's no need for tears. Here. I have a letter for you." He reached into his pocket. She hopped from one foot to another. He used to have sugar barley in his pockets, but he always made a game of searching for it.

"Oh, please, please," was all she could say.

"Easy now," he said handing her the letters. She tore open the one from Ireland. Her fingers fumbled.

"Oh, excuse me," she said remembering her manners. "But I must read this. It has been so long."

She read her father's words, but they made no sense. Her mother always did the writing. There was a roaring sound in her head. She read the words again, struggling to understand. A black veil fluttered across her vision. She felt herself being swept away. Her uncle caught her as she fell. He lifted her and carried her towards the house. An Indian woman came hurrying towards him, followed by some small children. He spoke to her in Guarani. She nodded and hurried to open the door for him. He laid Catherine on her bed and the Indian woman loosened her garments. She opened the shutters. A cool breeze came into the room.

Laurence looked at the letter. Thos Doyle, he thought. Tom Doyle, for God's sake. It was a sorry tale. He wondered how she had not known about all this before. He put it on the table in the kitchen with the other letter and stood awkwardly waiting. The children peeped at him around the door.

"Hello," he said, "and who might ye be?"

The little girl came forward.

"I am Sarah Cardiff," she said holding out her hand. "What did you do to my Mama?"

He stooped down. She stared at the black eye patch.

"Your Mama has had some very bad news. We must be quiet." He put his finger to his lips.

"What did you do to your eye?" asked the older boy.

"That's a long story," he said. "I'll tell ye about it some day. So ye are Catherine's children. Well, now!"

He asked their names and told them who he was.

"The baby is Thomas, but he is asleep," Sarah explained.

"I see," he said. "This is a great big family."

"We have ponies," said Richard, "and we have millions of cows." He spread his arms wide.

Catherine came into the room. She was barefoot. Her hair hung loose about her pale face.

"I am so sorry, Uncle Laurence," she said. "I haven't even offered you any refreshment after your journey."

"Don't worry about that," he replied. "I'm well used to travellin'. I'm sorry to be the bearer of bad news."

She put her hand on his sleeve.

"I am glad to see you all the same."

"Child," he said. "Your father is well and he cares about you. I read the letter y'see."

"But my poor brothers. What could have happened to them? And my poor mother. What are we to do?"

He said nothing. The children gathered around her wordlessly. She picked up the letter addressed to John. She might as well know what was in it. She opened it. It was from the bank, as she had expected. Things could not have been worse, but at that point it did not seem to matter. She put it face down on the table.

Guidai brought her a maté. She sipped and passed it to her uncle. He took it gratefully. She felt numb, waiting for him to propose a solution. They heard John's horse outside and the sound of his boots in the hallway. His spurs jingled as he walked.

She was grateful to him for the way he had taken the news and for his words of sympathy. To Laurence he was the soul of cordiality, addressing him as 'sir'. He made light of the letter from the bank.

"You should not have opened it," he said. "You should not distress yourself with these matters, particularly in view of the sad news of your family."

"But they threaten foreclosure."

"These are only words. The estancia would be of little value to them in this recession. They could never find a buyer. Anyway, I have had some word from Boxwell. We can expect to see him presently."

"You never told me."

"This is business, my dear. Nothing to concern yourself with. In the meantime you must write to your poor father. Please God, this one will get through."

"I hardly know what to say. Have you thought about his offer?"

"Out of the question. This is our home now, for better or for worse."

"What does Robert propose?"

"He would take over the debt in return for a share in the estancia."

"But he knows nothing of the business. What share does he want?"

"Sixty percent, but I will beat him down."

"Then Santa Catalina would be his."

She shook her head. "All that work. Where has it gone?"

"Times are difficult, but they will improve, I promise you."

She studied his face, wondering if he was talking only of prices.

"I promise you," he repeated earnestly, looking into her eyes. She looked away. She wanted to believe him but the thought of losing the land worried her. Again the notion of Elizabeth Boxwell, lording it over her in her own house, worried her. Would her children be hewers of wood and drawers of water for the Boxwells. All that work. Where did it go?

"I would like to see my father. Perhaps I should go home. I could go by myself."

"I am deeply sorry about your family," he said, "but consider the dangers. A woman travelling by herself. No, I could not allow it. Perhaps in time, when things settle down, we could all go together."

She knew that this would never happen, but the thought consoled her.

"If things pick up," he added, "Besides there are other things to worry about. Fierro tells me there are gavilleros active in the north. He feels that we should move the herd to the southern range for safety. You would wonder why we pay our taxes. The army is big enough, God knows."

He had so many things to worry about. She berated herself for seeing only her own troubles.

"What of the sheep?"

He bit his lip thoughtfully. "We may have to consider fencing."

"The gauchos would not like that."

"I know. It's just a thought. Anyway it would cost money, which we haven't got at the moment." He slapped his hands on his thighs and stood up. "Write to your father," he said gently. "It will make you feel better. I will see that it gets away safely."

She nodded. Her thoughts were already far away.

She watched him setting off with the children. They were laughing and chattering with excitement. Her spirits lifted again. Perhaps he meant it this time. Perhaps the shock of the news from home had changed him. She spent the day with her uncle, reminiscing about old times, talking of his adventures. She said nothing of the days when he had fought the savages. Guidai prepared the maté and sat with them in the shade. The story was different now. Catherine thought of the children hiding in the bushes and Fierro with his sword at the ready.

"Señor," asked Guidai. "How is it that you speak the Guarani?"

"Ah," said Laurence, "I picked it up on my travels, I suppose."

"And the eye señor? How is it that you lost your eye?"

"Ah, that," he replied. "An accident with a gun." He dismissed the topic with a wave of his hand. "I suppose I was a bit hard on meself over the years."

"Señor," she said. "You are old. You should stay here until you die."

Laurence laughed. "It's hard to kill a bad thing."

"You could stay, Uncle Laurence," said Catherine thoughtfully. In fact it was an excellent suggestion. She would be glad of an ally. "We would be glad to have you here."

"Ah," he said, "I'm a restless soul." I could never stay in one place."

"Señor," said Guidai, "you are needed here."

"But I am too old to work," he teased.

"You are little older than my Fierro and he is not afraid of a little work."

"I think maybe he is glad to go out in the morning. Glad of some peace."

"You are making fun of me, señor."

"Would I do such a thing?"

Guidai smiled. She said something in her own language.

"What did she say?" asked Catherine.

Laurence lowered his head.

"What did she say?"

"She said I am forgiven." He took a long drink of the maté.

"Will you stay?"

"I will," he said, "and gladly."

John returned earlier than usual and in his cheerful band of riders he brought a smiling Robert Boxwell. Robert raised his hat and waved to them. Gladly she went forward to greet him.

Chapter Three

Robert had plans. He had investigated matters thoroughly in Montevideo. He had spoken to experts. They all agreed that enclosure was the way forward, the alambrada, which had proved so successful further south. He was diffident at first, but his confidence grew. He would have been satisfied with a gentlemens' agreement, but the bank insisted on a signed contract.

"I'll give it ten years," he said. "In ten years you can buy me out. I'll probably move on to something else."

"Ten years," said John. "In ten years I will be a middle aged man. These children will be nearly adults."

"That will happen no matter where you are," said Robert in his practical manner. "This is a good deal for all of us. Do you know, my mother was trying to get me married. Every weekend, different young women. I feel I've had a lucky escape."

"Does she still ask about her umbrella?" interjected Catherine.

"Last seen heading south, with a fair following wind," said John. "It must be somewhere in the southern ocean by now."

"She does. She does," said Robert, laughing.

It was almost like old times. She took advantage of the good humour.

"I have asked Uncle Laurence to stay. He has nowhere to go. He says he can work as well as any man. He…" She paused. He looked at her in surprise.

"Excellent. Excellent. Of course. We can always use a good man around here, eh Robert?"

"I'm sure we can. Anyway, tomorrow you must show me around and then we must go to Montevideo for a few days to put things in order."

He made love to her that night. He was gentle and considerate and it gave her pleasure. She began to hope. She thought of the umbrella sailing bravely southwards and of how they had sealed their compact in the rain. It was all so wonderful then when the world was full of hope. Perhaps those days would come again and even better days, among friends, with their children growing about them. Middle age would hold no fears, or old age either. They would go someday, first class, as John had determined, to see her father and show the old place to the children.

He lay back and struck a match to light a cheroot. He chuckled.

"He's a fool of course. He has me over a barrel."

"Robert?"

"Yes. He could take the whole place, but he is too decent."

He made it sound like a weakness.

"But you will be fair with him too."

"Whose side are you on?" he asked lightly. "Of course I'll be fair, but I'll get the money to buy him out. I'll make sure that option is kept open."

"You are happy about Uncle Laurence?"

"Of course. Of course. We'll build a rancho for him, where he can be comfortable."

"I thought he could live in the house. He is family after all."

"No, no. A man like that would never be comfortable in a house. Think of the life he has lived up to now. He needs his own place."

She admitted that he had a point. She had no wish to push the matter. She was grateful for his good humour. She moved closer, enjoying the warmth of his body. She suspected that she was beginning to be happy again.

"I've been a bit of a swine at times," he said after a while. "You have no idea how much I regret it."

She shook him gently. "Don't," she said. The moment was too fragile.

"Things will get better from now on. I promise you." He stubbed out the cheroot, turning towards her. He put his arm around her. She moved closer, giving herself to him again. This was how it was meant to be.

"**G**uidai," she asked. "How did you know about my uncle?"

"Know what, señora?"

"Know about the thing for which you forgave him."

"The matanza, señora. Estrellita told me."

"But she is too young. How can she know?"

"She just knows. Fierro also knows things, but he does not say."

"And you forgive him?"

"He is a man who regrets what he has done. He has wandered the world since the matanza. With his one eye he sees more clearly what is right and wrong. I forgive him because that is what we must do, if we are to survive. Besides, he will be good to you and you need him."

Catherine looked at her, wondering how much she really knew. Guidai's face was expressionless. It was a thing she could do, retreating into her Indian self.

"But I thought your people always took revenge."

"The Charrúas are no more, señora. I am Christian now. This is what Nuestro Señor says we must do."

"Yes you are," said Catherine, humbled. She would learn from this simple woman. "And Estrellita? Is she Christian too?"

"She is, but she bets on two horses. With the life she has led she needs the help of all the gods." She smiled tolerantly. "She can tell you what is to come, but it is better not to know."

"She is a good person."

"That is what the men think." She shrugged. "She is a good washerwoman. I will take the basket to her now. I wish to speak with her about Rafael."

She gathered the clothes into the big wicker basket.

"Let me help you," said Catherine, putting out her hand.

"No. You are the señora. You must remember your place. The señora does not handle the laundry."

She elbowed her way out the door and set off towards her daughter's dwelling. It is hard being the señora sometimes, thought Catherine. She would have liked to go to the river with Estrellita, to do the washing. They could kneel there by the water, making suds, talking and laughing about men and their foolish ways. They would sing to the music of the river. Foolish nonsense, her mother would have said, but on such a fine morning it would have been pleasant and something to do while the men were away in Montevideo. In the meantime there were children to teach, a baby to feed, a house to be kept tidy and a room to be put in order for Robert, until he should decide where he would build his own place. The day was full enough.

Fierro was troubled. The horizon was closing in around him. Everywhere there were laws and officials. The old alcaldes were gone, the last relics of the Spanish. Now there were Justices of the Peace. He had never met one, but they were talked about at the pulpería. It was said that the government would soon control everything. He had never met an alcalde either, but it had been good to know that they existed, men of authority who could call up soldiers to deal with bandits and wandering gavilleros. All this government was making society fall apart.

He talked to his grandson, Rafael, about the old days, when the pampas belonged to the gauchos and before them, to the Indians.

"Why do you speak so well of the Spanish, Fierro?" asked the boy.

"Because they left us the animals," he replied simply. "Without the animals there would be no gauchos. Can you imagine how you would live without your horse? What would you eat if there were no cattle?"

The boy frowned. He patted the horse. Fierro admired his enormous spurs.

"You are a true gaucho, Rafael. There is no other life for you."

"If the alambrada comes, Fierro, what will you do?"

"I am old, Rafael. It is probably too late for me to do anything. But you? What will you do?"

"I will go north," said the boy defiantly. "The señor will not enclose me with the wire."

"Ah, the señor," said Fierro. Perhaps he had stayed too long with the señor. There was dark talk about how he treated the señora. Fierro would not repeat it, nor would he allow such talk in his presence, but he had heard the men nonetheless. It was said that the señor did not always respect his wife. Fierro wondered if he should stay with a man who was not noble towards his wife.

"Come with me," he said to the boy. "We will ride together and I will tell you how your ancestor came into The Banda, when the Spaniards brought the animals across the river."

This was the story the boy loved, the story of the African and how the people of the jaguar killed the Spaniard and took away his iron weapons. It was the African who brought the knowledge, all the way from beyond the ocean, the secrets that allowed his mother to read dreams and see the future in the smoke of the fogón.

Fierro returned after dark to report that there was stock missing. Gauchos bandeirantes, he said. Very dangerous men. He had followed the tracks northwards, but could not go too far because of the boy. Rafael was excited by the adventure.

"What should we do, Uncle Laurence?" Catherine asked. "I cannot send the men after them."

"There is not much we can do right now. They could be anywhere. "Fierro, do you think that any of the señor's men have joined with these thieves?"

Fierro shuffled, fidgeting with his hat.

"Well, Fierro. What is your opinion?"

"I cannot find the men who had charge of these cattle," he mumbled. "It is possible."

"But why?" she asked. "We have always been fair to them. Why would they do this to us?"

"I do not know, señora," he replied. "Perhaps it was from fear."

"Fear? I do not understand."

"Of the alambrada, señora."

They stood under the porch. The light from the doorway made a trapezium on the beaten earth. Rafael sat on his horse, looking down at them. The horse snorted restlessly. Estrellita came into view, driving her little wagon, bearing with her the basket of washing.

"Get down and help your mother," said Fierro.

"No," replied the boy haughtily. "That is not work for men."

"I apologise, señora, for my grandson. He has no father to beat him."

"It is not important," said Catherine stepping forward, but Laurence intervened. He swung the basket from the cart and carried it indoors.

"He is a wild boy, señora," said Estrellita. "My father will not beat him for me and I cannot catch him."

"He is a good gaucho," said Catherine kindly. Rafael smiled.

"Thank you Estrellita," she said taking some money from her purse.

"These papers I found in the coat of the señor," said Estrellita, accepting the coins. "They were in the coat where the pocket is torn. I think they are important."

"Thank you," said Catherine as Estrellita took her leave. "Fierro, come in the morning and let us discuss this matter. When the señor returns he will know what to do."

"Señora," he said, replacing his hat. He led his horse away, followed by Rafael. She noticed how easily the boy moved, in harmony with his mount. She went inside. Laurence was sitting by the fire, drinking a maté. He offered it to her. She sat down, suddenly weary. She rocked in her chair.

"This is a bad business," she remarked. "What are we to do?"

"It is to be expected," he said. "Twenty or thirty head. You will survive. No doubt it has happened before."

"Several times. John wanted to arm the men. He bought guns, but the Lanzas took them. But this is different. These were our own men."

He thought for a while. "Then you must hire others. New people. Not gauchos. There are many in the city, who would work for ye. Grow crops and get machines to harvest them."

"Ah no," she said softly. "Then we would lose all of our gauchos."

"I tell you there are machines to cut corn. Ye can still keep cattle, but ye can grow fodder for them, instead of lettin' them wander. It is the way of the future."

"The alambrada?"

He nodded. He took a long drag of the maté, looking into the fire. Catherine opened one of the folded papers. It had frayed at the corners to become a series of loosely linked rectangles. In the candlelight she could make out the arms of the Emperor of Brazil.

She laughed aloud. "You won't believe this," she said, passing it to Laurence, supporting the fragments on her spread fingers.

He tilted it towards the fire and bent forward, scrutinising the handwriting.

"What's this?" he queried. She told him the story of the Confederate colonel and his smartly uniformed troops.

"Ah," he said, examining the paper. "Maybe it's not too late to claim compensation. They say the Emperor is a fair minded man."

He rambled on about the time he had spent in Brazil, until he became conscious of her silence. He looked up from the paper. She was trembling and appeared to be fighting for breath.

"What is it child?" he said in sudden alarm. Wordlessly she handed him the letter. It too was frayed, to the extent that the firelight showed in bright crosses where the corners had worn through. He peered at it with his one eye. It was a message from another time, her mother's account of the drowning and the fatal cartload of woar.

"Ah, good God!" he said, looking at the date.

"But this is…this is years old."

"He knew," she said, as if explaining it to herself. "He knew all along. Why did he not tell me? Why?"

"I don't know, child," muttered Laurence. "Maybe so as not to upset you."

"No," she said and there was a controlled fury in her voice. "No. He resented my communications with home. He wanted to control me completely. I don't know. I don't understand. Why was he so cruel?"

Laurence expected the tears to come. He had always felt uneasy about her husband. From the teeth out, as they say. His words did not come from the heart. Catherine did not weep. This surprised him.

"What will you do?" he asked.

"He will not hurt me again. I will go home. I will take the children and go back to my father's house."

"That's a very big decision," he cautioned. "Should you not talk to him first?"

"No," she said. "I must go before he returns. If I stay, I won't be able for him."

Her hands were shaking.

"How will you manage?"

"I don't know. I don't know. I must get away from here."

"Easy now, child," he said taking one of her hands in his. "Think for a minute. Will you be able to live at home with people pointin' the finger at you and talkin' behind your back? Just think about that for a minute."

"At home?" she replied. "I thought this was my home. I don't care what people say. I have to get away from here."

"What about the children? Are they not entitled to a father?"

"I can't. I can't ..." she said. "I don't know. I can't leave them with him. I have to take them."

"Have you money for your passage?"

She shook her head.

"Very well," he said. "If that's what you want. I have money. It's no use to me. Take it and welcome."

"I can't. You would have nothing."

"Arrah, what do I need money for? You gave me a home."

"He would never let you stay, if I do this. He would hate you because of me."

"We'll see." He dismissed the idea. "How long have you got?"

"Two days. Maybe three. Of course there's no telling."

"Well then, you'd better pack some things. I will bring you to Fray Bentos. You can travel on a cargo ship. He would expect you to go by Montevideo."

She stood up. "Where do I start? Our whole life is here. Everything we own."

"Just do it," he urged. "Throw everythin' in a trunk, if you have one."

"I have." Doña María Jesús had sent one full of linen, a fine leather trunk of tooled Portuguese workmanship. She dashed about, gathering clothes for herself and the children, folding them hastily. She looked at her books. She would have to leave them. She picked up the Tennyson. His words, his tales of gods and heroes, of romance and noble knights, had soured. She tossed him aside.

"I must say goodbye," she said. "I will go now and say goodbye to Guidai and Fierro. Since I came into this country they have been kind to me. Everyone has been so kind." She paused. "And Estrellita. I must say goodbye to her and her children."

"Do that," he said gently. "It is important."

"I never did," she said and tears glinted in her eyes. "I never said goodbye to my mother or my brothers. That is why I am being punished."

"Now, now," he comforted her. "Go and talk to your friends."

She went in the darkness to the rancho of Fierro and his wife. She told them that she had to return to her father's house in her own land. She said that her uncle would stay, if the señor permitted and she asked Fierro also to stay and help.

"I know that you have thought of leaving," she said. "But the señor will need you."

She wondered why she cared. Realised that it was Santa Catalina she cared about. She had no wish to see it destroyed.

"Go with God," they said gently, understanding her distress.

She went down to the ombú grove. There was no chicharra complaining about being disturbed. She called softly, anxious not to waken the children. She pulled aside the leather flap at the doorway. Estrellita was sitting in the dim light of the fire.

"You have come to say goodbye, señora."

"Yes."

"I am sorry to see you go."

Catherine looked around. The hut was too big for Estrellita and her children. She recalled the faces of the gauchos on her first night at Santa Catalina.

"Sit down, señora" Estrellita pointed to the stool made of bones. Catherine sat down.

"You are remembering how this hut was crowded with men and you are thinking that it is too big and dark for one woman and her children."

Catherine nodded.

"The darkness is not empty," said Estrellita. "You want to know what is to become of you."

Catherine said nothing. The darkness seemed to crowd about her. She drew the stool nearer to the fir.

"Your children will be strong. They will help you." Catherine wondered about Sarah, John's favourite. "You will bring other children into the light also."

"And what of my husband?" she asked.

"He will return to you. The head of the family will always come back."

She felt the panic rising inside her. She would never be free of him.

"But some day you will be free. He will stay with you, but you will be at peace."

Her head spun. Was she wrong to go? If Estrellita could foretell the future then it was wrong to go. It was a sin to break her marriage vows.

"But now you must go, señora. It is necessary."

Catherine stood up. She held out her hands. Estrellita took them in her own.

"You are sad to leave this place," she said, "but it will always bear your name. Now take your children and go. You have little time."

Catherine hurried back through the long grass. She smelled the night perfume of her garden and her resolve almost crumbled. She wanted to stay in this place of beauty and magic, but she could not. She looked at the dark outline of her fine house. She knew that she would never see it again.

Laurence had the horses already hitched. They went together to rouse the children and dressed them for the journey. Sarah grumbled at being disturbed.

"Where are we going?" asked Richard.

"We are gong to see your grandfather. In Ireland," she added.

He whooped in delight, but Sarah scowled.

"Is Daddy coming?" she challenged.

"No dear. Not this time. Daddy is very busy. He will come some other time."

"I want to stay here with Daddy," she whined, but Catherine lifted her and bundled her into the coach. The boys climbed up in great excitement at this night time adventure. Laurence slapped the reins on the horses' haunches and their flight began.

Parakeets chattered and twittered in the eucalyptus trees, annoyed at this untimely disturbance. At the end of the avenue stood the dim figures of Fierro and his wife. They raised their hands in silent farewell. She looked back at them. The house was fading into the darkness. The parakeets subsided into silence.

The carriage turned onto the fine road built by the Welshman, Jones. The iron wheels rang on the gravel.

The sharp wind calmed her mind. The sails cracked overhead, as the sailors clambered in the rigging. They moved like spiders along the yards and the canvas rolled out with a sound like thunder. The land fell away astern as they moved out into the river. The masts of ships at the quayside, were hidden by a wooded promontory and soon only the great chimneys of the Liebig plant, with their rolling plumes of smoke, were visible.

The ship leaned with the wind. The prow cut through the brown water of the Uruguay. They were safe and free and bound for home.

Laurence rode out to meet the men returning from Montevideo. He figured that they would come across country from the pulpería. For some reason he felt that it would be easier to explain things away from the house. He took up his position on top of a small hill and waited. He lit a fire, putting a piece of meat to cook on a slanting stick. He peered into the distance.

He felt a sort of peace, now that she had gone. He would look after her interests to the best of his ability. Boxwell seemed an honest man. His influence could only be for good. In time, who knows? Maybe the wound would heal. He lay back against his sheepskin saddle, looking at the sky. An eagle soared on the rising air, circling in the enormous silence. Laurence chewed some meat. He wiped his chin. This is a good place, he mused. He watched a horseman far away, sending up a wraith of dust. A single rider. He cut another piece of meat and chewed on it. The rider was heading his way. He stood up, waving his hat. The rider obviously saw him or perhaps he had seen the smoke. He was heading directly towards the hill. It was Boxwell, the new man. He came up, weary and covered in dust. His white suit had taken on an orange tinge. He dismounted stiffly, flexing his legs.

"I'll have to get used to this," he gasped.

"Where is our friend?" asked Laurence directly.

Robert beat some of the dust from his jacket with the aid of his straw hat.

"He elected to stay at the pulpería. He says he will be home before nightfall."

"I would rather talk to him when he is sober," said Laurence ruefully.

"Why? What has happened?"

Laurence told him of the missing cattle and how some of their own men had deserted. Robert winced. The business was more complicated than he had anticipated.

"Also Catherine has gone. She has gone home to Ireland." He told him of the letter, of their flight through the darkness and of his own suspicions of what had gone before.

"The men talk you see. Probably they don't expect me to understand."

"Ah!" said Robert, rubbing his chin. "There will be the Devil to pay when he finds out."

"She asked me to stay to keep an eye on things," said Laurence. "I only have the one," he added in an attempt at levity.

"Yes, yes of course. You have my say so on that. Keep an eye on her interests. Good man."

"And himself. She thinks he will destroy himself and Santa Catalina with him."

"She cares for him then?"

"In a way, she does. But they are better off a few thousand miles apart. Maybe they will remember the good days and put away the bad."

"We must proceed carefully," said Robert. "He has a vile temper when he is crossed. Nevertheless, I am the majority shareholder, so what I say goes. You will stay. I would welcome your help. We can come to some agreement."

They shook hands. Laurence cut a slice of meat and passed it to Robert. Robert ate hungrily. He wiped the grease on the trousers of his white suit. He sighed contentedly.

"I think I like this life," he said, wincing as he remounted his horse.

Laurence kicked clay over the fire, treading it down carefully. He threw his saddle over his horse's back and cinched it firmly. He stepped into the stirrup, swung his leg over the animal's back and followed Robert down the slope. There were two eagles circling overhead, a good omen.

A steady wind drove the ship out of The Plate and northwards towards the tropics. She stood at the rail, watching the wake stretching astern, like a broad, undulating road, a road she could never retrace.

She thought of all those she had left behind and wondered how she would manage. Her father might not welcome four young children. There would be no Guidai to sit with her, sharing a friendly maté, no Fierro to marshal the men in the morning and lead them out to the jingle of harness and spur. The sun would never shine for her with such intensity, nor would she take her siesta in a cool, darkened room, or lie with her husband, listening to the sounds of her house.

There would be no Estrellita either, to dance and attract the eyes of the men. What was it she had said? 'Your children will be strong. They will help you.' That she could believe. Richard had taken immediately to life on board. He was good at minding his little brother, explaining to him what the sailors were doing, bearing up cheerfully under the cramped conditions of their quarters. But Sarah remained surly and resentful. She wanted her Daddy and she wanted her pony. She spent long hours moping in her bunk. She complained about the indifferent food and spurned the friendly talk of the sailors. There were times when Catherine wanted to slap her, but she was afraid that she might lose control. She would never slap her children, however trying they might be.

There was something else Estrellita had said. 'You will bring other children into the light.' There was a biblical ring to it. She pondered the phrase. 'Into the light.' That was impossible. She would never go back to John. It must have some other meaning.

She watched a flash of silver under the water, then another and another. They moved like arrows, keeping pace with the ship. She drew Richard's attention to them. He leaned on the rail. She held the back of his coat, fearful of losing him. The streaks broke the surface, flying fish. Long, thin gurnet, they spread their fins and sprang for joy, skimming from wavetop to wavetop, renewing their strength from the water and springing again, racing them home. She was impatient at the thought of the long weeks at sea, eager to begin a new life among old familiar surroundings.

Chapter Four

After the initial fury, John lapsed into a sullen silence. He brooded and drank. They avoided him. Laurence thought it better to move out of the house. He took one of the ranchos abandoned by the deserting gauchos. It suited him fine. He took a bundle of newspapers from the house and settled down to catching up on what had been happening in the world.

The Emperor of France was gone. Not puttin' the stuff in them anymore, he mused. There was a Life Insurance Act passed by the Parliament in London. Maybe he should have thought about that earlier. He grunted and turned the page. There was an engraving of a ship's lifeboat being launched into a wild and churning sea. Some women crouched in the stern. Loose blocks and tackle swung perilously near their heads. He thought of Catherine on the high seas. He hoped that she would not have to go through such peril. The oars looked frail, ineffectual wands against the surging fury of the waves.

The Berlin Geographical Society was busily preparing for the proposed Congo expedition, to be headed by Dr. Gürsfeld, the celebrated glacier explorer. The Germans, he reflected wryly, had their own way of going about things. A Swiss innkeeper found a gold nugget of forty ounces, inside a Californian ham. A fossil magnolia was found inside the Arctic Circle, as Professor Duncan explained in his final lecture to ladies at the South Kensington Museum, prompting speculation that the region had once enjoyed a milder climate. A strange and comical world, he thought.

He heard footsteps approaching. He went outside. Robert greeted him and asked him to give an opinion on some plans he had drawn up.

"I can't talk to John at the moment," he said. "He doesn't seem to be interested."

Laurence knew that he was being tactful. "You have wide experience of this part of the world. You would know what's feasible." He unrolled the chart, a fair copy of the original map.

He had divided the land into segments of between six hundred to a thousand acres each. Some sectors were watered by the river and ancillary streams, on which he had indicated dams and reservoirs. In others he had drawn wind pumps to suck water from the rocks below. Henry Jones's road was to be fenced on either side and the gaucho huts looked like the nucleus of a village. He had been busy.

"What does our friend say?" asked Laurence, nodding in the direction of the house.

"Not a great deal," replied Robert. "All he talks about is getting his children back. I'm afraid he descends to the foulest of language. I'm disappointed, I have to say."

Laurence shrugged. He knew that at some point John would resent the part he had played in Catherine's flight and would vent his anger on him. He was prepared, but in the meantime there were things to be done. He appreciated the way Robert respected his knowledge and experience.

"Right," he said, getting down to business. "You could increase the sheep to ten or twelve thousand. You could get forty or fifty tons of wool a year at that rate. Romneys. They'd be the ones." He studied the chart closely. "Now here we could sow alfalfa to fatten the steers. More cross-breds. Less risk of eye cancer. They fatten better than the pure Herefords. Bring the numbers up to fourteen or fifteen thousand. The land can take them." He could see a great future.

"If prices recover," said Robert. "If only we could find some other way of exporting meat."

"It will take money of course," said Laurence.

"Hmm," mused Robert. "It will of course. It will take time too. You think it can be done?"

"There's a few ifs. If prices recover and the bandits stay away. If himself gets off the drink and pulls his weight."

Robert furled the map again. "And if we have enough men to work the estancia."

He tapped the cylinder of paper against the side of his boot. He had abandoned city clothes.

"Plenty of ifs," he said thoughtfully, "but better than no plan at all."

"Aye," agreed Laurence, as Robert turned away. It was a funny thing he thought, to be making plans and talking about the future at his age. He should be sitting in some chimney corner, sucking on a clay pipe. He watched the sun dipping to the horizon.

"You bastard! You sent her away." He recognised John's voice. He turned to see him stumbling drunkenly towards him. He wore neither hat nor coat. His shirt front was stained. He had been on a batter for over a week and looked older than his years. Fortunately he was not carrying his usual rifle, but trailing on a thong at his wrist was his leather rebenque. He was looking for fight.

"Get off my land," he shouted, pointing his finger. "Get to Hell off my land." He stumbled under the force of his own rage.

"You're drunk," said Laurence, keeping the post of the awning between them. "We can talk about this some other time."

"We'll talk about it now. You came here to poison her mind against me. I want you out."

"Your partner has offered me a job."

Laurence braced himself. John steadied himself with difficulty.

"We'll see about that. I want you out of here." He grasped the silver handle of the rebenque, raising it menacingly. Laurence snatched up a length of firewood. He was too old for brawling, but he would still welcome a crack at this young bully. He had taken on some hardy men in his time. He was not going to be frightened by a man who could not hold his drink. He held the branch in front of his body, clenching it in both hands. The light seemed to fade suddenly.

"You're a fool," said Laurence. "You couldn't be honest with her, even about her brothers." He jabbed with the branch. "Come on," he challenged.

"If she hadn't gone spying on me, this would never have happened." His voice rose querulously. "She had no business spying into my correspondence."

"You're a damn fool. She wasn't spying. The washerwoman found the letter, where you were stupid enough to leave it."

Laurence laughed, taunting him. John swore.

"The bitch," he snarled. He swung the whip in a wide arc and stumbled over his own feet. He fell in an ungainly heap in the dust. Instinctively Laurence bent to help him.

"Take your hands off me," snarled John, clutching the upright post of the awning. He struggled to his feet, the fight gone out of him in his confusion and chagrin.

"Just you wait," he said, pointing an accusing finger. "I'll…" He could not decide what he was going to do. He backed away, swearing under his breath.

"To Hell with the lot of you," he shouted, stumbling away into the gathering darkness.

That bitch, he thought. That whore. That yegua. A hiding. A damned good hiding. That's what she deserved. She was the cause of all the trouble, flaunting herself like that, drawing men on. Laughing at them. By God he would put a stop to her gallop and her heathen mumbo jumbo. As the señor, it was his duty to maintain standards. A spy and a troublemaker. She could pack her bags and leave too. He didn't need anyone. She could follow the other deserters and take her brats north, to Hell off Santa Catalina land.

He saw the light in the ombú grove and the rage rose inside him, almost choking him. He clenched the stock of the rebenque.

In the quiet of the evening Estrellita prayed. She arranged the small candles in a circle before the picture. She knelt on the beaten clay floor. She wound the rosary around her two hands and prayed to the Virgin of the Chains, for the spirits of her people. She prayed for Jiménez and for her children, her angels, and for the señora also and her children, who had gone to the other side of the world, to a place where the sky was strange and where the Orishas had no power. In that strange place the Virgin had power.

The Virgin did not speak to her the way the Orishas did. She was silent and calm. She stood in her chains, becoming one with the poor and the oppressed. She would not reveal the future to Estrellita, but she accompanied her when she was alone. She was an Indian, who was worshiped by the white people. It was strange. Perhaps she was the daughter of a cacique, like Aymará. She prayed that the Virgin would take the señor away from them, that she would send him to the other side of the world. There was too much anger in the señor, too much hatred for those he had loved and too much hatred for himself. She prayed that the hatred would go out of him, before he destroyed himself and others. She closed her eyes, listening for an answer.

She felt a heavy blow across her shoulders and heard the crack of a rebenque, shocking her out of her trance. The pain shot through her like fire, paralysing her. She fell sideways to the floor.

"Blasphemous bitch!" She recognised the voice of the señor. She tried to raise her arms to defend herself. The rosary impeded her. The whip fell again, this time on her forearms and the side of her face. She gasped with pain.

He stood over her like a demon from Hell in the candlelight and the smoke from the fogón. He raised the whip a third time.

"Where are your children?" he demanded. She could not breathe to answer him. She tried to sidle away from him into the safety of the shadows. Her light cotton dress fell open. The whip fell across her bare thighs. She looked in horror at the raised weal springing up on her skin. It burned like the touch of the branding iron.

"Where are your children?" he shouted and she knew that he was insane.

"Señor," she gasped. "They are with my parents."

He looked around, lowering the rebenque. He seemed confused. He stared down at her, wiping his free hand across his mouth. He was breathing hard. She was too terrified to move, even to cover herself. A giant shadow loomed behind him, curving across the roof. The giant raised its arm. She waited for the blow, but it did not come.

He groaned a low, guttural sound. He lowered his arm. He backed away from her, feeling his way to the door. His eyes glowed in the light of the candles set before the Virgin. His skin was red, like that of an Indian. He went out into the darkness, never taking his eyes from her. The leather flap fell to. He was gone.

Estrellita crawled to a basin of water and dabbed some on the marks of the rebenque. She was shaking. The water was cool and welcome. She knew why he had come to her. She had known since the night of the fiesta and even before. She remembered how his fine stallion had scented her yegua, how he had tried to be angry with her. If he had asked, she would have comforted him, but now he could never lie with her and it would make him even more mad. She recalled how he had sat on his horse in the ford, watching her bathing with her children in the river.

She let the water trickle over her skin. He was a fine looking man, she thought, but she would not wish to have a baby with him. There was a demon inside him that would never let him be at peace. She touched the weal. The skin was broken. She looked at the blood on her fingertips. Her face was swollen where the lash had caught her. She put aside the rosary. The Virgin had not protected her when she needed protection. He would come back, she knew and she would turn to the other gods to keep her safe.

L aurence hauled the bucket from the well. Water splashed on his boots. He decided to build a windlass to raise buckets. This was too hard on the back. There were so many things to be done. He carried the bucket over and splashed water around the base of the oak sapling, sprinkling some on the flowers that Catherine had tended so carefully.

He could feel the heat building around him. He heard the call of the chicharra. He felt at home. He watched the woman, Estrellita, approaching. She waved her hand. There was something different about her.

"Señor," she called. "Have you seen my Rafael?" Her voice carried in the stillness of the morning. He put down the bucket and hurried towards her.

He could see that one side of her face was bruised. Under her dark skin he could see that the flesh around her eye was blackened and cut.

"Mother o' God, what happened to you, woman?"

She was gasping for breath.

"Have you seen my Rafael?" she asked again.

"Yes, he came early in the morning. He was looking for Señor Cardiff."

She put her hands to her mouth.

"He will kill him."

"Who?"

"Rafael. If he finds the señor he will try to kill him with his knife."

Laurence understood.

"He did this to you? Señor Cardiff?"

He reached out, touching the side of her face. She winced. "He did this to you?"

She nodded.

"I am ashamed," he said.

"No, señor. It is no fault of yours. But Rafael..."

"He is the husband of my niece. He is of my family. I am ashamed." His voice shook.

"It is not important, señor, but my own son is important to me."

"Have no fear. He will not find Señor Cardiff. The señor rode away in the middle of the night. We will not see him for a week or more. I will talk to the boy, before Señor Cardiff returns. We will both talk to him. We must keep them apart. I will see that the señor apologises to you. You have my word. Fierro will talk to the boy also."

She nodded. She was grateful for his concern.

"Rafael is gaucho. This has offended his honour."

"He is a boy. We will make peace between them. It is for his own safety."

She nodded again. She hoped that he was right.

"There is something in the house for that."

He indicated her bruised face. "Come with me. I will get some ointment." He smiled. "And maybe a maté."

She tried to respond, but the effort of smiling hurt. She followed him into the kitchen. He put water to boil on the stove and went to root in a cupboard. He returned with a tin of ointment and carefully applied some to the wound. His fingers were gentle.

"Please, señor." She took the tin from his hand.

He went to infuse the maté, taking his time and inhaling the aroma.

"Good," he said, probing it with the bombilla. He turned to her and saw the cruel weals as she spread the ointment carefully on her thighs.

"Ah good God!" he said, putting down the maté.

She drew her skirts down covering the injury.

"There is one more," she said, turning away and undoing her blouse. "I am sorry, señor, but if you could help me."

He looked at the ridge of skin across her shoulder blades and the smooth curve of her back. There was nothing of the coquette in her request for help.

He took some ointment on his fingertips and spread it across the wound. He felt the soft warmth of her skin. A painted savage, he thought. That was a long time ago. He felt the little bumps of her spine.

"I am grateful, señor," she said, covering herself.

"Ah, yes," he said awkwardly, feeling like a schoolboy. "No, it is nothing." He pulled out a chair, gesturing to her to be seated. He felt ridiculous, a man of his years, to be so embarrassed. He pushed the maté towards her and she drank. He watched her. She passed it back to him. He took a long pull.

"You are old, señor," she said directly. "You remember many things."

"I do," he replied.

"Do you think of the matanza of my people?"

"Every day," he said softly. "I think of it every day."

"And do you forgive yourself?"

At the time it was an adventure, a story to tell. Later it was a regrettable necessity. He had justified it to his peers. The Charrúas had brought it on themselves. They were too wild for the modern world.

"No," he said humbly. "I have not. This eye." He indicated the black patch. "This eye reminds me. I still see it with this eye."

"If you save my Rafael," she said. "If you do not let him go the way of Jiménez, then you may forgive yourself."

"Jiménez? Who is this Jiménez?"

She recounted the story of the colt, how Jiménez had made his fine new boots, how the señor had humiliated him and shot him with his rifle.

"This he will do to Rafael," she said. "He carries the rifle with him all the time."

Laurence pushed back his chair and stood up.

"I will go with Fierro to find him. Rest assured that we will let no harm come to him. You have my word."

He gave a small, formal bow, surprising himself. "Please excuse me," he said, picking up his hat and heading for the door. He blinked at the light, as he walked out from under the porch. Chicharra shrilled at him to hurry. He straightened his back and quickened his step.

Chapter Five

The farm was so much smaller than she remembered it. There were no vast horizons or soaring blue skies; no flowing herds sending up clouds of dust, with teams of gauchos nonchalantly urging them on. That was all like some dream, some story she had heard about a child who had run away from school to a strange, exotic country. She had to strive to recall the sounds and the smells and the excitement of her former home. She tried to communicate it to her father, but it was beyond his comprehension.

He was too happy to have her home, to be interested in such matters. That was all in the past. His life had taken such a turn, from the day that he had looked up from his reaping to see the side-car coming down the narrow road from Tomhaggard. There were children clinging to it and a woman holding a baby. He leaned on his scythe. There was something familiar about the cut of her jib. She waved to him and in fear and trembling he threw down the scythe and hobbled to the gate. The driver helped her down and she stood, holding the infant. She looked at him apprehensively. He put out his arms and came forward wordlessly, to embrace her.

The boys loved the strangeness of the farm. They explored the sheds and lofts, with Richard lifting his younger brother onto the high places. They ran in the upper meadow and drove the cattle in for milking. They explored the tumbledown castle, no more than a tower appended to a farmhouse, where two elderly Doyle cousins lived.

They searched the water meadow for snipe and shot at them with imaginary guns. Harpleats, their new grandfather called them, little darting birds almost impossible to follow with the eye.

They followed the margin of the lake with their mother, passing the cottages on the hill and the noisy forge, until they came to the sand dunes and the sea. She threw flowers into the cutting where the sea broke through into the lake, marsh flowers, that she had picked on the way. They said prayers for the uncles they had never known. They watched the tide tentatively accept the flowers, taking them away in a sudden retreat. The flowers swirled about and were carried out to sea. Catherine watched until they were out of sight.

"This is a dangerous place," she warned. "You must never come here alone."

They nodded silently, sensing her fear. They watched the streaks of foam on the fast flowing surface and they held her hands tightly.

Sarah never accompanied them on their adventures. She tried Catherine's patience to the limit. She sulked around the house, making herself miserable. She was often found in the apple loft where the little window in the gable end afforded a view of the avenue and the road beyond. She wiped the dust from the glass and sat there for hours on end, playing with her toys and humming to herself.

Catherine climbed the ladder and put her head through the trapdoor. She watched the child sitting by the window on an upturned crate.

"What are you doing up here?" she queried gently.

"I'm waiting for my Daddy," said Sarah, turning her back. "He will be coming to take us home soon."

Catherine climbed all the way up. She knelt beside her daughter.

"Daddy is very busy. He has so much work to do. It may be a long time before he can come here."

"I don't care," said Sarah. "I will wait for him."

She pointed. "He will come down the road on his horse, until he comes to the stream. Then he will jump his horse over the stream and he will come straight across the fields to the house and he will take us back home again."

"Do you not like it here?"

"No," she said obstinately.

"Do you not love your grandfather? He is very good to us."

Sarah shrugged and turned away. Catherine wondered if she should try to explain that sometimes people were not happy together, but the child was too young. She tried another tack. She made a story of how she had run away with John to a strange land, how they had got four beautiful children and how John had told her that she should bring them back to show them to their grandfather, because he was so lonely.

"Your Daddy was sad for my father. He wanted him to know you before it was too late. Daddy is a very kind man."

"Then why were you always fighting with him?"

Catherine was at a loss. Her little fiction had rebounded on her under the relentless logic of the child. She took Sarah's hand.

"Take your dolly," she said, "and come down for dinner. It's getting late."

Sarah struggled, trying to pull her hand away.

"No," she cried. "Daddy might come and I wouldn't see him."

Catherine retained her grip. She thought of nailing the trapdoor shut.

"If he comes I will tell you. I will even wake you if you are asleep."

"Promise?"

"I promise. Now come and have your dinner. No matter what time your Daddy comes, I will call you. I promise."

Sarah looked at her closely.

"I will see him first," she challenged. "I bet I will see him first."

"Take your dolly and let's go down," replied Catherine. She hoped that time would dim her daughter's memory, that she would find other things to occupy her. She helped her through the trapdoor keeping her arm around her as they descended the ladder, but on reaching the ground, Sarah twisted free and flounced away from her.

Tom was too diffident to ask what had happened. He held his happiness as one might hold a small creature in the cup of both hands, fearful of crushing it, reluctant to let it go. Out of loyalty, Catherine said nothing of the letters or of John's long deceit.

"I found the life too hard," she lied. "When I got your letter, it was the last straw. I knew I had to come home. It would not have been fair to John to force him to come. He has put so much into the place."

"So will you go back some day?"

She was silent for a while.

"Probably not," she said eventually.

"He is your husband. Your place is rightfully with him."

She poked at the fire. "I've missed a good turf fire," she said.

He let it go. "The offer still stands," he said. She nodded. She turned a sod of turf over in the fire. The flames singed and curled the protruding fibres. She arranged it carefully, watching the sparks.

"Do you still put a goose down the chimney?"

"No," he said laughing gently. "Not since the day it frightened you. I use a bit o' gorse now."

"She smiled at the recollection. It seemed a cruel thing to her, but the goose had emerged, sooty and furious, into the kitchen and she had jumped up on the table in fear.

"So my brother is well," he said changing the subject. "Did he ever say anything about Michael?"

"They just drifted apart, it seems. It is such a vast place."

Tom took out his pipe. He blew through it thoughtfully. "I dare say," he mused.

"But Laurence is well," she consoled him. "He has a home now. He was very good to me. We would often share a maté and he would yarn about home and his travels."

"A what?"

"A maté. It's the tea they drink out there."

"Ah, yes. We tried it but we ended up givin' it to the hens."

"I got very fond of it, I have to say. I wish I had thought to bring some with me."

"You could write to your husband. He could send you some."

She shook her head. "No, the post is not very dependable. There would be no point."

"Hmm," he said, resuming the filling of his pipe. "You know this place is yours, no matter what way the cat jumps. It's good freehold Doyle land and it's for you and your children."

"I know," she said softly, "but we are in no hurry. You'll be around for a long time to look after us."

He lit a scrib, touching it to his pipe. He sat back in his chair and stretched his feet towards the fire. He sighed contentedly.

On a sunny day she took the pony trap and drove the narrow winding road to Kilmore Quay. The boys were excited to see all the boats, the stacks of casks and the comings and goings of a busy fishing port.

They picnicked on the sand, only to be disturbed by foraging ants. They moved further down, closer to the water. She let the boys splash about in the shallows. She resolved to teach them to swim. Estrellita's children swam like little otters. The longing for Santa Catalina struck her, but she would not give in to it. She would bend herself to a life without John.

She watched the dark sails slanting on the horizon and listened to the shouts of her children. Sarah would have enjoyed the day if she had come, but she would not allow herself to experience pleasure. She looked out at the island, where the rebel leader Harvey had hidden with his family after the collapse of the Ninety Eight insurrection. Her grandfather was supposed to take him off to a ship lying to seaward of the island, but the soldiers had found him first. The grandfather saw them setting out and he knew that they had been betrayed.

But not betrayed in the usual way, for money or revenge. They were betrayed by the soap suds, when their maidservant threw the washing water out of the mouth of the cave where they were hiding. It was almost comical, to go on the run with a maidservant, but then the señora should never handle the laundry. Again she thought of Estrellita washing the clothes in the river and how John's betrayal had come to light.

They walked as far as the Forlorn Point. They marvelled at the gaunt ribs of some ship that had come to grief there. It was no more than a skeleton, overgrown with weed and stained with rust. The timber had rotted away from the nails. Iron sickness they called it. Some shipwright had saved a few shillings by using the cheapest nails. The boys clambered inside the rib cage, shouting at each other. They would sleep tonight, she thought.

She bought some fish at the pier. Some of the men recognised her and greeted her warmly, but she knew that they were talking about her when she turned away. She did not care. Her father did not reproach her, so why should she care what anyone thought? She drove home, enjoying the rhythm of the hooves and the swaying of the trap. She hummed a tune. Richard smiled at her.

"You got it that time," he said. "The note." She smiled and patted his head.

"I did. Didn't I?" She was pleased that he remembered.

"Got it that time," echoed William, not knowing what they were talking about. He yawned and rubbed his eyes. She slapped the reins. The pony broke into a trot. The light was fading as she splashed across the stream and turned into the avenue. The bees were returning to the hives with the last nectar of the day. The white gable wall gleamed in the light of the declining sun. She was home again.

She carried William into the house. He was already asleep. Richard ran into the kitchen and stopped abruptly. John was sitting at the table with his arm around Sarah. Catherine froze.

"There, I told you," said Sarah in triumph. "I told you he would come for us. I saw him first." She gave a little dance in her excitement.

They had been eating a meal. Tom Doyle was looking up, his eyes wide with concern. John stood up. He smiled and came to her.

"Catherine, my dear," he said quietly, kissing her on the cheek.

"You have come back," she said unnecessarily. Her heart was cold inside her.

"I have," he said gently. "I have been explaining to your good father that we have had our differences, but that is all behind us now. The fault was all mine as I can see, but I am willing to start again. I will make it up to you."

She looked at her father's anxious face and at her children. Sarah clutched at John's coat. The knuckles of her little fingers were white. She still had baby dimples in her hands. She looked up at her mother.

"I told you he would come back," she said again.

Catherine lowered her head. She was too tired to argue.

"If you say so," she said. He took the boy, William, from her arms.

"There, now," he murmured. "We must get this little fellow to bed." He cradled him gently.

Tom Doyle caught her eye. He raised his eyebrows questioningly. She shook her head. She had nothing to say.

"If you forgive me," said John humbly, "everything can be as it used to be."

She thought of Guidai and how she had spoken of forgiveness. There was something else she had said, or was it Estrellita? The head of the family. They would be at peace. Maybe there was something in her heathen prophecies. There was little else she could do. There was nowhere else to run to. She could not find the words. She nodded agreement. He kissed her again, pretending not to notice how she flinched.

"Well young man," he said to Richard, "show me where I should put your brother to bed." He patted Richard on the head. "Good fellow," he said heartily. "Good to see you again."

He followed Richard up the narrow stairs to the attic bedroom that had once been Catherine's. Sarah went with him, never loosing her grip on his coat. They heard his boots on the floor above and the creaking of the planks. She looked at her father.

"Maybe it's for the best," he said.

"Maybe," she said, sitting wearily at the table. She shook the teapot. It was empty. She was too tired to do anything about it. Tom rubbed the side of his nose.

"There is a farm o' land comin' available on the other side o' the lake. It would be convenient, you know. We could work the two holdings together."

"Wait," she said. "Say nothing just yet."

"Just a thought," he conceded. He fell silent at the sound of John and the children descending the stairs.

Manus Doyle knew the land of Liscreene better than anyone. He had worked that land all his life, for several owners. His wife had worked it, as had his children. The clay of Liscreene was under his fingernails. It clogged in his soul. At night he lusted for that land and tasted the bitterness of envy.

Manus was an angry man. At some time in the distant past he knew that Liscreene had belonged to his people. Somehow it had slipped from their grasp. Now he lived, one of the poor Doyles, in one of a cluster of hovels on the east side of the hill by the forge. The hovels were mostly occupied by Doyles and Manus saw himself in some ways as the chieftain of the poor branch of the family. It was his responsibility to keep old enmities alive, to poke the fires of envy at every opportunity. But his tribe was dwindling as one by one, his children and his cousins drifted away to America. Here and there where a roof fell in, the rough driftwood rafters pointed accusing fingers at the sky.

Manus could remember every cartload of woar that he had loaded on the strand and every harvest that he had reaped. He knew the sleek Friesian cattle that stood knee high in the lush grass of Liscreene. He climbed to the top of the hill in his free moments and, leaning on a stout ash plant, he surveyed the land that should have been his. From his vantage point, he could see the white gable of Tom Doyle's house. That land could have come to his family too, since the two sons were drowned, only the daughter, the wild one, had come back to claim it. But most of all, when he turned his back to the wind, his eyes travelled over the rich acres of Liscreene. He could have bought it too, if those sons of his, the tight fisted bastards, had sent the money from America. Rollin' in money they were, but too mean to remember their father. Everyone in America was rollin' in money.

He looked at the waters of the lake with its margin of swamp. There was talk of draining it, turning it into farmland. His fingers clenched the knob of the ash plant and his palms sweated at the thought. He would give anything to get his hands on some land. He saw the years flying by and he knew that the toil would break him before he could clutch a fistful of his own clay. But what made the bile rise in his throat was the thought of that man Cardiff who couldn't make a go of things in South America, hangin' his hat up in Liscreene, lordin' it over people with his pockets stuffed with Doyle money. He looked at the glassy surface of the cutting and at the weeds streaming with the tide. He wished the curse of Cromwell on John Cardiff, the new master of Liscreene.

Estrellita concluded that she liked her new life. This man was old and he had only one eye, but he was gentle and made no great demands. She had no regrets, since the day he had taken the wooden bucket out of her hand, as she trudged up from the river.

"Allow me," he said in his strangely accented Spanish and she had let him take it. Jiménez would have laughed at the idea, but Jiménez was dead. This man came to her with a lifetime of stories. She began to learn the language of the Inglés. He had some joke about learning a language, which she did not quite understand, but it had something to do with lovemaking. Sometimes, with Jiménez it had been like two tigers locked in a fight to the death, or maybe two dancers moving together in slow harmony, but this Lorenzo was gentle and considerate, like the cardinal bird, always looking back to see that his companion was safe.

He liked to read. He brought books from the house and made wooden shelves of sawn timber. He spent hours splitting a log, laboriously sawing a plank for his shelving. The timber was green. It warped as it dried, so that the shelf twisted, tending to spill the books onto the floor. He placed a counterweight, a large stone at one end and moved the books to a level place at the other.

He would sit in the sun, bending over the pages, following the words with his forefinger. His lips moved silently. She would lean over his shoulder and he would explain the words to her. She would repeat them when she was in a serious mood, but when she was playful she would rub her body against his back and murmur in his ear until he would put the book aside and come inside with her.

"Ah, woman, you are killing me," said Laurence. "You need a younger man."

He stroked her bare shoulder. His fingers strayed to the scar on her back.

"Does it hurt?" he asked.

"No. It is nothing now. Cardiff cannot hurt me ever again. You will prevent him."

"He is gone," said Laurence. "He has bought land in Ireland. We can forget about him."

He stroked the scar again, thinking of the anger that had inflicted it.

"And the señora? She is with him?"

"I understand that she is. Señor Boxwell tells me that they are together again."

"I am sorry for her," said Estrellita, turning towards him. She slid her thigh across his body and he felt himself being aroused again. She moved against him, caressing him gently.

"You would not wager me on a horserace, would you?"

Laurence laughed, "Good God, no. Why do you ask such a thing?"

"Cardiff, he did this thing. He is not hidalgo. He is not gentleman, as you say."

"A gentleman. No, he is not a gentleman. I have heard this story, but I don't believe it."

"Not a gentleman," she repeated carefully. "He is not a gentle man." She pondered the words. "No, it is true. I have spoken to those who heard him. His horse won the race and he received much money. The señora never knew what he had did."

"Done," he corrected. "What he had done."

She rolled on top of him, looking down at him.

"Old man," she said. "You will teach me the Inglés, but I will teach you many things also." She laughed and began to move her body on top of him. He reached up and drew her down.

John Cardiff took his morning ride on the strand. Life was good. He had a good horse under him again. He splashed through the shallows, where the cutting spilled out at low tide. Seagulls rose from their foraging among the weeds, wheeling and screeching overhead.

He saw a figure standing on the hill and scribbles of smoke from the low cottages. He recognised the labourer, Doyle. He had some tasks in mind for the man, a surly, idle fellow, but the best available at the time. He touched the horse with the tip of his rebenque. It responded. Just a tap. That was all that was necessary so long as the horse knew who was master. The waves flickered white at the edge of the tide as he turned towards home and breakfast.

Richard leaned on the pump handle. He heard the valve rattling empty inside.

"Put some more in," he directed and Sarah reached up to pour a jugful into the mechanism. He pumped again. There was a knack in it. He pressed slowly, firmly and felt it grip.

"Aha," he said triumphantly, giving a few short jerks on the handle. Water dribbled from the spout. The pump coughed and sneezed. They laughed. The water came in violent gasps, splashing into the bucket. Richard pumped until it overflowed, although he knew that they would have to tip half of it out to be able to carry it.

Sarah wandered in the long grass under the apple trees. The dew washed her bare feet gleaming white. She picked a handful of windfalls and carried them in a fold of her apron. She smelled one of them, savouring the sweetness and the earthy smell of decay.

"We can give these to our pony when Daddy gets it," she said.

"He won't get it," said Richard. "I just know he won't."

"He will. He will," she insisted. "He promised."

Richard concentrated on his work.

"I love the smell of apples," went on Sarah. "I used to sit in the apple loft in Grandad Doyle's house and watch for Daddy to come. I knew he would come for us. The apples make me think of that day."

"Just don't ask about a pony," said Richard. "He doesn't like people asking for things. It makes him angry."

"He won't be angry with me," she declared loftily. "I was the one who waited for him."

"What if he goes away again? What if he goes back home? I mean to Uruguay." He grappled with the notion of home. "I mean..." He paused.

"I will go with him. He couldn't manage without me."

"And what about the rest of us? Would you leave us all behind?" He was half teasing her.

Sarah said nothing.

"What about Mama? Would you leave her too?"

"We could all go," mumbled Sarah, frightened by the enormity of the decision. "Anyway, that won't be for a long time. We can all go home together. That's what we can do. He promised me that he would take me back some day, so you can come too and William and Michael and Thomas."

"And Mama?"

"She would have to come of course, but she would have to stop fighting with Daddy. She would have to come because she has a new baby inside her. The baby would have to come home with us."

This was news to Richard.

"How do you know that?"

"She told me. It's a secret so you're not to tell anyone."

"Well then," he pondered. "If the baby is born here in Liscreene, that means that this will be the baby's home. We will have to stay here until the baby grows up."

"That won't take long," she said airily. "It didn't take us long to grow up."

"You're not grown up," he scoffed. "You haven't even gone to school yet."

"I don't care," she replied. You think you're great because you go to school."

Richard shrugged. "It's nothin' great. I preferred when Mama was teaching us at the kitchen table with Miguel and Angelita. Do you remember Rafael?"

"He was very wild, wasn't he?"

Richard thought about Rafael. He had looked up to Rafael. It would be good to walk out of school like that, climb on a horse and look down at the master. Just jerk the reins and ride away with your spurs jingling, never to darken the door of the school again. Tangle the master with the bolas, if he tried to stop you. He thought of all the things he could do to the master, if he were a gaucho. The master would have feared Rafael's knife. It was only a daydream. He sighed.

"We will never go back," he said. "This is our home now."

"I will," she insisted. "If my Daddy goes back I will go with him. I don't care. I have to."

"Who will mind you if he gets angry?" queried Richard.

"He will never be angry with me."

Richard tipped the bucket sideways, spilling half the water.

"Give me a hand with this," he said, gripping the handle.

"I can't," she replied, holding her apron. "I have to carry these for my pony."

She walked ahead through the grass of the orchard. Richard struggled behind her with the heavy bucket. The water sloshed and the jug chimed against the side of the bucket. Sarah did not look back. The Grand Cardiffs, his mother said. There was one in every generation. The apples would be well rotted, he reflected, before she would see her pony. It was little she knew.

"*Hic est enim Calix Sanguinis mei,*" intoned the priest as the people bowed their heads. Catherine looked up. It was said that if you asked for something and looked up at the precise moment of the Consecration, that thing would be granted to you.

'The Chalice of My Blood - for the remission of sins.'

It was that same chalice that had lain hidden under the waters of the lake for almost two centuries, a chalice that had come back to comfort people with the promise of salvation. A priest had given his life to save it.

She prayed. She remembered how Mother Alacoque had told them of Christ in the Garden of Gethsemane and how beads of blood had stood out on His brow at the thought of the suffering to come; how He had cried to his Father 'Remove this chalice from Me: but not what I will, but what Thou wilt.'

It was a hard thought, to surrender to the will of another, even to the will of God. She had no will, she reflected. She was tied to John, to her children and to the tyranny of respectability. She could never betray to outsiders what happened within the four walls of Liscreene. She would never give them the satisfaction. She would keep it secret even from her children. Estrellita was wrong. John was very much the head of the family but they were not at peace. She prayed that the cup would pass from her, that she would not be devoured by bitterness, if only for the sake of her children.

She looked over at John. In the fashion of the country, the men knelt at the Gospel side of the church and the women on the Epistle side. His head was bowed. She noticed now in profile, he had acquired a second chin. He was still a fine looking man, tending towards distinguished, with grey hair at his temples. His moustache was greying too. He was dressed in the manner of a prosperous Wexford farmer.

She could not prevent him coming to her at night, even though they slept in separate rooms. On one occasion that she had locked the door, he had kicked in a panel, reaching in to turn the key. She had to invent a story for the children in the morning. She wondered how much they believed. Yet when they were together in the bed she recalled something of the feelings she had had for him and the joy of their lovemaking. It was not a thought for the Consecration, yet it would not go away. Her mind went back to the excitement of running away, their first night together and their coming to Santa Catalina. She wondered what she had done to make it all go wrong.

"*Pax Domini sit semper vobiscum,*" said the priest. She replied silently 'and with your spirit.'

Yet there was no peace, just an abiding fear, like the subterranean mutterings of a dormant volcano. She bowed her head, listening to the droning of the priest.

John squinted at the candles. He rubbed his eyes with finger and thumb. There was a halo of small candles around the statue of the Virgin. His head ached. His bleary eyes saw rays of light streaming from the statue. He closed his eyes again. He could still see the woman backing away from him in the candlelight and the sheen of her dark skin. He could hear the crack of the rebenque and her stifled cry of pain. He had wanted her then and she knew it. The bitch. Unfinished business. Some day, he vowed, he would have her, even if he had to thrash her to within an inch of her life. A witch, half Indian, half African. She would never laugh at him again. Maybe she had put a spell on him, an absurd idea, here in the house of God, in a rainy corner of south Wexford, amid the snuffling and coughing of unwashed peasants. He looked at the statue. The head was turned sideways, looking downwards. She looked disappointed, as if she could see into his mind. She wore no chains. He struggled with his thoughts. Estrellita had suckled his first child. He had seen her sitting in the sun with her breasts bare to the world, like the savage she was. Some day he would break her to his will, as he had broken others, as he had broken the wild criollo horses. He was still the señor. Despite what Boxwell might think, Santa Catalina was still his. Boxwell could wrap the land in the alambre de espinas, in the wire of thorns. He could turn it to a profit, but he would never be the señor. It took a different kind of man to be the señor, the conquistador. Boxwell was too soft. He was no more than a pen pusher. There was unfinished business there too. He would astonish them all some day.

The priest spoke of peace. There was little peace in his soul. He looked across at his wife on the other side of the aisle. He could not spend the rest of his life looking at her miserable face. It angered him to look at her with that constant reproach in her eyes. Long suffering, like the statue of the Virgin. He clenched his fist, sensing his strength. No one would tie him down. A man should take what he wanted while he still had strength in his body.

Catherine put the breakfast in front of him. He was always silent until he had eaten. She was glad to see him attending Mass. It had brought a routine into their lives, punctuating the weeks, something that had been lacking in their former life. He looked at the food thoughtfully. She waited. She felt apprehension rising inside her. There was something wrong. He had fasted too long. He complained that fasting gave him a headache. He took up a fork and speared a sausage.

"I was thinking at Mass about our first meal in Santa Catalina. Do you remember how Fierro brought you a cut from the asado.

"I do," she said, wondering where he was leading.

"Tell us about it," chirped Sarah and he told them again about the journey, the swollen rivers and the man who took off all his clothes to lead the wagons across.

"The baqueano," he said. "He can find his way anywhere, even in the darkest night."

"Are you a baqueano?" asked the child, wide eyed.

"No," he laughed, munching on his food. "Why do you ask that?"

"Well, you come home in the dark and you always find your way home, even when you come across the lake."

"How do you know I come across the lake?"

"I watch for you," said the child simply. "I know you have come across the place where the lake goes out into the sea. I see you coming from there sometimes."

There was a long silence. Catherine looked at him in alarm.

"That is a dangerous place," she said. "You should know better."

"Arrah, I only come across at low tide." He dismissed the matter with a wave of his hand. "It saves me a mile or two."

"You might fall into the water, Daddy," put in Sarah.

"I don't fall off my horse," he reassured her. "Don't you know that I am a gaucho?" He laughed. "Gauchos don't fall off their horses."

"I saw you falling off one night," challenged the child. "I think you were asleep and you fell off in the yard."

"That will do, Sarah," said Catherine sharply. "Finish your breakfast and go outside."

"But he did fall," she insisted. "I just don't want him to fall in the water." She looked from one parent to the other. Catherine put down her knife and fork.

"That will do," she repeated and Sarah saw that she had said too much.

John patted her on the hand.

"Two women watching me now," he said, smiling benevolently. "By the way, I have to go into town this evening. I have a meeting."

"What kind of a meeting would you have on a Sunday?"

"A Home Rule meeting. There's going to be an election. I'm backing Redmond."

"Since when have you been interested in politics?"

"Quite a while as it happens. There will be Home Rule at some stage."

"And everyone will be happy then, will they?"

He inhaled sharply.

"It's a matter of honour," he explained.

"Ah," she said. "I see." She ushered the children away from the table. They ran outside. "It has nothing to do with the fact that you can drink all night in that Home Rule club, I suppose."

He mopped the grease from his plate with a piece of bread. Round and round it went, pursuing every particle of egg and every smear of grease.

"You know what bothers me?" he said softly.

She tensed. He put the bread into his mouth and chewed slowly.

"The thought that I'm going to be looking at your face across the table from me for the rest of my life. It's no wonder I take a drink now and again."

He stood up and came around to her side. He put a hand on her shoulder. She did not look up.

"Expect me when you see me," he said lightly, kissing her on the top of the head. She made no move. She heard him going out. She heard him laughing with the children outside. She looked at the dregs of tea in her cup and the spent tea leaves clinging to the side. She pushed it aside and propped her cheek in the palm of her hand.

Richard touched her arm.

"Don't worry, Mama. I will mind you," he said. "If he falls in the water, I will look after the family."

Wordlessly she patted his cheek. He went to look out the window.

"He's gone," he said, "and I don't care if he never comes back."

"Don't talk like that about your father," she said. He looked at her.

"I know what he does," he said "I hear things."

"You don't understand. Don't talk about your father in that way."

"I still don't care if he never comes back," he said. He went out into the yard. He went down to the margin of the lake. He put up a snipe and aimed at it with a stick. "Bang," he said and the snipe jinked away from him. "Bang," he said again, wishing that they would let him handle the shotgun.

He met his grandfather on his way to the forge. Tom was leading his horse, a docile Clydesdale. He lifted the boy onto the animal's back. His legs splayed wide around the horse's enormous ribs.

"Did you ever sit on a fellow that size?" asked Tom, looking up at him.

"No. In Uruguay we had ponies. Even the horses were much smaller than here."

He gripped the mane, steadying himself against the swaying motion of the horse.

"Do you miss Uruguay?" asked Tom gently.

Richard thought for a while.

"We had friends there," he replied.

"Have you no friends here?"

Richard shrugged.

"Some," he said. "In school. They're all right, except for the Doyles."

"What's wrong with the Doyles?" He knew which ones Richard meant, the offspring of the poor Doyle cousins.

"I don't know. They just don't seem to like us. Sometimes they start fights. I have to mind William. And now Sarah."

"Don't pay any mind to them."

"They say my father hung up his hat. What does that mean? Why do they laugh when they say it?"

"Ah," said Tom. "They're just jealous. It doesn't mean anything. I'm afraid some of our cousins are only churls."

Richard savoured the word. He had never heard it before.

"Churrls," he said, mimicking his grandfather's accent. "I know what Rafael would do to them."

"Who's Rafael, when he's at home?"

Richard told him about the gaucho boy with his long knife, his silver spurs and his distaste for book learning.

"He'd be a dangerous man to have around, I dare say."

Richard kicked his heels into the horse's ribs, but it made no difference to its ambling pace.

"Rafael would show them," he said with a touch of envy.

They went along the waterlogged lane by the lakeside. Tom trudged through the mud, holding the bridle. They passed the cluster of cottages and Richard kept an eye out for the churls. He felt safe on the horse. He wished he had a bolas to entangle his enemies and drag them through the mud. A dog barked at them from a cabin door. A man, leaning on a half-door, raised a hand in greeting. Tom nodded to him and remarked on the weather.

"More o' the same," said the man with a resigned air.

"There'll be a bit o' work over beyond at the harvest, if you're interested."

"I might, at that," conceded the man and the bargain was made.

The man looked up at Richard.

"He'd be one o' them cowboys from America, I suppose," he said good naturedly.

"That he is," agreed Tom, "and a good one too." He patted the horse's neck.

"He has the cut of his Da," said the man. "A grand fella altogether. Sits on a horse just like his Da. The grandest man."

"Oh aye," said Tom. They moved on.

The horse left deep imprints in the mud of the unpaved lane and Tom's boots squelched.

"There now," he said. "That was a cousin of yours too. They're not so bad when you get to know them."

Richard made no comment. He had felt that the man was ridiculing him. Another churl, he consoled himself. He was glad that he had been looking down at him. His father would take no nonsense from them.

"Did you get your pony yet?" asked Tom.

"No. He says he'll get us one, but something always comes up. Sarah collected apples, but they all went rotten."

"They'd only give him wind. If all comes to all I could get it for you."

Instinctively Richard knew that his father would not like that.

"Ah no, Grandad. I think we should wait until Daddy buys it."

"Right so," said Tom, lifting him down as they stopped at the door of the forge.

The forge was built of stone and rough planks, many of them ships' timber salvaged from the strand. The door hung open and sagged at an angle. Wheels and bits of ploughs and other implements, leaned against the walls. Over it hung a great ash tree, hollow and scarred by lightning and yet, clinging to life, pushing out new growth every year, standing defiantly against the storms that raged in from the sea.

Richard looked up at the tree, marvelling that it could still be standing. There was a dark opening, like a cave, at the base and when he put his head in he could see daylight above. Tom explained that because the forge stood on the only high ground in the vicinity and because the clay was full of bits of iron, it attracted the lightning.

The smith, a powerful man in rolled shirtsleeves came out to them. His waistcoat strained across his belly. He lifted his cheesecutter cap and scratched his head. He inspected the horse's hooves and spoke to Tom. He led the horse inside. Richard watched from the doorway as the smith removed the old shoes. The nails squeaked as he levered them out. The smith looked up at him, smiling.

"Always stand close to him," he said. "If you're afraid of him he'll give you a woeful kick." He held the hoof on his lap, resting it on his leather apron. He spoke softly to the horse as he worked.

"Ha, Cardiff," said a voice. Richard looked around. "Never see a blacksmith before?"

It was a stupid question and he ignored it. It was one of the Doyle cousins, who had teased him at school, Ollie, a big soft boy with a malicious twist to his mouth. Ollie could pull your arm behind your back and make you helpless, while he laughed and whispered his insults in your ear. He could twist the skin on your wrist in opposite directions, making it sting like a burn. He was big, like his father, Manus, and carried an inherited resentment of anyone more fortunate than himself. What he lacked in intelligence or fighting skill, he made up for in weight.

"Ha, Cardiff," he said, nudging Richard's shoulder, daring him to take offence.

"Where's your father today, then?" he sneered, searching for a more telling insult.

Richard looked desperately to his grandfather. Tom was bent over the horse's hoof, in deep discussion with the blacksmith. Richard went to move further inside the forge, but Ollie caught him and pulled him out into the sunlight.

"Where's your father today?" he repeated. "Off drinkin', I suppose."

He jolted Richard with a short-armed punch to the shoulder. Richard stepped back and Ollie came after him. What was it the blacksmith had said? His foot struck against a piece of metal. In an instant he stooped and grabbed a length of iron bar, stepped in and struck Ollie a crushing blow across the face. Blood spurted from the bigger boy's mouth. He fell back and tripped. He put one hand to his mouth and spat broken teeth into his palm. He looked up in mute astonishment, putting up his arm to ward off a second blow. Richard stood over him with the iron bar.

"You say anything about my family again and I'll kill you," he said evenly. Ollie saw in his eyes that he meant it. He shuffled backward to a safe distance and got to his feet. He went to say something, but his mouth hurt too much and tears began to flow. He turned and lurched away down the lane. Richard dropped the piece of iron into the weeds. Tom came out into the light.

"That's Manus's young lad," he remarked, looking down the lane. "Did he give you any bother?"

"No, Grandad," said Richard. "No bother at all."

He wiped some rust from his hand. He felt good. He would have no bother from that quarter ever again, he thought.

Chapter Six

Manus came to complain. He showed Catherine the boy's broken teeth, his bruised and sorrowful face.

"That young lad attacked him," he said. "Attacked him with an eeren bar. He's dangerous."

Catherine looked at the boy. He was a couple of stone heavier than Richard.

"There must have been a reason," she protested. "Richard would never do a thing like that without a reason."

"He had no call to use an eeren bar," insisted Manus. "Young lads will voight, but an eeren bar is beyond the beyonds."

Catherine felt a stab of fear. The image of Jiménez flashed into her mind, history repeating itself.

"I'll speak to him, Mr Doyle," she said. "You may be sure of that."

"Aye. It will take more than that. His father should take his belt to him."

"I will deal with this, Mr Doyle," she said stiffly. "You may rest assured. Oliver, I'm very sorry about this. I would like you and Richard to be friends."

The boy shuffled his feet and looked down. There was little likelihood of that. "I'll make it up to you and I'll see that Richard apologises."

"Aye, well," said Manus. "Just see it doesn't happen again. I'll have the law on him if he attacks my lad again."

He turned away and Ollie fell in behind him. Catherine looked after them. Manus turned and spoke sharply to his son. Ollie broke into a trot to keep up with him. He had failed and let someone get the better of him. He had incurred his father's anger.

Had it not been for the severity of his injury he would have felt his father's belt for the shame he had brought on his family by this defeat.

John laughed at the story. It put him in unusually good humour. "Young lads will voight," he said mimicking Manus Doyle's accent. "So they will. So they will. But an eeren bar is beyond the beyonds."

It was true. The Doyles retained much of the Old Talk, which always seemed to amuse him.

"An eeren bar, by God." He went to the door and shouted up the stairs. "Come down here young man and explain yourself."

Richard came warily into the room. He stood by the door. He felt sweat on his forehead. He clenched his fists by his sides and looked at the floor. He began to count the nails in the boards, two by two.

"What's this I hear?" demanded John. "Your mother tells me that you attacked someone today."

Richard nodded. He looked from his mother's anxious face to his father.

"Tell the truth Richard," said Catherine gently. "I have told Daddy that I will deal with you."

It was some reassurance. John lounged in his armchair with his legs crossed. He seemed in a good mood.

"I hit Ollie Doyle," mumbled Richard.

"Speak up, man," said John with mock severity.

"I hit Ollie Doyle with an iron bar."

"Good Heavens!" exclaimed John, "an eeren bar."

"It's not a joke," Catherine remonstrated and John coughed.

"And why, may I ask, did you hit your school friend with an iron bar?"

He placed the tips of his fingers together.

"He's not my friend," said Richard hotly.

"Well, your cousin, then? I'm given to understand that you are blood relatives."

He glanced at Catherine, intending it as a barb, but her face was impassive. He liked to remind her sometimes of her less fortunate relatives.

"He's not my cousin. I don't want him for a cousin."

"Very well. Why then did you strike young Master Doyle with an iron bar?"

John was enjoying himself. He was prepared to play this thing out.

Richard looked at the floor again. "He was jeering me," he muttered.

"Aha!" said John. "Jeering you. And what precisely was he jeering about?"

Richard thought desperately. He knew that his father was on his side. If he repeated Ollie Doyle's jeer about John drinking, who knows what way things might go?

"He said..." he began.

"What did he say?" demanded John, with a touch of impatience coming into his tone.

"He said we shouldn't own Liscreene. He said the land belonged to his people."

It was no lie. Ollie had often made this assertion in school.

"I see. So you smacked him?"

Richard nodded.

"Hmm. His father thinks I should take my belt to you. Even my rebenque. What do you think?"

"I was sticking up for you. It wouldn't be fair." Richard looked at him defiantly. He held his father's gaze.

"Fierro," said John. "We have a man of iron here, my dear." He turned to Catherine, sharing the joke, but she did not smile. "Well Fierro, you will go with your mother and you will shake hands with Oliver and apologise to him."

"But..." Richard protested.

John raised a finger.

"We have decided to offer him some money for good will. Perhaps they can do something with his teeth. So you will shake hands with him."

He sat forward suddenly and punched the palm of his left hand with his clenched fist and laughed. "And every time he tries to eat his dinner he will remember what you did and he will be afraid of you."

Catherine turned away.

"Now go with your mother and do what she says." He stood up and went out, cuffing Richard lightly on the head.

"Fierro," he said, laughing softly. "A man of iron."

Richard exhaled slowly and the tension left him. He felt a great surge of longing for his father. He wanted to go with him. They could do things together as they had done when he was little. His father could hardly put him up on his horse in front of him though. He thought of Fierro the gaucho and was proud.

"It's nothing to be proud of," said Catherine. "What did Ollie Doyle really say? Come on. Tell me."

How did she know? He looked at her in wonder. She demanded the truth and eventually he told her. She hung her head in silence, her thoughts in turmoil.

"You still should not have hit him so hard," she ventured.

"He could kill me if he wanted. He's much bigger than I am. I had to do more than he would. I couldn't let him see I was afraid."

It was his father's logic. Beyond the beyonds. A question of honour. She felt helpless.

"We will go now," she said, rising from her chair. "You will shake hands with him and you will learn to control your temper."

"But I didn't lose my temper," he said reasonably. "I did what had to be done."

She did not press the point, for fear of opening a gulf between them. They went through the fields and down the watery lane to the cluster of cabins.

Ollie shook hands, more in awe of the fact that the lady had come to his house, than in any spirit of reconciliation. Richard did it out of consideration for his mother. Ollie saw in the other boy's eyes a warning that he had better be careful with his tongue. Manus pocketed the money with satisfaction, seeing an apology as a sign of weakness. He did not invite them inside, much to Catherine's relief. They walked home in silence.

The paradox was that she dreaded the days when John was in a good humour. When he was morose he went about the work of the farm with sullen diligence. She learned not to cross him, grateful that there was some kind of routine to their lives. He grumbled about the weather, about prices and about the politics of the day. He could become withdrawn, brooding for days and she could not reach him.

But when something happened to make him feel good he would head off to celebrate. It might be a chance encounter at a fair, or on a business trip to Wexford, or a political meeting, where a man could come close to the fringes of power; a place where a man could feel something of his own individual worth and his value as an indispensable cog in the great political machine. He had heard Parnell speak and was proud to have been in his presence. He had shared a drink with men, whose voices were heard at the centre of a great empire. He was somebody.

It could take him a week to come home from one of his jags, guilty and furious with himself and with anyone who looked sideways at him. Only Sarah could get through to him at these times. She would bring him a bowl of soup where he lay in bed shivering and unshaven. They were almost conspirators.

"Mammy says you should drink this," she said as he heaved himself up on his elbow.

He looked at the soup, grimacing. The room was stuffy with the rancid smell of whiskey breath. Sarah pushed the window up.

"It's a nice day," she said brightly. "You could fly your kite again if you like."

"What?" He took a small spoonful of soup and blew on it.

"You could fly your kite. Mammy said you were out flying your kite."

"Did she now?" He nibbled a piece of bread.

Sarah bounced on the end of the bed.

"Easy now," he said, steadying the tray.

"Will you make me a kite?"

"If you like." He put the tray onto a bedside cabinet and lay back on the pillow. "Later," he said, closing his eyes. "I'll come down later."

"And we'll make a kite."

"Yes, yes. We'll make a kite. Now leave me alone."

He could see them in the meadow with the kite soaring and diving in the blue sky. Catherine would wear her white dress. The children would run in the long grass. The world would be full of laughter and hope.

"And will you get us the pony you promised?"

"Yes, yes. Now let me get some sleep."

Some sleep, before going down to that sour disapproving face with its constant expression of accusation. No way for a man to live.

He tried to concentrate on the meadow and the happy laughing family, but his head ached. He wished the child would go but she wanted to talk.

"Were you very cross with Richard that time he broke Ollie Doyle's teeth?"

"Yes, I was."

"But he says you called him Fierro, the gaucho. He says you weren't angry at all."

"I was angry and I'll be angry again if you don't let me get some sleep."

Sarah stopped swinging her legs. She knew how angry he could be.

"Mammy was worried," she reproved him.

"She's always worried," he growled.

"Do you think Estrellita was a witch?"

"What? What are you talking about?"

"A witch. People said she was a witch."

"Nonsense," he scoffed. "Where did you get this nonsense from?"

"Richard says that Mammy told him she could see things that were going to happen even before they happened."

"Like a witch?" He was intrigued.

"She said you would always come home because you are the head of the family."

"Well, there you are. I am home."

"And that we will be at peace. That's what Mammy told Richard and he told me."

He pulled the covers up around him. He felt old and cold. So that was what she clung to, the ramblings of a half savage washerwoman. He felt a great sadness at what he had given her, a great sense of failure. He would do better.

"Go downstairs," he said to the child. "I will come down in a while and maybe we can make that kite."

He lay back on the pillow and tried to sleep. He heard the door click as Sarah went out. He listened to the silence of the house, thinking of the meadow with the kite soaring against the flying white clouds, but all he could see was the woman bathing in the river with her children and a humming bird probing the bright waxy flowers of the palo borracho. He could see the thorns protruding like blades from the bark of the tree. He heard chicharra's strident call. No one had ever seen the little bastard. The insect reverberated in his skull. He would find him, he determined. Some day he would catch the creature and find out what all the racket was about. He drifted off to sleep to the sound of the river breaking over the stones of the ford and the cries of children playing in the water.

Through the window came the metallic whirr of the reaping machine, as Manus turned the horses on the headland, starting another swathe. Ahead of him walked the children, on the look-out for nests, shouting and waving sticks to drive the corncrakes out of the way of the blades. It was bad luck, Manus said, to kill a corncrake.

Henry Jones felt his heart sink with the disappointment. "Ah no," said the one-eyed man, "they don't live here anymore. No, they went back home a couple of years ago." He spoke in heavily accented Spanish. Henry looked away. The place looked tidier than he recalled. There were neatly enclosed paddocks near the house and an enclosure for calves. There was a well tended flower garden and a fine young oak tree. The one-eyed man followed his enquiring gaze.

"You were a friend of theirs, I take it."

"Yes," said Henry, introducing himself.

"Ah," said the man, switching abruptly to English. "Jones the engineer. I heard about you. The road builder." He put out his hand. "Laurence Doyle," he said. "You might as well come in. I dare say you've been on the road long enough."

Henry felt a childish pleasure at the fact that they had remembered him. He dismounted and stretched.

"Things have changed," he remarked.

"That they have," agreed Laurence, ushering him inside. "The boss is away so I'm keepin' an eye on the place."

"The boss?"

"Aye, Robert Boxwell. He's Cardiff's partner."

"Ah, so they haven't sold up completely?"

For some reason the news made him feel better.

"Estrellita," shouted Laurence, changing to Spanish. "Get this hungry man something to eat." There was a clatter of dishes in the kitchen by way of reply.

Henry made to decline.

"No, no. She'd be offended if you didn't take somethin'. She started cookin' half an hour ago. Said we would have a guest. And here you are."

"So you live here then?" queried Henry.

"No. We just mind it when the boss is away. We have a place of our own."

Henry wondered about the plural and the man's easy air. He sat down and accepted a drink. Laurence stretched himself in the rocking chair, contemplating his glass.

"So what do you hear of the Cardiffs?" asked Henry, impatient for the story.

"Well," said Laurence, taking his time. "I'm sort of, the long lost uncle. I came in towards the end, you might say." He spoke of the letters, of Catherine's distress and how she had fled in the night. Henry listened intently.

"I have to say, I thought he treated her shabbily from the beginning. I don't wish to engage in backbiting, but there was an episode in Mercedes, some wager over a horse. I thought it quite disgraceful." Henry sighed. "She was little more than a child at the time. I have to say I thought him a bit of... a bit of..." He was reluctant to speak ill of Catherine's husband. "No, there is no other way to put it. He was a scoundrel. A young scoundrel."

He took a sip of his drink, dismayed by his own vehemence. Laurence regarded him with interest.

"What brings you here anyway?" he asked.

"Oh, the railway. There are plans to run a railway to Fray Bentos."

"An English railway, I'll be bound."

"Of course. They are the only ones with the money."

"When will this be?"

"It should have been done ten years ago but there was too much commotion in the country. Perhaps another five or ten years. I can't say for certain. I'm not privy to these things. I just survey the ground."

"I see. Will it pass near this place?"

"Probably," said Henry shortly, more interested in getting back to the story. Estrellita interrupted them and they went into the kitchen. He was surprised to see that the servant sat down with them, surprised too by the easy familiarity between the pair. He regarded the steak that lay in front of him.

"Have some praties," invited Laurence, passing a bowl of boiled new potatoes. Henry realised that he was starving.

"We grow a few down by the river," explained Laurence.

"I grow them," interjected Estrellita. "This old man sits in the sun and gives me advice. He says the potato is from Ireland, but I tell him he is a fool."

Henry concentrated on his food. He wanted to get to the subject of Catherine, but not in front of the servant, however familiar she might be.

"When I was last here," he began, "there was an Indian woman working for Mrs Cardiff. What became of her?"

"That was my mother, Guidai. She went with my father Fierro."

"The gaucho? They left? Why was that?"

"It was too much for them, the alambre de espinas. My father, he tried to be a farmer but he could not. He could not walk with his spurs and he did not like to be without them. He did not like to open and shut the gates every time he went on his horse. He had stayed too long, so one day he took my mother behind him on his horse and he left. With him went my boy Rafael, who also would not be a farmer."

"But you stayed. Why did you not go with them?"

She looked at him frankly. "I have work to do here. I have things I must do for Señora Cardiff and I have found this old man, who loves me very much."

She put her hand on Laurence's arm, smiling at him. "So I stay here."

Henry cut his meat carefully into squares.

"I'm on probation," said Laurence lightly. "If I behave myself, she will let me stay." He laughed.

"I see," said Henry slowly. "I see."

"You have come because of the señora," said Estrellita, looking him in the eye.

"To pay my respects, yes. To see if I could be of service to her, yes."

"You can be of service to her. She is not happy. You can help her some time."

"If I can help her in any way, of course."

He felt uneasy about discussing such matters with a servant, no matter what irregular relationship she might have with Catherine's uncle.

"It's all right," said Laurence. "Estrellita can read between the lines."

"How do you know she is not happy in her new life?"

"There was one letter, maybe a year ago. I could tell from the tone. She has six children now." He shrugged. "So I suppose things must be all right between them some of the time."

"No," interjected Estrellita. "His love for the señora died when he discovered his own weakness. He punishes her for his own weakness. These children did not come from love."

"You're not suggesting…" He did not know what she was saying. "I mean she loved him very much as I recall. I would never have regarded him as weak."

"Yes, she loved him. She still does, in a way. She still hopes that he will become the man she thought he was and he punishes her because he will never be that man."

"No, no. I cannot accept what you are suggesting. He has his faults but he would never lay violent hands on a woman."

A look passed between them and Henry knew that it was true. He remembered how Catherine had flinched from John's touch. Damn the man! He was a scoundrel. There was no other word for him.

"I could show you the letter," offered Laurence. "You can read it yourself. I'll go and get it for you." He got up from the table, leaving Henry sitting awkwardly with Estrellita. Laurence went out into the sunlight heading towards the ombú grove.

Henry looked about. He noticed a cracked tile. He coughed. "So your parents have gone and your boy. You must miss them."

"It was better for them to go. I would not want them to go into the city. They would be nothing in the city only poor country people. In the north they are still themselves."

"And the other gauchos? Are they still here?"

"Some. They have become farm workers. It is not the same. Soon there will be only machines, I think."

"Not for a very long time," Henry consoled her. "There will always be need of horses and good men."

"But you are bringing this machine that runs on the iron. Nobody will need horses when this thing comes."

Henry pondered the situation. He wished the man would return.

"You wish your boy to remain a gaucho?"

"I wish him to be himself. He may become a bandit. I do not care so long as he is happy. I do not want him to belong to anyone else. He must do what his heart tells him."

"I see," said Henry, not at all sure that he did. The boy might become a bandit, to be hunted down by the military. It would perhaps have been better to stay in the security of a steady job.

"And you, señor. Have you done what your heart tells you?"

"Look here! I say! This is preposterous."

"You have come here out of your love for the señora." She raised the palm of her hand, stifling his indignation.

"Perhaps if you had come to her sooner. Perhaps if you had spoken of what is in your heart you might also be happy."

Henry tried to protest.

"You know that what I say is true."

His head spun. He saw himself reflected in her dark pupils, two insect sized images of himself.

"You may still do something for her," continued Estrellita. "Some day I will send you to her with a message and you must go. No matter what you are doing you must leave it and go or she will never be at peace."

"Yes," he said. "I will." Hope sprang inside him. He blinked and looked away. "You may call on me at any time, if I may be of service to Señora Cardiff."

He phrased his words carefully, fearful of what he was thinking.

She smiled. "That is good," she said rising to begin tidying the table.

My Dearest Uncle, Henry read. He adjusted his reading glasses, conscious of their eyes upon him.

I write to you to let you know that I am well and to say that I hope you are too. I hope you have moved back into the house, as I know you could not be comfortable in your little rancho. I am happy to think that you would treat our house as your own.

I have six children now, five boys and Sarah. They are well too and getting very big. We have the farm, Liscreene, fornenst my father's land. It is good land as you may remember. If you could see us you would think we were gendrize.

I am very skilled at making things. I make all the clothes for myself and the children. You would be proud of how I manage. My father is well too but he is getting old. He has been very helpful to us, but is not able to do too much any more. The boys help him as much as they can and he has men working for him, some of the cousins from down at the forge. A lot of the cousins have gone to America and are doing well there. I am glad for them as life has not always been good to them here.

There are so many things I want to write about. I think of you often and of our lovely home. Please, remember me to Fierro and Guidai and their daughter, Estrellita. I remember their kindness to me at all times and I think of the days when I used to teach the children their letters. I wonder if Rafael ever went back to the books. I doubt it. Please ask his mother to remember me to him if you see her. My father asks if you have ever heard of Uncle Michael. I suppose not. The pampas is a very big place. I hope he has found a home as you have.

If you write to me, write care of my father at Lingstown or care of the post office at Bridgetown. The woman there is a friend of mine and will keep the letters for me. I hope you are attending to my garden. I can see it still when I close my eyes and I can hear the sounds of Santa Catalina. When I am tired or downcast I close my eyes and I am there.

    My love to you,
     Catherine.

Henry removed his glasses and folded them. He rubbed his eyes. He slipped the glasses into his top pocket. "Gendrize," he said. "What does that mean?"

"Gentry," replied Laurence. "It's an old dialect word, the Old Talk of South Wexford, where we come from."

"I see." He saw her fading from him, sinking back into dialect, ensnared in a strange language.

"It's her little joke," said Laurence. "She is having a little joke at her own expense. It is a little joke from home to cheer herself up."

"I see," said Henry again. It cheered him too to think that her spirit was still strong.

"Gentry. They must be doing well all the same. Did you write to her?"

"Ah, I did. I'm not much of a hand at it, but I did. I told her all the good news and how things are going here, more or less. The boss writes regularly to himself."

"I notice she never mentioned him. I presume he is still there."

"Oh, he's there all right. You can tell from the way she never mentions him. Maybe some day he'll take a vagary. She'd be better off if he did."

Laurence told him of the saying about the Grand and the Mad Cardiffs and the ways of the Irish gentry.

"You need money for that carry on. Me bucko knows what side his bread is buttered on. He's waitin' to get me brother's land too and then we won't be able to talk to him for gosther. Gentry, how are ye."

Henry listened to the diatribe, not quite sure of the nuances, but he appreciated that the tone was in general, derogatory. He pictured John as a corpulent and debauched minor squire, breaking the back of his horse as he rode to hounds. The idea comforted him in a spiteful way, but always, his thoughts came back to Catherine and her plight. He imagined himself going to her and taking her away, with her children. Six children. It gave him pause. Six children would somewhat disturb his bachelor existence. It was not a practical idea. He revised his daydream. She was embroiled in family life. She would never leave her children, no matter what happened, but some day, he reasoned they would leave her. He wished that he was more impetuous, less careful, more in fact, like John Cardiff, in a way.

"You will go to her, when I ask." Estrellita broke into his reverie. It was almost as if she could read his thoughts. He nodded.

"We will leave you, señor. Your bed is prepared. We must go home."

They rose to go and Henry got to his feet. He gave a polite little bow to Estrellita. He concluded that he had underestimated her and wondered, with unwonted humour, if Laurence had told Catherine all his good news.

He lay for a long time listening to the sounds of the night. He thought of Catherine. He saw her clearly as he had first seen her, a child in her hooded school visite, on the wet, sloping deck. She was clinging to the rail, bracing herself against the roll of the ship. Her hair blew across her face. She brushed it aside. Her cheeks were red from the wind. He had never seen a creature so beautiful and happy and his heart had lurched inside him.

He cursed himself for the careful, pedantic fellow he was. He had named the stars for her, explaining how they moved in the blackness of space. He heard their music, but he could not dance to it. He had seen her hurt in Mercedes when the wretched fellow had gambled a kiss for the horse and he had followed with the maidservant instead of striking him down in the dust as he deserved. He had seen her, a grown woman, dueña of Santa Catalina, yet flinching from contact with the man. A cold hatred suffused him as he thought of what he would like to do to him.

He pictured the ocean that lay between them, the gale whipping the spray from the crests of the waves and he swore that some day he would find the means to go to her and avenge the wrongs that had been done to her. But he did not know what to do. Maybe Estrellita would know. She seemed to understand, as if by instinct. A wild trick of her ancestors. He could not remember where the phrase came from. He drifted off to sleep dreaming of the ocean and sails booming in the wind.

Sarah could remember the day things changed for her. It was the day he made the kite. She knew now that he was drunk at the time, but then she thought he was being funny. He had taken a linen blind from the sitting-room. It was a room they rarely used. He said nobody would notice. He cut it up with a razor blade and got some laths to make the frame.

"Just wait till you see this," he said, gluing the thing together. "I was always a great hand at kites."

He whistled as he worked. She watched him with rising excitement. She had always loved his plans and adventures. She remembered how they used to go on expeditions to the pulpería with their ponies. He would whistle or even sing, when they were riding home. Sometimes it was dark when they got home. She thought of how she had loved her magnificent stumbling father and how he would laugh, steadying himself at the door.

The kite would be fun. They could fly it in the meadow. They would all be friends again and there would be no more fighting.

He surveyed his work proudly.

"There now, I told you," he said holding it up. "That's how the Chinamen make them." He rolled the flittered blind and replaced it on the hooks. He tapped the side of his nose, inviting her into a conspiracy. "Not a word to your mother. She'll never notice."

Sarah giggled at the enormity of their secret. They went outside. There was a stiff breeze off the sea. The kite fluttered at his side, struggling to escape. The boys came to watch. He handed the kite to Richard telling him to hold it aloft, while he ran backwards, putting a tension on the string.

"Up," he shouted. Richard released the kite. It jerked skywards, then whipped through a quadrant of a circle and hit the ground. He ran to inspect it and tried again. It took erratic flight only to settle gently into the long grass. He removed some twists of newspaper from the tail, little bow ties, intended to give stability. This time it rose and then swooped low in a circle like a wild horse on the end of a lunge rope. It hit the ground. The frame was knocked slightly askew.

"Damn!" he muttered and set the frame to rights. He eyed the angles and pronounced it airworthy. "It will fly, if we have to stay here all day." He bit his lower lip in annoyance.

They launched again, with Richard jumping as high as he could to give it a start. It swung upwards as he paid out more string. The children cheered and clapped. The kite jigged and lurched. It fell out of shape. It swooped and dived, skimming over their heads. The tail of newspaper flailed behind it. They ducked. It came back at them and they scattered.

She could still see little William running. His bare white knees bobbed as he struggled through the long grass, like someone running in a nightmare. He looked up at the kite. It seemed to turn to attack him. It dived at his legs and in panic he kept running, kicking the frail framework to matchwood, as it entangled him, until the kite was a dead thing, a bundle of litter in the grass among the buttercups and pale blue cornflowers.

Then his father beat him.

"What did you do that for you little ...?" He used a word that she had never heard before. "You little bastard." It was a venomous word. The boy was too terrified even to cry.

"It wasn't his fault," said Richard but his father rounded on him.

"Do you want the same, you young pup? Keep a civil tongue in your head."

He shook William by the shoulder, pushing him in the direction of the house. "Get inside you," he said and the boy ran a couple of steps under the impetus, then stopped, unable to decide where to go. Sarah realised that she had not moved. She had been laughing when the kite landed in front of William. She had her hands to her mouth in shock.

"Get inside," he shouted again. The words blasted William backwards. He closed his eyes. She could see that he was shaking.

She found herself moving forward. She took his hand.

"Come on William," she said and he followed her.

"Get inside the whole damned lot of you," he said. "That's the last time I'll make anything for you. Ungrateful pups." He kicked the wreckage of the kite and swore. The children hurried towards the house. Sarah looked back. He was looking after them. She quickened her pace.

They went inside. William burst into tears. They made a protective circle around him, unable to think of anything to say. Sarah patted him awkwardly.

"He didn't mean it," she said but she knew that her words were hollow. It was part of the business of keeping things going, that they had all unconsciously subscribed to.

Catherine found them. She asked what had happened. Richard explained. She hugged William and wiped his tears.

"That does it," she said, standing up. She set her jaw in a way that they had never seen before and went outside, but he was gone by the time she reached the meadow.

Sarah remembered the day in every detail and how she had watched for his return. She prayed for the first time, that he would not come back. Not until his anger had cooled. She prayed that her mother would say nothing. William had recovered, although he sniffed at times to remind them of what he had suffered.

But he came home and there were loud voices in the night and she closed her eyes, wishing that they would stop. She remembered how she had watched from her grandfather's loft, wishing for her father to come home. She recalled the sweet smell of the apples. She thought of the apples she had stored for the pony that never came and she sat at the window and prayed that he would fall from his horse, where the tide cut through into the lake as the land gave way to the sea. She wished that the water would sweep him away and she knew that she would go to Hell for wanting this thing, but it would be worth it to see the oppression of her mother taken away.

She could no longer abide the smell of apples. It made her sick inside. She remembered the little, slow moving flies that emerged from the brown, decaying apples and how they died in droves, on the cold window panes, with the first frost of autumn. She longed for the father she remembered and wondered where he had gone astray. She wanted to go with him in the moonlight, with her brothers on their ponies and William safe in his arms, singing as they crossed the river, looking up at the ombú grove and the lights of home. But he had taken all that away, kicking it to pieces like the shattered kite in the meadow.

Sarah had a sense of grim foreboding. Richard was to go away to school. He was finished with the local master. His mother insisted that he would go to Wexford as a boarder, to make something of himself. Richard resisted, saying that he would stay and work the land for them; that he was big enough to do a man's work. His father grumbled about the expense, but was prepared to put up with it. She knew that her father respected Richard and was to an extent, wary of him. It was something about the boy's quiet determination. They all drew on Richard for something and Sarah wondered how they would manage when he went away.

She went to talk to Richard for reassurance, where he sat on the high-backed settle, cleaning his shotgun. He was so proud of that gun. His grandfather gave it to him, showing him how to use it and how to respect it. Richard was looking forward to Autumn and the shooting, refusing to accept that he would be incarcerated in school, as the geese honked overhead and the snipe darted in the long reeds.

John drove homewards in a cold fury. He had heard them laughing about him in the hotel. 'A fine speech,' they said, 'but Cardiff has no bottom. All for show, but a toper nonetheless. A country farmer aping the gentry.' They were wrong. He would show them. He wished that he had ridden to town, but he was not so comfortable on horseback anymore. He accepted that he was getting heavy. It gave him something of a presence, but it precluded him from taking the short cut across the mouth of the lake.

He passed the entrance to Tom Doyle's lane. The old scoundrel was taking his time about dying. John thought of how he could use Tom Doyle's money, but the old man was disgracefully healthy, if a little slow on his feet.

He resented Tom too, because Tom had done the things he knew he should have done himself. He kept a pony for them on his land. He taught the boys to shoot and took them to the hurling. He drove Catherine to church as often as not and the children looked to Tom when things were difficult. He fixed their toys and told them stories of the old days, of Catherine and her brothers, of his own brothers in South America and of the Wexford sailors who went to all parts of the world.

Tom Doyle had robbed him, John concluded. He had deprived him of a father's right to the affection of his children. He had poisoned their minds against him and listened to the endless whining of their mother. All because he had put up the money for Liscreene. Expected a man to be down on his knees in gratitude for the rest of his life.

He put his hand in his pocket and drew out his brandy flask. Engraved silver, a shrewd investment, that came in handy at horse races or dreary political meetings. It dulled the boredom of the other speakers and sharpened his wits for the fray. He had put down many a heckler with the aid of that flask. He drained the last of the brandy. It put a finer edge on his sense of injustice. They were draining him dry. Doyle should look after the school fees, since he put himself in the place of their father. Maybe the boy could go in as a scholastic; feign a vocation to the priesthood; hoodwink them for a free education. The idea amused him. He would put it to Catherine. He remembered a fellow who had done that, but the plan backfired. Backfoired. Where had he heard that before? Yes, it backfoired. He was turfed out on a decimation. Every tenth man turfed out, for somebody else's offence. A kind of poetic justice. Still it could be worth a try.

He dismounted and opened the gate. He led the horse through. He noticed that the bridle was worn and shabby. He went back to close the gate. It always irritated him, this opening and closing of gates. It more than irritated him. It made him angry. He was used to wide open pampas. He would show them.

He climbed back into the trap. He was breathing hard from the small exertion. He rapped the horse's haunches with his rebenque and rattled along the avenue to the house. He was in time to catch Manus Doyle, the idle scoundrel, sneaking off home. He gave him charge of the horse and went inside.

Catherine looked up from her sewing. She knew that he was annoyed about something. She waited. He threw his hat down on the table and clattered the rebenque beside it. The fine silver handle shone in the lamplight. The rebenque was an affectation, which annoyed her. He carried it instead of a whip, a serviceable instrument in its proper place, in the hands of a gaucho, but in Wexford it was just looking for notice. Putting on airs.

"You could tidy this place up," he growled.

"I'm working," she retorted. The room was impeccable. She looked at this stranger in her house, a heavy-set florid man with a flowing moustache. His collar was too tight and the buttons of his waistcoat strained. He reminded her of someone she had once known, a fair-haired boy, who laughed and quoted Tennyson. He once stood on a bollard in the rain and promised her the world.

"Working? What is this?"

He snatched the half-made garment from the table. A pin stuck into the ball of his thumb. He swore.

"It's for Richard," she said. "It's a jacket for school."

"No son of mine is going to school in home-made clothes." He flung the garment to the floor. "He will dress like a gentleman."

"If you gave me the money," she said, her face white with fury, "I wouldn't have to make everything, would I? If you weren't off gallivanting and making your silly speeches and throwing money away at the horses and buying drink for every corner-boy in Wexford…" She paused for breath. "And God knows what else you get up to."

"How dare you speak to me like that? he roared catching her by the arm. Spittle flew from his lips. "Don't ever speak to me like that."

To Hell with it, she thought.

"So they turned you down," she laughed. "You didn't get the nomination. Maybe you should have taken your rebenque to them. That would knock the smirk off their faces."

He gasped for breath. His eyes bulged with rage and she thought he would choke. He seized the silver handle and brought the lash around savagely. She fell under the force of the blow.

He raised it again, bringing it down with all his strength across her shoulders. She put up her hand to ward off another blow. He stood over her, looking down, as he drew back to strike.

She saw murder in his eyes. She saw the plates on the dresser and the low beams of the ceiling. There were horse brasses and a little horse shoe for luck, nailed to the beams. She saw the plates disintegrate into a million fragments. The fragments flew out from the shelf like a burst of stars, as a shot reverberated in the room. The fragments cascaded musically to the stone floor, blue and white, Willow Pattern, coloured Indian Tree, her favourites.

She saw John frozen into immobility with the rebenque still raised above his head. She thought of a statue of a Trojan warrior, an illustration from *The Graphic*.

"Enough," Richard said. "That's enough."

The statue came slowly to life. John lowered his arm. He turned to the boy.

"If you do that again I will kill you," said Richard evenly. "It stops now."

John gasped for breath. He tugged at his collar. He looked at Richard in astonishment, trying to muster his anger for a fresh confrontation.

"I have another barrel," said Richard. "If you raise your hand again to any of us, I promise I will kill you."

Catherine got to her feet. She looked from one to the other and at Sarah who was standing with one hand raised against the back of the settle. The boy held the gun level. He did not blink.

John threw the rebenque on the table. "Put that thing away," he said gruffly. He worked at the cravat and removed his high wing collar. He looked at the collar studs in the palm of his hand.

"There's no need for that," he said, sitting down wearily. He jiggled the collar studs in his fist. "There's no need for that," he said again and his voice was flat.

Richard lowered the gun and broke it open. Sarah sneezed at the smoke. Catherine clutched at her shoulder. The pain went right through her, even to the tips of her toes, but she would not cry. She motioned to the children to go out. She looked at her husband, but he would not meet her eye.

"So I was right then. You didn't get the nomination."

"You were right." He gave a bitter laugh. He tossed the studs, like dice, onto the polished table-top. "Home Rule will have to come without my help. They were laughing at me." He gathered the studs again and shook them. He tossed them and Catherine felt her irritation rising. She was no longer afraid of him.

"About that," he began awkwardly. "About what happened there."

"We can talk about that in the morning."

"I didn't mean to…"

"It doesn't matter. We can talk about it in the morning. I'm going to bed."

She turned at the door. He was still sitting, jiggling the studs in his hand. His eyes stared vacantly at the polished surface. She closed the door quietly and went to bed.

In the morning he was subdued, almost humble. He ate his breakfast in silence. He looked at the children with a hang-dog expression, but said nothing to them. Catherine almost laughed in his lugubrious face. She knew that he would go through his phase of contrition, before becoming his old self. But this time it would be different. She knew that he had believed Richard; that he had come to a turning point. Things, she was sure, would be different from now on. He stood up diffidently.

"That bridle is badly frayed," he said. "It could be dangerous. I have to go and get a whole new harness." He hung his head, still not meeting her eyes. "If there is anything you want from town." He scuffed the toe of his right boot on the floor.

"No," she said. "I don't think so." He went to the door.

"Oh yes," she remembered. "We need tea. Bring back some tea."

He nodded. He looked at his family as they sat around the breakfast table. The children stared at him, wondering about the events of the previous night. The smaller children were still in their night shirts. They had spoons in their hands.

"Tea," he said. "Right." He nodded to them and went out, closing the door quietly behind him. They never saw him again.

As the days passed, Sarah feared that her prayer had been answered. They searched the beach and even dragged the lake, but there was no sign of him. There were no wheel tracks on the beach where he might have taken a short cut. Tom Doyle looked out to sea where his two boys had been lost. He would not wish that fate on any man, even his son-in-law. He went back to where the men were dragging the lake with a grapple. The water was too shallow to hide a horse and trap.

He went further afield, enquiring of everyone he met by the roadside. Eventually he came to the town. He was always a bit diffident in this busy seaport, always a bit nervous as a countryman, of going over the mountain to Wexford. It was no great mountain, but big enough to make him feel a stranger.

He went to the Peelers, but they had nothing to report. He went to the bank. They told him that Mr. Cardiff had been in right enough, but obviously, they could not discuss his affairs with anyone. That was reassuring in a way. He went back again to the Peelers in desperation.

"Ah yes," said the constable. "We made some enquiries. That Mr. Cardiff. We know him all right. A great man for the politics. Yes indeed. We had a report that he was seen boarding the Liverpool boat about a week ago. Yes, last Tuesday to be exact."

The Liverpool boat, thought Tom. Maybe this time it was all for the best. He felt a kind of relief and headed home to break the news.

So Estrellita was wrong, thought Catherine. The head of the family was gone and yet they were more at peace than before. He was gone and she was short of tea. She would have to do something about that. She felt her spirits lifting. She was glad that she had not gone with him on the Liverpool boat. She wondered where he would go, what money he had taken with him and what he had left in the bank. She asked her father to drive her to Wexford to begin the task of putting her affairs in order.

"I'm afraid he can, Mrs. Cardiff," said the bank manager. "As the law stands, everything belongs to your husband."

Catherine sat in stunned silence. The manager watched her anxiously. He felt like a traitor. As a boy he had pulled the legs off a daddy-longlegs. One at a time, until the insect was reduced to a leg on one side and a wing on the other. It had been fine amusement, but he still remembered how guilty he felt. He had stepped on it to obliterate his guilt. He thought of it now. He coughed.

"And the South American money," he said.

Her eyebrows went up. She stopped twisting her handkerchief.

"What South American money?" Her voice shook.

"We received a bank draft every six months from a Mr. Boxwell in Montevideo, in favour of your husband."

So Robert had turned a profit after all and was too decent to conceal the fact.

"We can show you the figures," said the manager, slipping into the plural, as if to spread the blame among others. "It was quite a respectable sum."

She made a dismissive gesture. So that too was gone.

"It's not important anymore."

The manager rose and went to the door. He called the porter ordering him to bring some tea for Mrs. Cardiff. He spoke sharply, as if the fellow had fallen down on his work. He returned to his desk. There was more. Just the last wing and the creature could hobble away with its solitary leg.

"You are aware…" he began. There was no other way to put it. She was a fine looking woman still, he thought. "You are aware that he has sold the farm." The leg, not the wing. It buzzed in a circle.

She shook her head.

"I don't understand."

"Confound the man," said the manager, going to the door. "Where the Devil is that tea?" he shouted. Customers in the main hall looked in his direction in alarm. He sat down again drumming his fingers on the desk, wishing himself elsewhere.

"Liscreene. He sold Liscreene?"

The manager looked at the papers on his desk. "I'm afraid so," he mumbled. "Some American gentleman, he told me. From Cincinnati, I believe. Yes, Cincinnati."

Accuracy was important in matters of business. He shuffled some foolscap sheets, tapping them into a neat bundle, making sure that all the edges were in line.

"Yes indeed. Cincinnati."

The porter brought a tray with tea and biscuits. The manager directed him to put it on the desk. He thanked him twice, regretting his outburst.

"Thank you," said Catherine. Her mouth was dry. Her cup rattled in the saucer as she lifted it. 'Tea, right.' That was the last thing he had said to her. She drank. He would never hurt her again. It was a heavy price to pay, but he was gone.

"We don't owe anything to the bank, then?" she asked.

The manager shook his head.

"Good," she said. "That's a good start." She heard herself saying the words and wondered where they had come from. There was nothing more he could do to hurt her. He could go to Hell. She put down her cup and stood up. She swayed and steadied herself. The manager made a convulsive move to take her arm, then drew back, anxious not to offend. She took a deep breath.

"When can I expect the gentleman from Cincinnati?" she asked with a wry attempt at a smile.

"I'm afraid I have no idea," said the manager. "That would be a matter for the lawyer."

He showed her to the door and shook hands, assuring her that he was at her service at any time. He watched her going down the steps. She held her head high. Her back was straight. He retreated to his office and put the file in his desk. He finished his tea. It had gone cold.

Catherine heard the pounding on the door. It was the front door. She had been waiting for it. She opened it. Manus Doyle stood on the step with his stout ashplant in his fist. His son, Oliver, stood slightly behind him, grinning with a mouthful of jagged teeth.

"I want you out by the end of the week," said Manus. Oliver's eyes were bright with triumph.

"What is this, Manus?"

"Liscreene belongs to us now," said Manus. "I have the papers, if you want to see them."

"No, that won't be necessary." It made no difference who took the roof from over their heads. "We'll remove as soon as we can."

"The furniture is ours," said Manus. "Every stick."

She nodded. "Very well." It would be a kind of relief to be shut of the place.

"By the end of the week, or I'll have the bailiffs in." He turned away and Oliver fell into step behind him. He stopped and rubbed his chin. Oliver said something and Manus cuffed him heavily behind the ear. He came back, taking off his hat.

"You were always fair to us, Mrs. Cardiff. You can take as long as you need."

He shuffled his feet awkwardly. He was not enjoying this as much as he had imagined.

"Take as long as you need."

"I appreciate that, Manus," she said softly, "and I hope you have better luck here than we had."

He looked closely at her. He saw that she meant it. He had come to gloat, but he could not.

"Aye," he said, "and thank you M'am."

He put on his hat and turned away. He walked briskly, with Oliver keeping his distance.

Catherine leaned against the door frame. She watched them until a bend in the avenue took them from her sight.

"This is your home," said Tom. "Of course you'll stay here." "But we will be in the way. You won't be able for the noise."

"I've had me fill of silence," he said simply. "Sure, where else would you go?"

"I don't know. I wanted them to get an education."

"And so they will. So they will."

She wanted him to say she had brought it all on herself. She wanted his absolution.

"I know what you're thinkin'," he said. "You're thinkin' you brought this on yourself."

She nodded.

"And now you've been punished. Isn't that so?"

She nodded again.

"Well then, that's that. You're still a young woman. You have fine children and you have your health. You can't blame the child that you were at the time, for everything that happened."

It was a new concept. She had once found a snake skin on the ground. A víbora, down by the river. She had always been a bit worried about snakes in the long grass. Estrellita had shown her the places to avoid. It was like a long glove of the kind that fashionable ladies wore. The scales were translucent, with a pale imprint of the original pattern. She had picked it up out of curiosity, but had not liked the feel of it. It was as if the snake had wriggled free of its old self, leaving it to bleach in the sun.

"I will be all right," she said. "I am well able to work."

"And tell me one thing," said Tom gently. "Would you have missed it for the world?"

"He was so beautiful," she said and for the first time, the tears came. "I miss him, but I don't want to see him ever again. I miss the man he used to be."

"There now," said Tom awkwardly. "You're safe here. You're stronger now than you were then. I'll back you, whatever you want to do."

There was absolution but no blame. If there was fault, it lay with the child she had left behind, the child who had seen the world turning under the vast dome of the stars, the child who had put everything on the hazard for the love of a boy, who shone like an angel. She wept for the child she had once been and for the boy who had slipped away, like the snake, sloughing off his old, diaphanous skin.

Chapter Eight

He drank by himself in the saloon but it did nothing to lift his spirits. He dined alone, avoiding the other passengers, inviting none of the usual shipboard familiarity. He travelled first class at thirty five pounds sterling for a single fare. He was not troubled by sea sickness on this fine, new twin-screw steamer, cutting through the waves at seventeen knots. The ship did not roll and pitch like the paddle steamers of old. He stepped ashore on the quayside of the new harbour at Montevideo, impatient to stretch his legs and reclaim what was rightfully his.

He walked through the streets, noting the scaffolding and the new buildings. He stood in the plazas, where families strolled in the evening time, three generations together, enjoying the coolness. He listened to the piping cries of the children and the splash of fountains. He stopped and gazed at a phalanx of hibiscus bushes and the bright extravagant flowers that held their perfection for so short a time. He took lodgings and contemplated his return to Santa Catalina.

He came out into the bright morning sunshine. His feet crunched on a carpet of insects that had fallen from the trees overnight, large brown cockroaches that studded the flagstoned pavement. The thought of so many lives so casually crushed, made him more morose.

There were soldiers on the streets, toy soldiers in green and navy, with white webbing. They lounged and chatted, looking expectantly up the street. Bandsmen rested their instruments on the ground. There was an air of holiday. A crowd had gathered. There was a murmur of conversation. He stopped idly to see what was going to happen.

Officers, resplendent in gold braid, called out along the street. The soldiers straightened up and fell into line. They stood impassively as the band struck up. It was a slow and sonorous march, raucous and heart-rending. A bass drum marked the time with a low insistent beat. The brass wailed a sad lament.

John felt the hairs standing on the back of his neck. From behind the rank of soldiers he watched the escort approaching, moving with the hypnotic hesitancy of the funeral march. He saw the gun carriage and the coffin draped with the flag. Gleaming brass shells stood upright around the coffin, evidence of the army's new Krupp field guns. He was impressed. He saw the cavalry, the coaches and the faces of the women draped in black.

"Who is this?" he asked of a bystander.

"This is Don José Aguirre, a great man of our country. He was a general in the Great War and a senator in the government."

He began to walk, keeping pace with the procession. He saw the women alighting from the carriages and the colour party removing the coffin, moving like automata in formal respect. He heard the orders of the officer, harsh in the stillness of the morning. He recognised Doña María Jesús. He knew her by her erect bearing, this woman who had been instrumental in saving his life. He should wait and speak to her after the ceremony, but he was ashamed. She would ask about their little Catalina and he would have to lie.

He turned away. The music swirled in his head, a haunting soul-searching wail. The old soldier was gone, gone to wage eternal war with the Indian who had eluded him. They would stalk each other through the night sky, the gaucho and the hunter with his upraised club. The idea surprised him. It must have been something he had read long ago. He looked at the faces of the people, silent in respect and he envied the dead man. He wondered who would turn out to bid him a last goodbye. He realised that he needed a drink, even at that early hour. He sat on a bench in a plaza and took out his flask. A thrush in scarlet red trousers, foraged among the fallen insects. Zorzal, they called him, the sponger, the simpleton. He was in good company, he reflected and drank again.

He dreamed that he was inching his way along a high scaffolding. Catherine held his hand.

"From up here we can see the whole city," he said.

"Look at all those people down there." She pointed to the workers digging foundations and laying blocks. There were men levelling the streets. Traffic moved between piles of bricks. A military band snaked in and out between the horses and carts.

"It will be very peaceful," she said, "in our new house."

He clung to a jutting piece of moulding. He brushed loose rubble from it to improve his grip.

"Be careful here," he warned. "It's very narrow."

Her fingers slipped from the moulding and she fell away from him. Down and down she went, striking the bars of the scaffolding until she struck the ground. He looked down at her. She wore a bright blue blouse with a white collar. She had made it herself. She lay still among the rubble. He could not get down. He shouted to the people below, but they could not hear him. They were too busy with their work. He shouted again and a strangled cry came from his throat. He sat up and opened his eyes. He could still see her falling away from him, tumbling and spinning as she struck the bars. The bass drum sounded in his head.

He looked at the woman in the bed beside him, with a sense of revulsion. She snored. There was a smear of rouge on the pillow. He shook her into wakefulness.

"Get out," he said, thrusting a handful of notes at her. "Just go."

She checked the money. "Paper money," she sneered. "Not worth a polvo." She dressed herself without another word and left, slamming the door behind her. He wondered what her name was. He washed and dressed and packed his belongings for the journey.

The coach lumbered along the gravelled road. He would give the Welshman his due. The bridges made life easier. He looked out on fields of grain and brown sorghum. He lurched against the passengers on either side as the coach swayed from side to side. It was no way for a man to travel. He resolved to rent a couple of horses at the pulpería in order to arrive in a manner befitting the señor.

Estrellita saw the rider coming out of a stand of trees on the crest of a ridge. He was leading a second horse with some bags on its back. He paused to open and close a gate in the wire fence. A herd of cattle parted to let him through.

She wriggled her toes in the red soil. The potatoes shone white, where she had turned over the stalks. The river sparkled in the sun. He followed the line of the fence, until he came up to where she stood, with only the wire between them.

"So you came back, Cardiff," she said. She noticed how he had got heavy. His hair was grey. He eased himself painfully, standing for a moment in the stirrups.

"I have come back," he replied. "I have come back for what is mine."

She polished a potato between her fingers, brushing off the dry red clay.

"It is fitting," she said. "The circle is almost complete."

He looked at her, not comprehending.

"What nonsense are you talking about?"

"You have not yet seen the jaguar."

He snorted in derision.

"There are no jaguars any more. If I see one I will shoot it. You may be sure of that."

"Perhaps," she said, dropping the potato into a basket. "Perhaps."

"And you, madam. If you are to stay on my land, you will do so on my terms."

She shrugged her bare shoulders. She still retained that animal grace that had obsessed his mind before, a feline grace like a black jaguar, perhaps.

"Candombera," he said. "You will dance to my tune."

She shrugged again. "You are the señor," was all she would say and he wanted to strike her again for her insolent manner. He kicked the horse's side and continued along the fence searching for a way through. She watched him turn and come back.

"Where the Devil is the gate?" he asked, feeling foolish and angry.

She unhooked a section of fence, letting the posts fall flat and gestured to him to go through. The horses stepped carefully through the gap.

"You must learn to live with the alambrada, Cardiff," she said, smirking at his irritation.

He splashed across the ford and went up the slope towards the house. Estrellita went back to her work.

"You should have let us know, man," said Robert. "We could have come to meet you." He shook John's hand cordially. "What of Catherine and the children? I take it they are following directly."

"Not just yet. So how are things here?"

"Oh, you'll see a lot of changes. We'll go out tomorrow and I'll show you around."

"There's no need," said John. It rankled that Robert was offering to show him around his own land. "I'll find my own way. What of the gauchos? How have they taken to the changes?"

"Ah," said Robert ruefully. "Most of them have gone. A few stayed on. Dismounted cavalry, you might say. We have mostly new people, immigrants. You won't have seen the village, since you came across country. Quite a settlement. Now there's talk of a railway."

"I've been listening to that kind of talk for years," said John gruffly. "So things are looking up."

"Yes, indeed," said Robert with boyish enthusiasm. "The country is much more settled. Still a bit of trouble now and again, but we live very quiet lives here. Lorenzo keeps the men busy. He has made an excellent capataz."

"Lorenzo?"

"Yes. Your wife's uncle. He stayed on. He has proved to be invaluable."

"That old scoundrel. I trust he isn't living in this house."

"No, not at all," laughed Robert. "He lives with Estrellita in the ombú grove. You know the place. He's very much at home there, I gather."

To his surprise, John felt a sudden jealousy. This information was unexpected.

"He's welcome to her," he said. "She's running to seed." He laughed harshly. "This railway, you say?"

"Yes, we've had a few visits from your old friend Enrique Jones. He is working for an English company now."

"Jones? And how is he?"

"He seems fine, but tell me about yourself and Catherine and your children. How are things back home?"

John made a dismissive gesture. "You know. Parish pump politics. Some jackanapes makes a speech and the crowd go about opening each other's heads with their blackthorn sticks. Comic-opera stuff. I had little time for it."

"And Catherine?"

"Well, well. She more or less sent me on ahead. She could see that I was never at ease in Ireland. You know how it is. Itchy feet."

"Indeed I do," agreed Robert. "I have a kind of hankering to try Brazil some day. Emeralds, you know, gold, rubber, that sort of thing."

"Maybe you could collect my debt from the Emperor," said John with a dry laugh. "With interest it could be worth a few shillings."

Robert smiled. "It's around here somewhere, I dare say. But you must have something to eat and some rest. It's been a long journey. Then we can look over some figures. Liebig is expanding all the time. The next thing will be refrigeration. It's all the talk nowadays. If that comes, we will be able to sell all over the world. Just imagine that." He rubbed his hands. "And that box there. Liebig cards. I've been meaning to post them to your children. I remember how much they enjoyed them."

He went to look for Estrellita to get her to prepare some food. John lifted the lid of the box. It was stuffed with the coloured cards, a treasure-trove. Flower girls; children sitting on globes of the world, holding jars of the famous extract; methods of preparing poultry; girls in flowing dresses, standing in shrubbery; historical figures; a journey through the Caucasus and even more notable Belgian town halls.

He wanted those cards. He wanted to go home, empty the box onto the kitchen table and watch his children scrabbling through them, making sets and arguing over swaps. His hands shook. He put the cards back in the box and secured the lid. He put his head down on his arms and fell into a fitful sleep. Robert woke him and placed a plate of potatoes and meat in front of him. He ate ravenously.

Laurence came in and sat opposite him. He was tanned and wiry. His hair was grizzled. He wore a gaucho knife tucked into his belt, but his clothes were more European, workaday, serviceable clothes. He put his hands on the table.

"I heard you were back," he said. John looked up from his food. He made no reply.

"I just want to say this. If I had my way I would cut your throat. Make no mistake, I could do it, but she says no. But if you so much as lay a finger on her again, I will. That I promise."

He knew that his words went home, but still John said nothing. He chewed on his food, looking at Laurence with a strange, detached gaze. Laurence felt an urge to force the issue, to slap the plate to the floor and demand an answer.

"I suppose there's no point in askin' how Catherine and the children are gettin' along."

John blinked. He pushed the empty plate away and stood up. He noticed that a piece of the cracked tile was missing. He tapped the tile with the toe of his boot.

"Have to do something about that," he said pensively. He clicked his tongue as if at some minor irritation.

Laurence went to the door.

"So long as we know where we stand," he said. He waited for an answer.

There was none. He went out.

It was all there, thought John. He had travelled over the sea to Troy. He had seen the pilot stars. The great Achilles was dead and now the Cyclops was threatening to kill him. The idea diverted him. He wondered if his Penelope would wait for twenty years, spinning in her bower to keep the suitors at bay. He doubted it. Ulysses, however, was the most cunning of all the Greeks. He would prevail.

"Daddy," began Catherine, "I've been thinking." He knew what was coming.

"I will have to move to town. The children will have to go to secondary school."

"How will you support yourself?"

"I can sew. I'm a good seamstress. I can make outfits for all the fashionable ladies of Wexford."

She said it lightly, although she wondered herself, how she would manage. She wanted him to say no, so that she could argue and convince herself that she could do it.

"You know," he said, "it's time I saw a bit o' the world meself. It's time I went over the mountain."

She looked at him in astonishment.

"Aye," he continued, amused by her reaction.

"I've been thinkin' along them lines meself. I'm thinkin' if you could put up with me, we could buy some place in town. You could run your business and the children could go to school."

"But the farm? What about the farm?"

"Ah sure look at me. How could I keep it on? It wouldn't be fair to keep your boys here just on my account. I can rent it on conacre. If one of them wants it when he's a grown man, he can have it."

She was silent, stunned by the enormity of what he was suggesting.

"But we have been here for generations. There have been Doyles here since God knows when."

"And there can be again if they want it," he said reasonably. "But there's too many ghosts here for me right now. Later maybe."

"Conacre? It would still be your land?"

"Ours," he corrected her. "It will be ours for as long as we want it. The land has been good to us, but land can destroy people too. It can drive people demented. Look at all this Boycottin' and murder. Look at poor Manus. The soul in him was twisted for the want of land. Look at ..." He was about to mention John but checked himself.

"I know what you're saying. But you could never..."

"I gave it me best, but it's time now to try somethin' else. I want to sit on the quay and watch the ships. I want to ride on the railway and see Dublin again before I die. I want to talk to people and I want to see you back in the world. Is that too much to ask?"

He had turned it, so that she was now the benefactor. He was giving up everything he had held dear and making it sound as if she were bestowing some great gift on him.

"We can do it," he urged. "It's for the children."

She could not refuse. She remembered the fish and the tinker children and his furtive kindness. She nodded agreement.

"I like the railway," he said smiling like a boy. "We could have a fine time."

He lit his pipe with a lucifer.

"Great yokes, these," he said puffing away. "There's just one thing though. I want to be buried in Tomhaggard near your mother. You wouldn't know who you'd be associatin' with up there in Wexford."

"But she's in …"

"I know. She's with her own kind down the road, the Wrays and all the Protestant Boxwells and the like. But we can visit each other, can't we?"

Catherine felt her skin prickling at the thought.

"We can go strollin' by the lake at night and talk with all the Doyles that ever was in Lingstown. That's not so bad now, is it?"

"It's not so bad," she said quietly.

"And sure you'll do well," he went on. "I bet all the ladies will flock to your door."

"I bet Elizabeth Boxwell will anyway," said Catherine with a wry smile. "She'll be pleased to see me."

The house had a bakery on the ground floor. She took a room above the bakery for her work. Tom made heavy weather of the stairs to the top of the house, but from his window he could see the masts and spars of the sailing ships. The children were as happy in school as any normal children could be. The nuns took a special interest in Sarah, no doubt because of her mother's notoriety in the history of the school. Sarah showed an aptitude for languages and the nuns were impressed also by the bit of Spanish that had stayed with her.

Elizabeth came to call. She had married well and always dressed in the height of fashion.

"I just wanted to hansel your little business. I'll recommend you to all my friends." She pulled off her gloves.

Kiss my arse, thought Catherine. That was another expression she had heard at the fair, a kind of disparaging comment on the price asked for a beast or for the price offered. She would have liked to say it aloud.

"That would be very good of you," she said demurely.

Elizabeth looked around. "You've made so much of the place," she said approvingly. "I have some things I could send over if you like. Curtains and the like."

"No, no. Not at all I wouldn't hear of it." Kiss me arse. "I'm making curtains, as it happens. I have all the material."

"Well, you know. If there's anything you need."

"You're very kind and I am glad to see you again. You look so well." She was pleased too. She had always enjoyed fencing with Elizabeth. Elizabeth had won in material terms, but she was still unsure. There was an aura around Catherine, a sense of experience and adventure that Elizabeth envied. They took tea together and Elizabeth probed for information.

"Robert is very bad at communicating. I would slap him if I met him. Is it something in the air out there?"

"I'm sure he's very busy. It is a vast place you know."

"Do you think John has gone back there?"

Catherine shrugged. Elizabeth wanted the details and Catherine would not oblige.

"To think that I introduced you. I blame myself."

"There's no need. I made my own choices."

"You were so brave."

"Well, it's over and done with now."

Catherine buttered a scone, one from Mr. Godkin downstairs. Elizabeth was disappointed. Catherine seemed too contented, for someone who had suffered so much. She must be keeping it all in. It was her duty as a friend, to draw her out. She was entitled as a friend, to all the shocking details. She needed to know, in order to pass the story on in the strictest confidence of course, to all her acquaintances. But Catherine would not give. She would not accept sympathy. It was most frustrating.

They discussed patterns and the importance of collars. Catherine took some measurements. Elizabeth, she noted with malicious satisfaction, was getting stout. She had been plump as a girl, but plump hardens into stout. No matter how much Elizabeth might own, no matter how important her husband might be in the commercial life of the town, she would always be stout, while Catherine could eat Mr. Godkin's scones with salty country butter running off them and she would still be tall and elegant. There was some justice in the world after all.

They embraced affectionately and Elizabeth went downstairs, but Catherine knew that she would be back, armed with sympathy and charity, to renew the duel. She looked forward to it.

"Where did you meet my mother?" she asked Tom.

"Ah now," he said, leaning towards the fire. He poked at the coals, leaving the iron to heat in the glowing cavern. "It's a long story."

"We have the time."

"Dorothy's father as you know, was a Protestant minister."

"I know."

"Well, when he was a young man he had the roof burned over his head during the Ninety Eight."

"I know. I heard about that."

"Well anyway, after things settled down they built the chapel for him again and didn't he get married. Fierce civil the Protestants were around here for a long time after the Rising. After the hangin' and all that, they tried to convert the people. Her father got on with everyone. A decent Protestant, as they say. The best in the world. He had no time for militias or yeomen or any o' that class o' thing. Live and let live."

"So how did you meet her?" He was inclined to ramble away from the point.

He chuckled. "Ah you know. The paughmeale."

"The what?"

"The harvest-home. We used to call it the kissing-meal, the paughmeale. The Old Talk do you see? Her father wanted to be on good terms with everyone. He went to all the celebrations."

"The kissing-meal. I never heard of that."

"Ah well. The Famine put a stop to a lot of the old ways. The old language too."

"And that was where you met her?"

He smiled. He drew out the poker. The tip was red. He ignited bubbles of tar on the smoking coal. Each bubble hissed giving off a jet of smoke.

"Your mother was a young girl once as well, you know. She wasn't always as strict as you remember."

"And did her father approve?"

"Let's say things took their natural course. It became necessary for us to get married."

"The paughmeale? Was there a scandal?"

"Aye. Then the bad times came, the potato blight and it didn't seem to matter very much."

"And her father died from the fever."

"Aye. In the workhouse."

"Were you always happy together?"

"We were." He put down the poker. "So you see, we have a lot to talk over even still, although they won't let us be buried together. We'll have great gossip to tell each other."

"The paughmeale," mused Catherine. "So that was why she worried about me and John."

"I suppose."

"At least we got married first," she said with a touch of disapproval.

He spread his hands in surrender.

"You have me there," he admitted. "You have me there." He laughed. "It's funny how things turn out." He went back to his contemplation of the fire.

She thought about old ghosts strolling by the lake. She wondered if she and John would ever meet again in another life and stroll together, all enmity put aside, gossiping like long separated friends. She hoped they would. They might find another silver cup under the water of the lake and they could drink a spectral toast to each other.

She went to the window and looked down into the street. Lamplight fell in dim circles on the pavement. There were women laughing in the street, soldiers' wives spending their weekly allowance. They were medlio, as the locals put it. A woman looked up at her and cackled. She waved a bottle.

"God bless the oul' Zulus anyway. If it wasn't for them we'd never have a penny." She cackled again at her good fortune in having a husband in the army. They moved on up the street. Their laughter faded away. Catherine closed her eyes. She saw herself looking down into a street, a crowd with a head on a lance and the man shouting about Berro the outcast, the murderer of Venancio Flores. She remembered the smell of the sick room and how she had misjudged John. She wished that she could be back there with him in that city, where people had gone mad with hatred and killing. She wished that she could be there to sponge his brow and hold a glass to his lips. She wished. She wished. She wished that she had met him at a paughmeale and tumbled with him in the straw; facing the anger of their parents, with chaff sticking out of their hair; that they had settled together, two country people raising their children in peace and obscurity. She did not know what she wished. She wanted to hear chicharra, to see the herd coming to the river and the bright cardinal birds, always in pairs, darting in the branches, looking about, looking out always for each other. She wished for some word.

Granillero came to call, the candombe doctor with his top hat and long-tailed coat. His white beard descended to his chest. She listened for the drums, expecting him to break into his shuffling dance. He was carrying his black bag. Granillero raised his hat. He spoke.

"Good afternoon, madam," he began. His eyes were anxious. "Allow me to introduce myself, I am Dr. Cardiff, John's father."

"Oh," she said.

"I have no wish to intrude but …"

She saw the hunger in his eyes.

"Please come in," she said stiffly, stepping back into the hallway. She brought him up to the sitting room. He wheezed on the stairs and her stiff manner softened. He sat down.

"I must begin," he said without preamble, "by apologising to you."

"There is no need."

"I should have called long before this, but to tell the truth, I was ashamed. It is difficult for me to admit it. When one has worked in a place and earned respect, it is painful to see a member of one's family do something low and despicable."

"I don't think he could help it in the end," she murmured.

He looked at the ground, leaning both hands on his walking stick.

"I don't know everything that happened between you, but I can guess. He was always headstrong."

"We had good times too," she said. "I have six fine children. I would not change things."

He coughed. "I understand," he said. "Your parents came to me, you know, all those years ago and I was unable to help them. I have felt bad about it ever since. They were distressed and I gave them nothing but easy words."

"You lost a child also," she said, seeing his distress. "I was to blame too. He was too young for responsibilities. Maybe if he had gone by himself, he would have had time to grow up."

He turned the idea over in his mind. "Perhaps," he said thoughtfully, "but then you would not have had your children and I..." He paused. "I would have no grandchildren. I would very much like to meet them."

She started. Maybe he had come to claim them. He might go to law to take them from her.

"I would understand if you did not want this. My son has deprived me of my entitlements."

"I am at fault too," she said. "I deprived you of your son. I took him away from his studies. I will not deprive you of your grandchildren. They have gone with my father to look at the ships, but I will bring them to meet you. I must warn you, they are a noisy brood."

He smiled. He looked like a benign leprechaun, with his long beard.

"Like the base Indian, in Shakespeare," he said quietly.

"A base Indian?"

"Yes. Who threw a pearl away, richer than all his tribe."

"What Indian?" she asked, puzzled.

"Oh, nothing. I'm just rambling. You must excuse me." He coughed again. "I have received a communication," he said awkwardly. He picked up his black bag, placing it on his knees. "I am long retired," he explained, "but the bag has grown to my hand. I carry it for ballast."

He undid the buckles. "It is addressed to you, but the people in Bridgetown had the good sense to send it on to me."

He took out the package and handed it to her. She knew the writing. She looked at it and at John's father. He said nothing.

She picked at the string, breaking the sealing wax.

"If you would prefer…" he said rising.

"No, please," she said. "There will surely be some word."

She undid the string and opened the paper. It was a box of the coloured cards. There was no note. She gazed at them, remembering her little school in the blue tiled kitchen.

The doctor looked at them, not comprehending.

"Is there no letter?" he asked, with a note of disappointment.

She shook her head. "The children will be pleased," was all she said.

He stood up. "I will leave you now," he said, taking up his bag and his top hat. "I look forward to meeting the children."

She went downstairs with him and opened the door. They shook hands.

"I am sorry there was no letter, Catherine," he said. "May I call you Catherine?"

"Of course," she replied. "I will bring the children on Saturday, if you like."

"Splendid," he said, raising his hat. "I shall order a cake from the excellent Mr. Godkin." He went towards the shop door.

She smiled. Definitely Granillero. He gave a little skip and went in the door. She listened for the drums.

Sarah came home from school. She looked at the cards. "Is that all?" she asked.

Catherine nodded. The girl took the box and went to the fireplace. She tipped the contents into the flames. Catherine made no effort to prevent her. She saw the cards shrivel and all their bright colours fade to brown, to black, to wisps of ash. They crumbled and vanished.

"We don't want anything from him," Sarah said. "We're fine as we are."

"Ah, Sarah," was all she could say.

Sarah looked at her defiantly.

"You would let him back. You're too soft."

Catherine avoided her eyes. She was thinking of happier times.

"We're happy now," insisted Sarah. "He will only disturb us again. Don't try to write to him. He's gone."

"But…" began Catherine.

"No buts. If he ever comes back, we will have to leave you."

It was a fact. Catherine knew the girl was right. She had always been John's favourite too, which made it the more painful. Estrellita was wrong. They could never be at peace together.

"Let's go for a walk," she suggested. "If I stay here I'll have Elizabeth in, showing me the latest fabrics from Gask and Gask in London." She mimicked her old school friend. "I always order from Gask and Gask of Oxford Street. Just look at this silk. Three shillings and ninepence a yard. It's so important to buy the best. Kiss me arse."

"Mother!" said Sarah in astonishment. "What did you say?"

Catherine laughed. "Never you mind. It's just an expression."

Sarah frowned. "I never heard you talk like that before."

"I'm sorry," said Catherine, "it won't happen again." She was still laughing and Sarah put aside her disapproval.

They walked up along the river, watching the oarsmen at practice. The sun was shining. It hurt her to watch them.

"Your grandfather Cardiff called today," she said. "He wants to meet you all."

Sarah sniffed.

"He seems a nice old man."

Sarah sniffed again. "I don't want to meet any of the Cardiffs," she said. "I have no time for them."

"Give him a chance."

"No. I won't go."

She knew it was useless to argue. Sarah had a will of iron, when she made up her mind.

They turned towards home.

"That's the shop door where I hid from the cattle, the day I ran away with your father."

"I don't want to hear about it," said Sarah. "Maybe my grandchildren will enjoy the story, but it frightens me. What would you say if I did that?"

"You're too young. I was seventeen at the time."

"An old woman," scoffed Sarah. "Did you not think of others?"

"No," replied Catherine. "I didn't. I thought only of your father and what a great adventure it was."

"Well then, you were stupid."

"If I had not run away, you would not be here. You would not even exist."

"I wouldn't care."

"You would not be here to not care."

"This is a silly argument," said Sarah. She walked on, looking at the pavement.

"You are alive," said Catherine gently. "No, I don't want your father back. I could never live with him again, but neither can I waste my life being bitter about him. Neither must you. You have so much ahead of you."

It was like a sermon, she knew. Sarah set her face into her stubborn expression. She bit her lower lip. She was so like John.

"I won't go to see my grandfather Cardiff."

"Maybe later," suggested Catherine.

Sarah shrugged.

"Maybe someday," said her mother. "Don't close the door."

Sarah shook her head. "I won't go," she reiterated.

Richard found the wrapping paper.

"What's this?" he demanded.

Catherine could think of nothing to say. She felt like a child.

"Liebig cards," said Sarah. "I burned them." Her face glowed from the fresh air.

"You had no right," said Richard. "What did he say?"

"There was no letter," said Catherine.

"He didn't even ask about us? He couldn't give a damn." Richard set his mouth in a hard line.

"Now, Richard. Let's have none of that language."

"I'm sorry I didn't shoot him when I had the chance."

"Don't talk like that," said Catherine sharply.

"Sarah was right. We're better off on our own."

"Anyway they would hang you, up in the gaol," put in Sarah maliciously. "And your eyes would pop out."

"Stop it," said Catherine, her voice rising. "I won't have that kind of talk in this house." They subsided into silence. Richard crumpled the paper and threw it in the fire.

"Maybe you were right, Sarah," he conceded, "but you'd think he would write a word or two."

"You're both soft," said Sarah.

Richard looked at her. She would have shot him, he mused. She was always his favourite.

"Go and find the others," said Catherine. "Tell your Grandad its time for tea. I'm half afraid he'll run away with them on some schooner." She smiled, lightening the mood. "It's a family failing."

They responded to her levity.

"Were there any Hannibal cards?" asked Richard. "I needed two to complete the set." He looked at Sarah. She raised her eyebrow. "Ah well," he said. "Can't be helped." He put his hands in his pockets. "Time was I thought they were the most important thing in the world. It's funny how you grow out of things. I mean, you want something so much. Then you get it and then you throw it away. Come on Sarah. We'll go and fetch the others."

Off they went, clattering down the stairs. What was it the doctor had said? She thought of him as Granillero. That hat was taller than President Lincoln's. It was in the old style, almost a stovepipe. Something about an Indian, who threw a pearl away richer than all his tribe. But they were only Liebig cards.

She picked up the string and the shards of sealing wax and tossed them into the fire. The wax sizzled and exploded. Indians in the firelight; Gauchos, their faces lit like demons. Another time and a world gone forever.

He chose to live almost as an outcast on his own land. He preferred the solitude of the pastures furthest from the house. He took to the enclosing of the land with fierce determination. He patrolled the line of the fence relentlessly, checking for gaps and marked out where the men were to erect the poles to enclose the northern range.

The work took him to the furthest limits of Santa Catalina land, along the River of the Forlorn. Beyond lay the hills.

'There you may meet the jaguar.' The wagon driver said that years ago on that memorable journey to their new home. Somewhere in those hills a legendary jaguar slunk through the espinas de la cruz, or couched in the shadows of the ñandubay. There were few trails through the thorny scrub of the hills. Horse and rider must go draped in leather to survive the thorns. He looked towards the line of hills and wondered if the jaguar ever took any of his stock.

He took the carcass of a lamb and disembowelled it. He left the fleece in place. He scraped up hot ashes with a tin plate and packed them into the rib-cage and the cavity of the abdomen. He pulled the flap of skin across to hold them in place. He pushed the lamb into the ashes of the dying fire. The fleece began to singe. He went about his work.

At dusk he returned and threw more wood on the fire. He rolled the carcass from the pile of ash. Smoke reeked from every orifice of the creature's body. He looked at it. Even the eye sockets smoked. The eyes were shrivelled and sunken.

I am in Hell, he thought. This is what it is like. The pain of loss and the pain of sense. The priest had explained it to them in vivid detail. The fires of Hell, burning forever, forever replenished. He laid on the horror and then despatched them to confession, before the effect could wear off. But the pain of loss is worse, he said. The knowledge that you would never see the face of God, coupled with the knowledge that the Just, the mealy mouthed bastards, were up there having a great time. The priest never put it quite that way, but that was what it seemed to boil down to. The worst thing was the knowledge that you had brought it on yourself. There, beside the River of the Forlorn, John Cardiff saw his vision of Hell.

He took his knife and peeled back the skin. The meat was done to perfection. He carved a chunk and lay by the fire, propped on one elbow. The sun fell away. The stars came out. It should have been different. His boys should have been there to learn from him, to look up at the night sky and ask him the names of those other worlds. They should have been there to share the meat, and to listen to the story of how they had come there, the battle by the river, the Gatling gun and the merry jape of hiding the horse in the kitchen to outwit the rebel soldiers. But too much of the story was built on lies and deceit.

In the morning he found the broken fence and the tracks of cattle and horses leading north-eastwards towards the hills.

"There are soldiers at San Martin," said Robert. "Perhaps we can enlist their help."

"That's twelve miles in the wrong direction," replied John. "Already they have a headstart of forty miles. If we wait for the soldiers we will be giving them time to cross into Flores. They could reach the Negro in two days and that's the last we'll see of them."

"How many are they?"

"I make it five. I'm no tracker."

"How many cattle?"

"Forty or fifty head. I can't be sure."

"These are gavilleros, John. Dangerous men."

"They're our cattle," said John fiercely. "We can't let them away with this."

"We should send for the soldiers." Robert scratched his head. "Let's see what Lorenzo has to say."

"Damn Lorenzo. I'm going after them anyway." He dismounted and went into the house to get a box of shells.

Laurence came in from the paddock.

"What's all the commotion?"

Robert told him what had happened. John came out with his pockets bulging with bullets.

"Are you coming or not?" he snapped at Robert.

"Wait," said Robert. He went into the house.

Laurence looked at John.

"Go to San Martin. Tell the officer that we're heading northeast. He'll pick up the trail through the hills. Tell him to hurry."

"Send someone else," said Laurence. "I'm comin' with you."

"What in blazes for? You're too old for this."

"I promised your wife I'd keep an eye on her interests. I suppose you qualify, up to a point." He said it without warmth.

"You'd better get yourself a weapon then. There's a couple of shotguns inside, for all the good they'll do."

He went to get a man to ride to San Martin. He saw Estrellita standing among the ombús. She was watching him. He felt a shiver run down his spine. He saw Laurence on horseback, go to her and say something. He pulled the horse away and cantered back to the house. She did not move, a white-clad figure against the bright green of the trees. There was no one this time, to say goodbye to him as he rode off to battle.

They followed the tracks without difficulty as far as the River of the Forlorn. Darkness compelled them to halt. They made no fire. The Moon, the merest sliver of lemon, lay on its back. They spoke in low voices by the purling river, afraid that sound would carry in the profound silence.

"I have never discharged a weapon at another man," admitted Robert. He chewed on a length of tasajo.

"Don't worry," said John. "You'll do no damage with a shotgun. It's only for show."

Robert was relieved.

"What about you Lorenzo? Have you ever seen action? I mean with guns?"

Laurence cut a length of the leathery meat. He chewed slowly.

"We don't want to talk about that class o' thing."

"But did you? insisted Robert. He needed reassurance.

"A long time ago," replied Laurence. "I don't talk about it."

Robert was rebuked. "Maybe we were too hasty. We should have brought some of the men."

"They wouldn't come," said Laurence. "Remember they were gauchos, some of them. They wouldn't turn on their own kind. These are gauchos bandeirantes."

"They're thieves, whatever way you look at it," growled John. He lay back, resting his head on the sheepskin of his saddle. He looked up. The moon was weak and watery.

"Maybe the soldiers won't come," said Robert. "What do we do then?"

"Go to sleep," growled Laurence. "We'll worry about that in the mornin'."

They lay in silence for a long time.

"I mean, if the soldiers killed all the bandits, then they would be out of a job. Maybe they keep enough of them alive to ..."

"Be quiet," said Laurence. The man was beginning to get on his nerves.

"If anything happens to me," John began hesitantly. "I mean if I don't come back from this, I want you to promise me something."

The two men listened attentively.

"I've had a lot of time to think. I haven't had a drink for a long time so I've been able to think clearly. I know what you think of me, but I ask only one thing of you."

"What is it, old man?" asked Robert, always prepared to think the best of people.

"I want you to see that Catherine and my children get my share of the estancia."

A silence fell between them.

"Of course, old man," said Robert. "You have my word."

"Write it down," said Laurence. "And sign it."

"I have a gentleman's word," said John angrily.

"The word of a dead gentleman doesn't amount to much. We may all be dead. Write it down."

He unstrapped a saddlebag and took out a book. He struck a lucifer and touched a twist of grass for light. He opened the blank fly leaf and took a pencil from his pocket.

"Write it down," he said, handing the book to John. It was the Tennyson. John made no comment. Some work of noble note may yet be done.

He wrote. 'Being of sound mind.' There were formal phrases for this kind of thing. He asked Robert to sign as executor. Laurence signed as a witness. They were satisfied.

Laurence made another twist of grass and lit it. John continued writing, until the fly leaf was full. He wrote on the title page, in between the florid decoration. The flame died. He put the book into his pocket. His fingers stroked the fine calf leather. She had tired of Tennyson, he reflected.

They found a horse with a broken leg. Its throat had been cut. A black cloud of flies swarmed about the carcass and the puddle of congealed blood.

"That should slow them up a bit," said Laurence.

They pressed on along the narrow trail. The thorns plucked at them. Bright birds darted in the trees. A small deer jumped up and sprang into the dense scrub.

"The Welshman says he's going to drive a road along this ridge," said Robert. "All the way to the Negro."

John grunted.

"Make life easier for the bandits," said Laurence dryly.

"And for the military," retorted Robert. "On balance, I'd say it's a good thing."

John raised his hand to silence them. He pointed. In the distance they could see a cloud of dust. They left the trail and pushed through the scrub, cutting across country towards the distant cloud.

"They're heading for the Arroyo Grande," said John. "They'll probably try to cross in the morning. We should hit them before they get down out of the hills. We can get ahead of them."

He spurred his horse and they followed. He seemed filled with a sense of purpose. There was an air of calm about him. He led them down through a narrow defile between the thorn trees and by late afternoon they were ahead of the plodding cattle. They could hear the animals lowing for water.

They left Laurence with the horses and crept forward to the top of a ridge. The cattle were confined in a hollow, with a small pond in the centre. They stood contentedly, knee deep in the water. There was a fire some distance from the water and figures moved about it.

"Four," whispered John. "I thought there were more."

"Should we call on them to surrender? We have the advantage of surprise," Robert whispered in reply.

"Not a chance. They'd vanish at the first sound. These are professionals. Our only chance is to hit them at first light. Sitting ducks. Get as close as we can."

Robert's mouth was dry. He said nothing.

Laurence could hear someone wriggling through the long grass. He crouched in the shadow of a bush and slid his long knife from its sheath. He heard the low tinkle of spurs. A figure crawled into the clearing where the three horses stood hobbled. He slid towards them. His scarf was pulled over his head. The horses snuffled and shied away.

Laurence moved swiftly, dropping on the man and driving his knee into the man's back, bearing him to the ground, winding him completely. He laid his knife to the man's throat and turned him over.

"Rafael!" he exclaimed, still holding the blade under the man's chin.

Rafael could not speak, because of the weight on top of him. He swallowed. He looked up at Laurence without fear.

"Rafael," said Laurence again. "What are you doing here?" He removed his weight, slowly withdrawing the blade. Rafael watched him warily, like a trapped animal poised for flight. He raised himself on his arms, still gasping for breath.

"I need a horse," he said simply.

"Ah Rafael," said Laurence. "This is not the way to get a horse. This is not the way to live. Why are you with these men?"

Rafael looked at him defiantly. He was a powerfully built young man. He wore a short beard in the gaucho style. Laurence pointed the knife at the ground. Rafael made no move to escape.

"Is Fierro with these men?"

"No," replied Rafael with indignation. "My grandfather is not a thief."

"And you?"

Rafael looked away.

"You would steal our horses?"

"I need a horse," said Rafael again.

"If you are caught they will hang you. The military will surely kill you. They are coming right now. This man Cardiff will shoot you like a dog."

"I am not afraid of a man who would beat a woman. If I see him, I will kill him first. I will kill him because of my mother."

"There may be a time, but it is not now. You must get away from here. The soldiers are not far behind us."

"I have no horse," said Rafael. "Anyway, I cannot desert my companions."

"You will hang with your companions if you stay here. Where is your grandfather?"

"North," said Rafael. "He went north."

"Go to Fierro. He will show you a better way. Do this for your mother. I will set you free. I will give you my horse."

"You could not hold me here, old man," said Rafael.

Laurence stood up. Rafael got to his feet.

"Make no mistake, Rafael, I could. I am giving you this chance. Take my horse and go now. I will tell them it was stolen."

"Why do you do this, Lorenzo? Is it because of my mother?" Rafael's defiance was gone.

"For your mother, yes, but also for myself. I need to do this for myself. So if you go now, quietly, you will repay my debt."

Rafael shook his head. "I do not understand, but I will do as you say. There will be another day for Cardiff."

Laurence stooped and undid the hobble. "Go to Fierro and learn better ways," he said. He stood up and handed the reins to Rafael.

"Go back and get Laurence," whispered John. "I'll stay here to watch them. Don't make a sound."

Robert moved back carefully. The trigger snagged on a twig. The gun recoiled in his hand as the report shattered the stillness of the evening. The men at the fire leaped up. John swore. The men ran.

He levered a shell into the breech and fired. Someone returned fire. A bullet whistled through the bushes overhead. The men were running and firing with pistols, to little effect. The cattle at the pond began to stir and mill about in alarm. They began to move away from the noise.

Robert's hands shook. He broke his gun and inserted another cartridge. He fumbled and snapped the gun shut. He saw a horseman coming straight at him, at full gallop. He stood up and fired. The man lifted backwards, under the full force of the discharge. He was silhouetted against the low sun. His hands flailed desperately at the sky as the horse went from under him. He hit the ground with a sickening smack. Robert stared at him.

"Come on," shouted John, "They're getting away." He levered and fired again.

"The horses," he shouted and began to run down the slope. His voice was almost drowned in the bellowing of the cattle and the snapping of bushes as the animals panicked and began to stampede out of the hollow, down the slope towards the clearing. They crashed through the scrub and the thorns in a wild avalanche of heaving sides and tossing horns.

John's breath came hard. He looked back. He saw Robert immobile on the ridge. The animals came on, their eyes rolling. He ran. He saw a rider break from the clearing, crouching low over the horse's neck. He fired. The rider zigzagged down the slope and found the narrow trail.

He saw Laurence holding two of the horses. "Come on, man," he shouted, leaping into the saddle. "Get away from here." He set off after the rider, at full tilt down the slope. He could see the flash of a white shirt. He fired and levered as he galloped, steering the horse with his legs.

The cattle smashed into the clearing and, too late, Laurence realised what was happening. They came at him from his dark side. He turned to run. He fell and the hooves, sharp as blades, thundered over him.

John saw the crests of the hills illumined in resplendent colours. He saw the sapphire sky, darkening to amethyst. He saw the scarlet ceibo and birds hovering by the yellow blossoms of the palo borracho. The horse rose and fell under him as he followed the white speck in the distance. He saw the espinas de la cruz, like an avenue of crosses against the evening sky.

In a stretch of open country he saw a figure, an old man, naked except for a ragged cloak of fur. His skin was dark. His hair was bound with a strip of animal hide. He whirled his bolas. John heard the thrumming of the cords, like the wings of the humming bird. The black balls made an unbroken disk over the man's head.

The horse stumbled as the cords entangled its legs. John pitched forward. The bones of his neck snapped as he hit the ground. His hands grasped at the earth, as the blackness engulfed him. Sepé, the Jaguar, looked down at the stranger, who had taken Laján, the Place of the Ombú. He retrieved his bolas from the struggling horse. The white speck faded into the gathering dusk as Rafael fled northwards. The shadows stretched longer and longer as the sun teetered and fell into darkness.

Catherine heard hoof beats as she lay in her bed. The house was silent, save for the ticking of the clock. Someone was in a hurry. Far away at the edge of town, someone was riding at a reckless speed, at breakneck speed. She listened, following the trail of the rider, down the hill, down by the Bull Ring, down onto the quays, thundering along by the ships. Some bad news. A dispatch rider. War declared. Someone in need of a doctor, a priest. Up the street. Iron shod hooves on the wet paving stones. Some soul on the point of departure into that great void, had sent this urgent messenger to fetch the priest.

Up the street. She heard the outer door to the street crashing in. The hooves pounded on the stairs and the bedroom door exploded in a shower of splinters. The horse reared over her. There was no rider. The silver hooves descended towards her. She screamed, but no sound came. She closed her eyes and raised her hands in terror.

There was silence, except for the ticking of the clock. She could feel her heart pounding. She reached for the box of lucifers and lit a candle. The room was as it had always been. Rain spattered against the window-pane. It was winter.

She lay in the candlelight and wondered about her dream. Was it a dream? It was high summer in Uruguay. She looked at the clock. It would be evening time over there. She must have been dreaming about the gauchos coming home from the pastures. They would be singing in that nasal style they liked so well. The insects of the day would be giving way to the insects of the night. The birds would be flying to their roosts in the eucalyptus, except for lechuza, the solemn little burrowing owl. She would be in her garden. She would water her flowers and the gallant little oak tree.

The rain slashed at the window. She wondered what might have happened to the rider. She shivered and pulled the blankets around her. Perhaps there had been some soul in peril. Some soul in need of encouragement, before setting out on that last great adventure. Some soul. Some poor soul. She crossed herself and prayed. She hoped that it would find a true baqueano to guide it to its destination. She closed her eyes and drifted into a fitful sleep.

Days later, Robert came home on foot, exhausted and haggard. He brought the two bodies, tied across the back of the one horse he had managed to retrieve. He was happy enough to let Estrellita make the arrangements, disgusted as he was by the stench of death and the flies that had followed him for much of his journey. He slept for a full day and woke in time to see the two pine boxes lowered into the ground on the slope above the river.

"We did not wish to disturb you, señor," said Estrellita. "Everything has been done. I have sent for the priest in Dolores, but we could not wait for him."

"It was good of you," said Robert. "I am sorry that you have lost your good friend."

"He did a good thing, señor," she said. "He has paid his debts."

Not a bad way to go, thought Robert.

"And this poor unhappy man?" He felt instinctively that Estrellita could make sense of things.

"Cardiff may yet repay his debts," she said. "They are many. The circle is not yet closed."

Robert frowned. He still had power of attorney. There was something he should do.

"But you, señor. You are troubled."

He looked around. A skein of geese honked overhead as they slanted downwards to the river. The grass swayed in the breeze.

"I can no longer stay here," he said softly. "I have spilled blood on this soil"

"You are not the first, señor."

"There is a man out there somewhere. I could not find him. His bones will whiten in the sun. I can no longer stay at Santa Catalina."

"You are tired señor. Go back to the house and I will bring maté to console you."

He nodded, glad that there was someone to tell him what was best. He went back and sat by the fire. She brought the maté to him. It jolted him from his torpor.

"You said that Lorenzo did a good thing before he died. What good thing was this?"

"He saved the life of Rafael, my eldest boy."

"When was this?"

"Just before he was killed by the animals."

"But how can you know this?"

"The Orishas tell me."

"Ah!" He wondered who they might be. "Can you tell me what I should do?"

"No. Sometimes I know what will happen and sometimes I do not." She took the maté and sipped. "You must decide for yourself, señor." She passed the gourd back to him. "I will leave you now, señor."

She left him deep in his troubled thoughts and went back to her hut. She looked at the ant hills under the roots of the ombú. The hormigas were busy below ground, yet there was no sign of rain.

Aymará sat in the shade of the colonnade. She watched the fish flicking on the surface of the ornamental pond. She thought of many things. She thought of how they had fished in the Great River and of how they had followed the herds across the endless grasslands. She saw the flocks of ñandú, gigantic birds, swifter than the horses of the gauchos.

The servant came quietly on his sandalled feet.

"There is a woman here who wishes to speak with you, señora. I will send her away if you say so."

Aymará flicked her fan. "No, I will speak with her."

The servant went away and returned with Estrellita. Aymará studied her closely. Her eyes were growing dim. Her memories were clearer than the world about her.

"You wanted to speak with me."

"Yes," replied Estrellita. "I have come to tell you that your brother, Sepé, has been taken by the military. They have brought him to Montevideo."

"No," gasped Aymará. She put her hand to her breast. "How do you know this?"

"I am the daughter of Fierro and Guidai. I hear about things that are happening. It is true what I am telling you."

Aymará grasped her cane and stood up.

"I must go there to speak for him. My sons have powerful friends."

She looked at Estrellita. She saw a poor peasant woman with a bundle under her arm.

"I must tell you first, what has happened and then you must do something for me. I have not the money to do this thing so I have come to you. We are the last of the Charrúas."

Aymará sat down again. She rang a small silver bell. The servant came noiselessly to her side.

"Bring a chair for this lady," she directed "and some food and drink. She has travelled a long way."

Estrellita sat with her in the shade. She told Aymará the story of what had happened. She told her of Catherine and of John and how their lives had changed. She spoke of Robert and of how the death of the man weighed so heavily upon him. She told of how Sepé, the Jaguar, had surrendered to the military. Surrendered with honour. His task was done. He would stand trial for his actions and would vindicate his vanished people.

Aymará listened intently. It was a far cry from the convent in Buenos Aires or the opulent life of a great estanciero. They had kept the faith, her brother and this barefoot peasant woman.

"I must go to Montevideo to speak for him," she said again. "I will do as you direct and I will send for you when I return."

Estrellita rose. She touched the old woman's forehead with her right hand in benediction. "I am grateful," she said and turned away. The servant opened the door, holding it back to let her pass. The fish made circles on the surface of the pond.

Moreover, the estancia, I am happy to say, wrote Robert *is free of debt. I am enclosing the deeds so that you may decide how to dispose of it or, perhaps, return to manage it yourself. I consider myself amply repaid for my investment. I shall seek my fortune in some other place. I plan in the immediate future to remove to Brazil.*

May I say once again, that I am sorry to be the bearer of bad news. It may be some consolation to you to know that he must have died instantly. We have ensured that both he and your uncle received the full benefit of the Church's rites, as you would have wished.

I have appointed a manager, on the advice of my attorney, to administer the estancia for you, until you decide what is to be done. My attorney here in Montevideo will carry out your instructions to the letter.

It was John's last wish that you should know that he regretted his actions and his behaviour towards you and his children. I know that he suffered great remorse, as is evidenced from the pages enclosed. He wrote these on the night before his accident and extracted a promise from me that I would send them to you. You will excuse me for having read them, but as you can see, they contained several instructions for myself. I venture to suggest that they are proof of the intensity of his remorse and the violence of his affection towards you.

He signed himself as her obedient servant and read over the missive again. 'Violence of his affection,' he mused. It suited the situation. It was a sorry tale of a bungled expedition. It told of his own remorse and of how the dead man, lying somewhere in the Hills of the Forlorn, was driving him from the place that he had come to call home.

He went out into the street. The news stands carried the story of some old Indian cacique who was on trial for the murder of nine soldiers and three government officials. It hardly seemed likely that one man could have killed so many, unless of course, he had lain in wait for them individually. He had heard of a man at home in Ireland, at the height of the land agitation. The man specialised in the assassination of landlords. He lay in wait behind a bush and shot his victims like a fowler. "If he's a good man," he was reputed to say, "I'll shoot him for ten shillin' and if he's a bad man, I'll shoot him for nothin'." Couldn't say fairer than that.

He posted the letter and wandered about the streets. He dined alone and read the newspaper. There was an etching of the Indian cacique and an account of his misdeeds. It was as if some strange fossil had been turned up, or a fish, long thought extinct, had come flopping into the light of day, in some fisherman's net. It was a further proof, the newspaper said, of the efficiency of the army of the Republic, in bringing miscreants to justice.

Robert wondered about that. He had reported his own misdeed to the military, only to be greeted with a shrug and a laugh. By rights he should also be up there in the dock to answer for his actions. He could defend himself for what he had done, but he should be obliged at least to answer for it. The life of a man should not pass merely with a shrug and a ribald remark.

The Indian was a fierce looking character. His eyes were deep-set, below heavy brows. His jaw protruded pugnaciously. A dangerous man to encounter on a lonely road at night. His crimes were of long standing. There was a suggestion of an amnesty. It seemed that as time passed, murder became less heinous. The victims faded with the passage of the years and the murderer lived on to justify his actions and enjoy a certain notoriety. They should hang the fellow, thought Robert with uncharacteristic severity. Nobody should get away Scot-free for such a crime, let alone an amnesty and a profitable career touring the world, lecturing on the injustices suffered by the indigenous people, as was being suggested by some. Did Caine appear before the crowned heads of Europe to justify his crime? Did the Wandering Jew turn a pretty penny in concert rooms and opera houses, regaling audiences with lantern slides of his travels? Robert shook his head and muttered. He was beginning to talk to himself. He put aside the paper and finished his meal. Tomorrow to fresh woods and pastures new.

Chapter Ten

Young Manus Doyle from Cincinnati made an offer for the house at Lingstown. Manus Doyle the Second, he styled himself, after the American way. He was an agreeable young man, who paid the rent on the nail. He had managed to see beyond the green hedge, as Tom would say and his mind had broadened as a result. But some atavistic need had brought him back to put up the money for Liscreene and work Tom Doyle's land on the ancient system of conacre.

They turned him down. Catherine could not part with the house. She loved to travel down at holiday time, open all the windows and let the wind from the sea blow through it. She brought the children to see her mother's grave. Dorothy lay in the Protestant graveyard, back with her own kind. There were Boxwells there too with their own private crypt. Army men, imperial administrators, a governor of Dacca. Dorothy would have little to say to them, but she would not go in awe of such grandeur either. They put flowers on her grave out of respect for the grandmother they had never known.

Elizabeth Boxwell had a little ivory table. It had belonged to that distant cousin, the governor of Dacca. She was very proud of her ivory table. Her people had consorted with nabobs and princes. Catherine thought of her stool of bones and the company of simple working men. The vulgar expression came to mind again. There was something about Elizabeth that always brought it to mind.

On the road by the ruined castle they met the post-mistress taking her Sunday walk.

"Oh," she said, "I'm glad to see you again. I was going to forward it on to Wexford."

"Forward what?"

"A letter. A very important looking letter from South America. From Montevideo."

It was as if a cold stone had dropped to the pit of Catherine's stomach.

"If you would like to walk back with me now I'll get it for you."

"No," said Sarah, before Catherine could reply. "It's miles to Bridgetown. We can drive over tomorrow."

Catherine assented. "It's a bit late," she agreed. "We'll come and collect it tomorrow." Her mind was in turmoil. She wanted to go there and then and tear it open. She wanted to devour its news, whatever it might be. Perhaps, perhaps he had sent the tea.

"Very well," said the post-mistress. "I hope it's good news and all." She was disappointed that her curiosity would have to wait another day. She had looked at the letter from every angle. She had held it up to the lamplight, but she had been unable to make anything out.

They walked on in silence for some distance. They came to the stream. The boys wandered on ahead and Sarah sat down beside her mother.

"Do you really want to hear from him again?"

Catherine shook her head. She could say nothing.

"It can only mean trouble. We don't want anything from him. We're fine as we are." She did not trust her mother. She was too forgiving. Before they knew anything he would be back, roaring and shouting around the house and falling drunk on the stairs.

"You have to let go," she said. "You'll never be strong until you let him go."

"I have" said Catherine. "I have let him go."

"But you still want to hear from him, don't you?"

Catherine nodded. "No. Oh I don't know what I want. I used to think of him as Art O'Leary. I told you that story, didn't I?"

Sarah nodded.

"When he would go away I would be afraid that he might fall off his horse and be killed and the horse would come back to me, like Art's horse came back." She stopped and gazed into the distance. "And I would leap onto the horse and go to find him."

She twisted her hands together. "She drank his blood, you know. Art's wife. She was that distracted by grief."

Sarah grimaced.

"I had a dream once. A dream of Uruguay. There was a horse. It doesn't matter." She clasped her hands around her knees and sat silently, rocking gently back and forth. A little smile twitched at her lips.

Sarah looked at her. "Don't open the letter. It can do no good."

Catherine plucked at a blade of grass.

"Did he ever show you how to do this?" She slid the blade of grass between her two thumbs and blew on it, producing a wavering squawk. She blew again.

"He showed me that trick the first day he ever came here. He could play *The Conquering Hero*. It was the only tune he could manage." She laughed. There was a faraway look in her eyes. "We had a picnic down by the lake and your grandfather sat at the gable end, keeping his eye on us, smoking his pipe, moryah."

"We're better now," said Sarah softly taking her hand. "Let's go home."

They went together over the little bridge and along the avenue, but Catherine was not easy. She wanted to take the pony-trap and gallop along the leafy roads to Bridgetown, pound on the door and rouse the postmistress from her bed in the middle of the night and have her grumble and rattle her keys while she fumbled with the lock of the little thatched post-office.

Sarah took a candle and climbed to the apple loft. Nothing had changed. There were still apples stored there, the property of Manus Doyle the Second, of Cincinnati. There was an earthy smell of seed potatoes. She looked out of the little window. Spider webs had reclaimed their rights on it. She could see the avenue, the bridge and the stream that he had splashed through on the day he had come back. She wondered if he might come again and take them all back to Santa Catalina and the wide, open spaces, with eagles circling overhead. A breeze from the window blew the candle out. She struck a lucifer, cupping her hand around the flame. The flame guttered and died. She struck another. She looked at the spear of light and wondered. Great yokes, her grandfather always said. She blew gently on the flame.

It made a tiny sound like a far-off conflagration. She frowned. She blew out the flame, went down the ladder and out into the night.

Richard drove them to Bridgetown early in the morning. He was excited, but neither Sarah or Catherine had much to say. Sarah yawned and sat in brooding silence. Catherine looked dreamily at the passing hedgerows. Richard kept his thoughts to himself. He could never understand women. This could be the most important letter they would ever get, yet these two were treating the whole thing with indifference.

"Mup there," he said to the pony, slapping the reins.

The post office stood in ruins. Onlookers hung about with their hands in their pockets. Children walked diligently in every puddle of water, wriggling their bare toes, enjoying the excitement. Two policemen stood with their hands behind their backs. They leaned towards each other in serious conclave. The black rafters, fallen out of place, poked at the sky.

"Oh, Mrs. Cardiff," said the postmistress, "I don't know what to say. Everything is gone. This is terrible."

Catherine said nothing. She did not know if she was relieved or disappointed. Everything was put on the long finger. She would wait. Richard went into the ruined building and kicked things around in a vain search. He cursed under his breath. There was nothing but charred timber and a scorched brass weighing scales. He kicked it in frustration. It jangled like a bell. Sarah sat impassively in the trap, looking at her hands.

The post-mistress spoke to the policemen. They looked at Catherine with interest. It was a good story, one of those little ironies to add spice to a mundane report.

Richard came out of the ruined building. He wiped his feet on a tuft of grass and got back into the trap. He drove home in glum silence. Catherine saw him wipe a black smudge from his cheek. She thought she saw the glint of a tear. He wiped angrily with his sleeve and spoke not a word.

"Well, that's that," she said as she dismounted from the trap. She put up her hand to help Sarah alight by the little swaying step. Sarah looked into her eyes.

"Maybe it's for the best," said the girl. "Don't be too disappointed. We'll do fine."

"You're probably right," agreed Catherine. "We must get on with our lives."

Richard unhitched the pony and turned it into the paddock. He leaned on the gate watching the pony for a long time.

Catherine had the house to herself. She listened to the noises of the town, wheels trundling and the clip-clop of hooves. A steamer boomed its mournful note, signifying departure. She wondered where it was bound for. Her thoughts verged on the morose. People came and went, going about their business, but she remained. Soon her children would go from her and she would be left alone, her life's work done. Tom would be gone too. Her fingers would gnarl with arthritis and she would no longer be able to earn a living. She would be thrown on the charity of friends. She checked herself. Now wait a minute. I'm not yet forty. I can fend for myself for a while yet. She would not yield to Elizabeth and accept her charity. Not by a long shot.

She thought about her children, especially Sarah. Manus Doyle the Second had a great notion of Sarah. That would be a good one. The bonds of consanguinity were loose. The Doyle cousins were far removed by blood and penury. What of Manus Doyle the First though? Prosperity had made him a more civil man. Even Oliver had improved. She smiled inwardly at the fact that Oliver now cultivated Richard's acquaintance on their visits to Lingstown. Perhaps it was all a ploy to cajole the land from them. She wondered. Sarah had plenty of time on her hands. She entertained no passion for young Manus. It was hardly likely that she would run away with him to Cincinnati. Still, you never know.

She pinned a length of ribbon along a lapel. Lapels were back. She held the pins in her mouth. It was a task more conducive to reflection than conversation. Each person is moulded by his work, the sailor, awkward and rolling on land, the bandy-legged and usually limping, gaucho, his bones imperfectly set after many a fall. Herself with her mouth pinned shut, keeping her thoughts to herself. She thought of galley slaves, made monstrous and deformed from years of working without change, chained to starboard or to port. She thought of Elizabeth made stout by lack of work, her tongue ceaselessly clacking in her head about the hardships she had to put up with.

The knocker clacked downstairs in the hallway. Her again. The customer is always right. She removed the pins from her lips and went down. There was rain on the fanlight. Good enough for her. She would probably borrow the umbrella to get home. It was only fair in a way. She opened the door.

The man raised his hat. Rain dripped from the brim.

"Mrs. Cardiff," he said. "How do you do?"

"Enrique," she exclaimed, shocked into Spanish. "Henry Jones. Oh my goodness! What are you doing here?"

"I came to pay my respects," he replied with rain running down his face. "I was in the vicinity."

"Henry Jones," she repeated, taking his hand. "Henry Jones."

"Do you think I might step in out of the rain?" he asked diffidently.

"What?" She was still holding his hand. "Oh, the rain. Yes. Yes, of course. Come in."

He stepped into the hallway and she invited him to remove his coat. He hung it, dripping on the wide branching hall stand. He put down his black leather bag and put away his cane.

"Come upstairs and tell me all your news," she said, leading him up to her work room. He sat by the fire. She handed him a towel to dry his face. She sat down opposite him.

"Henry Jones," she said. "I can hardly believe it."

Henry coughed and stood up. He spoke formally, slightly bowed, with his hands behind his back.

"I wish to extend my sympathy to you on the loss of your husband."

She heard the steamer-horn again. There was a man who always went to ten o'clock Mass, who blew his nose like that. Always after the Consecration, when the heads came up again. Boom, boom, until the rafters shook, children giggled and parents looked sternly at them. Boom, boom, went the steamer. She often felt like giggling herself and the children always looked at her to see if she could keep a straight face. It was one of the attractions of ten o'clock Mass in Rowe Street.

Boo-o-o-m, went the steamer in a last, long-drawn-out farewell. It swung away from the quayside. Water surged between its sides and the land. It fell away into mid-stream, turning its bow to the ocean. She went to the window. She could see the mast over the rooftops and a little blue flag at the truck. Grey smoke twisted in the breeze. All bets off.

"How did it happen?" she asked.

"I understand it was a fall from a horse. I am not too familiar with the circumstances."

Probably drunk, she thought, but kept it to herself. There was a kind of inevitability about it. So that was it.

"When did it happen?" she asked and her voice shook.

"About a year ago, I understand. Just at sundown, I was told. I am so sorry. I presumed that you already knew."

She shook her head. About sundown. She remembered her dream. It was raining. She dreamed of Uruguay and the men returning in the evening light. They were singing. A horse had come from far away and threatened to trample her. Somebody on an urgent quest. The hairs stirred on her scalp.

"May the Lord have mercy on him," she murmured, crossing herself.

Henry looked diffidently into the fire.

"I suppose I did know, in a way. There was a letter, but it was burnt in a fire before I could read it."

"Ah yes. That must have been from his partner. I understand that he is looking after everything."

She came back to her chair, gesturing to him to sit down again.

"I will write to him," she said, "though I'm afraid there could be nothing but debts, if John had any hand in the managing of the business." She smiled sadly. It was disloyal of her she knew, but it could make little difference now. "Robert is a good man. He will do whatever is for the best." She wondered how the children would take the news.

Henry sat in an awkward silence.

"I must have Mass said for him," she said after a while. "Not ten o'clock."

"No, of course, not," Henry agreed, uncomprehending. It was probably some Papist thing.

"But you," she said after a while. "Look at you after your journey and I haven't even offered you a cup of tea."

"Of course. Of course," he said. "I had almost forgotten. The sad news put it out of my mind, see. I have something for you, a gift, you see, from some friends of yours. Excuse me."

He went quickly down the stairs and returned with the black bag.

"She said that you would enjoy this." He took out a package and handed it to her. She unwrapped it carefully. She sniffed the contents.

"Yerba maté," she sighed. "I don't believe it."

He was pleased by her reaction.

"Who sent this?" she asked.

"Your servant, the Indian woman. African, I was never too sure. She brought it to me and asked me to take it to you."

"Estrellita. She asked you to take a packet of yerba to me and you came all this way, just to deliver it. Seven thousand miles!" She looked at him incredulously.

He blushed.

"It happened to coincide with business," he said. "No, that's not what I mean. There was something else."

He took a box from the bag and handed it to her. She opened it and took out a silver maté on a silver stand. It was the size of a large teapot. She gazed at it in amazement. The surface was plain, unadorned silver work with an inscription in Spanish, 'Para consolarnos'. "It's beautiful," she said. "I could never use it."

"She said that you must," said Henry. "It is a gift, she said, from the last of the Charrúas. You must drink the maté and think of all that has happened to them and to you, she said."

"Estrellita? But she could never afford something like this."

"There was someone else," he said. "A princess of the Charrúas. They have sent it as a gift, so that you will remember them. You must taste the maté. Those were my instructions."

"Instructions!" Estrellita had a way of getting people to do her bidding. "How did she find you?"

"I was engaged in the building of the railway. It has started at last, you may be interested to know."

"I can't imagine a railway at Santa Catalina. It just doesn't fit with my memories of the place."

"There was no proper road, if you recall," Henry reminded her.

"And then you came along."

"Indeed."

"You have left your mark on the country, Henry. You will be remembered."

"And you too. Your name will always be there."

She held the maté in both hands.

"But what of John? He loved that land."

Henry was silent.

"Poor John," she said softly. "So how did she find you?"

"We were laying track," he said. "There was a locomotive and a wagon load of timber. I saw this woman approaching. I noticed that she was barefoot. I thought I recognised her. She came up to me directly and gave the maté to me and told me to bring it to Señora Cardiff."

"So you did?"

"It took me a little time to get free of my commitments."

"So you left everything to bring this to me."

"What else could I do? I had given my word. It was a matter of honour."

"You had given your word?"

He nodded. "Some years ago. Yes."

"What else did she say?"

"She told me of your husband's death and of the Indian Princess and how she remembered you. She wanted to send you this gift to console you, she said. Then she looked at the railway tracks and remarked that they would bind the country together. The fierro, she said, will bind the country together. Quite a philosopher, if I may say so."

"Well then, if these are the instructions, I must boil the kettle."

She went into the other room. He looked around at the work spread out on the table. He drummed his fingers on the arm of the chair. She came back, holding the maté by its stand. She sat down again. Steam rose from the vessel. She sniffed it languorously and sighed.

"It's been so long. I know I should leave it for a while, but…"

She put the bombilla to her lips and sipped. The taste hit her palate. It was the smoke of the fogón, the cigarillos of the gauchos, the smell of horses and leather, of cattle and the clear wind of the pampas. She breathed slowly through her nose. It was John's panatella and the incense of High Mass in Mercedes on the day they had christened their first-born, under the eyes of the Virgin of the Chains. She sipped again. It was the smell of the soil opened for seed and the taste of the waters of the River of Silver, seeping from the heart of the great forest. It was the taste of gunsmoke and of poor broken Paraguay.

She felt the tears coming to her eyes. She felt the chains slipping away and she wept. Henry bowed his head.

"I am sorry," she said after a long while. "You must have some." She held out the maté and he drank, looking at her over the rim. She dabbed her eyes.

"I'm sorry," she said. "I was quite overcome. It was so kind of them to think of me. Estrellita remembered how much I enjoyed a maté."

He passed it back. She drank again.

"You say you had to get free of your commitments? When do you return?"

Henry coughed. "Well, you see, I may not go back at all. There is plenty of work for people like myself. There are railways building everywhere, you see."

"But you are Uruguayan. You said so yourself."

He shrugged. She passed the maté to him again.

"I remember," she said. "I remember on the ship, Don José said that you were going there to find gold and jewels. Did you find many jewels?"

Henry looked into the fire.

"Just one," he said softly. He chewed a fragment of leaf. "Just one."

"You sound as if you lost it again," she teased.

"But I keep looking," he replied. "I keep looking for it."

"So you have bound the land with roads and iron bridges. And now railways."

"Perhaps I have bound it too tightly. When I saw it first, when you saw it, it was different."

"What will you do now?"

"I have had certain offers made to me over here. Railways are the future. I have learned the necessary skills in my travels."

"A journeyman," she said lightly.

"A journeyman," he agreed. "Now I must go. With your permission, I would like to call on you again."

"I would be very happy to see you again, Henry and I hope you find your lost jewel."

She laughed and the serious look went from his eyes.

"I hope so too," he said. He held out his hand. "I must say goodbye for the moment but I hope to see you again before too long."

He took his leave. She returned to the fire and the maté. She neglected her work. She took long draughts through the silver bombilla. Her heart was warmed by the kindness of the Indian women, those last remnants of the Charrúa people, the people of the Jaguar. She was touched also by the kindness of the diffident Welshman, who had come so far to deliver a wondrous gift. Para consolarnos. She felt at ease. She drank again.

Chapter Eleven

The train stopped at Arroyo Grande. They were loading cattle. Memory stirred. Sarah looked out at the milling herd. Eyes and noses, tossing horns and men on horseback driving the animals forward. She heard hooves thundering on wooden ramps and the passenger carriage rocked.

"There will be a delay," said the inspector, moving down the corridor. He stopped at each door to announce the news. He opened Sarah's compartment. He spoke in English.

"There will be a delay, señora," he said. She nodded in acknowledgement. She was in no hurry. She listened to the yelps of the herdsmen. She could smell the cattle.

"Shall I close the window, señora?" asked the inspector. He knew how fastidious these English women could be.

"No, gracias," she replied, and he withdrew. It was a river of cattle. Their white, staring eyes seemed to regard her accusingly. Soon they would be meat, frozen and packaged to feed the teeming populations of Europe. Meat for the factory towns and the armies of the Empire.

Memory stirred. Her mother's story of that journey and the baqueano swimming the river with the oxen. A naked man, she said, plunging into the winter-swollen river. The ostriches on the skyline and her father going out with an empty rifle to shoot one, to the amusement of the drivers. The gaucho with his herd of cattle. A young girl looking at the stars and lying beside her new husband.

Sarah closed her eyes. She could remember when she had become fascinated by the silver maté. She polished it. She could see her face in it. She could not drink from it because of the smell. The maté looked back at her, although she knew it was her own face. The nose was bigger because of the rotundity of the vessel. "Hello!" she said as you might call to an echo, recognising yourself in the answer. "Hello!" she said into the neck of the maté. Her voice reverberated. She lowered her voice and spoke in sepulchral tones. "Hello in there!"

It was a game they played. Her younger brothers loved the tone it produced. The maté got a bit battered, because of the game. Catherine was angry with them, scolding them for dropping it. The stand became crooked from frequent handling. When the yerba was finished, she put the maté on the high mantelpiece over the fireplace, out of reach. When they looked up at it they could still see themselves looking down.

The maté watched over them as they grew up. It saw Richard and William leave home for America. It saw Thomas leave for America and Frank. It saw little Michael going off to sea as a cabin boy, staggering backwards under the weight of his canvas bag. It saw Henry Jones return again and again until finally, Catherine consented to marry him.

But always Sarah remained. Manus Doyle married somebody else. Tom passed away, full of years. He lay near his two sons, fornenst the chapel, as he said himself, the chapel of the Tintern monks, other Welshmen who had come, following instructions. They brought the chalice that had lain in the lake. It all fitted together like a jigsaw. Tom could see the Mass-Rock from where he lay. It was where the people went after Cromwell's soldiers destroyed their chapel. He was within walking distance of Dorothy. He had a lot to tell her.

Henry Jones had come with that other silver cup. He had brought peace to Catherine. He built the railway from Waterford to the new port at Rosslare. He supervised the building of the harbour. He pointed out the need for a second pier, but the money was not there. "It will be grand," they said and Henry threw up his hands. He advocated a new bridge across the river at Wexford, "All in good time," they said. He looked at the lake at Lingstown.

"I could drain that lake," he said. "It would make excellent farmland. I could put an engine on either side, with a chain to pull a plough across."

"You keep your hands off my lake." Catherine warned him. She pinched his arm. Henry smiled his gentle smile. The lake was safe.

Sarah heard her singing again. She could always reach the high notes.

Sarah thought of Grandfather Cardiff, Granillero as her mother called him. She never went to see him. Now it was too late. She had known one grandfather. That was enough. He was the only man she trusted, with the exception of her brothers, of course. Now they were all gone, scattered to the four winds, but she remained, teaching school, keeping her house tidy and visiting her mother and Henry in the old home at Lingstown.

Tom would have enjoyed this journey. He loved the train. It opened the world up to him. He went to Dublin on one occasion with her. They saw the Queen-Empress driving in the Phoenix Park. The woman beside them ostentatiously turned her back as Victoria's carriage drove past. Flags waved as the people hailed their monarch with wild enthusiasm.

"Well now," said Tom, "isn't that wonderful, marvellous?"

She took him to see the great exhibition celebrating the glories of Victoria's reign. There were machines and factory-made goods of all descriptions. There were people from all over the world. There was an elephant from India, with coloured paint on its face. There were lions from Africa and Zulus. There was a village set up in the park, a Zulu village some said and others argued that they were Somalis. It made no difference. They all belonged to the Queen-Empress. There were mounted police from Canada. They showed off their riding skills. She could not decide whether their scarlet uniforms were the most impossibly glamorous uniforms she had ever seen or quite the silliest. They wheeled in perfect formation and she wondered if that was the approved method of apprehending criminals in Canada.

There were Red Indians who sat by their wigwams with arms folded. They looked grave and wise. They were not very exciting. In a booth in a corner of the main exhibition hall they saw Sepé the Jaguar, the last chief of the Charrúas.

"See Sepé the Jaguar," shouted the showman. "Sixpence to see Sepé the Jaguar drinking from the skull of his enemy. See Sepé the Jaguar, slayer of a hundred soldiers."

It was too good to miss.

"Wonderful, marvellous," said Tom. He took out a shilling.

They were not real skulls, just crude wooden imitations. The Red Indians were said to have real scalps dangling from their wigwams. "They're real scalps," said the people pointing in awe. Some scratched their heads, just to check that everything was in place. The Red Indians looked on impassively.

This was a little old man, thin and shrivelled. He wore only a loin cloth and a ragged fur cloak. His skin was almost black. His eyes were dull under dark, overhanging brows. He looked at them listlessly.

"Sepé the Jaguar," announced the showman. "The terror of the pampas." He gave a short account of how Sepé had terrorised the settlers in Uruguay; how he had come in the night with his fierce warriors; how he had been hunted for years and how eventually, he had been captured in a terrible battle in which, single-handed, he had killed dozens of his enemies.

He tapped his cane and the old man took up a skull and drank from it. It looked like beer. The audience shivered in horrified delight.

Sarah's heart went out to him. He looked at her over the skull and his eyes seemed to see into her soul. She felt soiled and guilty from the tawdry exhibition. She wanted to apologise to him, to step over the low paling and draw the cloak over his thin shoulders. She wanted to shield him from the eyes of the spectators. But she was helpless to do anything. She heard a buzzing in her head and blackness swarmed before her vision. She could see nothing but the sad eyes of the old Indian. She hurried out into the light and the fresh air. She wanted to go home. Tom took her arm and led her away from the place of gawping faces and pointing fingers.

She asked Catherine about Uruguay and the Charrúas. She listened to the stories yet again. Time and life with Henry Jones had taken the edge off Catherine's pain. She had forgiven John, Sarah knew. The story had become an old romance, an old legend, something a poet might invent. Catherine spoke of Aymará, the princess, and Estrellita. She told her how Estrellita claimed to be able to read the future, but that sometimes she was wrong. She told her how Estrellita always said that John would come back to her.

"You remember Estrellita, of course. You remember how we had our little school in the kitchen and how I tried to teach Rafael to read."

Sarah nodded. She remembered. She remembered too her father's betrayal. She would never trust anyone fully again.

"And Estrellita was a Charrúa?"

"I suppose so. Her parents were gaucho but before that they were Charrúa. They adapted, you see."

"Is it true that the Charrúas drank from the skulls of their enemies?"

"Oh, that was some old story. Some pishogue. They said that you could never be at peace until you drank from your enemy's skull. But this is morbid stuff. Tell me. What do you think of this man Carty? He'd be a good match for you."

"I dare say," replied Sarah. "A good solid businessman. With the emphasis on solid."

Jack Carty was a good deal older. A decent man, kindly, if rather dull.

"You're not getting any younger," said Catherine. "Are you going to go on as an old maid, teaching school until they carry you out in the box?"

Sarah shrugged. "Can I ask you something?"

"What?"

"Are you happy now?"

"I am," said Catherine.

"And do you ever wonder what happened to Santa Catalina?"

"I've let all that go. Henry says that the land probably reverted to the state. That is, if Robert abandoned it. I don't know. He never answered my letters. If he stole it from us, he probably needed it more than we do. Let him have it. If he left it, then somebody else, who needs it, is working it now. It's gone, one way or the other."

"And you are at peace? You have no curiosity to go out there again?"

Catherine lowered her head. "Too many ghosts," she murmured. "Estrellita said that she spoke to the ghosts of her own people under the ombú tree. I would be afraid to disturb old ghosts."

Sarah took the maté to Mr. Sachs, the jeweller.

"It's a very fine piece," he said, holding it up to the light. He pulled his spectacles down to the tip of his nose and turned the maté this way and that. "Difficult to value you see, as there is no hall-mark. Hmm."

"I don't want to sell it," she said. "I want you to repair it. Can you remove the dinges?"

He scrutinised it again.

"Difficult," he mused. "You see the dinges are on the outside but they don't appear on the inside. That tells me that there are two layers. Very curious indeed."

He took a long calliper and measured the thickness of the silver.

"Hmm," he said again. "Colonial, is it?"

"Uruguay," said Sarah.

"It looked rather Spanish right enough. The inscription, of course."

"Can you repair it?"

"I can try," he said, "but I promise nothing. I will have to remove the base."

"I would be grateful if you could do something. It has been in the family for quite a while."

She left it with him.

Mr. Sachs could do very little. He polished it up nicely and straightened the stand.

"I'm afraid I wasn't able to remove the dinges. It appears to have been built around some kind of wooden template. Ivory perhaps. It was difficult to see. I would be afraid to do anything for fear of making things worse. It could be bone."

Sarah bit her lip. It could be bone.

"I would leave it, if I were you," said Mr. Sachs. He held the maté in both hands. "Every little mark tells its own story, you know. I have no doubt this dinge could tell a story."

A story of two small boys throwing marbles across the room, trying to roll them into the maté. There was a fight, a scuffle and the maté was bowled across the floor. Catherine had been furious with them. "Look what you've done," she scolded and they hung their heads in shame. "Look what you've done."

Sarah could still see them, crestfallen, yet keeping their eyes on the marbles, in anticipation of further arguments. The maté was put back over the fireplace.

It could be bone. She took it home. She gazed at her reflection. They said she had the look of her father.

"Hello in there," she said quietly. "Hello in there," she said into the vessel and her voice rang. She thought of Sepé the Jaguar far from his home, a curiosity to be pointed at and laughed at. "I will take you home," she said to the maté. "Then maybe you will be at peace."

The whistle blew. The train lurched forward, past empty stockyards and men idling on their horses, watching the great engine taking the strain. Grey smoke unfurled, blowing back along the train. A smut flew in through the open window, lodging painfully in her eye. She removed it carefully with the corner of her handkerchief. She looked out at the fertile fields and the trim meadows, wondering what she would find further down the line.

She stepped down from the train. The inspector handed down her bag.

"Will you be staying long in Santa Catalina, señora?"

"I'm not sure."

"Tomorrow there is a train back to Montevideo."

"Thank you," she said.

He blew his whistle and the train moved off again. She saw the doomed animals peering through the slats of the wagons. They depressed her. Catherine was right. She was mad to come on such a journey.

She looked along the track. Something caught her eye, a procession of black ants carrying segments of leaves. The sun bore down on her from the cloudless sky. The rails shimmered in the light. The ants struggled over the iron rail. The leaves slanted like miniature sails, a green flotilla on a shining river.

"It is going to rain señora," said the station master, coming up to her quietly.

"What?"

"The hormigas. They know when it is going to rain. They bring their tortas fritas under the ground." He laughed. "In this country we eat them when it is raining."

"Hormigas?" she asked, not understanding.

He laughed again. "No, tortas fritas. We eat them to comfort us when it is raining. Para consolarnos."

"But it is so hot."

"The hormigas are never wrong." He smiled and looked along the track where the mirage flickered like an expanse of ruffled water.

She remembered. Tortas fritas in the kitchen, the kitchen where the horse stamped on the blue tiles the day the soldiers came; the blue tiles of Calais, which her mother had loved so well. "Blue tiles from France, just for gosther," she said, happy in her fine new house.

Something stung her sharply on the foot. An ant, black as a blackberry pip, had taken exception to her presence. It had bitten her, even through the lisle stocking. She stooped and brushed it away. The bite stung like fire. She lifted her skirts and stepped back. The ants had reached the platform, triumphantly bearing their plunder through the grass and broken cinder.

"You are waiting for someone, señora?" enquired the station master.

"No, not exactly. I was hoping to hire a cab."

"Ah," he said, smiling sadly. "There are no cabs. We are a very small town. But wait. I will ask this woman to drive you to where you wish to go."

He went to talk to a woman sitting in a small cart. A young mare stood patiently in the shafts. He came back.

"She is going to the mill," he said. "She will take you to where you want to go. She says she has been waiting for you." He picked up the bag and conducted her to the cart. The woman pushed back her straw hat and smiled down at Sarah. Her face was creased and wrinkled from the sun.

"I have been waiting for you, señora," said Estrellita. "You are welcome."

"Estrellita," said Sarah, reaching up to take her hand.

Estrellita stopped the cart on the broad road. Wagons lumbered past on their way to the mill.

"Listen," she whispered.

The sound of childrens' voices came to them on the still morning air. They were singing.

"That is our new school. All my grandchildren go there. They are great scholars."

"I am a teacher," said Sarah. "The school is the life of your town." She realised how much she loved that sound. Coming up the street she could always hear her pupils shouting, at play in the school yard. She listened again.

"You have no children?" It was more like a statement.

"No."

"You must have children," said Estrellita. "You must have children to carry on your story. There is a good man waiting for you. You must marry him." She made it sound like an order.

Sarah laughed. She might or she might not marry Jack Carty. All in her own good time. Stolid was the word for him, but he might break out too. No man was to be trusted, except perhaps Henry Jones. Except of course, Tom Doyle. Except naturally, her dear brothers.

"There is a good man for you," said Estrellita. "It is time for you to heal."

She drove on. The childrens' voices faded.

"I am beginning to wonder why I came."

"Wait," said Estrellita.

She turned into the avenue of eucalyptus, enormous towering trees. Birds twittered in their untidy bundles of straw and twigs. A hornero peeped from its improbable blob of a nest. The parakeets squabbled.

She saw the house and a tall oak tree. There were flowers everywhere. The white walls gleamed. A palm tree towered higher than the roof. The vanes of a wind pump rotated lazily.

Estrellita got down from the cart. She was old, thought Sarah, old and bowed by toil. Maybe she was a witch. Estrellita spoke to the people in the house. They came over and shook Sarah's hand. They bade her welcome.

"She is peregrina," said Estrellita. "She is searching for peace."

"Ah," said the woman of the house, "come inside and tell us of your travels."

No, they had never heard of a Boxwell or a Cardiff either. They gave her food and maté. She drank, concealing her distaste for the liquid. She could never understand why her mother enjoyed it so much.

"There is a room for you, if you wish to stay" said the woman. Sarah looked around. Little had changed. The windows seemed lower. She could see out, without having to cling to the window ledge.

"She will stay with me," said Estrellita. "We have much to talk about."

It was settled. She would sleep in the hut under the ombú.

She showed her the two stones on the slope by the river. Sarah prayed for a while, although there was anger inside her. She remembered Laurence and how he had taken them on a wild journey through the night.

"He was a good man," said Estrellita. It was enough of an epitaph. He needed no inscription.

"And my father?" asked Sarah.

The woman paused. "There are three things yet to be done."

Sarah knew better than to ask. They returned to the hut.

"Wait here." Estrellita went inside. She opened a small leather trunk and took out a broken circlet of rusty iron. Sarah heard chicharra, like an angry starling in full voice. She looked up into the ombú. Estrellita came out.

"This is the first iron ever to come into The Banda. It is the collar worn by my ancestor, the African. My Charrúa ancestor set him free. Come with me."

She walked down through the long grass to the river. She threw the collar into the water.

"Why do you do this?" asked Sarah.

"Because we are free. The water will wear it down. It will rust. The river will take it north to where my parents lie. It will flow into the River of Durazno and into the River of the Forlorn and on and on until it becomes part of the River of Silver. Its many pieces will go who knows where. They will be free also."

Sarah listened. It was a comforting thought, although she could not say why. It began to rain. They went back to the hut. The rain spattered on the roof in playful staccato. Thunder rumbled.

"Give it to me," said Estrellita. She reached out her hand. The tendons stood out on the back of her hand. "The maté. Give it to me."

Sarah obeyed. She was not surprised. She undid her bag and took out the maté. Estrellita took it outside. The heavens opened and rain battered on the roof. Estrellita returned. She poked the fire of the fogón.

"You must eat," she said. "Then you must tell me of your life and that of the señora."

Sarah sat on a rickety stool, cunningly devised of cattle bones. She drew near to the fire. She told of how they had fared since leaving Santa Catalina. She kept nothing back. It made her feel better. She had never admitted to anyone else how much her father had hurt them. She chewed on the meat. The shadows gathered around them. Estrellita went out. She returned with the maté brimming over with rainwater.

"Drink," she said.

Sarah shook her head.

"I know what it is," she said.

"Drink it," said Estrellita. The firelight touched her face. Sarah could see a raised weal on her right cheek. It ran from the corner of her eye to her chin. She had not noticed it in daylight.

"It is the clean rainwater of Uruguay. You must drink it and then tomorrow you will begin your journey home. You will be strong again."

She held the rim of the cup to Sarah's lips.

"Drink," she insisted. "Drink it now."

Sarah turned aside, like a child avoiding a foul-tasting medicine.

"Drink it," said the dark woman. The shadows moved in the flickering light and Sarah drank. The water was cool and refreshing. Estrellita drank.

"La paz sea contigo," she said softly. "Now there is one thing more."

The rain had stopped. It was dark outside.

Estrellita took a spade. They went through the wet grass to the two stones. She dug a deep hole beside one of the stones. The moon was low. The stars glittered in the vault of the sky. She placed the maté in the hole and covered it over.

"His work is done," she said. "He has paid his debts." She took small candles from the pocket of her apron and lit them one by one, from a lucifer match. She placed them carefully in a ring, encompassing the two low mounds of earth. She handed the last one to Sarah. Sarah knelt and put the candle into the final space. Estrellita touched her hand.

"You are well again," she said gently. "The circle is complete."

dottle